# Blood Forest

# Blood Forest

## GERAINT JONES

MICHAEL JOSEPH
*an imprint of*
PENGUIN BOOKS

MICHAEL JOSEPH

UK | USA | Canada | Ireland | Australia
India | New Zealand | South Africa

Michael Joseph is part of the Penguin Random House group of companies
whose addresses can be found at global.penguinrandomhouse.com

First published in Great Britain by Michael Joseph 2017

001

Copyright © Geraint Jones, 2017

The moral right of the author has been asserted

Set in 12.5/14.75pt Garamond MT Std
Typeset in India by Thomson Digital Pvt Ltd, Noida, Delhi
Printed in Great Britain by Clays Ltd, St Ives plc

A CIP catalogue record for this book is available from the British Library

ISBN: 978–0–718–18481–0

www.greenpenguin.co.uk

Penguin Random House is committed to a
sustainable future for our business, our readers
and our planet. This book is made from Forest
Stewardship Council® certified paper.

To Mum

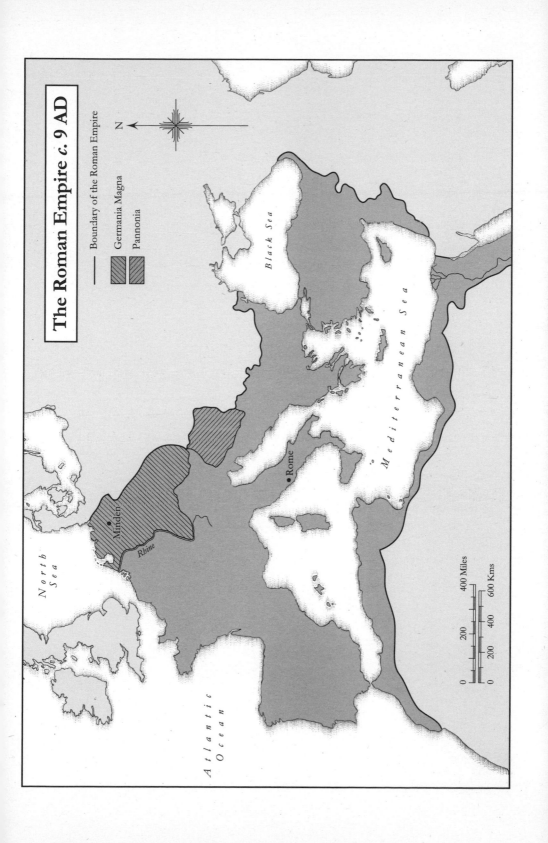

The Roman Empire *c.* 9 AD

Boundary of the Roman Empire

Germania Magna

Pannonia

N

North
Sea

Atlantic
Ocean

Black Sea

Mediterranean Sea

Minden

Rhine

•Rome

0     200     400 Miles

0     200     400     600 Kms

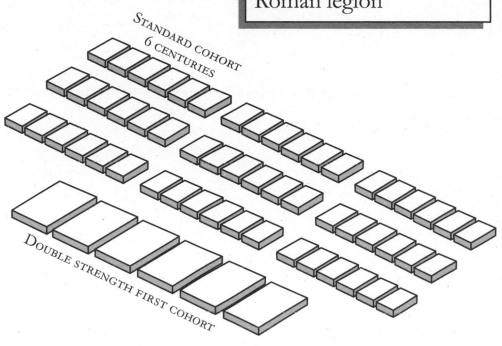

Structure of the imperial Roman legion

STANDARD COHORT
6 CENTURIES

DOUBLE STRENGTH FIRST COHORT

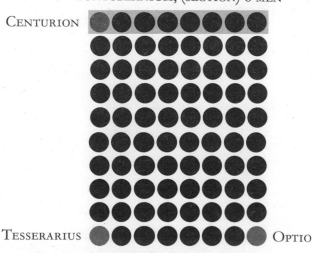

CONTUBERNIUM, (SECTION) 8 MEN

CENTURION

TESSERARIUS                                OPTIO

CENTURY, 80 MEN

# Prologue

An army was dying. An empire was being brought to its knees.

The soldier was at the heart of it, always had been, and though he was ignorant of the scale of the tragedy in which he found himself, he had seen enough of his comrades fall to come to the inevitable conclusion.

'We're fucked.' He smiled at the man beside him.

It was a hollow smile. The Empire meant nothing to him. Enlightenment? Romanization? Fancy words for corpulent politicians. His world was the section, the mates on his shoulders. His world was the few feet to his front, seen over his shield's lip.

'Here they come!' A centurion called the warning as a wave of men burst from the concealment of the trees.

They were big men, a head taller than the Romans, and their charge from the raised banks only made them look more like giants. The soldier noticed that these were fresh troops, unbloodied, their eyes still sparkling with life, not yet acknowledging the truth that they could die on this track.

'Brace!' the centurion called, and the soldier overlapped his shield with his neighbour's, putting the weight of his body behind his front leg. His limbs were weakened yet they obeyed. He felt the slip of the mud beneath his sandals, and ground them in deeper, every inch of push and shove a matter of life and death.

The soldier caught his neighbour's eye. Three days ago, this comrade had been a young warrior. Now the stubble of his unguarded throat had grown white.

Eyes back to the front: the Germans were a few paces away, their faces screaming, cursing, twisted by both hatred and the scent of victory.

They clashed. It was shield on shield, grinding, creaking, splintering. It was metal into flesh, the resistance of bone, suction as the blade was drawn free. It was gnashing teeth, spitting faces, eyes dead with resignation or ablaze with defiance.

It was battle.

Time became meaningless for the soldier; he measured life in breaths, and so he had no idea how many gore-soaked minutes passed before the line of Roman soldiers finally broke, the Germans pouring into the breach, the fight descending into a melee of individual skirmishes.

Warrior after warrior came at him. Most were a blur – cut, parry, thrust, move on – but some details were etched into his mind: a Roman staring quizzically at the stump of his arm, hacked off by a German axe; a woman, a whore from the baggage train, holding spearmen at bay with wild swings of her own staff; a mule, thrashing in agony, eyes bulging from its skull in terror. Brushstrokes of battle on a canvas of war.

'Rally, rally, rally! Form on me! Form on me!' The soldier heard the harsh call for order and saw the broken line of soldiers fighting their way to his side. He did not know it, but the barking voice had been his own. Like the well-drilled strokes of his sword arm, the soldier's tongue had acted on its own initiative.

The small knot of men stood firm as the tide of German warriors swirled around them. Other groups of soldiers closed ranks, shields overlapped, swords and javelins held in shaking hands. The circling carrion birds watched as this stronghold of armoured men was besieged by a rolling sea of enemies.

A lull in the battle. Men still died, but the initial clash dissipated into a handful of skirmishes and the dispatching of wounded. Tortured cries for mothers rang out in every language of the Empire. The soldier knew battle, and he knew that this lull was an inhalation before further exertion. The fight was not over. The forest seemed to hold its own breath, waiting for the next move.

It came from the head of the track. Thunder. The thunder of hooves.

German cavalry charged forth, pouring into the narrow space between the trees, sweeping up Romans who had survived three days of horror only to die trampled beneath hooves or spitted on the end of cavalry spears.

The knots of men broke in the face of this force, discipline replaced by the animal instinct to flee. There might be safety in the trees. They might yet live . . .

Some men resisted this urge. Forced it down with clenched teeth. They were the backbone of the legion. 'Get back, you cunts! Get back!' the centurion called, only to be silenced as he disappeared beneath a trampling steed.

The soldier's group split apart. Only a half-dozen stood with him now. The survivors of his own section: men who had slept, ate and shat together so often they were almost of the same organism. Their solidarity now bought them respite, for the cavalry mounts swerved around the unyielding shields, leaving the diehards to go in search of easier or more glorious prey.

And there was nothing more glorious than a legion's eagle. The silver totem was the soul of the legion. As the soldiers died in the dirt, or fled for the trees, the eagle wavered, the standard-bearer forced by wounds to his knees. The bearskin cloak about his shoulders was thick with matted blood.

The soldier saw the man sag, a witness to the last stand of the infantry who fell in defence of the eagle. Only when the standard-bearer made no further move to fight did the soldier realize that the man had died with his hand on the sacred staff. The boot of an enemy cavalry trooper was enough to push his body to the dirt. The wild-maned warrior hefted the totem into the air, cheering himself hoarse, and his countrymen broke from their slaughter to revel in the capture of one of Rome's most sacrosanct possessions.

But the soldier was no longer watching the eagle.

He hadn't turned away through anguish. Another of the standard-bearer's charges passed through his vision. A charge that had slunk, unnoticed, into the deep green shadow of the forest.

It was a mule, and the soldier knew what the boxes on its sweat-shined flanks contained. The legion's pay chests. In this forest of ghosts, they offered the soldier a promise of being reborn.

He took it.

# PART ONE

# I

I'd seen worse places to die.

It was a shaded grove of oaks, monolithic and ancient, the expected chorus of birdsong conspicuous by its absence. Between the high branches stretched a blue to match the eyes of the people born into this land of sweeping forests and angry rivers: the Germans.

I had met the first of them far from here, and though the faces of those warriors had blurred with time, I recognized their guttural growling language and their imposing physical traits: the thick beards, thicker shoulders and muscular limbs. Compared to my own, now nothing but gristle and sinew, they appeared god-like.

About their own gods, I had known nothing until this morning. Now illuminated, I wished only to go back to blissful ignorance.

Because the German gods enjoyed sacrifice. Human sacrifice.

I had been spared the sight of the act, mercifully unconscious of what was happening so close to where I rested my head on a pillow of dirt and fern leaves. It was the smell that drew me, the smell of cooked meat, and my hunger had overcome my inclination for solitude. I had approached what I presumed to be a campfire, intending to beg or steal some food, depending on the appearance of those at the feast.

What I had found was a banquet for the gods only. I counted six bodies in six charred wicker baskets, suspended above fires that were now nothing but ash. The bodies were roasted, shrunken, but the cross-slung leather belts on their hips told me that they were Roman soldiers. I knew because I had stood in the ranks myself. Six of their comrades were staked out to the floor, their feet touching to form a circle, bellies slit and entrails piled upon their chests.

Yes, I'd seen worse places to die, but this manner would take some beating, and the sight of slippery innards and torn muscles sent my vision reeling. I puked, but only a handful of half-digested berries fell pathetically on to the forest floor.

I looked again at the men on the dirt, seeing faces twisted by pain and indignity. How had I not heard their screams?

And how had I not heard the hoof beats?

They were nearly upon me. I looked towards the far end of the grove, seeing flashes between the trees of horses and armour.

Shit. Roman cavalry.

I turned and cursed. My line of retreat was cut off. I saw them coming through the trees now, a skirmish line of infantry soldiers. They hadn't seen me, eyes lowered and scanning the undergrowth ahead of them. They were the beaters, but their quarry was long gone, and so only I would be flushed on to the grateful spears of the cavalry.

I looked at the circle of bodies. I knew what I had to do, and yet I hesitated, even as I began to hear the Latin voices of the soldiers calling to one another.

'Stay in extended line! Put a javelin through that bush! Scan the treetops!'

No, they would not miss me. I had no choice.

I knelt beside one of the staked men. He was in his late

forties, probably close to the end of his enlistment; his lips were torn open where his own teeth had gnashed in agony. This close, I noticed the insects crawling over his exposed organs, and the deep mine of his emptied stomach.

I plunged my hand within, finding the liver. My knife was tiny, a couple of inches only, and blunt. Blunt because it had served me well. It did not fail me now, on this last task. The liver came free. I drove the knife inside the man and left it there, and then I slid into the undergrowth.

My hiding place was a thick tangle of thorns, and they suited my purpose. I pulled off what was left of my tunic, pushing it beneath roots and soil. I turned this way and that, feeling the barbs prick and tear at my skin. The first few drops of blood formed my mask, and as the blood ran freely, a memory came with it; I pictured sun-drenched hillsides above a pale blue sea, my limbs spotted with blood as I pushed through the snagging bushes, the baying of dogs on the wind.

The barbs dug deeper.

I stilled when I saw the two men enter the grove. From living on the frontier of Rome's Empire I recognized the thick array of decorations and ornaments on the man's shield: he was a prefect, the third-highest position in the legion, and the only one that could be reached by a man not born to the senatorial upper class. He must have served upwards of thirty years on Rome's front lines, for he was perhaps fifty years of age, and he'd even come to resemble a legionary's shield: solid, a little worn at the edges, with the slightest of bulges along the midline. Even the shield's iron boss was a reflection of the officer's bulbous nose.

But it was the man with him who held my attention. Though half the age of the Roman, the cavalry officer led the way, power and authority coming off him in waves. Only those born into nobility carried themselves with such assurance. Yet the man was tall, with blond hair to his shoulders. German nobility, then, from a client kingdom of the Empire.

I watched him as he studied the cages, and their occupants. I saw a smirk appear on his lips, though he did well to hide it from his companion. He pointed out the leather belts, coming to the same conclusion as I had done myself.

I willed myself to be still, patient, and listen. I opened my mouth, mastered my breathing, and blocked out the background noise of troops rustling in the undergrowth.

'He's a soldier, but he's not one of mine.' The veteran shrugged. 'All my work parties are accounted for. Detachment from one of the forts on the Rhine, maybe?'

'Only twelve of them?' the tall German posed.

'Maybe they're the First Legion. Thick as pig shit, that lot. Sir,' he added, before seeming to address the manner of the men's deaths. 'Six in the cages, six with their guts out.'

There was a question behind the statement, and the cavalry officer answered it. 'I can't tell you what significance that holds, I'm afraid. Maybe none.' He shrugged. 'What I can tell you, Caeonius – and you can take these words to the governor yourself – is that I shall put my best men and trackers on finding the savages who did this. Judging by the state of the bodies, and the warmth in the timber, I don't think they can be more than a day ahead, if that.'

The prefect – Caeonius, the German had called him – nodded vigorously, partly in agreement, but more so in anticipation of retribution.

6

Following hundreds of years of conquest, all the world knew that the Romans had an unquenchable thirst for vengeance. I knew that the wrath of Rome would come to these forests with more certainty than the decay of autumn.

'I'll get the men to bury the bodies, sir.' The old soldier offered his junior a departing salute, but paused on his heel at the unexpected reply.

'Don't,' the cavalry officer stated simply.

I could see Caeonius politely rephrasing the words that he'd caught on his lips as the German knelt beside one of the torched cages. He motioned that the Roman do the same; joints clicked as the gruff veteran conceded.

'Here.' The nobleman gestured below the rim of the cage. 'There's a wedge of wood held in place by the frame. Once the frame moves, this rope here' – he pointed to an inter-twined length of vine – 'will bring down deadfall on whoever moves it.'

'Deadfall, sir?' Caeonius asked as the cavalry officer scanned the canopy above.

'There.' He pointed, without triumph. Above them, a heavy branch stood at an unnatural angle from the others. I'd spotted it myself, and if the German was also looking for such traps, then perhaps we did have something in common – a shared heritage of dirty warfare. 'From that height, you're dead if it comes down on top of you,' he added.

'Is nothing sacred?' the veteran grumbled, doubtless yearning for the days of shield on shield. Ironic that he stood on ground revered by those who were indigenous to these lands, though Romans were known for their destruction of cultures, not their embracing. 'Thank you, sir,' the prefect

7

eventually added, obviously meaning it. 'I'll have slaves move the bodies.'

They were at the staked soldiers now, a mere ten paces from my refuge. Behind me, I could hear the line of legionaries moving slowly, but coming closer. So close to the grove, they would not expect to find anyone, now, but how could they miss me?

It was time.

I stood.

'You.' I addressed the two officers, lifting a legionary's short sword in my shaking hand. The shake came from nerves, but made me look like a man on the edge of sanity.

The two officers turned, the Roman reaching for his own sword, but the German waved him down with an open palm. The noble's face was at first astonished, but the open mouth slowly twisted into a wry smile, as if he were the only man privy to the Empire's greatest joke.

'You,' I repeated, my voice unsteady. It was the first time I'd had cause to use it in weeks.

I saw them looking at me, marvelling at my naked body. I had discarded my tunic, and the only thing covering my skin was a sheen of deep, red blood. I had bitten into the liver, gagging on the cold flesh, and used the organ as a leaking sponge to turn myself from decrepit beggar into a figure of nightmares.

'You.' I spoke a final time, pointing the sword at the German and blinking blood from my eyes. 'Who are you?' I faltered.

He raised his hands, slowly, palms open, and spoke in a voice that was both commanding and friendly. If he saw a ghost, rather than a man, he betrayed no sign of it. 'I am

8

Arminius. I am commander of a cohort of Roman auxiliary soldiers, Cheruscan cavalry, to whom I am also their prince. I am German-born, but a citizen of Rome. Who, my friend, are you?'

I let the sword drop to the dirt, the last of my feeble strength fleeing.

The act was over.

'I don't know.'

# 2

I passed out shortly after and woke up within the bleached confines of a campaign tent. Once a soldier, I'd slept under the waxed goat-hide before, but more than this I recognized the sounds outside the tent as belonging to an army in the field. The tramp of hobnailed sandals; the clink of metal on metal – tent stakes being hammered into the ground; the bark of orders, some in Latin, and some in a language I could not understand.

So, I was within the ranks of the German auxiliaries.

And now, from looking about the tent, I realized I was within the home of their commander, Arminius. It seemed as though he lived the simple life, which undoubtedly made him popular with his men, but his status as a leader was marked out by the presence of a campaign chest and table, over which was stretched a map.

A map! Where was I? My destination lay north, but skulking travel through thick forests had made navigation by the sun difficult at best, and I could only hope that I had not strayed south, and deeper into the Roman Empire.

I had to know. I had to see it.

Instead, my eyes were pulled to the tent's flap, which swooped open, Arminius entering with a warm smile that seemed at odds with the intensity of his eyes.

'Did I wake you?' he asked me in a Latin far more pure than my own.

I decided silence was my ally, and slowly shook my head.

'Good. Wine, then?' He had begun to pour before asking, and now thrust a cup into my hand. I hastily moved back as I realized his intention of sitting beside me on the pallet bed.

'To your recovery,' he offered, and took a deep draught. 'You've had a long road.'

I mumbled a thank you, and drank long myself. It was a good wine, and as it splashed down my throat I had the briefest glimpse of home: Mediterranean sunshine, warm hillsides, blue waters. How long?

'Thank you,' I said again, meaning it, but the words came out as a sadness. Arminius mistook it for confusion.

'You passed out there. We thought you were dead, for a moment.' He paused, a dark flicker across the eyes. 'Those men you were with. Your comrades?'

I shrugged. Silence was my ally.

'A detachment of battle casualty replacements from the Rhine garrisons,' Arminius explained, and then paused, his intense eyes burrowing into my own. Fearing scrutiny, my instincts cried out, telling me to flee this man. It was obvious that my disguise would not fool him, and I would die, screaming. Always screaming. I felt the cup in my hand. I could hit him with it, then go for his throat. I could—

'You're a soldier, my friend,' he told me, cutting short my murderous fantasy. 'You were a naked one, but your sandals were legionary issue.'

I looked at my feet. New sandals of uncreased leather. Doubtless the metal hobnails below them would be shining. I felt a pang of loss for my old pair, great comrades, then cursed myself for not disposing of them sooner, and concealing my past.

I shrugged, unconsciously touching the tunic that had been pulled over my head as I slept. It was dyed a deep red – the ideal choice for hiding blood.

Arminius followed my eyes, and read my thoughts. 'Can't have you running around the camp naked. Not like the Britons.'

The Britons. As a child, I had known one of their kin well. He was a slave, and from him I had learned of his people – fierce tribes across a northern sea, free from the rule of Rome, its taxes and its retribution. Julius Caesar had crossed the waters some sixty years ago, establishing trade and alliances with the southern tribes, and I wanted only to follow in his footsteps. To place myself beneath the shadow of white cliffs, and out from under the hate-filled gaze of Rome's eagles.

'The detachment you were with,' the German went on. 'Some of them were veterans. Scars,' he explained. 'You have scars yourself, soldier.'

*Soldier.* It was impossible for me to lose that identity. Even if I had not been wearing the sandals, any veteran could read the story carved and nicked into my skin, and this German was well versed in war, I knew it.

'I am a cavalryman. I've been in the saddle as long as I can walk. As a cavalryman, my friend, I like to move forward. You must do the same. There may be things in your mind that cannot, or do not, want to be found. So be it. Move forward.'

I nodded numbly at the words. Words that I knew to be folly.

Time has a way of wiping the slate of our memory clean. Given enough of it, even the face of our own mother becomes a blur. But the terrible things? The awful things? The things that we wish to forget? Those we can never overlook. Those are the things that haunt us whenever we close our eyes.

12

'You need a name,' he said abruptly. 'How about Felix? The lucky one?'

I nodded, accepting it. Felix was as good a name as any other. Arminius seemed galvanized by my naming and got to his feet, pouring more wine and laying the half-empty skin down on the map. My heart beat faster as I thought of the answers that lay within its ink.

'You have a name, and now you need an occupation. I'd be happy to take you in myself, Felix. My unit is made up of Germans from my own tribe, the Cherusci, but this I could overlook. From your legs, however, I take it that you are no cavalryman?'

I shook my head, and he either took that as a *no*, or *I don't know*. It mattered not. He had a home for me.

'The Seventeenth Legion,' Arminius announced. 'Your party was destined for the Eighteenth, but . . . I feel a fresh start is better for you.'

I didn't understand the change. Wherever I ended up, as an individual I would arouse suspicion. People would want to know where I had come from and why I was alone. Battle casualty replacements rarely appeared on their own.

A head appeared through the tent's flap. An ugly head, belonging to a German. He said something to his prince in their own tongue, and then the gnarled visage was gone.

'Berengar says that your new commander has arrived,' Arminius informed me. 'But before you leave, I have some business with him myself. Please, Felix, relax here. Take some more wine. My home is your home.' He put out his hand, an uncommon gesture from officer to soldier, but what was common about this prince? I accepted it, a little startled.

13

'Until we meet again, my friend,' he told me, departing, and leaving his words bouncing around my skull. *Until we meet again* – just a common farewell, or did it mean something deeper?

I had no time to ponder. Instead, I rushed to the map. It was brilliantly detailed, outlining rivers, roads, towns and forts. There was only one problem – I did not know where I was.

Still, at least from the area depicted I could deduce that I was in the province of Germania Magna, a collection of client kingdoms to the east of the Rhine. This gathering of German tribes paid taxes and tribute to Rome. Some, evidently including Arminius's own people, even provided troops to serve in the Empire's auxiliary cohorts, the soldiers who provided the bulk of the army, leaving the heavy infantry of the Roman legions to act as shock troops – both the spearheads of campaigning armies, and the lynchpins of the Empire's frontier defence.

If I were in Germany, then I could dare hope that I was heading in the right direction – it was likely that the army was poised on the edges of the Empire's control, and that lay to the east, and north. Perhaps it was the wine, but I felt a little light-headed at the thought.

Treading lightly, I stepped towards the tent flap. Holding my own, I could hear the breathing of two men outside: sentries. From the bellows-like exhalations, they were big men. Straining harder, I could hear two voices in conversation.

Putting my eye to a gap in the material, I saw that one was Arminius, relaxed yet commanding. The man facing him was a bundle of nervous, bitter energy, encased in the body of a centurion, identifiable by the transverse crest of his helmet, which shone with the sun. A striking figure, this was evidently my new commander. Though Arminius was senior to him, it was a rank outside of the centurion's own chain of command, and I wondered what Arminius had over this man that allowed him to pull his strings.

With a sinking feeling, I realized that it was a question I'd have time to contemplate. I was held only within a structure of hide, but with the sentries at the flap, and with Arminius and the centurion a few paces away, I may as well have been imprisoned in one of Rome's deepest dungeons.

With nothing else for it, I reached for the wine.

# 3

At the beginning of summer, the town of Minden had been populated by a few hundred members of the Cherusci tribe, the German people who swore fealty to Arminius's noble family. As he had done in the previous two years' campaigning seasons, the governor of Rome's German provinces, an aristocrat by the name of Varus, marched three of his five legions from their stone-walled bases on the Rhine, and paraded them in supplicant territories to impress German enemies and allies alike. On Arminius's advice, the governor had chosen Minden as the location for this year's summer camp, turning it into a temporary tented city for twenty thousand soldiers.

Minden had been a small town when the Roman army had encamped on its doorstep. It was still a small town now, but one with a disproportionately high level of prostitutes per capita. Some were locals, keen to take advantage of the business that had fallen, and now lay grinding, in their laps. Others had dogged the army from its winter bases on the Rhine, followers of the eagles as much as any soldier in the ranks. They were not alone, being accompanied by musicians, magicians, thieves and the unsanctioned families of the soldiery – it was forbidden for legionaries to marry, but commanders chose to turn a blind eye so long as the union caused them no headache.

To cater for the literal thirst of the troops, every other hovel in Minden had styled itself as an inn, while those that did not were used to lock away the innocence of the town's young women.

I was told all of this by my new centurion, Pavo. He was young for that rank, which suggested that he was either extremely capable, or well connected. He carried himself with confidence, as befitted his rank and handsome looks, but his contemptuous eyes betrayed a man consumed by bitterness.

Our journey through the German camp had begun in silence, Pavo taking charge of me as one would a stray dog, with rapid hand gestures and grunts. I walked on his shoulder, playing the part of the lost, but I caught the slightest twists in his neck as he contemplated his charge. He was intrigued by me, and so, as we approached the main encampment of the army and the town of Minden, he had buttered me up with talk of the settlement and that summer's campaign.

There had been no campaign, was the thrust of it. Governor Varus had brought the three legions from the western Rhine in a show of force intended to keep the quarrelsome German tribes in their place, but instead of marching the length and breadth of the territories, Varus had been content to pitch his tents and hold court at Minden, accepting tribute from the loyal tribes and turning a blind eye to those who remained absent. From my own experience, I knew that there were some amongst the Germans who were doing more than merely ignoring the Roman presence.

'So what now, sir?' I asked the officer.

'You say something?' he asked, his mind clearly drifting.

I nodded respectfully and repeated my question.

'Now?' he grumbled. 'Now we pack our kit and march back to the Rhine. A whole bloody year without any plunder.'

Plunder. So that was his weakness. Pavo was either greedy, debt-ridden or, more than likely, both. Could this be the source of Arminius's influence over him?

Now that I had finally opened my mouth, Pavo put on his best smile to set me at ease. 'I heard about the grove, and the men they sacrificed,' he told me, feigning sympathy.

I wasn't surprised. Soldiers gossip like fishwives, and doubtless the tale had already spread across the army.

'Now, you arriving on your own, it's going to raise questions.' He stopped at this, putting a comradely hand on my shoulder. 'You don't need to worry about any of that, all right? You have a problem, you come to see me.'

I nodded thanks, and we fell back into step. Evidently, this man felt that I had some kind of connection with Arminius. I wondered about the prince's interest myself, but I could only place it as intrigue in the mind of a benevolent leader.

We entered the camp through the open wooden gate. There were sentries on the archway above it. Earthen ramparts, topped with a fence of stakes, ran from either side. The grass of the turf had knitted, indicating that what should have been a temporary camp had indeed stood in position for months.

Through the gate, and the camp followed the familiar plan of all Roman encampments. An open road ran unobstructed through its centre, from the northern gate to the southern. In the centre of the camp was located the headquarters buildings, likely where the governor would be residing. The soldiers were tented in the same manner as they were broken down into units of battle: legions into cohorts, cohorts by centuries and centuries by sections. It was Roman logic, and the legion's discipline, at its best. I had never stepped foot inside this encampment before, but from the turns we made into the neat, tented alleyways, I knew exactly where we were heading: the quartermaster's, better known in the ranks as the QM.

The man himself stood behind a long wooden counter, its surface scuffed by the kit of thousands of soldiers. He was built like a slab of marble, his skin pale and blotched by birthmarks. In my life, I have found that those born ugly tend to extremes of either joviality or anger.

'What the fuck do you want, Pavo?'

The quartermaster inclined towards the latter disposition.

'Kit him out,' Pavo told the man, jabbing his thumb towards me.

'I've not been told we got anyone new coming in,' the big lump growled. 'Who is he?' he pushed, talking as if I were not standing a mere two feet away from him.

'He's one of mine. Kit him, and we can sort out the rest later.'

'Humph. Stores is for storing.' The corpulent quartermaster uttered what was undoubtedly his mantra, but started to reach for equipment behind the counter of his storeroom none the less.

'Titus been back?' Pavo asked the man as the pile of equipment began to grow in front of him.

'This morning. You see him before I do, make sure he comes to see me. Way things are going around here, could be a scrap on soon, and if he dies without cutting me in, I'll skull-fuck his rotting corpse.'

Pavo ignored the threat of defiling bodies to pick up on the first thing the quartermaster had mentioned. 'What scrap? The governor's packing up. We're going back to the Rhine forts.'

'He was, but things are changing. Bodies are piling up, and in some nasty ways. Yesterday, group of engineers scouting a bridge – hacked down to a man. Some nasty shit in the forests, too. The goat-fucking savages burned them alive, the bastards. I've gotta sort out the funeral rites, as if I don't have enough to be getting on with.'

I tried not to swallow, but I needn't have worried. The quartermaster had forgotten I was there; his words were for Pavo only. For his part, the centurion mastered what must have been an overwhelming urge to look my way.

'Doesn't mean there'll be war, though. Varus is a lazy bastard.'

'He is, but that German ain't.'

'What German?'

'Arminius.'

Pavo's act held, though I could feel the interest come off him like a wave of heat. I could only hope my own wasn't as obvious.

'Roman name?' asked the centurion.

'Yeah.' The quartermaster nodded, hauling a set of rusting chain mail on to the table. 'He went to Rome as a hostage from his daddy and uncle, the chieftains. Took the name, then took rank with the cavalry. Bloody good soldier, from what I heard, but anyway, Varus thinks the sun shines out of this German's arse, and the German's got some scores to settle with the other tribes.'

'Says who?'

'Rumour mill.' The big man shrugged. 'If it's bollocks, though, then it's bollocks coming from a lot of different mouths.' He surveyed the pile in front of him, and finally deigned to notice my presence. 'Sign here.'

He pushed a ledger towards me, and I ran an eye quickly over the contents: heavy javelin, short sword, dagger, helmet, leather bag, string bag, T-shape carrying pole, all placed within the slightly rounded shield. There was a price set next to each item, and it would be deducted from my pay. That was fine by me. I didn't intend on being around that long.

I signed with a cross next to each article, feigning illiteracy. It never did to give away too much, especially to your superiors. Let them think you're an ignorant peasant, and they'll talk as freely in front of you as they would a mule.

Pavo gave a grunt as a farewell, and I hoisted the shield and its contents from the counter. My arms and shoulders ached instantly from the burden, which must have weighed in excess of seventy pounds, but I could not afford to draw attention to myself through a show of weakness.

'And tell that bastard Titus to come see me!' followed us out.

Mercifully, it was a short distance to the century's tented lines, and yet my back ached as though I'd been trampled by a horse.

Pavo commanded the Second Century of the Third Cohort, its position marked out by a standard of cloth placed at the end of the tented lines. The tents were large, made of waxed goat-hide that had bleached in the summer sun. There were twelve tents for the century, ten housing sections made up of eight men, with an individual tent set aside for Pavo, and another for his optio, the unit's second in command.

Pavo led me to the tent furthest from his own. Outside it, scrubbing armour, were two soldiers barely older than boys. They sprang to a rigid attention as Pavo approached, but the centurion ignored them. He had been quiet since the talk with the quartermaster, evidently chewing over the notion that there could be war.

'In there,' he told me, and left.

I felt the eyes of the two young soldiers on me as I placed my burden on the ground. I had been in this situation before, years ago, and I had learned the hard way that it would not do to go staggering into the tent, exhausted and aching. Instead, I caught my breath, rolling my shoulders in their sockets, and all the time feeling the eyes of the two young legionaries upon me.

It must have been clear to them that I was a new soldier, as they were, but my age and appearance gave them pause for thought. It was not unusual for older men to be recruited by the legions, particularly by force during an hour of need, but by arriving I had elevated them from the lowest of the low, and they were busy trying to decide if they were therefore obliged to put me in my place, as they had endured themselves upon arrival. Certainly they thought of it, and one even came as close as to open his mouth, but one look from my worn-out eyes was enough to silence him. Inside the tent, I knew it would be different.

I picked up my equipment and pushed through the entrance.

# 4

The tent was bleached by the sun, the thin skin allowing the late summer's sunshine inside, and saving me the necessity of having to pause at the threshold to allow my eyes to adjust.

I had expected to find five men within, given that the section was made up of eight, and two were outside, but I found only four.

Two were lying prone on their bedrolls, one snoring lightly, while another two were playing a game of dice, the pile of coins small, low stakes between friends to pass the time. All four were veterans, evident from the fact that the youngsters outside were cleaning their armour, and by the silver plates stitched on to their legionary belts.

At first, they didn't seem to notice me, probably assuming that the movement at the tent flap had come from one of the novice soldiers. Then, when there was no noise and movement to mark my exit, heads began to turn my way.

I stood there, my equipment in my aching arms, and met their gaze. I held it, feeling the inquisitive hostility for a few seconds, and then casually broke it, casting my eyes around for a place to lay my burden. I found it in the far corner, which meant walking past the veterans. I did so without acknowledging them, and I felt their eyes tracking me as I moved. I expected an assault at any moment, either physical or verbal, but none came. That could mean only one thing: their leader was not present.

I placed my equipment into the tent's corner, as gently as if laying down a child. I took great care in rolling my blanket on to the packed-dirt floor, and then, with effort, I forced myself to close my eyes, assuming a look of serene comfort.

I felt the hard stares through my closed lids, but I heard nothing. I was disappointed. I just wanted it to be over.

I waited hours and, in that time, I feigned sleep. The act was exhausting, my body tense, awaiting the inevitable. During that time I heard three of the men come and go, while the other snored blissfully in the opposite corner. Outside, I could hear the sound of brushes on metal as the boy soldiers cleaned armour, the cloying smell of their wood-ash polish wafting into the tent.

It was a shadow that gave away the appearance of their leader. I felt the light above me darken, and I hoped that it was a cloud passing the sun, and not the silhouette of what must be a huge man. From the sound of his voice, steel dragged over gravel, I would be disappointed.

'Who the fuck are you?'

I deigned to open my eyes, and willed my face to stay neutral. It wasn't easy.

His head was grazing the tent's top, his shoulders as wide as a century in battle formation. I was surprised to see that, despite this mountain of flesh, the man had a handsome face, though one which was now twisting in distaste. I noticed the deep crow's feet about his bright eyes, and the olive skin, and surmised that this brute was a veteran of the desert legions. How had he come to be here, surrounded by rivers and forests?

I pushed the absurd question from my mind. I had to concentrate on surviving this encounter with him, not chronicling his service.

'Who the fuck are you?' he repeated, taking a step closer.

I saw that his veterans were on his shoulder, waiting to take their lead from this man. The two youngsters were watching at the tent flap, continuing their military education. Besides myself, only one other man was lying down – the sleeping soldier, who was now propping himself up on to his elbows, an amused smile on his pursed lips.

I decided that it was time for action.

I stood slowly, giving them no cause to overreact. Doubtless the novice soldiers would have reported that the centurion himself had escorted me to the tent, and this anomaly would be the only reason that I was not currently having my face trampled into the dirt.

'You're in my tent, you ignorant bastard.' His voice was low, thunder on the horizon. 'Fucking answer me.'

I did, but not in the way he was expecting.

I planted the crown of my skull into his mouth – I couldn't reach the nose – and I felt a lip burst beneath the pressure. In the same movement, I reached down for my iron helmet, planning on bringing it crashing into the side of his head – if I could deliver a crushing, rapid assault on their leader, then maybe the others would back down – but he was faster, and harder, than I'd expected, and the helmet was only halfway through its arc when he recovered and threw his right fist into a savage uppercut.

I half stepped to my left, but even the glancing blow was enough to send my eyes bouncing in their sockets and a jet of blood shooting from my mouth where a rotten tooth was knocked loose.

The helmet completed its arc, but the power had been taken from my swing and the aim gone awry, so the metal thumped harmlessly into his shoulder, and then he was on me.

We went down into the dirt, and his comrades, their courage found and blood up, dived down with us. On the floor it was a blizzard of punches, kicks, elbows and bites. It was hard to know who hit whom, a friendly elbow no less damaging than an intentional one, but I caught enough that were aimed for me. I managed to get my teeth into the flesh of somebody's ear, but before I could tear it away, I felt something crash into the bone beside my eye socket, and I slipped into the black void.

My unconsciousness was a short one, for when I came to I could still hear the panting of the men I had brawled with. I was in that beautiful moment where my body was so traumatized that the pain had not yet materialized, and so I kept my eyes clammed shut, marvelling at the copper tang of blood that ran over my teeth and dripped into my throat. Evidently, the big man had noticed that red liquid, and didn't want me to die.

'Roll the bastard on his front before he chokes.' I felt rough hands grip me and turn me over. My nose pressed into the dirt, and I cheered inwardly to know that it had somehow escaped the fight unbroken.

I heard the tent flap being pulled open and the light increased. A familiar voice came with it. Centurion Pavo.

'What the fuck have you done to him, Titus?'

Titus. So the big man was Titus, the soldier the quartermaster had been so interested in.

The man shrugged. 'I can explain.'

'Please do.'

'He went for me. The other lads saw it.'

To this, I heard an echo of agreement.

'Is he dead?' Pavo asked them.

'No,' Titus replied, his tone betraying a little disappointment.

'He didn't forget how to fight, then,' Pavo mused out loud. He then raised his voice, addressing the tent's occupants as a whole. 'Look, he's in your section, so you'd better make it work. Titus, my tent. The rest of you, sort him out.'

Pavo left, the big man in tow. The other veterans lifted me on to my blanket while I mumbled incoherently, not entirely out of deception. I was badly hurt from the beating, shapes and colours drifting in front of my eyes. I would have happily dropped into unconsciousness again, but now the pain had arrived, a burning column of agony that marched the length of my body.

It didn't desert me for the next two days, during which I drifted in and out of sleep, soon to be woken by sharp pains in my skull, my eye feeling too big for its socket. In this time I heard the men talk, my 'comrades', and I was often the subject of discussion.

'He's mad. He's tough. He's a bad omen.' So, they had discovered where, and how, I had been found. That could work in my favour. If they were superstitious men, they would be more likely to leave me, and my past, alone.

On the second day in the tent I couldn't keep my eyes closed any longer. I felt pus weeping from one of them, a fact confirmed when one of the veterans – a real ugly bastard with pockmarked skin and a sagging neck – began wiping at the corners. From the rough strokes, it was evidently a duty, rather than an act of charity.

'Will he lose the eye?' I'd heard Titus ask, a knot in my stomach. The other veteran had mumbled, 'I'm no surgeon,' which told me nothing.

'It would be good if he did,' the section commander had added. 'Can't have a one-eyed bastard in the fighting lines. Pavo'd have to move him to the baggage train or something.'

'If he loses it, he loses it,' the ugly veteran had replied, in a tone that indicated he would not hasten my blindness.

I learned a lot about the section during my few days in the blankets.

The leader, Titus, was absent much of the time. The others didn't seem to know where he went, usually, only that he came back with coins, and shared a few with his comrades in return for them covering his duties within the camp. Pavo often called the man into his own tent, but no one was aware of the nature of their conversations. Likely, however, it was tied into those same coins.

As my eyes recovered, I was able to put faces to the names and voices I had become acquainted with. Lying on your back for days, and in search of any distraction from pain, you can learn a lot about people.

Titus's four friends and followers were veterans, known as salts, or sweats, throughout the legion. The most outspoken of this clique was Stumps and, like most comedians, the twenty-something-year-old soldier was a sullen pessimist at heart. He had lost a couple of fingers during a skirmish with German tribesmen the previous summer, and from the way that he went on, it was he who was bedridden with injuries.

Rufus was of Gaul, a red-headed Celt who kept an unofficial family on the camp's outskirts. He was a quiet man, which I took to mean that he was an unhappy one. He was also a *duplicarius*, meaning that he received double pay. To be the beneficiary of this award, he must have pulled off some heroic deed.

One of the younger veterans was a fanatic, worshipping both the legions and the Roman deities. During some of his sermons on the enlightenment that Rome was bringing to the barbarian people, I wished that my ears would give up as well as my eyes. I had heard that shit too often in my past, and knew where it led. The uncompromising soldier had been named Moonface for his pale skin and wide, oval visage.

The veteran who wiped the pus from my eyes was known to his fellow veterans as Chickenhead, for his pinched face and the sagging flesh of his neck. He was eight months short of completing his twenty years' service, and so he was exempt from most duties. He'd put in the miles and the fights, and so Pavo seemed happy for him to see out his remaining days from the relative comfort of the tent.

The two younger soldiers were Micon and Cnaeus, but I saw and heard little of them, as they were essentially the slaves of the section, usually burdened with cleaning, cooking and completing any unsavoury duties that came along. As always with young soldiers, it was hard to gauge their true nature, as they were awed into silence and obedience by the veterans, whom the boys looked up to as demi-gods.

The section's final member was unofficial, but held a higher office than all. He was Lupus, a grey-haired kitten, ward of Chickenhead in particular. During the veteran's regular dozes, the cat would curl up alongside him, or in the ugly man's iron helmet. In the evenings, Chickenhead would feed it with slivers of meat bought from his own purse.

'I'll move back to Italy when I muster out,' he told me as he wiped at my eye. 'And Lupus will come with me. He'll have a whole farm to roam then, won't you, Lupus?' Chickenhead beamed. He was referring to the plots of land given to soldiers on their retirement, often barren tracts on the fringes of Empire. 'Think of all those mice!' the soldier teased. 'Think of all those mice!'

On my third day in the section I was at last able to prop myself up on my elbows, the aches still present, but subsiding. The swelling around my eye had reached its climax, and though it was still shut from the puffy skin, the weeping had begun to slow.

The veterans were playing dice when Titus entered. He cast me a desultory look before turning to the sweats, his open face betraying conflicting emotions: excitement and angst.

'Oh, shit,' Chickenhead murmured, reading the signs.

'What is it?' Stumps pressed, before groaning when he got his answer.

'War,' Titus told them flatly. He seemed unsure of how he should react to the news. 'It's going to be war.'

## 5

Where Titus had come by that information he did not share with or in front of me, but it seemed as though there was something to it, as for the next two days Pavo had the century brought together for drill.

Still invalided out from my beating, I was excused the first day's manoeuvres, but on the second, Pavo put his head inside the tent to see me.

'Can you walk?' he asked with a little delicacy, still unsure of my relationship with the evidently powerful Arminius.

Despite the ache, I got to my feet to show that I could. It wasn't out of bravado that I did so, but because I knew my best chance of slipping away from army life was in the field. To get there, I would have to show that I was fit for duty.

'I can walk, sir.'

He made a noise that didn't sound at all convinced. 'Just your tunic. No armour. We'll see how you go.'

I got on well enough. The purpose of drill is that the movements of battle become as ingrained in your mind and body as breathing, and battered and bruised though my muscles were, they remembered the moves as well as those of the other soldiers. We practised as a century only, simple manoeuvres such as going from column to extended line, or facing attacks to our flanks.

Half of the eighty men of the century seemed to be seasoned veterans, men in their early thirties with ten years' or more service under their belts. Now clad in their war gear, many of these sweats displayed decorations on their armour, Titus, Chickenhead and Rufus amongst them. The Gallic redhead had been awarded the Gold Crown, which explained his status as a *duplicarius*, and the subsequent double pay.

Perhaps two dozen of the faces in the ranks had barely begun shaving, and it was these soldiers that caused Pavo and his second in command, the optio Cato, to go red-faced in rage.

The usual subject of their ire was Micon, of my own section. The spotty, gormless youth seemed unable to tell his left from his right, his wrong-footed actions causing the same chaos in the ranks as Hannibal's elephants had inflicted on our forebears.

'Micon, you little prick!' Pavo roared. 'The next time you fuck up my formation, I will track down the whore who gave birth to you and shove you back inside that mess between her legs!'

During breaks from the drill I sat by myself, but I was not forgotten. Titus was clearly as popular in the century as he was in the section, other veterans looking my way as they asked the big man the inevitable questions. They didn't know how to take me, but I was happy enough to be left alone. The beating I'd endured had been worth it, and they knew I wasn't one who could be walked over. Easier for them to save themselves the trouble and forget about me, unwanted though I was.

I listened casually as they swapped stories of past conquests, both military and sexual. Beautiful women were described in intimate detail. Former comrades were discussed with hilarity. Combat was spoken of with narrow, faraway eyes. Throughout the army, and throughout every legion of the Empire, this ritual would be repeated daily. It was more than simply a way to pass the time – it was the mortar that bound the troops together. I recognized it. I missed it.

At the conclusion of the second day of drill, Pavo had us formed into two ranks, forty in each, with the front rank kneeling. He liked to see the faces of his men when he addressed them, whether because he enjoyed talking man to man, or because he did not trust his men to listen, I did not know.

'Is it going to be war?' Chickenhead blurted out before Pavo could begin. The centurion bit back irritation. Clearly, here was a man who commanded on sufferance of the veterans in his ranks.

'Not as you'd know it, Chicken,' Pavo told him, attempting to take back the initiative. 'We're going back to the Rhine forts, and—' He stopped at the loud chorus of groans and raised his hands for quiet. 'We're going back to the Rhine forts! From the march, raiding parties will be dispatched against the tribes that haven't paid tribute this summer.'

'And what about us?' a veteran called. From overheard tales, I knew that the man had campaigned against the German tribes before. 'Are we in these parties?'

Pavo shrugged. 'I don't know.'

'So there's no bloody loot?' Stumps grumbled, the sentiment echoed by several other voices.

'I told you, I don't bloody know,' Pavo protested.

'So what *do* you know, boss?' Titus asked him with dripping sarcasm.

Pavo visibly bit back a retort.

'Tomorrow, as a century, we march out to the River Lippe. We're to join a detachment of auxiliaries already there, and hold a bridge on the river. Repair it, if necessary, so that the army can use it on its move back to the Rhine.'

'If we're holding a crossing on the river' – Titus spoke again – 'then we're not going to be in any raiding party, are we?'

Pavo was forced to shake his head. 'It doesn't look like it, no.'

And at this, the veterans in the ranks let loose a hail of abuse at the army, Germany and the goddess Fortune. With no prospect of pillage and plunder from a whole summer's campaigning season, the men's patience was at an end.

This was the true face of Rome's glorious legions.

I was alone again, sitting on the dirt of a track that ran through open countryside, the fields grazed low by cattle. At this time of year the beasts were as fat as they were going to get. Most would be slaughtered and salted before the lean season of winter began to eat into their meat, with a few held back by the tribesman for breeding.

We'd left camp at dawn, marching out as a century, and now I yearned to rub at shoulders pinched by armour, but I refused to show weakness to those who sat apart from me, no matter how blistered and raw my skin. It was down to their indifference that the armour had become a burden. Without a second man to help me dress in the protective steel, it sat loose and awkward on my shoulders, the edges of the plate rubbing at the skin beneath my tunic. My campaign kit, a burden far heavier than my banishment, was piled alongside me, shield held upwards by my heavy javelin. A javelin that I dreamed of ramming into the guts of my 'comrade' Titus.

Somehow, the other troops were able to ignore me, while simultaneously using me as the subject of many a debate, the soldiers armed with an endless supply of suspicion and scorn. They talked as if I weren't there, and in my mind, I was not. I was a continent away, but the men of my section did not need to know that.

That morning had shaken loose memories that I had hoped forgotten: the tramp of hobnails; the dirt kicked into the air and into my throat; the jingle of equipment; and the bump of shield on javelin. It had brought it all back. I don't know what I had begun to mutter to myself, but it was enough to convince the more superstitious of my companions that I was somehow possessed by spirits. By now, they had all surely heard how I had joined the legions – the bloody apparition from the grove of the gods – and some were active in their quest to be rid of me.

'Hey, boss,' Stumps called to Pavo, who was passing by. 'How long do we have to keep him with us?' He jabbed his stubby fingers towards me. 'He's bad luck.'

Pavo ignored the soldier, turning instead to Titus. 'Titus, if I get one more question about this from your section, I swear I will dry-fuck you all with this bastard javelin.'

'Yes, boss,' Titus replied absently to Pavo's back, before resuming his conversation with Rufus. The subject, I was sure, would be me. Choosing to ignore it, I watched instead as the centurion made his way to the head of the short column, the size of which drew derision from the more salted soldiers.

'This isn't a bloody war,' Chickenhead complained, speaking through a mouthful of hardtack biscuit.

'Oh, here we go.' Stumps laughed, before pretending to stifle a yawn. 'Time for the story 'bout how Chickenhead and General Drusus beat a million Germans and saved the Empire.'

At the head of the column, Pavo was conversing with a cavalry soldier. The mounted troopers acted as the army's messengers, and I was more interested to know what orders we were receiving than to listen to another round of endless bickering between the two veterans.

'I didn't say there was a million, did I?' Chickenhead retorted, the skin of his neck flapping earnestly. 'When did I ever say that? Go on!'

From a cloth sack slung about Chickenhead's chest, the kitten, Lupus, poked his head out at the consternation and raised voices.

'Get your tunic out your arse, mate, I was only having a laugh with you,' Stumps protested, wiping at his face. 'No need to go spitting your scoff all over me.'

'I'd like to hear about Drusus,' the section's youngest soldier, Cnaeus, put in, with the eagerness of youth.

I knew of Drusus, and that he was a legendary commander who had led the legions in Germany almost twenty years before, defeating the tribes in huge, bloody battles. Battles that Chickenhead had evidently been a part of, but now refused to be drawn on.

'No. Not now. Ask Stumps about the time he broke his arm in camp, and cried like a little bitch.'

'Oh, fuck off, you grumpy shit,' the accused man snapped.

Titus interceded before Chickenhead could follow with his next insult. 'Shut up. Pavo's had his orders.'

I let my eyes wander back to the head of the column. The left lid was still half closed, but my vision had returned well enough for me to see the cavalry soldier spurring his mount away.

'Prepare to move!' Pavo called, and a ripple passed along the line as men hauled themselves to their feet, the sentries from outside of the main body rejoining their sections. I made an effort to get to my feet faster than the others; childishly, I was desperate to show them that the beating had taken no toll. Titus must have suffered enough of his own hidings to know that I was bluffing, and grinned.

'Ready for another few miles?' He asked the question to the section, but his eyes met only mine. 'Only another eight until we make the fort.'

I refused to give him the pleasure of a rise. We were out of camp now, just eighty men, and I needed only to bide my time, and wait for a chance to present itself. My service with these soldiers would be short-lived.

Chickenhead was unable to hide his own feelings quite so well, and clucked in disgust at the tiny column ahead of him. 'When Drusus took us east, you couldn't see from one end of the army to the other.'

'Probably because you were sleeping, as usual, you lazy twat.' Stumps laughed, but the exchange was cut short as Pavo's voice rang out across the German countryside.

'Century, by the left, quick march!'

I stepped off as one with the other men, embracing the pain in my legs and savouring every mile. I endeavoured to lose myself in the tramp of hobnails against dirt, my eyes fixed on the bundled pack ahead of me. Each step carried me away from what I had left behind. I could only hope that, over the distant horizon, I would find a new beginning, away from war, pain and death.

I laughed.

The march was not an enjoyable experience for me. Not because of the agony of my muscles, or the eye that began weeping again as kicked-up dust clogged the corners, but because of the reason I had crossed a continent alone. The reason that I wanted to be away from these soldiers while they were still soldiers and not brothers.

It was my secret. The dark infection that gnawed its way through my core.

I drove the heels of my palms into my eyes, focusing on the pain and little else. Eventually, the darkness faded.

We arrived at the fort with a few hours of daylight to spare, having pushed the pace beyond the regular marching speed. From my own experience of officers, I expected that came down to Pavo being in a sour temper. He certainly had that look about him: what should have been a handsome face twisted into a sullen snarl. He'd likely pushed the pace hard, willing some man to fall out and give him the excuse to vent his spleen, but though a few had faltered, none had crumbled, and now our column drew level with the River Lippe.

'They call this a fort?' Moonface spat in derision.

He had a point. The outpost was little more than a shin-high earthen rampart, with a tangle of withies forming a barricade along the top. There were no towers to speak of, and the outline of sentries was visible behind the makeshift barricade. From the shape of their oval shields, these guards appeared to be Roman auxiliary troopers, men recruited from provinces under Roman control, but not themselves citizens of the Empire. That title would be bestowed upon them should they survive the twenty years of their enlistment. A quarter cohort of these auxiliary infantry, some hunderd and twenty-five men, held this bastion beside the waters of the River Lippe.

Moonface grimaced, unable to resist a further insult. 'They couldn't keep a German's fart out with that barricade.'

'You'd be surprised,' Titus countered, stifling a yawn. 'That wood's as tough as your mum's tits. Bastard to try and break through. It'll take the wind out of any attack.'

'It wouldn't stop disciplined troops,' Moonface snorted, unable to back down, but not willing to confront the bigger man about the insult to his mother's bosom.

Chickenhead smirked. 'Well, what a good thing I don't see any around.'

'Century!' Pavo called from the head of the column. 'Halt!' The halt was ragged, doing its best to prove the veteran's point. 'Section commanders on me!'

Titus acknowledged Pavo's call with a grunt, and trudged wearily in the centurion's direction.

'We've spent all summer on our arses,' Chickenhead mused, returning to his subject. 'We're the rabble around here, not the Germans. It's bloody embarrassing.'

'Oh, tell it to your old mate Drusus,' Stumps teased.

'I think he's buried somewhere along this river, isn't he?' Rufus mused in his usual hushed tones.

'He is,' Chickenhead answered with a reverence that made him forget Stumps's jibe. 'At the fort of Aliso.'

I listened to that piece of information with some interest. As a boy, yearning to be at war, stories of the campaigns of Drusus had rung in my ears.

'Didn't he fall from his horse?' the youngster Cnaeus asked, hoping to be included in the conversation between veterans.

'Why are you talking, you snot-faced shit?' Moonface snapped, but Chickenhead was keen to talk on the subject of his esteemed former commander.

'He did. No foe could take him in battle, and the gods were anxious for his company,' he said, head nodding vehemently. Moonface, if nothing a servant of the gods, added his own violent head movements.

'You mean he got pissed and fell out of the saddle?' Stumps asked, managing to maintain a straight face. Before the pair of believers could fall upon him with their bile, Titus returned.

'Whatever it is, shut up, and let's go.'

We followed him, tramping through a gap in the fort's defences, and into our temporary new home.

As we went, I cast my eyes to the river.

My escape.

The most menial and least desirable jobs in the legions fell to the newest troops, and so I found myself with Micon and Cnaeus, the two boy soldiers who were ten years my junior. The age mattered not, only that the veterans in the section considered the three of us outsiders, and so we were handed the burdensome task of erecting the section's tent, while the veterans used their javelins to spit chickens that Titus had sourced from the locals.

Out of earshot from the sweats, the youngest members of the section were unsure how to behave around me. Yes, I was an outcast like them, but for different reasons. Micon's head might have been full of air, but I could see that Cnaeus was an astute youth. He watched my practised motions in setting up the campaign tent, the gears of his mind evidently clicking. What did he see? A veteran, or a man who was simply used to working with his hands?

I felt the unspoken questions, but I had no desire to answer them. Talk leads to friendship, and I didn't need friends. I didn't *want* them. Why? Because friends die, and you live. It's the cruellest joke in the world, and I had had it played upon me enough times that I was sick of the punchline.

No, I'd grown used to living within my own mind. Sometimes I didn't like what was in there, but it was familiar, and familiarity was always comfortable, no matter how disturbing.

I stood back, my good eye appraising the construction of waxed goat-hide. Titus would find no legitimate fault in it, but he sauntered over to try, lips greasy from the chicken in his hand.

'The lines aren't tight enough.' The big man gestured, using a chicken bone to point out a rope under perfect tension. 'Here.' He handed me a pick from a basket of engineering instruments. 'We need a shit-pit. Chicken's delicious, but it won't want to stay inside forever.'

I kept my face neutral, but an image swam into my mind of the pick ploughing down between Titus's amused eyes. I savoured it a little too long.

'Try it.' He smiled, knowing what was going on inside my bruised skull.

I did not, but instead walked away to complete the task. The weight of the pick felt good in my hands. My muscles ached, and I welcomed that pain as I brought each swing hard into the dirt, picturing the smashed skulls of Titus, Moonface, Rufus, Stumps and that hideous bastard Chickenhead. At a moment like this, I knew it was best not to fight it. Just let the anger take over. I brought the pick down, over and over, picturing other faces. Other men I yearned to kill. Before I had worked my way through all that hate, the pit was deep enough to hold the shit of the entire army.

Bile spent, I felt the familiar hollowness. I made my way back to the section's tent. They'd held back no food for me, as I knew they would not. I was too exhausted, too beyond caring, to make my own, and so I collapsed on to the dirt, spurning my bedroll. Around me, the men of the section snored on, for once silent and oblivious to the stranger in their midst.

I closed my eyes, and within moments fell into my own black void.

# 6

I woke to a kick in the ribs.

Titus, of course.

'You're waking half of Germany,' he told me.

The lump looked prepared to deal me another kick, perhaps expecting that I wouldn't have taken kindly to his methods of waking me, and so my words took him aback. 'Thank you,' I told him, meaning it.

I wasn't thanking him because he'd kicked me in my chain-mail coat rather than my exposed head, but because he had broken me out of something that I could not escape myself.

I knew that I'd been screaming.

'There's a spirit in him,' I heard Moonface whisper to Titus, deep-rooted fear in his voice.

The section commander ignored the superstitious soldier, keeping his eyes fixed on my own. 'Get out to the rampart and take over watch from the young one. Maybe the rest of us can get some sleep.'

I made my weary muscles move. There was no way that I could sleep again now, and I would not want to in any case. The nightmare had taken as much of a toll on me as the march, and I felt empty, my bones grinding against joints, pestles in mortars.

Picking up my arms, I found Cnaeus on the rampart; the keen young soldier challenged me with the first part of the night's watchword. 'Three.'

'Bears,' I answered, completing the security measure.

'It's an inn,' Cnaeus told me, not that I had asked. 'All the sweats go there.'

'I see.'

It was the longest conversation I'd ever had with him, but even that small exchange was enough to spur him on towards comradeship. Bollocks.

'I heard screams. Did they wake you?' he probed cautiously, having no idea it was my own nightmares that had curdled his blood.

'They did,' I answered, turning my gaze out into the black of the night, and hoping that would be an end to it.

'It's been quiet,' Cnaeus pushed on. 'Haven't seen a thing.'

'You wouldn't,' I replied, offhand. I noticed Cnaeus sagging a little at the implied criticism. 'None of us would. This is their land.' I pulled at the armour on my chest. 'And they're not weighed down with this. They can slip around like ghosts.'

I instantly regretted using that last word, and we fell into a void of silence which the young soldier hesitated to climb out of. Eventually, he found the nerve to try.

'They say you're a ghost,' he offered to the darkness.

'And how many ghosts do you see standing shagging sentry duty?' I asked, tired. Tired of the conversation. Tired of the life.

'Where did you soldier, before?' he asked, pushing his luck.

A push too far.

'Go get some rest,' I told him, betraying a tone that was used to giving orders, and having them obeyed.

He did as he was bid, leaving me to stare into the darkness.

It beckoned me. I could slip away tonight. It would be two hours until I was relieved. Maybe Pavo would check the lines, but he didn't strike me as the sort.

But no. Not tonight. The nightmare had drained me. I wanted only to look into the black.

In the morning, we set to work on the bridge.

The river was the width of five horses standing nose to tail, a dark silver in the late summer. Hollowed banks betrayed its winter savagery, but now the current was lazy, the river's floor smooth. Birds darted along the water, snatching at insects. The treeline of the southern bank was alive with their song and chatter.

My hobnailed sandals felt their way along the silt, searching for a firm footing. I was stripped to my loincloth, the water slapping gently under my chin. Titus, much taller, had his head well clear, his eyes inspecting the bonds of the wooden pontoon bridge.

'Worked on bridges before?' the section commander asked me.

I shrugged, then realized the motion would have been hidden by the river's murky water. 'No,' I answered, flatly.

'Then how you learn to do that?' Titus pushed, pointing at a lashing between timbers.

It was time for a barb.

'It's tying rope. Any idiot can do it.' It was obvious who I was implying was the idiot, and Titus cast sharp glances to the river's banks and bridge. Half the century were present, many stripped down to their tunics or less, all engaged in the bridge's maintenance. The other sections of the century, fully armoured, were pushed further out as a protective screen. One set of prying eyes was one set too many for what Titus had in mind, and I smiled as he forced his anger down into his thick chest.

'Well, seeing as you did such a good job, you can retie the rest of the sections.'

'I've been in here for hours,' I protested, not wanting him to know that I'd got what I wanted.

'Are you refusing to obey an order?' he asked with glee, knowing that such a refusal would give him a legitimate reason for putting me in my place.

Anger was so easily manipulated.

'No.'

'There's a good boy.' He took hold of the bridge and hauled his big frame out of the water, the muscles of his back bunching beneath the scarred skin.

The work was harder alone, but that was how I wanted it. This way, I was able to secrete rope beneath the timbers. Rope that would bind a few planks together and take me along the river. All I had to do was slip away from my next sentry duty.

I saw Titus join the rest of the section. They were on the southern bank, stacking the rotting timbers that we'd replaced that morning. No orders had been given as to what to do with the surplus beams, and Titus had considered how best to turn them into a profit.

'I'll talk to the auxiliaries later,' he'd told the other veterans of his group. 'We'll get a cart from them – have to cut them in, of course – and try the local farms.'

'But it's rotting?' Moonface had observed.

'That's why we're gonna paint the stuff,' Titus had told him, as if speaking to a child.

'What about Pavo?' Rufus asked his friend.

'That arsehole will do as he's told.' Titus's words dripped scorn for the century's leader. It would all have been very interesting, if only I were staying.

As I got back to work, the rope chewing at the puffy skin of my hands, I felt Titus's eyes on me often. I didn't know for sure why he hated me, and wanted me gone, but I had my suspicions.

Titus, quite clearly, was involved in some business outside the legion. As he wasn't permitted to conduct any other kind of work, that meant it was black market, and so Titus knew secrets, kept secrets, and recognized when others were doing the same. He recognized that *I* was doing the same, and a last thing Titus wanted was attention drawn to the section and his own dark dealings. If an accident could befall me, then he would be all the happier. If it could not, then he simply needed to ride me to the point where I would snap, and give him justified reason for killing me in self-defence. These things happened in the ranks. Titus and the witnesses would say their piece, there would be a lot of head-shaking and tutting from the officers, and there the matter would end, with my body in a shallow grave, a spadeful of lime for company.

Titus needn't have worried. I would save him that bother.

I strained hard at the rope to close the knot. The labour kept me warm in the water, but my hands had pruned, the wet skin coming apart with the work. I watched the droplets of blood fall into the water, to be quickly carried away by the current. They mesmerized me. One after another. Drip after drip. I swallowed, suddenly nauseous.

I did not know why my stomach felt as if it were rising into my throat, or why my head throbbed as if there were an army inside, besieging the walls of my skull. I only knew that I had had this feeling before, during my long journey.

Fuck. Perhaps I was dying?

I closed my eyes, squeezed them tight, willing the sickness to go away. It wouldn't, and so I went back to my task with vigour, attempting to fill my mind with the actions, willing nothing to enter my body but the feel of the rope in my hands.

Eventually it worked, but the thumping in my chest did not subside. Something was wrong. I became aware of another sensation.

It was one I was well used to, developed since childhood and honed on the far side of the Empire.

I sensed eyes on me.

It wasn't Titus. It wasn't any of the section, consumed as they were by their stacking of timber.

Then who? What? Something had changed. I would stake my life on this sense. I *had* staked my life on it, and I was still drawing breath.

It was out there, an indicator of combat – the presence of the abnormal. The absence of the normal.

Fuck. The birdsong, in the southern treeline.

It was gone.

The German spearmen spewed out of the greenery a moment later, a dozen of them, their war cry bouncing across the water.

One second there had been order, the Roman troops bustling like ants over the bridge and their tasks. Now, as savages screamed murder, there was chaos.

Soldiers, stripped of weapons and armour, raced for the fort's safety on the northern side of the bridge as a trumpeter blew a series of desperate, ragged notes.

What had happened to the outpost of sentries, I had no idea, but neither did I care. My chance had arrived! I just had to swim with the current. I would be clear, and there would be no pursuit. Pavo would assume I'd died in the assault.

But something, perhaps a primal sense of retribution, made me look back to where the section had been stacking timbers. Maybe I wanted to see Titus die. Maybe.

Instead, I saw the big man pull his section together, marshalling them behind the stack of timbers. Their weaponry out of reach, he was urging them to pick up tools to defend themselves.

The Germans had reached the bridge now, their spears plunging into the backs of the few Romans who had been too slow to outrun them or throw themselves into the water. One of these fleeing men, eyes wide in terror, screamed into my face as he waded through the neck-high waters. 'Move, you stupid bastard! Move!'

But I didn't move. I watched men squirming on the end of the German spears. Spears that were between the section and the bridge. My section – *my* section? – were the only troops on the southern bank now, while on the north a squad of armoured Romans had appeared to block off the bridge. The German spearmen, bare-chested and bearded, showed no intent to take on this new force, but turned their attention to the men sheltering behind the timber.

They came with a roar, blood up and sensing easy prey. The section, picks and axes in hand, waited to greet them, but the longer spears of the Germans would surely make it a one-way fight.

Then, speartips split seconds from plunging into flesh, the German charge was halted as Titus, bellowing like a boar, hurled one of the timbers into the onrushing men. It tumbled end over end, striking one in the head, knocking the long spears down into the dirt.

'Leg it! Fucking leg it!' Stumps shrieked, and the section followed his charge to the bridge and freedom. They passed the Germans close enough to spit on them, but Titus's action had bought them inches to escape and, in battle, an inch was enough. They would survive. All of them.

If only Cnaeus had followed.

But he was young, desperate to be accepted by his comrades and to prove himself a warrior. As the others thundered over the bridge, their hobnailed feet inches from my head, Cnaeus stooped to pick up a discarded javelin and shield, and turned back to face his enemy.

Four of the Germans had stopped to haul up their comrade, knocked senseless by Titus's timber. Another three were busy picking over corpses for loot, convinced that the Romans on the northern bank would hold their position. That left four, and at these spear warriors, hard-looking men all, Cnaeus charged.

He had courage. The young ones always do. Courage, and enough stupidity to break the banks of the river. Perhaps, as he made his assault, he realized as much, but by then it was too late. Stupid bastard. Stupid, stupid bastard.

I couldn't watch him die.

I pulled myself out of the water, my eyes on a German who had pushed himself ahead of his comrades, doubtless as young and eager to prove himself as Cnaeus. They came together in a clash, spear on Roman shield, javelin on German. My stomach lurched at a noise I had heard magnified a thousandfold.

Cnaeus held his own, strong legs braced. As I ran I collected a pick in my right hand, putting my momentum into the swing as I tossed it; the tool took the second German in the chest, enough of a blow to discourage him from the fight, and then I was on Cnaeus's shoulder, pushing him forward, smelling the wine-soaked breath of the German on the other side of the shield, his own comrades doubtless moving to take us in the sides.

'Keep pushing!' I shouted into the boy's ear, and rolled left, surprising the man who had drawn a dagger and was aiming to plunge it into the exposed neck of my comrade. *Comrade!*

My hand grabbed the tribesman's as he shouted something into my face that I could not understand. I used my mouth to better effect, sinking my teeth into the bridge of his nose, feeling the bristles of his beard rub at my lips. I tore away. Most of the nose came with me. Blood pooled down the face as he howled in agony, thinking of the pain, not his dagger, allowing me better command of his fist; I twisted the blade towards its owner. At the same time I drove my knee up into his groin – his body sagged with the blow – before my left hand gripped his lank hair, pulling him towards the blade. I felt it bite, pulled him onwards, and the steel found a soft spot between bone. When he stopped struggling I chanced to look down, and saw that the blade was buried in the side of his head.

Of the other combatants, there was little sign. At my own intervention the armoured troops had been ordered forward, and the spearmen had fled, leaving their doomed friend locked in my embrace.

For the second time in a week, I found myself drenched in another man's blood, and with open-mouthed Romans staring at me as though I were a phantom.

'What?' I shouted at the closest soldier, who took a step back at my hostility.

He was right to. I wanted only to kill.

It was the big man, Titus, who realized I was now a danger to my own side as much as I had been to the enemy.

'Felix.' He spoke to me from behind. 'Felix.' He had to say it again, the name still alien to me.

'What?' I screamed, turning so hard on my heel that it pulled the dagger free from the dead man's skull.

And then I saw what – a pick handle.

Titus slammed it down.

# 7

Titus brought the pick handle down and across, driving it into my stomach, and the wind from my lungs. I sagged, the dagger dropping to the wooden boards of the bridge. Before I could recover, he threw me like a child into the river.

Gagging as I was from the blow, I sucked in a deep mouthful of water and liquid blocked my throat and nose. I was only vaguely aware of something splashing down beside me, gripping my jaw and hitting my back. Water and bile coughed up to run over my chin.

'Felix,' Titus said to me, holding my head as if in a vice. 'I had to do it. You had a murdering look.'

Not now. Now I was simply drained. Hands gripped me from above, hauling me back on to the timbers. I lay flat on my back, panting. My head lolled on the boards, and I saw the dead face of the German a few paces away, the bristly beard I had felt against my skin now thick with his clogging blood.

Soldiers were standing about him, prodding with their sandals. They were the younger men, eager for their first look at a slain enemy. At the far end of the bridge, legionaries on their knees spoke final words to comrades who had died spitted on German spears.

It hadn't been a battle. It hadn't even been a skirmish. But for those who died, it had been enough.

It had been enough for Cnaeus, too. The young soldier came over to me now, a wobble in his step, knees ready to give. On his cheek, he had a speck of vomit missed by the back of his hand.

'Thanks,' he told me. I waved him away, angry.

Pavo had arrived, and cast a look of annoyance at the dead German.

'How the fuck did they get by our sentries?'

The answer came later. I was inside the fort, leaning back against my shield, a wineskin in my hand. Pavo's exchange with me had been short, but he'd excused me from duties for the rest of the day.

Two carts rolled inside the low ramparts, four Romans in each. A section, their throats slit. Their own weapons had gone, as had their armour, but doubtless they would have been unbloodied. Clearly, these men had been surprised, gathered and then butchered like cattle.

Amongst the bodies was a veteran, grey temples, open eyes staring up at a cloudless sky. Titus saw him, and let out a cry of fury. 'You stupid arsehole, Macro! You stupid fucking arsehole!'

Chickenhead followed my look. My actions on the bridge had not won me acceptance by any means, but they had earned me a weary kind of tolerance.

'Comrades in the desert war,' he told me, as if that explained everything.

To a veteran, it did.

The camp was quiet that night. Here and there was a muffled sob from one of the younger soldiers who had lost a friend, but the overriding sense within the troops was that of simmering anger. They had lost eleven comrades, and none of those deaths could offer the consolation, however tenuous, that the men had died in combat, facing their enemies.

Three had been skewered like trout in a stream. Eight had their throats opened, doubtless while they had knelt. From my own look as the carts had passed, I could see evidence that at least one had shat himself.

Soldiers needed to find nobility in death, but today they had suffered death for death's sake. It did not make for a happy group.

Titus talked to no one. The death of his old comrade had hit him hard, and he barely moved, eyes fixed on the dagger he had driven into the ground.

Moonface had offered prayer, endless prayer, petitioning the gods and his ancestors for their aid in bringing vengeance on the foe. Stumps, pessimistic at the best of times, had predicted doom for all, until the usually quiet Rufus had snapped, telling him that he'd slit Stumps's throat himself unless he shut his fucking face. Only Chickenhead retained his usual character, finding comfort in the companionship of his faithful kitten.

We buried them in the morning. Simple graves, a little downriver. Titus, and other veterans, promised that they'd come back for their comrades and see them enshrined on the Roman side of the Rhine in a mausoleum befitting their service. While the auxiliaries held the fort, the graves were safe enough, but men feared they would be desecrated if no Roman forces were present.

And desecration was popular that day. I do not know who was responsible – not our own section – but the German I had killed did not survive the night intact. His body was hacked apart and fed to the four pigs that the auxiliaries raised within the fort. It didn't matter to me. He was an enemy, he had tried to kill me, and now he was lining a pig's stomach. At least he had control over part of that destiny, which is more than many people can ask for.

Once the bodies had been placed in the grave, a comrade spoke on behalf of each soldier. As in all of the army, a soldier's relationships were closest within his own section, but links grew throughout the century and legion, particularly for those men who had served the longest. Some would be on their second twenty-year enlistment, and now, as he moved to the graves to speak on behalf of his friend Macro, I learned that Titus was one of these 'two-timers'.

They had served together as boy soldiers in the desert provinces of Judaea and Syria, a hit-and-run war against an unseen enemy, the conditions as hostile as the people. During one skirmish, Macro had broken ranks, fighting his way on to a rooftop where he was able to bombard the enemy spearmen with tiles. That quick thinking had forced the locals to give ground, enabling the Romans to regroup, and doubtless saving many of their lives. For his actions, Titus's friend had been awarded the Gold Crown. At the end of their enlistment they had departed the desert, and each other's companionship, with sadness – a sadness only matched by the joy of being reunited when both men had come to the Rhine to follow the eagles once more. Why there was a break in Titus's service he did not say, but I could make my own assumptions on that. If I was right, then it would not do to press him on the subject.

The other eulogies were shorter. Beside Marco's long and venerated military career, there was little to say about the younger soldiers, whose day of death had been their first taste of combat. And, unlike Titus, the comrades of these younger men were uncomfortable addressing the century, their words sometimes hushed, often choked.

I tried not to listen. I had no need to listen. I had heard such things many times before. Had I not been the speaker? Names and faces fought fiercely to break into my mind: Varo; Priscus; Octavius; good men doomed to bad deaths. I did not even know what fate befell Centurion Marcus. I could only hope that his end had been quick, but I had seen enough in those few days of war to know that that was a fantasy. No, it was not a time I wished to recall, and so instead I concentrated on Titus, painting in my mind the reasons for his leaving the desert, only to rejoin army life in Germany.

The funeral rites complete, we fell to work on the fort's defences. This wasn't so much for our own protection – the general opinion being that the Germans were cowards, and would only engage in one-sided hit-and-run skirmishes – but because the auxiliary commander had begged Pavo for legion expertise in their construction, doubtless fearing what would become of his garrison if he was tasked to hold on through winter. Equally doubtless in my mind was that Pavo would have extracted a price for our labours.

Our own section – *Titus's* section – were throwing up dirt on to the southern rampart when the troop of cavalry arrived, a familiar face at the head of the dirt-flecked horsemen.

Arminius, his eyes as sharp as a wolf's.

'Felix!' he called to me with evident delight.

Around me, men stood to attention at the approach of the officer, and yet I felt their eyes, wondering how I, a common legionary, was held in such esteem by this nobleman.

I wondered as much myself.

'Sir,' I managed.

He dismounted, clasping my hand in comradeship. 'I've brought you a gift!' He beamed, gesturing to one of his horsemen. I recognized him as the ugly sentry from Arminius's tent, Berengar, but it was what lay behind the trooper that the German was referring to.

Prone in the dirt, attached by a rope from the saddle, was the body of the spearman Titus had hit with the timber. It was hard to tell at first, given the state of the corpse, which must have been dragged some miles, but the pattern of his cloak gave him away.

'Where's Pavo?' Arminius asked of me.

'His tent, sir?' I guessed.

'Show me.'

As we walked through the camp, men snapped up from their duties to stand to attention in acknowledgment of the officer. He didn't let one go unremarked, smiling and offering salutations to the troopers. Here, I thought to myself, was a man who knew that men would follow *him* and not his rank. It was noble birth and the class-based system of the Roman Empire that had given him his position, but Arminius would have risen as a leader had he been born to the lowest peasant.

'Felix, how are you recovering?'

'Mending well enough, sir,' I answered.

He smiled as he took in my black eye. 'Of course.' He placed a friendly hand on my shoulder, his voice lowered so that it was for my ears only. 'The grove. Have you remembered anything before that? Where you came from? How you got there?'

His eyes were kind. His interest was generous.

And yet . . .

'No, sir,' I lied, not wanting to reveal the weaknesses in my armour, even to this man.

His smile returned. 'Maybe in time,' he said, and then turned to greet a new arrival.

Pavo, evidently alerted to the arrival of the cavalry, saluted the German prince, his usual scowl only slightly suppressed.

Arminius greeted him, expressing sadness at the loss of the centurion's men. 'Tell me what happened.'

Pavo did and, to my discomfort, included my own action in the skirmish. At the mention of my charge in defence of the young soldier – Pavo did not know Cnaeus by name – Arminius's face took on a reverent expression.

'The gods spared you in that grove for a reason.'

I could only nod, numb with embarrassment and appalled by the attention.

Then it was Arminius's turn to tell of how he'd come across the spearman who was now acting as a sled. 'I've had my boys out for days, looking for the savages responsible for the killing in the grove.'

'You think this was the same group?' Pavo asked.

Arminius shrugged. 'There are a lot of people here who don't care for Rome. I wouldn't want to say. In any case, we were following a blood trail and found that one. His friends must have caught sight of us, and abandoned him.'

'And the others?' the centurion pushed.

'The trail died in a village. They would have discarded their weapons, and blended in. Nobody gave them up.'

'So raze the village,' Pavo said, as if it were the most obvious solution in the world.

'That will turn a hundred more against us,' I heard, then turned ashen as I realized it had been my own voice. 'I'm sorry, sir.' I addressed Pavo. 'It's not my place to speak on it.'

'No, it's not,' he answered with a cold look.

'But he's right,' Arminius said gently. 'Our army is the greatest in the world, Pavo, but we need to use it in the right way. How many times have we crushed an uprising by force, only to see it spring up again as sons avenge fallen fathers? Let us show the tribes that Rome is the way. Let them see the benefits of open trade, and security. Do this, and they will police themselves. Troublemakers will be brought to heel by their chieftains before blood is spilled.'

Pavo did not look impressed by the argument. His mindset – of bloody reprisal – ran deep in the legions. 'And what if the chieftain's the troublemaker, sir?' he asked, poker-faced.

Arminius laughed, and slapped the centurion on the shoulder. 'Chieftains are above all greedy, Pavo. They wouldn't bite the hand that feeds them.'

Pavo only nodded in deference to the ranking officer, and the talk of strategy died.

'So, you have a body?' the German then asked. Pavo immediately became fascinated with the links of his chain mail as he explained how the pigs had been fed. Arminius didn't seem to care.

'What about his equipment?'

Pavo led on through the fort and then picked up the spearman's shield from amongst a pile of firewood. Arminius studied its swirling pattern of paint.

'The Angrivarii tribe,' he grunted with anger and surprise. 'Up until now, we suspected it was only the Sugambri behind the attacks.'

'So the rebellion is spreading?' Pavo asked.

'I wouldn't quite call it a rebellion, Pavo. But the animosity, yes, it seems to be spreading.' Our small group lapsed into silence as Arminius seemed to consider the implications. 'The section you lost, can you take me to where they fell?'

Pavo nodded, and from the look that Arminius gave me, I assumed that I was to follow. My centurion noted my presence, but made no protest. Collecting a half-dozen of Arminius's cavalry for protection, we made our way out across the bridge and south to where the picket line had been placed on a small rise within the treeline.

Beyond the woods, which were only a hundred yards deep, lay open fields. They should have seen the enemy approaching.

'No,' Arminius told us, then showed us why. His troopers had found the hides, shallow depressions in the earth amongst the trees. 'They'd lie up in here overnight. Cover themselves with these branches. Your sentries were looking across the fields, not behind them.'

There were expert trackers amongst Arminius's troop, men who knew the countryside as if it were their own skin, any blemish obvious to their trained eyes. They pointed to small, fist-sized indentations in the dirt. Besides the indentations, no skill was needed to identify the congealed red matted against the forest floor.

'They forced them down on to their knees here,' Arminius concluded. 'Then slit their throats.'

'Why didn't they call out?' Pavo asked, almost to himself.

'That close to death, maybe a man becomes a sheep. Maybe he hopes that if he does as he's bid, then the end won't come to him.' Something in his voice betrayed the prince's first-hand knowledge of such affairs. I had seen enough myself to know that he was right.

'What now?' the centurion asked, observing the ants that trudged through the red slime.

'Now,' Arminius told him, 'I will ride to Minden. Governor Varus needs to hear the news that the Angrivarii, or at least part of that tribe, have taken up arms. Then? Then, Pavo, I am not so sure.'

'Varus doesn't want a war, does he?' Pavo asked with disappointment.

Arminius shook his head. 'It may be that he has no choice.' He turned to me then, as warm and beguiling ever. 'It's good to see you restored to yourself, Felix. Walk with me,' he offered, and then grinned as he took in my swollen eye. 'You should be careful what you bump into.'

We stepped towards the river's banks. The water rolled by lazily, undisturbed by the rumour of war.

'Tell me what you think?' the prince asked me.

'Of what, sir?' I looked over my shoulder, because I felt eyes on me. They belonged to Titus, and I imagined his mind ticking as his huge frame leaned back against the fort's wall.

'Your friend?' Arminius smiled, looking again at my bruised eye. I shrugged, and he went on: 'Tell me what you think of the tribes. The trouble. The governor.'

'I know nothing about Governor Varus,' I confessed. 'The tribes?' I shook my head in sadness. 'You said that the chieftains wouldn't bite the hand that feeds them, but if enough of the tribe want to bite, then the chieftain can either face the legions, or his own people.'

Arminius nodded slowly at my words.

'You only kill Roman soldiers if you want a war, sir,' I concluded. 'One way or another, this season or the next, they'll get their wish.'

'Is that what experience has taught you?' he pushed, his eyes on the river's calm waters.

I bit back my first answer.

'It's what common sense tells me. And history. Somewhere, there is always war. It seems as though it is Germany's time to suffer.'

'Or Rome's,' Arminius countered with a sad shake of his head.

I shrugged. Rome had become such an irrepressible force on the world that it was hard to imagine her military might failing to conquer any foe. Year after year, the Empire's borders continued to expand across the world like spilled ink on paper.

'I fear that the army underestimates their foe, Felix,' Arminius told me. 'The German tribes are fierce warriors. Should it come to it, they will not easily be beaten.'

'Better that they lose quickly. At least then the suffering is shorter.'

'There are more kinds of suffering than battle wounds and death, Felix. Many of them worse,' the prince mused. Then Arminius came to a standstill. He gazed with reverence across the lush green countryside. 'It's beautiful, isn't it?' he asked me.

'It is.' It was.

With a sad sigh, Arminius placed his hand on my shoulder. When he looked at me, blazing blue eyes biting into mine, his words sparked a fire in my gut.

'Then we shall have to fight for it. Side by side.'

And with those words, I knew that I would die for him.

# 8

Arminius galloped away with his men shortly after, leaving the spearman that Titus had felled with the timber prone in the dirt. Titus pissed on the corpse, spat on the mangled face, and then the pigs were fed.

They ate noisily, squealing in delight at their unexpected windfall. Stumps watched them with a snort of angry laughter, addressing the hunched forms of his fellow veterans. 'Well, someone's come out of this trip happy.'

The next morning, a cavalry trooper arrived with a message for Pavo. The centurion called his section commanders together, and they, in turn, broke the news to us.

'Prepare to move,' Titus explained sourly. He was still sullen from the loss of his old comrade. 'They're gathering the legions at Minden. We're marching.'

'Where?' The question blurted from several mouths.

Nobody knew, but we saw the signs of the army's departure a long time before we reached Minden. Herds of cattle, sheep and goat were being driven towards the camp, the farmers hoping to get what they could for the beasts before the hungry mouths of the soldiers were on the opposite banks of the Rhine. The century marched through the shit of these animals, along roads built by the sweat and ingenuity of the legions. Many Germans might have resented the Roman presence, a few seemed to contest it, but none would rail against the roads and bridges that the eagles laid in their wake.

At times, the century would be pushed aside on these packed roads, the hooves of a cavalry mount thundering by. Titus and the other sweats would call out to these troopers for news. If the messenger was not in too much of a hurry, or if Titus should happen to have a wineskin in his hand, then they would rein in their steeds, coming to a walking pace beside us. In this fashion, we heard fragments of what lay ahead for the legions.

It appeared as though Governor Varus had changed his plans, and the army would not move back to the Rhine via the string of forts along the River Lippe, where the legions could be kept resupplied by boats. Instead, the army was to head north, into the lands of the Angrivarii, the tribe that had assaulted our century at the bridge; it looked as though Arminius's message to Varus had got through.

The prospect of some limited campaigning raised the spirits of the troops, and there was a notable surge in the pace of the march. Perhaps this would be a chance to strike back at the people responsible for the murder – for that was what it was – at the river. For men like Pavo, it offered the scent of the elusive plunder.

I was buoyed by the news myself – north! A plan of action began to form, and I felt myself pushing the pace of the man ahead of me, willing him on towards the camp and the information that I wanted.

'If we're not following the river, resupply is going to be a pain in the arse,' Titus mused.

Little that I knew of the man, I suspected I knew enough to recognize that he was smelling some opportunity for profit.

'That's a cohort up ahead,' Chickenhead said, his veteran's eye picking up a sizeable force of soldiers by the dust kicked up in their wake. A cohort was made up of six centuries, slightly under five hundred men, and was a considerable fighting unit.

'Why are they going south?' Stumps asked, giving voice to my own thoughts.

There were no answers for us, and as we neared Minden, we saw several other detachments, all considerable in size, heading south from Minden and away from the intended direction of Varus's thrust against the Angrivarii.

'Maybe the messengers were wrong?' Stumps queried, but he knew as well as the rest of us that those men would be the best informed in the army.

The late-summer day was warm, and by the time we arrived at the camp gates our faces were dirty brown with dust, rivers of sweat running along our spines and down into the cracks of our arses. I felt good after a week of legionary rations nourishing my body. I must have been the only man in the camp to be glad of the hardtack biscuits, but after months of living on insects, berries and whatever unfortunate animal I could trap, the tough mouthfuls felt like an emperor's banquet, and energized my muscles.

Within the fort, huge areas had been emptied where cohorts had packed away their tents and marched out. We soon learned the reason for this exodus. Titus called out to a familiar face and the veteran fell in alongside us, expressing his relief to know that Titus was not amongst the dead of the bridge before telling us of the troop movements.

'They've gone to garrison the River Lippe forts over winter, and the towns.'

'The towns?' Titus was as thrown by this as I was myself. Garrisoning a fort was one thing, and their very purpose meant these camps were often situated close to the same strategic resources that encouraged the growth of settlements: ports, rivers, junctions, mines. But it was almost unheard of to garrison the towns themselves, at least with sizeable units of front-line-grade troops.

'Governor Varus's idea.' The soldier shrugged. 'We want them to be sheep, we got to show we're the shepherd. That's what he said.'

'He's not done anything like that before,' Titus replied. There was a question behind the statement.

'Lads reckon that German talked him into it.'

'Arminius?' I asked, unable to help myself.

Titus's friend nodded. 'Rumour mill says his people got some kind of feud with another bunch of goat-shaggers, and he's talked Varus into smashing them up for him.' He turned his attention back to Titus. 'I don't know, mate, I just hope there's some bloody loot in it. Been a long couple of summers, you know?'

Titus told his friend to find him later for a drink as our under-strength century came to a ragged halt in an open area of camp set aside for our tents.

Pavo, the red crest of his helmet blowing slightly in the evening breeze, could not wait to be rid of us. 'Section commanders, get your tents up and kit squared away. Nobody leaves the lines. I'm going to get our orders.'

Chickenhead snorted. 'He didn't even bother to fall us out.'

'I'm going,' Rufus told Titus, and nobody tried to stop him as he slipped away without a further word to visit his family on the camp's fringe.

I caught Titus's eye and got the meaning. Back here, within the ramparts of the camp, there was nothing to gain from provoking him except another beating.

'I'll get the tent up.'

Pavo returned a few hours later. Possibly, getting his orders had involved wine, a lot of wine, or more than likely he had made a stop at an inn on his way back from headquarters, spending the coins he had extracted from the auxiliary commander in return for the century's work on the fort's defences.

His reddened face pushed its way inside our tent, growing ruddier still as he realized that only I and the two young soldiers were present. 'Where's the rest of 'em?' he slurred.

'Sentry duty, sir,' I said, to save him face in front of the younger soldiers.

He knew as well as I did that they were away drinking, but he caught on and accepted the rescue. 'Ah, yes. Yes. You two,' he sneered at the boy soldiers, 'fuck off and find me some chicken.'

They got to their feet quickly, reaching for their mail and arms.

'You don't need that shit! Just get me chicken!'

They scuttled out, Micon on the heels of Cnaeus, the leader of the pair.

'And wine!' the centurion called after them.

I expected him to go then, back to his own tent, but to my surprise he sat down on the bedroll opposite me, observing through eyes that had narrowed into slits. He was more the worse for wear than I'd thought.

'You all right, sir?'

68

'You know you're the only one who calls me that?' he answered quickly, the words unexpected. '*Sir.*'

I didn't know what to say, and so I kept my mouth shut. More wine than man, he had enough conversation for the both of us.

'I mean the young ones do, yeah, but they don't mean fuck all. The salts, though. You're the only salt who calls me sir.'

So he'd worked that out. Fine. I wasn't about to help him piece it all together.

'I'm just older, sir. I'm no more a sweat than those two boys.'

'Oh, save the bullshit. We're both outcasts in this century, so let's talk like fucking men.'

I nodded, but I kept my mouth shut. I had nothing to say to him. Nothing truthful, anyway. Maybe with as much wine in me as he had, things would be different, but I was sober, and I saw an opportunity to take advantage of my commander. 'You've achieved something most soldiers never do, sir. Men are jealous of that.' I was buttering him up: he was not immune to compliments, but he was bitter.

'Achieved what? I've never even fought in a bloody battle. I know it's not my fault, I didn't have any bloody choice about when I was born, and when the legions would take me, but still! Look at that bastard Chickenhead. He looks at me, and he sees a puppy. Why do you think I let him lie on his arse all day? Because if I don't, he can make trouble for me! The other salts listen to him because he's been there, and done it. And Titus! Titus . . .'

He trailed off, and I didn't push him. I knew what he was: a sour man with lofty ambitions. Doubtless he'd got his position by being a better soldier than his peers. Fitter, harder working, and a better arse-kisser. Such things can take you so far, but that ceiling was low, with eighty men below you, and a fat, corpulent class above, their positions secured by noble birth, and no amount of skill or grovelling could see you reborn.

Pavo had gone quiet, his eyes closed. I hoped he'd fallen asleep, but it seemed as though he was simply taking a moment for contemplation.

'I need this war. I don't know if it's even going to *be* a war, but I fucking need it. I can't stay where I am for the rest of my days.'

I nodded at the truth of his words. War took life, but it gave birth to careers. Pavo's ambitions seemed set to the highest rank of the legions, but he was in competition with dozens of other centurions, most of them his senior in terms of age and experience. To reach the top he needed war, and lots of it – dead men's sandals and glory. I could see by how much he yearned for it that it was something he had never experienced.

Even a drunk could see the distaste etched on my face. 'You've seen war, haven't you?' He smiled. 'You're as salty as any of them.'

He thought on this as he held back what I hoped was a belch, but I suspected was vomit. Once gathered, he continued. 'You know, if you told them, they'd accept you. Why are you hiding it?'

I held my tongue. Pavo sneered, drunk and amused.

'I have an idea why, but it won't do either of us any good to say it, so fuck it, hey?' he slurred. 'I'm going to need good men.'

The centurion got to his feet. Unsteady feet. He placed a hand on my shoulder, whether to support himself, or me, I didn't know.

70

'Forget who you were, if you need to. But when we do finally get out there, and I've got my war, then be who you are.'

He stopped at the tent flap. For a second, the usual harsh snarl was gone. I glimpsed the man, stripped of the ambition.

'No one should die amongst strangers,' he told me.

It wasn't until later, much later, that I understood the words were intended for his own ears.

# 9

Cnaeus and Micon returned from their errand. From the look of relief on their faces, Pavo had been happy with what they'd brought him. From their pouts, however, I suspected that the food and drink had been provided from out of their own pockets. No surprise there. That was the way it went in the legions. If these two youngsters could climb to Pavo's rank, or Titus's status, then they'd be the ones dispatching boy soldiers to acquire chicken and wine. Until then, they'd have to suck it up.

They did and, run down as they were by the march back from the Lippe, not to mention the constant graft on the section's behalf, the pair were soon asleep.

I was glad of their slumber, for two reasons.

First, because ever since I had saved his life at the bridge – and I say that as simple fact, not hubris – the boy Cnaeus had been looking at me with something close to reverence. On the times that he'd come close to addressing the matter, I'd given him a look of what I hoped passed for cold-blooded murder, and that had been enough to kill the unwanted conversation in its infancy. Still, the puppy-dog adoration was uncomfortable even if it was given in silence, and so was one reason I was glad the young soldiers were asleep.

The second was because I did not want it known that I was about to leave the tent. With perhaps the exception of Rufus, who gave me the impression of being an avid family man, the others in the section were still absent, presumed drunk. Regardless of their destination, I doubted that any of them would make it back much before sunrise. It was now time for my own excursion, and so I stepped over the sleeping forms of the boys and out into the starlit night.

My first stop was Pavo's own tent, and I found what I had expected to see: the centurion, snoring loudly, a half-eaten chicken in his lap. With a final look about me, I made my way inside.

My search was short, and fruitless. A map was what I wanted. I would have been surprised if Pavo, at his rank, had possessed one of a large enough scale for my designs, but the chance his drunken stupor had offered was too good to pass up. I was not surprised to note that there were no bags of coins or signs of wealth within the tent. Either Pavo was a master at concealment, or he was broke.

I had no money of my own, and I would need it for what I had in mind. Still, it was not an insurmountable problem. I had a feeling I knew where to get it.

The camp appeared deserted as I walked along the tented lines. The sentries were pushed out on to the distant earthen ramparts, while the broke and the boring slept in their tents. Any man wanting a drink would be in the town, surrounded by loose women and, I hoped, looser tongues.

Finding the quartermaster's was no problem, its location seared into my memory from other encampments and from the painful strides I had taken with the burden of equipment in my arms. As I had hoped, a glimmer of candlelight shone from within. For the protection of the legion's goods the engineers had erected a wooden structure for the stores, and I rapped the panel beside the open door.

'Who the fuck are you?' growled the quartermaster, his birthmarks shifting with distaste.

'Need a loan, sir,' I told him simply. As I expected, this caused no consternation.

'Well, come in then.'

From the quartermaster's interest in Titus, I had the feeling the pair conducted business together, and where there is black-market business there is money, and where there is money there are loans.

The quartermaster would not be retiring a poor man, and it was a hefty rate I agreed to; I'd be paying back double what I borrowed.

'There's gonna be a payday before we break camp,' the slab of a soldier told me. 'You'll pay me then.'

I didn't need to ask what would happen if I didn't. Men like him always held others in their pockets. Men who'd break fingers, or slit a throat, to be forgiven their own debts.

What I wanted to ask for was more information on the army's planned movement. The quartermaster would be in the know, but I'd need to tread carefully, coming across as just an interested foot-slogger and nothing more.

'So there's a date set, sir? For us leaving?'

He shrugged. Transaction over, he only wanted me gone. I sat still, patient and earnest, giving him the impression that the quickest way to get rid of me was to send me away with some titbit of information in my ears.

'Couple days, tops. Plans to be finalized.' He made it sound as though he was privy to those plans. Perhaps he was, or perhaps he enjoyed elevating his station.

'You know where we're going, sir?'

'North. Now fuck off.'

It didn't do to push, and so I did as I was bid.

Entering Minden I saw that I was hours late to the party; many soldiers were already vomiting in the alleyways, or bartering hard with the business-savvy whores. The working girls avoided me, sensing my sobriety. Drunk and horny, powerless against their desires, that was how they liked their clients.

'Where's the Three Bears?' I asked a soldier who was supporting a comrade, the pair staggering as if escaping battle.

'Next street down, on your left.'

I nodded thanks, and made sure to give the area a wide berth, because that inn was the favoured watering hole of my own century.

Instead, I found an establishment that had been a German home a few months before. The inside was crowded with soldiers, legionaries and auxiliaries, standing and sitting on oak benches, wine flowing freely from skins and across the bare breasts of fair-haired whores. Never known for their restraint, the mere rumour of war had been enough to send the soldiers into an orgy of decadence. I remembered the feeling: you can't take it with you, so why not enjoy your last few days on earth? Most of these soldiers would not be truly fearing death, but the excuse for excess was enough. Let the wine and tits flow.

I edged my way to what served as a counter, a long table set against the far wall. Behind it, the German proprietor was flanked by two hulking Roman soldiers who were making a little extra on the side; the inn's owner was savvy enough to know that the local muscle would never be as respected as the army's professional warriors.

I put a coin on the table, and was handed a mug of bitter wine, the kind that makes you want to drink more if only to forget the taste of the last cup. I settled in to wait. I would stay here until the crowd began to thin, men falling on their backs to sleep or fuck. By then I would be a part of the wine-soaked furniture, and with luck Fortune would have guided me to an inn where the keeper was a talker. Until then I drank, slowly, and I watched.

I wasn't the only one.

I found him at the end of the bar, a gnarled veteran, a Roman, perhaps forty years old. He was beside a taller, silver-haired comrade, but neither talked much, they simply watched me. Why?

It was too early, but my sense of unease overcame me. I slipped the German an extra coin for my next drink.

'The two in the corner. Were they here before me?'

He nodded, which was all I got for my coin. Money well spent. I had not been followed.

But who were they?

I tried to put it out of my mind. Perhaps they were simply wondering why a Roman was drinking alone. Bored, they were making conversation, and I had provided a topic. Yes, that must be it.

My attention was quickly pulled to the front of the room, where a fight had broken out between a group of Roman infantry and German cavalry. It was a good fight, the men just drunk enough to withstand pain, but sober enough for their punches to aim true. As the other soldiers cheered them on, I felt myself smile. For a moment, I was there with my old comrades, Varo throwing men around as if they were empty tunics. It was we who were fighting, having each other's backs, the black eyes a badge of honour to be laughed about the next day.

The two groups were finally pulled apart, and I recognized one of the men restoring order as the large German who had guarded Arminius's tent, and had dragged the body of the spearmen behind his horse: Berengar. If he recognized me he gave no sign, and, the scuffle over, the drinking resumed. I turned back to my table.

And found the two Roman watchers seated beside me.

'Comrade,' the silver-haired one greeted me.

'Brothers,' I acknowledged, lifting my cup, trying to appear more drunk than I was, then turning my head from them in an attempt to break the conversation.

It didn't work.

'I know you.' The shorter, gnarled man spoke. His words were not condemning, simply intrigued. I felt the safest course of action was to humour him.

'Then you're a lucky man.' I smiled, splashing wine out of my cup.

'But not from here,' he wondered aloud, and my stomach began to knot.

'Oh?'

'What legion you with?' the taller of the pair asked.

'Seventeenth. I'm new,' I explained, with a gesture about me, making a show of my lack of companions.

'You look like you've got a few miles on you.'

I smiled. 'I was married.'

They smiled too, but I could see that, in the depths of their minds, old memories were being dragged to the surface.

'Well,' the shorter one concluded with a look towards the whores, 'I can see why a married man would come here. Drink?'

I took a long, saddened look at my cup, now drained. 'I need to get back to camp. My centurion, he's a real bullshitter.'

The veterans smiled their understanding, and I got to my feet. I'd only taken a step when the silver-haired man had his epiphany.

'Pannonia! That's where I know you from! You were Eighth Legion!'

'Not me, brothers.' I smiled again and turned away, but a hand gripped my shoulder.

'It's him!' the shorter one spat to his friend, anger rising. 'You piece of shit!' he snarled at me. 'You were—'

I didn't let him finish, smashing my elbow into his mouth. His knees banded like a newborn foal and his friend instinctively caught him as he fell, giving me the chance to bolt for the doorway. I could not be sure if they were alone, and to be exposed would see me die in the most painful way imaginable, so it was without thinking that I pulled the purse from beneath my tunic and cast the coins into the air as I ran, the silver rain bringing excited cheers from soldiers and whores alike. I was instantly pained at the loss, but I hoped that my life was a worthy investment.

I was in the alleyway a second later. A few calls to stop me rose above the cheers but, distracted as they were by the money on the floor, nobody listened. Nor did anyone in the street. The soldiers had come into town to drink and screw – why should they care what went on between others? I resisted the urge to run, knowing that it would draw attention from any policing patrols of the camp guard, and so I was only at the end of the alleyway when the silver-haired soldier stepped into the night.

Shit. His friend was with him, stumbling a little, but otherwise recovered. I went for the first turn I could find and took flight. The hobnails of my sandals sounded like hammers on anvils, but with a head start, and in the tangle of dark streets, they had no hope of finding me.

It didn't matter.

Somebody knew my secret.

# IO

The next day, at dawn, an ill-tempered Pavo called reveille. The other men of the section grumbled, hung-over, but I was anxious to escape the tent, which was thick with the smell of stale wine, and staler farts, and so I was the first into the morning's wan light.

I had slept fitfully, the adrenaline from my chance meeting taking time to dissipate. Then I had been woken time and again as the men of the section stumbled in. To my relief, they'd drunk enough to pass out quickly; I'd been expecting another showdown with an inebriated Titus. Rufus was the last to arrive, his gentle footsteps padding in shortly before reveille had been called. He was sober, having spent the night with his family.

The century formed up on parade, several soldiers swinging on their feet like corn in the wind. Farts erupted from up and down the lines, and at least one man in the rear rank twisted to vomit on his heels.

'Glad to see you're all well rested,' Pavo snorted through the side of his mouth. He'd passed out earlier than most, and as a consequence he looked one of the more human of the century. He didn't bring up the fact that men had disobeyed his orders and left their tented quarters. Better, in his mind, to skip over the incident and pretend it had never happened.

'Now we're back,' he continued, 'we're getting worked into the fort's guard schedule. From noon, you'll split down into sections to provide checkpoints and roving patrols in Minden.'

He saw some of the men smile knowingly to their comrades, and growled, 'Roving patrols doesn't mean you do a fucking crawl from one inn to another. Now the army's moving there's a lot of people coming in, and a lot going out. Be on the lookout for anything suspicious. Spies, thieves, deserters.'

After ordering the two boy soldiers to clean the equipment of the veterans, Titus and his clique fell with glee back on to their bedrolls. Chickenhead, I now noticed, had never even bothered to rise, Lupus purring contentedly on the ugly man's chest.

With the youngsters cleaning, I awaited some order of my own from the section commander. Latrine duty, perhaps, or cooking the section's breakfast. None came, and Titus must have felt my surprised eyes.

'Get some sleep,' was all he told me, his voice infuriatingly impartial.

I lay down, expecting some trap, but there was none. Within moments, the big man was snoring along with the rest of them.

Confused by the sudden neutrality towards me, I simply lay on my back, watching the hide of our tent grow lighter as the sun climbed higher.

With armour scrubbed bright by Cnaeus and Micon, Titus led our section into Minden. Pavo had instructed him as to our destination, and we took up position on one of the town's arteries, our orders to question those coming and going. If necessary we would search their goods and persons.

I was paired with young Micon to search the outgoing, while Cnaeus and Stumps searched the incoming. Titus and the remaining veterans leaned against the wall of a hovel, watching the traffic and the performance of the searchers. I had hoped to question these civilians, perhaps discover what I had been unable to find the previous night, but none spoke Latin, or at least none admitted to as much.

During a quiet spell I noticed that Titus's group had been joined by two young boys. They were red-haired, and from the way that they shuttled back and forth to the man, it was obvious that these adolescents were Rufus's children. It was forbidden to marry in the ranks, but many a soldier had an unofficial family that followed with the army's baggage train. It would be a brave commander who would try to upset the status quo: he'd have a mutiny on his hands if he did so.

The task of searching the outgoing carts was monotonous, but I embraced it. After the shock of being recognized in the inn, I was glad of a task in which I could lose myself. That being said, instinct is a hard beast to tame, and I felt my eyes on stalks whenever a soldier appeared in the periphery of my vision. Should those men come across me I would have no choice but to run, die or, more than likely, both.

Such thoughts in my head, I took a moment to look over my shoulders and assess my surroundings. There, with Titus, was a familiar figure, but not one from which I needed to hide. It was the quartermaster, taller and wider than even Titus, though his bulkier frame was padded out with fat. They seemed to be on cordial enough terms: two men passing the time of day. It was only later, when a cart covered with a hide sacking came towards me, that they interrupted their conversation and approached.

I was just about to pull back the covering when Titus's hand squeezed me gently by the elbow. 'This one's fine. Let her through.'

Low profile that I wanted, I was happy to oblige.

Micon, however, had ears of cloth to match his brain, and tugged back at his own corner of the sheeting before Titus or the quartermaster could stop him.

They'd been buried beneath hay, but the bumping on the road had shaken enough straw free to allow a glimpse of the cart's contents. Swords. Chain mail. Arrows.

In one smooth movement, Titus was able to pull the covering back into place, while simultaneously delivering a backhand across the startled Micon's face.

'What did you see?' Titus growled into the boy soldier's ear.

'No-no-nothing,' he stammered, and, slow as he was, that was probably true. Titus knew that I was a little quicker with my wits, and his eyes met mine.

'Straw,' I said simply.

The cart went on its way, soon clear of the town, and the quartermaster, face twisted in anger, stomped off in the opposite direction.

'Moonface,' Titus called to the veteran. 'Take over from him.' He gestured towards me. 'You. Let's take a walk.'

It was a short walk into a narrow alleyway off the main street. From the drying vomit on the dirt, it seemed there was an inn nearby.

'What did you see?' Titus asked me again.

'Straw,' I told him, straight-faced.

He seemed content with that, but if he believed in the silence of a man he had beaten, he must have had better reason to do so than my word.

'Twelve,' he finally told me, smiling slightly. There was guile there, and more than a little smugness.

The conversation had broken ranks, and I had no idea why, or to where. My face told him as much.

'That bloke, the one with the birthmarks, he's the quartermaster,' he told me, beginning his explanation, 'and a bent bastard. Sells the straw, like you saw. But you know what he's really good at?'

I shook my head.

'Keeping records. He's really good at that, because he's a quartermaster, and this is the Roman army, so you better be bloody good at keeping records.'

Now I had a horrible feeling that I knew where he was going. My fingers twitched, involuntarily, towards my dagger.

'The quartermaster, he doesn't just issue sandals and javelins. He's got other responsibilities, and one of those is putting dead boys in holes. That meant getting the names of your mates from the forest, so they could get a proper burial. They came from the First Legion, so that's where he had to send for his answers. When he got them, I asked him about these comrades of yours. You know, the ones you can't remember?'

The movement of my fingers was no longer involuntary. I'd have to kill this big bastard.

'I lost a friend the other day. A good one. We went through it together. He was a good fucking man. Seeing him coming in on that cart, with his throat torn open like he was nothing more than an animal—'

84

He stopped. He was picturing his comrade, and struggling.

'Since then, every time I close my eyes, I see that. I don't know if it's revenge I want, or what, but I want *something*. Now, *you*? You come out of a forest with twelve bodies, twelve comrades. You scream in your sleep every night, and I wonder if, maybe, you really are that fucked up that you can't remember it at all.'

This was the point. He was either going to let it go, or force me to kill him.

'Twelve.' He repeated the number again. 'That's how many they recorded as sent from the First Legion, to join up here as casualty replacements. Guess how many bodies the quarter-master put into holes?'

I didn't, and so he answered for me.

'Twelve.' Titus looked me up and down, but it was intrigue in his eyes, not malice. 'So where did you come from?'

And there it was.

I looked for an opening. The neck? He was too tall. The groin, then? Yes. I'd go for his groin, and the artery within.

'So, I've got straw, and you've got problems counting.' He was almost smiling now. 'Embarrassing for us both, if these things came out.'

He was offering me a truce, but I wasn't about to take it. I was waiting for the second his guard lowered, just enough, and then I'd ram the dagger into his groin, and I'd be gone, on the run, and probably dead before the day was out. Fuck it. Better to die with a fighting chance than to have them come for me in my sleep. I'd seen crucifixion. I wouldn't suffer that fate.

Movement came from the end of the alleyway, and Titus turned his head to see it. Here was my chance. My fingers gripped the dagger, but the words kept the blade in its scabbard.

'Uncle Titus!' It was Rufus's boys, their ruddy faces alive with excitement. 'Uncle Titus!' they called again, unaware that they had just saved the man's life, and probably mine into the bargain.

'What is it?' he called back.

'We found a dead man!'

The boys were wrong. They hadn't found a dead man.

They'd found three.

They were in a pile of manure; a stiff arm had been uncovered by a scratching dog. The sullen beast now watched us, protesting with a feeble growl at being denied its dinner.

'Shit way to go,' Stumps snorted to himself. The others ignored the pun.

'Dig him out,' Titus ordered, looking at me. 'Moon, go and get Pavo.'

The grave of dung was shallow, and I decided that the quickest way to extract the body from shit was not to dig, but to pull, and so I took a hold of the stiff wrist – still warm, thanks to the manure – felt for purchase with my sandals, and tugged backwards. The body began to slip out, face down, the dirtied red neck-tie marking the corpse as a soldier. Though short, the man was heavy, and by the time he slithered out like a newborn I was breathing hard. When Titus put his sandal to the body, and rolled him on to his back, I almost stopped breathing altogether. My drinking companion from the inn. The man who had known my secret. A corpse, his throat opened with a gash that was the same livid red as his features.

'There's another,' I heard Stumps say, despite the beating of blood against my temples.

I knew the identity before he was pulled from the filth

and dumped without ceremony alongside his comrade. The silver hair was stained brown from pig shit.

I felt light-headed, washed over with relief, but with a deep, foreboding instinct that told me a greater sin had been committed to save me from my own. Why, I did not know. When the third body was discovered, the questions that seared my skull threatened to overwhelm me.

Pavo arrived then, giving me a sidelong look, doubtless wondering why I – the veteran he knew me to be – was so pale at the sight of a few bodies. He turned his gaze to the final corpse to be dragged from the dung.

'A centurion,' he noted when Stumps produced the vine cane that was a symbol of the officer's authority.

'Stumps. Search them,' Titus ordered.

'They're covered in shit. Get one of the young lads to do it,' he protested.

'They don't know what they're doing,' he explained, before grunting impatiently: 'Forget it. I'll do it myself.'

Expert hands patted down the bodies, checking all the hidden areas where a pouch of coins could be concealed. He found nothing. Even the soldiers' belts had been taken, doubtless for the silver plates that marked them out as veterans.

'Robbed and dumped here,' Titus concluded to Pavo.

The centurion nodded. 'Come up behind them, slit their throats, take their loot, and shove them in the shit. Probably a bunch of auxiliaries,' he concluded.

He sent for a cart, happy with his conclusion and eager to hand the stiffs over to the care of the quartermaster's department. As the bodies were loaded on, the open eyes of the shorter veteran seemed to burn bright with hate for me. I couldn't meet the look and banged against the cart as I turned away, but if Titus noticed, he made no comment.

'Get back to your checkpoint,' Pavo ordered, and the section did so, the bodies soon forgotten. Crime and death were a part of life on the frontier.

Stumps cast his eyes over the manure. 'I mean, really, getting your throat ripped open so someone can have a few more drinks? That's no soldier's death.'

The sweats muttered agreement, and shrugged. What else was there to say?

As the day's light began to fade, the late-summer sky a ribbon of pink against the thatch of the town's hovels, we were replaced at the checkpoint by another section. These soldiers grumbled, sour at being denied a night at the inns. But one of their sweats grinned at our veterans. 'Hopefully we can shake down some of the locals, make up for it tomorrow night.'

'Three Bears?' Titus suggested to his companions, drinking foremost in his own mind.

Rufus shrugged with his usual economy. 'Wife.'

Chickenhead also declined. 'I've got to get back and feed Lupus.'

'Shit,' Titus snorted, 'I don't know who's more in love, you or Rufus. How about you? You look like you could use a drink.'

It took a moment for me to realize that the big lump's words had been intended for my own ears, and I was too taken aback to immediately decline.

'Well?' he pressed.

There was an angle in it for him, I was sure, but the section commander was right – I could use a drink. Gods, I could use a drink.

And so I fell in behind Titus, Stumps and Moonface flanking his broad shoulders. As Stumps discussed the size of his comrade's oval head, I searched my mind for the cause of Titus's invitation.

Inevitably, I kept coming back to the pile of manure and the three bodies that had slithered from its depths. But if

Titus wanted to kill me, why let on that he knew my secret? It made no sense, and I expected I'd find out soon enough, but as it happened, it was the secrets of our high command that were exposed that night.

The source was Metella, the proprietor of the Three Bears. Unlike the German inn that I had visited, this Roman dispensed with security guards, and little wonder – her forearms were as thick as Titus's, and no less scarred.

'She's got the face that launched a thousand ships.' Stumps smiled, catching my appraising look of the innkeeper. 'Course, they were rowin' fast as fuck in the opposite direction.'

He had to shout to be heard above the din, for the tavern's space was crowded with legionaries, and his tactless words were caught by their subject. The big woman grabbed a tight hold of his ear and his smile quickly turned to a grimace.

'Funny boy, hey?' She grinned before bouncing his head off the counter top.

Titus and Moonface roared with laughter, and the big woman's eyes sparkled with mirth. When she eyed Titus, there was a healthy dose of lust in there, too.

He told her about the dead men in the pig shit, and I did my best not to pass out from relief, and revulsion. It gave me no satisfaction to know that the men's death meant my own survival, but neither was I about to run to Pavo and confess my sins.

I was snapped from my reverie by the feeling of eyes on me. Four sets. The others had ceased their conversation, and were simply observing me. What had I missed?

'So you're the one, eh?' Metella asked, casting a disappointed eye over my gaunt features.

'The one?' I managed.

91

'From the forest. The bloody one. The ghost. You don't look like much of a ghost to me. A skeleton, maybe.'

The others howled with laughter at her jibe. So, this was the reason Titus had brought me here: to show me off to his friend, an object for scrutiny.

'I should be going,' I murmured, but the big man's hand shoved me back down on my stool.

'Ah, sit down and have some wine, you grumpy bastard,' he told me, before turning to the innkeeper. 'You've hurt his feelings! Must be a free drink in that.'

'Sure,' she replied, passing me the cup. 'But it's going on your tab.'

Titus made no protest, and as I drank deep of the bitter wine, the pair continued in their trade of camp gossip. I ignored most of it – I didn't know any of the characters – until one name caught my attention.

'Arminius,' she repeated, at my insistence, and then turned back to the others, 'was a fucking riot at the governor's dinner, apparently. Young Arminius is there, and a bunch of other commanders and chieftains, then this one German storms in, telling Governor Varus that Arminius is a traitor, and he's plotting to see us all off.'

'Who came in?' Titus asked, seemingly unflustered by the accusations.

'I forget the name, but he's the same tribe as Arminius, a bit higher up the ranks. Think he's his uncle, maybe? Fuck knows. They're all inbred, these bloody Germans.'

'Our nobility's no different,' Stumps offered.

'That's true.' She nodded, chins wobbling. 'But don't interrupt, or you'll get another clout.'

'Sorry.'

'That's interrupting, isn't it? Anyway, the uncle wants Arminius put in chains, but Varus won't believe a word of it.'

'What happened?' I found myself compelled to ask.

'Nothing. Turns out Arminius had eloped with his uncle's daughter a few months back. The old man was just pissed off, and wanted to mess him around.'

'Family, eh?' Stumps shrugged, ending the conversation, at least for their clique. I couldn't drop it so easily myself. Arminius, accused of treason.

I found that hard to reconcile with the man I had met, however briefly. A man who had offered me – to whom he owed nothing – such kindness and compassion.

I knew treason, and traitors. Arminius was not the type. A family feud was all it was, spilled into the governor's lap because of the high station of the actors.

By the time I'd convinced myself of this, Metella and the veterans were on to topics new, discussing the occasion when Moonface had been fleeced by a whore, later revealed to be a man in drag. Ridden by laughter as they were – with the exception of Moonface, whose mug was on the verge of curdling – none noticed me slip away and out of the inn's back door.

As I traced my way through Minden and into the army's camp, the thought of treason was still foremost in my mind. It was still there when I lay on my bedroll, despite clenching my eyes tight, and begging it to leave me be. It was still there when, hours later, I finally fell into the darkness of sleep.

Was it any wonder that I woke screaming?

I wanted to scream, but there was no sound. I wanted to die, but death would not take me.

Ribs snapped. Skin and muscle tore, and still I could not scream. My voice was not my own to control. It never had been.

The eagle's wings emerged from my shoulders, bloodied, torn and decayed. They took me to the air, but their beat was heavy, a brutal omen, like the drums of war.

Airborne, I could see my friends. My brothers. I reached out. Beseeched them for help.

Some ran. Some stood as if petrified, faces etched in horror at the vision I had become, a once handsome face reduced to a human jaw, a bloodied, bear-like snout dripping saliva and hot breath from above.

My friends ran, or stood, and I reached out to them. I wanted to hold them, to tell them it was me, their friend, their brother, but where I reached, bodies fell. My hands had always been weapons, held weapons, and now they were reddened talons with the fine points of swords.

This wasn't *fair*. This wasn't my doing. If only someone would *listen* to me, talk to me, then I could explain all this. This monster was not *me*. But they would not stop. They would not listen. They never had, even though they *knew*. Instead, they fled and, one by one, silently wailing as my wings beat against the heavy air, I killed them.

Husks of comrades danced upon by flies looked back at me, damnation and betrayal in their dead eyes. I needed to escape, now more than ever, and so I beat the wings harder, each snap of the bones threatening to bring forth a scream that would never come. I needed to scream; I knew that. It would be my release. My salvation.

The wings took me higher, higher. Below, a forest stretched in every direction, closer to black than green, its canopy as dense as a formation of assaulting shields. Fruit hung from the trees. My eyes adjusted. The fruit was decaying, fly-blown. It was men. Soldiers. Women. Children. It was *my* fruit, born from the seeds I had planted. The same seeds that had taken root in my back to sprout the wings of the damned.

A roar, and I snapped my head up.

The horizon was growing red, and an immense wall of thunder was approaching. It was a wave, as high as any tower, and it was crashing through the forest, uprooting the ancient trees and carrying with it the bodies.

I knew that I must climb higher to escape it, but now the wings failed me, their beat becoming weaker. They shed feathers, which mocked me in their gentle spirals towards the earth. The wave roared closer.

Blood. A wave of blood.

I tried to close my eyes, but they would not obey. Instead, I watched the wave come closer, closer, trees and bodies churned in its red froth.

It was upon me.

I screamed.

# 14

The nightmare left me nauseous, as it always did. My breaths came shallow and ragged, as if the weight of a horse were upon my chest.

In the darkness of the tent I saw two sets of wide, white eyes upon me. They were terrified: the eyes of Micon and Cnaeus.

Another pair opened and, as my own sight adjusted to the gloom, I saw that these belonged to Chickenhead. Again, we were the only four present within the tent.

'You woke Lupus,' he told me, his tone as dull as his stare. In the man's hands, I could make out the shape of the agitated kitten, struggling.

'I'm sorry,' I finally managed, still fighting for air.

The veteran got to his feet, cooing to his feline companion. His fingers had wrapped around the throats of enemies, but now they gently stroked his friend. Eventually the kitten calmed, and the old soldier turned his attention to me. 'Outside.'

I followed, the cool air welcome on my livid skin.

'Here.' He handed me a cup, and I muttered thanks.

'This is water,' I told him, surprised.

'You start drinking now, you'll never stop.'

I nodded at the wisdom in his words. We drifted into silence, the cup soon drained. As he refilled it, I turned my eyes up to the skies, where the usual canopy of stars was eclipsed by a shadow of thin cloud.

'How long?' he asked.

I was too tired to offer resistance. I accepted the cup, and the offer of a veteran's ear that came with it. 'I'm not sure.'

'But they're getting worse?'

I nodded, and he must have seen the movement in my silhouette.

'For two years, after Drusus,' he told me, referring to the campaign of the famous general, and what must have been the first taste of battle for Chickenhead, the boy soldier. 'The same one, over and over . . .' He paused, and I thought his revelation was at an end. It wasn't.

'Fifteen legions we took into Germany, the strongest force in the world. The tribes stood, we scrapped, and by the time I was nineteen I'd lost count of the men I'd killed. I was fine with that. I *loved* that. But it was the other things that kept me awake for the next two years. The *raiding parties* – a nice name for butchering the local men, and raping the women.'

His voice had gradually grown weaker, echoing as if he were descending into the shaft of a mine. He took the cup from my hand and sipped, swilling the water around his mouth and spitting it on to the dirt.

'This German girl, she couldn't have been older than fourteen. First woman I'd ever been inside.' I felt his sickened smile in the darkness. 'Isn't that something?' he concluded.

'You got past it,' I said steadily, aching to know how.

'I did?' he replied with an empty laugh.

I thought our conversation would die there, the veteran doubtless picturing the young German girl he had raped when he was not much more than a child himself.

'I've been stationed here my entire service.' His voice creaked. 'I've even been through that village again. When my

97

twenty's up, I'll go back to Italy, but I'm not stupid enough to think that she won't come with me. That's the problem with what's inside your head. It has to come with you. Don't kid yourself that a few miles makes any difference.'

He was the first of the veterans in the section to talk to me as a man. Traumatized as I was from my nightmare, I was too shocked to see the sweat's candour for what it was – a recognition of a kindred, tortured spirit. But if I was shocked by the veteran's behaviour up to that point, his next gesture threatened to overwhelm me.

'Here,' he offered, holding out Lupus. 'Hold him. Give him a stroke if you like. It helps.'

I took the struggling kitten in my hands, feeling the power of such a tiny creature hidden beneath the fur. With some encouragement from Chickenhead, the animal calmed, and I tentatively began to stroke its head and ears.

The veteran was right. It helped. Concentrating on the kitten's tiny beating heart, my own returned to its usual rhythm, the threat of its bursting through my ribs at an end.

'Thank you,' I said, my eyes on the kitten.

'You saved that lad,' he offered by way of explanation. 'He's young, and that makes a boy do stupid things, but he didn't deserve to die for it. If it was one of the others did what you did at the bridge, they'd be getting an award.'

I grunted at that, knowing the truth in what he had said. 'Regardless. Thank you.'

'Don't tell the others,' he answered, an edge of steel to his voice. 'Bring him inside when you're done.'

He left me then, the life of his most treasured friend in my hands. I stayed in that spot, stroking and cooing, until the sky grew amber with the dawn.

As I turned to step inside the hide structure, I felt a wave of troubled uncertainty wash over me.

'Fuck,' I growled beneath my breath, angry at my nightmares, and at myself. Angry, because I would no longer see the veteran as a soldier, a faceless killer in steel.

I would see a comrade.

## 15

That morning, formed up on parade, Chickenhead made no mention of our talk. He was his usual self with the veterans, a part of the whole and yet aside, and I wondered which, if any, knew that the most gnarled sweat amongst them suffered with the savage memories of his early service. Likely none, I surmised. Weakness was something we hid from those closest to us, no matter the cost.

Pavo approached the front of the parade, a creeping smile displacing his usual scowl. Titus knew his centurion well enough to read that omen.

'We're getting paid.'

And he wasn't wrong. After Pavo had informed the century of that fact, and once the cheers had died down, we were marched to the centre of the fort to receive the third and final instalment of that year's wage.

For a legionary, this pay would be three hundred sesterces, but the annual salary of nine hundred would suffer deductions for anything from equipment loss to donations towards a funeral fund. Every soldier grumbled that should they die for Rome, the least the Empire could do would be to bury them from out of its own pockets, but the reality was that each man was anxious for a good send-off, so that his spirits could be content and venerated by his ancestors. The last thing anybody wanted was to be a discarded corpse on a battlefield, and so the funeral funds and mess bills were paid despite the grumbles.

Arriving at the centre of the camp, we joined the other centuries of our own legion and cohort, the men filing slowly along to receive their pay. Though these soldiers belonged to the same unit as the troops of my own century, they were mostly strangers, the section being a soldier's close family, and the century his extended.

As we drew nearer to the desks, my eyes were drawn to the gathered standards of the legions. These sacred totems had come from the hands of the emperor, and were topped by eagles crafted from silver, the bird of prey chosen because it was sacred to the god Jupiter. Each of these standards was a shrine in itself, but gathered here, under the watchful eye of the standard-bearers, the sight was almost too much for a reverent soul such as Moonface.

'Such magnificence,' he uttered in adulation.

Stumps poked him. 'It's a bird on a stick.'

Only after Titus reminded Moonface that a fight would result in a docking of pay did the enraged man stand down.

I took in the sight of the standard-bearers, one for each of the three legions in camp. They were formidable-looking warriors, chosen for their heroism and dedication. The standards were prized by enemies the length of the world, and so the standard-bearer would always be found where fighting was at its thickest. The faces of the men were hidden from me by thick cloaks of bearskin slung over their shoulders, the snouts terminating in a peaked cap that set the wearer's face into deep shadow. I shuddered at the sight of them.

These standard-bearers were also responsible for their legion's coffers, for the majority of men elected to hold most of their pay within the safety of a fort's walls. When it came to my turn to make my mark and take the coin, the issuing centurion's eyebrows raised as I stated that I wished to withdraw my full stipend.

'There's not much to spend it on in the forests, lad,' he offered gently, hoping to change my mind.

'I'd like to hold it, sir,' I lied. 'See how much my life is worth,' I added with a smile.

'You're going to be disappointed, lad,' he told me, and was not wrong. The weight of the coins was pitiful. I looked at Pavo, whose own pay would not be much higher. No wonder he aspired to be *primus pilus* – the First Spear, and most senior centurion in the legion, with an annual salary of one hundred thousand sesterces.

With the money tied in a purse, and snug inside my tunic, I took my place on the side of the parade square, and waited in formation as the other men were paid. My eyes drifted from the chests of coins to the eagle standards, and the men that carried them. There were but twenty-eight legions in the whole of the Empire, and to be one of the few standard-bearers was an honour like no other.

Mesmerized as I was by this elite, it took me a while to realize that our entire century had passed by the pay chests, and yet we remained on the square. Titus must have wondered at the reason himself, and quietly called to Pavo for the answer.

'The governor's coming out to make an address.'

And so we waited in the sun, for hours it seemed, the square slowly filling with soldiers. They were smiling at first, anxious to be paid, but the smiles turned sullen when they understood that they'd be kept from the wine and whores to wait on Governor Varus's oration.

I was in the front rank, so when he did finally arrive, in the late afternoon, I was afforded a good look at a Roman who, by his position, was one of the most powerful men in the world. As Governor of Germany, Varus commanded five legions, and more than double that in auxiliary cohorts. All in all, it was almost a fifth of the Empire's fighting strength.

But strength was not a word that could be attributed to the general's physical self. He wore armour, though I expect the aim was to give his body a harder look, rather than protection. His features were dark, the aquiline nose testament to his noble birth. Beneath this hook, an extra chin shone with sweat born from the effort of wearing battle attire. I have seen many leaders, and on first glance it seemed as though this one was more inclined to the court than the campaign trail. Little wonder the army had been inactive, and the German tribesmen had grown bold.

Governor Varus now took his place on a dais, his strong voice at odds with his physique. As a noble, he would have been trained in oratory from a young age.

'Brave soldiers of Rome!' he began, and I groaned inwardly. Behind me, I heard Chickenhead snicker.

'Let me tell you of the glory that awaits us!' Varus went on, and so began a tedious detailing of his grand plan.

The wasted summer, it seemed, had been a ploy to lure out our enemies. The change of route to the Rhine, eschewing the forts and supplies on the River Lippe, was a feint that would catch our foe off guard.

'He could spin a bloody cloak with his arsehole, this one,' I heard Stumps pipe up beside me.

It was true enough. Varus glossed over all of the shortcomings of his campaign, painting them as strokes of a master tactician. Despite Pavo's repeated sharp glances, Stumps couldn't resist a further jibe.

'If he'd invited the Germans for this speech, they'd already have surrendered.'

Perhaps Varus believed that this hot air was what the common soldiers wanted to hear. Officers and nobles, after all, rarely connected with the men below them, but in a sign that he was not totally oblivious to the desires of his troops, Varus now assured the ranks that there would be plenty of loot on the campaign, and that they were free to take from the Germans whatever they could find.

'They pulled the feathers!' Varus yelled above the cheers. 'Now let them feel the eagle's claws!'

'At least the end was good.' Stumps grinned. 'Bit of loot! Don't mind if I do.'

We were dismissed, and marched back to our tents.

As Titus counted the pile of coins in front of him, Stumps pushed the big man on his feelings towards the coming campaign.

'We better march soon,' Titus answered, stifling a yawn. 'Every bastard in Germany must know what's coming, and the longer we delay, the longer they've got to go burying their good stuff.'

'They'll be burying their sons and fathers soon,' Moonface added with relish.

'Oh, give it a break, you camp-fire hero,' Chickenhead chided him. 'Your sword's seen about as much action as a virgin's cunt.'

Stumps gave a deep bark of a laugh and slapped his friend Moonface on the shoulder. 'He got you there. Next time it'll be "I was on the fort walls, when you were in yer dad's balls!" Ha!'

'I'm surprised you haven't shat yourself yet,' Chickenhead spat at Stumps, unhappy to be mocked.

'About what? This whole thing's a riot. Like Titus said, the Germans have had all the warning in the world. That's all this is, a cock-swinging contest. They've got theirs out, now we'll get ours out.'

'Please don't,' Rufus interceded.

'We get ours out,' Stumps continued, miming the action. 'They see it's bigger than theirs, and everyone goes home happy.'

'You ever thought of running for the Senate?' Titus asked his comrade, before getting to his feet. 'I'm off to see Pavo.'

'Why?' several voices asked at once.

Titus answered by tossing a pair of dice into the air. 'He got paid too, you know? If I don't take it, some other bastard might.'

He was about to step out of the tent, but stopped, eyes on the two young soldiers who were polishing his armour. 'You can leave off that tonight, boys. Where we're going, doesn't pay to stand out. Get yourself into town. Here.' He reached inside his purse and tossed a coin to each of them. 'Get a whore on me.'

The youngsters smiled coyly, unsure of how to react to the sudden generosity.

'Could be the last chance you ever have to get your dick wet,' Titus told them as he left. The boys' smiles slid off their faces.

The section commander's exit began the usual exodus: Rufus to his family; Stumps, Chickenhead and Moonface to the Three Bears.

'You could buy an army of whores with that money you took out,' Stumps informed me.

'I'm just going to stay here,' I told him, not that he gave a shit.

'Fine. Play with yourself then, you tight bastard,' he snapped as a farewell.

Now that the veterans had departed, Micon and Cnaeus talked in hushed tones, obviously discussing what they were going to do.

'Go to town,' I told them a little irritably, sick of the whispers. 'Titus is right. You could be dead soon. Go and get drunk, get laid, but do something.'

They did, and I was at last alone. I was hoping that Chickenhead would have left Lupus behind, but evidently the kitten had been invited to the Three Bears along with the veterans, and so I had nothing to do but think, and contemplate the coming campaign.

We were going north and, unlike Stumps, I did not believe the Germans would simply be content to look at our cocks, as he had put it. No, they would contest our presence, not in battle, but with hit-and-run attacks. Our army would lose a few dozen men, a hundred at most, and Varus could say that he'd persecuted his enemy and achieved his goals. As governor, he was first and foremost a politician, and, like all politicians, he knew how to weave the strands of defeat and failure and turn them into a cloak of personal victory.

My own victory would be coming soon, I knew. When the army hit its northernmost destination, then I would slip away, and continue my own journey. Fortune had been kind, and I was sure that the money I had received that day would pay for my conveyance across the sea, and to the land of the Britons.

The thought of that land gave me a rising sense of hope, but also one of trepidation. I had never set foot on those lands. From long conversations in my childhood I had a grasp of the language, but how many years had it been since those harsh words had left my tongue? I would be as much a stranger there as I was here, with nothing but a name to give me hope of sanctuary.

Still, it was my best chance – my *only* chance – of salvaging something from a life that had begun with such promise, before my naivety and optimism had been ground to dust beneath the heel of Rome's legions.

And yet, something Chickenhead said to me had struck a blow. He couldn't know of my plans – no one did – but maybe he could see enough to recognize a man on the run.

It was with this thought in mind that I decided I must seek out familiar companions, and inspiration. With luck, those comrades were here within the fort. I had seen them that day, taking pride of place on the parade square.

And so I went to talk with the eagles.

# 16

The three legions' standards were set back in an alcove on the fringe of the parade square, the silver eagles brought to shimmering life by the candlelight. The parade square itself was seemingly deserted, but I knew that there would be guards in the shadows – soldiers drawn from each of the legion's first cohorts, the body of men that carried the sigils into battle.

On the hallowed ground of the alcove, a handful of legionaries knelt before the totems that embodied the spirits of their legions, past, present and future. The standards were a symbol that, no matter what befell these individual soldiers, their memory would live on through the legion.

It was bullshit, I told myself. Absolute bullshit. And yet I had come here. I had been drawn here. I needed to see the standards. To touch them. Why?

I reached out.

'Evening, brother.'

The words came from over my shoulder, and though they were spoken as a greeting, there was a force and order behind them, my hand dropping involuntarily to my side.

I turned, and formally greeted the man who had spoken. 'Standard-bearer.'

The peak of his bearskin cloak cast his face into deep shadow. Beneath the darkness, his jaw was angular, nicked with scars. Here was a warrior.

'Go ahead,' he allowed, seeing that I'd retracted my hand.

With his permission I reached out, my fingers touching the silver, feeling the lines of the feathers, a work of master craftsmanship.

'They're cold,' I said to myself.

If he heard my words, he made no comment, mistaking my mask of loss as one of reverence.

'Your devotion does you credit, brother, but paydays are rare, and in these last few years, battle even more so. Tonight is a night to be with comrades.'

'I am,' I breathed, tracing my finger along the crest.

'What's your name, brother?'

'Felix,' I told him, breaking my touch. The lie came more naturally now.

'The lucky one.' A thin smile appeared above the scarred jawline. 'A good thing for a soldier.'

'Better to be heroic,' I offered, taking in the awards that were affixed to the man's armour.

He shook his head, the snout of his bearskin exaggerating the small motion. 'Plenty of dead heroes. Better to be lucky.'

Though they were hidden from me, I knew from the tone of the man's words that his eyes would be as dead as my own. He left then, perhaps uncomfortable at allowing even the smallest of insights into an armoured mind.

I listened to the tread of his sandals as he disappeared into shadow. His duty was to these standards, and to his legion. While the other soldiers were drinking and whoring, laughing and arguing with comrades, he would stand sentinel, unaided, over the legion's soul. It was the greatest irony of the legion – the man who held the eagle lived apart, fought single-handedly, and died alone. Despite his obvious courage and heroism, I pitied him.

I turned back to the eagles.

I have no idea how long I stood there, picturing standards held above the bloodshed of battlefields a continent away. Long enough that the praying soldiers had left, and I was alone with the watchers in the shadows.

At first, so deep was I in the past that I thought the sound of struggle was nothing but a vivid memory.

I was wrong.

They brought him across the square in chains, a silent hooded figure dragged by a mob of a dozen burly Germans. At their head was a chieftain, identifiable by the thick golden torque hanging across a chest that could have been carved from oak. The only noise came from the tramp of their boots; the men's lips were sealed, twisted into looks of grim determination.

My hand went to the dagger on my belt, but a voice beside me willed me to be still.

'Steady, brother.'

The standard-bearer. Closer now, I saw his eyes for the first time. A killer's eyes, focused yet lifeless.

I followed their gaze, and saw that, in the darkness, a group of Roman soldiers had followed the Germans. Their swords were sheathed, and yet they were clearly agitated.

'Nineteenth Legion,' the man beside me said. 'They have the fort's guard tonight.'

Following their chieftain – who was evidently uninterested in the collection of silver eagles – the Germans came to a stop in the centre of the square; the tall captive was forced down on to his knees.

At the square's edges, the Romans fanned out, facing inwards, watchful yet held back by doubt. There was a century's worth of soldiers, and they could have overcome the Germans – powerfully built as they were – in mere moments.

'They must value the hostage,' I thought aloud.

'Or the hostage-taker,' the standard-bearer answered, observing the chieftain who wore golden wealth around his neck and arms. 'Maybe both,' he continued. 'You don't bring a hostage into the heart of a Roman camp unless you place a lot of worth on his head, and your own.'

A further century of Roman soldiers arrived, but still they made no move against the Germans. The tribesmen held their ground, immobile, thickly bearded statues in chain mail.

A centurion, his sword sheathed, strode up to the chieftain, and did him the courtesy of a small bow. They conferred, words lost to me, and the officer returned to his men. Considering that there was a man clad in irons, with two hundred armed warriors in attendance, it was all very calm.

And then the cavalry arrived. Six of them.

They were Germans, and I knew them well – Arminius's men, but their leader was absent. Instead, his large bodyguard Berengar rode at the head of the handful of troopers, his ugly face twisted in a snarl.

As the horses came to a stop, the stomp of their hooves echoing in the night, Arminius's warrior yelled something in German that could only have been a challenge. The chieftain's face showed his distaste, but he held his tongue, as well as his ground. Signalling with the slightest movement of his head, the hood was pulled from the captive, and I had my first look at the hostage.

Arminius, of course. I had known it the second his soldiers appeared. Nothing else could have caused the angst they displayed so openly.

The prince's face was bloodied, and yet he smiled. He smiled at his captors and, turning his head, he smiled at his six loyal men on horseback.

And they charged.

No weapons were drawn, and I expect they hoped to use the bulk of their horses to press through the body of men, grab Arminius, and ride to safety.

But the chieftain's men were handpicked – the best warriors his tribe had to offer. With no orders needing to be given, they pulled into a tight knot of shields, Arminius and the chieftain at its centre, and, seeing the solid object ahead of them, the cavalry mounts pulled up, turning and rearing.

Immediately the hostage-takers burst from behind their impromptu shield wall, taking hold of reins and riders. One man was felled by a flailing hoof, but the others had momentum on their side, and in seconds, three of Arminius's men were out of the saddle.

The rescue effort had ended in failure, to the dismay of the prince's bodyguard. From their howls of rage and torment, I could only conclude that they did not expect their leader to survive the night.

I should have stayed where I was. I should have left the German bastards to it.

But loyalty is a potent drug, and I was already running.

I ran into the rear of the melee. The pathetic cavalry charge had come from the opposite side of the square, and it was German backs I faced, not shields. Even the chieftain was struggling to pull the remaining troopers from their saddles, and so there was only one man between myself and Arminius.

As I said, these Germans were seasoned warriors, and the principle of all-round defence was one that they knew well. Not allowing himself to be sucked into the scrap ahead of him, one warrior had kept his eyes on the shadows to their rear. He saw me coming from thirty paces away, which was twenty-nine more than he needed to decide how to kill me.

But he couldn't kill me. The violence in the square was no more bloody than a wrestling match, though I sensed that life was somehow at stake. Obviously under orders from the chieftain, the men were at pains to subdue their fellow countrymen with fists and elbows only, and so there was no way that the solitary German warrior could gut a Roman in the centre of the army's fort.

It was this indecision that let me beat him. The man finally attempted to tackle me as I was a pace away, but I'd expected his dive, and feinted to the side, pushing down on to his back so that his momentum ploughed his face into the dirt. With that simple move, and as the last of the cavalrymen were pulled to the ground and beaten, I was at Arminius's side.

He recognized me at once, but the smile slid from his face as I drew my dagger and held it to his throat.

Instantly, the square was still.

'What are you doing, Felix?' The words were as cool as a winter stream, his intense eyes betraying not a flicker of fear.

I didn't answer. I wasn't sure myself. Plans formed in a split second of adrenaline and emotion don't usually hold up well to scrutiny.

Seeing the blade pressing into the skin of their hostage and prince, the Germans stilled, breathing heavily.

The chieftain, bushy eyebrows creased in puzzlement, repeated Arminius's query in heavily accented Latin. 'What are you doing?'

'Back off, or I'll kill him.'

'You'll kill him?' There was an edge of amusement in his voice.

Perhaps I'd miscalculated. The big man seemed to be considering the proposal with some seriousness.

'Maybe it would be better if you did,' he finally mused aloud, confirming my fears.

'Uncle,' Arminius said, ignoring my insistence that he shut up. 'You're wrong about this.'

'Don't talk to me, whelp,' the chieftain spat, face quickly creasing with anger. 'It's only the feelings of my idiot girl that has kept your head on your shoulders.'

So this was the uncle – father of Arminius's eloped bride, and chieftain of the Cherusci tribe, to which Arminius belonged. There could be only one reason that the chieftain had put Arminius in chains. One reason he had brought him here, and one person he had come to see. Realizing who, and why, my world felt as if it were about to fall out of my stomach.

Why had I done this? After every poisonous decision, every painful mile, I would die screaming on a crucifix. Why?

But I knew the answer well enough.

Loyalty. As deadly as love.

The man I feared arrived moments later. I feared him not because of his prowess as a warrior – he had none – but because his power was immeasurable. Since donning the uniform of the legions, my life had been placed indirectly in his hands. Now, it was hanging from his manicured fingernails.

'Governor Varus,' the chieftain greeted him.

Varus wore a simple toga, the expensive silk pulled tight around his spreading waist. His face was neutral: he was a politician, after all. The armoured troops that flanked him were enough of a reminder of his power.

'Segestes.' He spoke, tiredly, to the chieftain. Then he greeted the hostage: 'Arminius.' There was no mirth in his voice.

I braced myself.

'And who are you, soldier?'

I attempted to pull myself to attention, while continuing to keep the dagger's point at the prince's throat. What a sight I must have made.

'Beg to report, sir, Legionary Felix, Second Century, Second Cohort of the Seventeenth Legion, sir.'

'And my friend, governor,' Arminius added.

'Your friend?' Varus asked, clearly believing that the shock of arrest had addled the mind of his German protégé. 'So what is he doing?'

'Saving my life,' Arminius told him with a smile that threatened to light up the parade square. 'I think you can lower the blade now, Felix,' he suggested.

'Yes, yes,' Varus insisted. 'Put the blade away, soldier. There will be no bloodshed, not here. Not against this man.' These words were directed at Segestes, but the chieftain was not about to back down.

'Varus, this man is plotting against you! He is a snake, a treacherous snake. You must imprison him before he leads you to ruin!'

The governor winced at being addressed by his name, but let it slide, maintaining his composure and using his most calm yet convincing tone. Politics, always politics.

'My friend, this is a member of your own family we are talking about—'

'He stopped being family when he became a treacherous shit!'

'—and I understand that you are justly offended by his actions with your daughter, but Arminius is a loyal officer.'

'He's loyal only to himself!' Segestes thundered, clearly struggling to stop himself attacking his nephew. 'By the gods, governor, if you won't imprison him alone, then take me too. Put chains on every noble in my tribe, and those that claim fealty. I will gladly suffer the dungeons if it stops this worm from leading the army to ruin, and bringing bloodshed to my lands.'

There was something about the man's words, the sheer conviction, that stopped my heart. I could see that Varus felt it too, and the governor had to look into Arminius's eyes for reassurance that the accusations were false, despite their venom. I looked at those eyes myself, and they were the eyes of a man at peace with the world. A man of his word. When I saw that, I believed again, and my heart resumed its thumping within my chest. Varus saw the same. He almost sagged with relief.

'Release him.' He spoke so softly that he had to repeat the order.

Segestes's look could have set the world on fire. He turned that gaze on to his nephew, spat, and then spun on his heel, his men following in his wake.

Unbound, Arminius stood, and I felt his hand squeeze my elbow. His voice was so low that only I could hear. 'Felix, no matter what, no matter when, you have a friend in me, and a place by my side.'

'I owed you one, sir.'

'You owed me two.' He smiled, leaving me confused, but that was the end of our conversation. Varus embraced Arminius, the governor abandoning dignity, such was his relief at the release of a man he adored.

They walked away together, Varus with an arm over the young prince's shoulder, the two centuries of soldiers following in their wake. Arminius's loyal soldiers, battered but buoyed, limped behind with their horses.

I was left, forgotten, my eyes on the back of the enigma. When I rushed to his side, I had told myself that I was repaying a debt – balancing the books – but when he had called himself my friend I had believed him, and treasured the connotation.

I watched him go until he was consumed by the hungry shadows at the far end of the parade square. Slowly, I sank to one knee, breathing deep of the night's air.

'Lucky, and heroic.' It was the standard-bearer, the mouth beneath the shadows pulled up in amusement.

'Just fucking stupid,' I groaned.

'Yes, that too, but lucky beats stupid.' He offered his hand. I gripped his forearm, and he pulled me to my unsteady feet. 'Just don't push it too far.' He looked towards the shadows. 'These Germans will be the end of us.'

With that warning in my ears, he took his leave. The next time we would meet, the fur of his bearskin would be matted with blood.

I looked down at my hands. They were trembling, adrenaline I had not even known was there now seeping out of my body. Despite the shaking muscles, I felt a surge of heat and purpose course through my body. I had saved a worthy man's life.

I did not know that in doing so, I had condemned an army of others to their graves.

# PART TWO

# 17

I'm sure the average citizen has a romantic notion about how an army looks when it takes the field, its thousands of soldiers moving as one, a horde of individuals fused for a single purpose. After all, this is the image our rulers have pushed since the early days of the Republic, the bombast only growing under the Empire. We see it painted, sculpted, and acted out: the conquering heroes, sandalled legions stamping beneath the eagles.

Perhaps, from a distance, that is how it appears. Or perhaps, if you are a citizen of some other land, it seems more like a venomous, multi-limbed insect inching its way across a landscape, stripping the fields and laying waste to the towns.

Yet this beast is not romantic, or mystical; it is not a single creature, but a cluster of hollow-eyed individuals. Evidence of this humanity grows stronger still during a halt, when the limbs of the insect will be pissing and shitting alongside the trail, or even in place, depending on the degree of discipline on which their commanders insist.

On the move, the sweat-coated soldiers at the head of the column hold a blessed position. They may be the first to walk into any ambush, but that is better than following in their wake. During the dry months, the vanguard's advance kicks up dust that sinks into the throats, eyes and ears of those who trail them. In winter, the van's shod feet churn any track into a viscous sludge through which the following soldiers have to slither and stamp, all while carrying a pack made heavier by the rain. The warriors of the rearguard will have the honour of marching through an army's worth of piss and shit, their open sores and numerous blisters soon rife with painful, pus-weeping infection.

Perhaps, if the dust is spread by the winds, or the soldier can raise his head from out of his exhaustion, then he may glimpse the rest of the army as it crosses some stretch of high ground, but on the whole, all the marching trooper will see is the men to his front and flanks, whether he is part of a group of twenty or twenty thousand. Only the aristocratic officers, and those with the highly dangerous job of cavalry scouts, will have the slightest notion as to the scale of the army. But, for a veteran and salt like Chickenhead, there are ways of making an educated guess.

'Fifteen thousand,' he told the section between shallow pants. 'That scout said we're about a quarter way from the front, and there's already a load of shit on the track.'

'You're not wrong,' Stumps agreed with a grimace. 'Think the scouts have traded in their horses for elephants.'

'You used that one last summer,' Chickenhead replied tiredly. 'You're boring me now.' Like all the other men of the section, his voice came from behind a legion-issued red neckerchief, tied about the face to keep out the dust cloud that had risen from the dry summer track.

'I'm surprised you can remember a year ago, you old shit,' Stumps countered, but when no reply came from his comrade, the younger veteran turned to Titus, who marched on his shoulder. 'You reckon he's right?'

Titus's mind seemed to be on other matters, his feet moving automatically. Stumps pressed again, and the big man finally slid from his reverie.

'What?'

'How many in the army? Chicken reckons fifteen thousand.'

'What does it matter?' Titus rumbled, and Stumps clearly decided it was best to let the lump drift back to his own thoughts.

'How many miles you reckon a soldier marches in his career?' he asked Chickenhead instead.

'A lot.'

'Depends where you're stationed,' Moonface suggested. 'I reckon up here we put in a lot more miles than the legions down south. Comfy life out in the desert.'

'What the fuck would you know about the desert?' Titus snarled, catching the conversation.

'Nothing,' Moonface admitted reluctantly.

'Yeah. Nothing. So shut your fucking mouth.'

We tramped on in silence, or at least devoid of conversation. Despite men's efforts to secure their gear, helmets bounced off shields, scabbards off armour.

'We sound like the world's shittest musicians,' Stumps observed.

I tried to concentrate on the pack in front of me, wanting, like Titus, my mind to rise above the column, for the march had not brought with it the elation I had expected.

That was because, mere hours after the incident on the parade square, I had been sought out in my tent by one of the quartermaster's minions. I had hoped that with his logistical workload of preparing for the legion to decamp, he would have been unable to call in my debt until we reached our winter quarters. Of course, by then, I planned to have been long gone, using my collection of coins to pay for passage to Britain, and what I hoped would be a new beginning. Instead, I had handed my purse to the ill-tempered loan shark.

'Dead men don't pay debts,' he'd grunted, noticing my appraising eye on the line of sullen solders behind me.

'You think the Germans will stand and fight, sir?' I'd asked, appealing to his vanity. As I'd expected, he couldn't resist the opportunity to display his insight.

'Stand and fight *us*? No, not enough of the tribes making trouble. But these goat-fuckers didn't bring Drusus and his legions to a standstill by being cowards. They'll know what these raids of theirs will have set off, whether Varus is a lazy bastard or not, and so they'll have some surprises for us, I'm tellin' you. Anyway, I'm taking no chances. You're two short.' He snorted this final statement, his birthmarks darkening with anger. After fishing the coins from my pockets, I was near destitute once more.

The army had broken camp the next morning. After a summer of inactivity, it was a blizzard of commotion, doubt-less due to Varus's eagerness to be on the road before Arminius and his uncle could resume their family feud. Word of the night's stand-off had already begun to filter through the tented lines, but my century remained ignorant of my own involvement, and doubtless that was for the best, as Titus was already irritable. The other men of the section had no idea why, and even Rufus gave his close friend a wide berth, organizing the section's decampment himself while Titus sat alone, digging his dagger into the earth in aggres-sive contemplation.

With the tents and stores packed on to mules, Pavo marched the century out to a wide field to join the cohort. From there we joined the remainder of the legion, and even with the discipline and organization of the army, it was still a stop-start affair, the sun high in the sky by the time the host finally marched away from the hovels of Minden. Doubtless its citizens would be glad to see the backs of the drunken, sex-crazed soldiers, while at the same time missing the business and the coins they had brought in the wake of their excess.

For my own part, I had waited for this moment to break camp since fate had shoved me into the legion's ranks – it was my opportunity to move closer to the coast, and Britain beyond it – but my near-empty purse was a problem, and after hours of thought, I had come to a troubling conclusion: I could desert with next to nothing and hope for the best, or I could steal from the very men I was beginning to see, despite my best efforts, as comrades.

I didn't like the choice that swam inside my head, and so I searched for some distraction by breaking the silence that had become expected of me. 'It's seventeen thousand.' I spoke loud enough for the rank ahead to hear me over the din of the march. 'Seventeen thousand troops, and about three thousand civvies in the baggage train.'

Stumps twisted to look over his shoulder. He was not overly fond of me, taking his lead from Titus, but he was also bored, and as desperate for conversation as I was. I would have to do. 'And you know that because ...?'

'Saw the lists in the quartermaster's,' I lied, not wanting to give away that the information had come, following Arminius's release, from the standard-bearer at the eagles, or my reasons for being there.

Stumps nodded at this, as if it only confirmed what he already knew of our strength. 'He did you a favour, I reckon,' he shouted back to me.

'Who? The QM? How's that?'

'We got a long march. You wouldn't have wanted those coins weighing you down!' He laughed, and I could imagine the sly smile beneath the red cloth. 'Hey, don't look so upset!' he went on. 'Only another four months till the next payday!' Stumps cackled at his own barb, doubtless hoping I would reply. 'Where are you from, anyway?' he asked when I held my tongue.

'I don't know,' I lied.

'You don't know, eh? Well, you don't sound Italian, and you don't have ginger pubes like Rufus, so you're not from Gaul. Can you really not remember?' he pushed.

'Nothing before they found me in the grove,' I lied again.

He thought on that for a moment.

'I saw a bloke go mad once.'

'Who?' Moonface asked.

'Not in the legions,' Stumps told me. 'When I was a kid. My neighbour found out his wife had been fucking his brother. Killed them both, and the two kids. When the smell got bad enough they found them in the house. The guy was still there, living in his own shit, talking over and over about how he was sent by the gods to do it.'

'Maybe he was.' Moonface, a religious man, shrugged. 'She was fucking her brother.'

'Her brother in-law,' Stumps corrected.

'Still.'

'Well, I think he was just plain mad. Like this one,' he concluded, with a bob of his head towards me. Then the man turned his eyes to the front, our conversation over.

If only the march had been so short.

It was sixteen miles of dusty, shoulder-numbing foot-slogging. With an army so large, any delay or halt towards the head of the column had a rippling effect along the body, so it was impossible to establish the usual pacing of four miles an hour, with regular stops to piss and take on a mouthful of water or wine. Instead, men took the chance when they could, though none but the most desperate wanted to leave the column to shit, aware that the marching beast could lurch back into motion at any minute. Like many others, I used the unexplained pauses to lean forward with my hands on my knees, taking the pressure from my shoulders and allowing the blood to move freely. It was a veteran's trick, taking away the time-costly motion of stripping kit to achieve the same effect, and Micon and Cnaeus were soon copying the older soldiers.

Our track that day had taken us north through flat lands and open pastures, and so it would have been a simple task for the pioneers and surveyors at the head of the column to find a suitable location for that night's marching camp. When we arrived, the advanced party of engineers had already laid out the markers that would denote the placement of each century – the legion's tented layout would be exactly as it had been at Minden, or any other station in the Empire.

'I hope to bloody Jupiter, and whatever local god wants to listen, that it's not us who has to build the rampart,' Stumps groaned, referring to the earthen defences that would have to be erected about the camp's entire perimeter.

Perhaps it was the Germanic deities who granted his wish, as Pavo informed us that our century would form part of the half of the army to stand guard in full battle dress, while the second half completed construction of the rampart and tents.

'Better off if we'd done the diggin' tonight,' Chickenhead told the section. 'It'll be our turn tomorrow, now, and you're always stiffer on the second day.'

'You remember what stiff is, old 'un?' Stumps grinned, grabbing at his crotch, but, drained from the day's march, no one rose to the horseplay.

The section formed into a single rank, looking out over the peaceful German countryside. It was late evening, the sun still bright and the air warm. A bead of sweat trickled down alongside the cheek-plate of my helmet, and I pushed a finger inside to wipe it.

'So you're human after all, eh?' The rare words came from Rufus, a wistful smile on his ruddy face.

'I'm human,' I replied cautiously, unsure why he had broken tradition and addressed me; the red-haired Gaul usually seemed to place a high price on words with even his closest companions. Perhaps he was seeking distraction from the thought of parting with his family, as they, like most of the army's followers, would journey to the Rhine via the River Lippe and its string of Roman-occupied forts.

He took my measure for a moment longer; then he turned his gaze to the southern end of the growing encampment. I followed his interested eyes.

There was a troop of cavalry approaching, moving in stops and starts, seemingly addressing the work parties of men who had stripped off their armour and substituted javelins for picks.

'Some bloody inbred officers, inspecting the work and inspiring the troops,' Stumps surmised sarcastically.

'No.' Chickenhead shook his head, appraising with a salt's eye. 'The gentry are built like stalks. Those are big men. German auxiliaries.'

'Bollocks,' Stumps retorted. 'Why'd they be checking the defences? Coin says you're full of shit.'

Chickenhead assented with a nod, the sallow skin of his neck flapping with the vigour of the motion.

'Bollocks,' Stumps said again, a few minutes later, this time because the riders were clearly in sight, and clearly German. They stopped at the leftmost section of our century, and I saw a finger point in our direction. The cavalry moved towards us, but it took me a moment to recognize their leader, his face cast into shadow beneath his helmet.

It was Berengar, Arminius's bodyguard. 'Felix,' he greeted me, chewing over his Latin.

'He's bloody famous with the goat-fuckers, this one,' I heard Stumps whisper over my shoulder. Fortunately, the words were missed by the German, who outweighed even Titus.

Berengar's eyes sought out our own giant now, figuring Titus as the section commander, and addressed him: 'Orders from the prince. I talk to this one.' And, without waiting for a reply, he tugged on his horse's reins so that the beast walked away from our lines.

I turned to Titus.

'Go,' he grunted with remarkably little interest. Whatever was on his mind was clearly bothering him deeply, but that was a puzzle for another time.

I left the line, joining Berengar beyond hearing of the Roman troops. The German swung down from his saddle, the speed of the movement rendering me defenceless against his surprise attack.

He embraced me, and the air left my lungs in a cough. When he finally stood back, I saw that his eyes were wet.

'Thank you,' he told me, before deciding that his attempt at Latin had not done justice to the meaning of the words. 'Thank you,' he stressed again.

I was too taken aback to speak. Putting a paw-like hand on my shoulder, Berengar took it as an invitation to continue.

'Arminius is a father to me, but also a brother, a son and a friend. You understand?' He gestured to the cavalry troopers behind him. 'To all of these men. You saved his life. You are also, now, my brother.'

I could feel that the words were genuine, and heartfelt. Exactly the kind of words that made me so uncomfortable that my skin burned and itched with anxiety. 'Where is he now?' I asked, desperate to avoid more gushing adoration.

'He rides to the tribe,' Berengar answered, after considering his words. 'He gathers the warriors, and then he will come back. Join the army.'

'How many warriors?'

'Enough,' he answered, with a shrug.

'And you?'

'We stay. Varus needs guides. He needs German help, but he does not like to ask.'

'But he likes Arminius.'

'As a son,' Berengar agreed.

'Will there be battle?' I asked finally.

The big German seemed to weigh the question, and his answer. He even looked up at the clouds, as if attempting to divine the weather.

'Arminius is a son to Varus,' was his final answer, before pulling me into another embrace. 'You have a good friend in him, and a brother in me. Remember this.'

With those words hot in my ears, Berengar pulled himself into the saddle and led his troopers into a trot northwards.

I couldn't understand why his words had left my stomach sour and churning. Like the droplets of blood at the bridge, some visceral reaction had been caused by a reason I could not fathom. My head began to throb, my heart thumped, and I knew that on this march towards uncertainty, I could at least be confident of one thing: that despite the sweat and toil of this day, I suddenly dreaded the prospect of sleep.

I knew that the nightmare was coming.

# 18

'You're awake.' Chickenhead greeted me in his matter-of-fact tones, his pinched face and gizzard emerging from the section's tent flap. It was before dawn, and my eyes, red-rimmed with fatigue, would still be hidden from him by the fading darkness.

'I am,' I replied simply.

The veteran lowered himself on to the ground beside me, rubbing at the toes of his bare feet. 'You can't keep that up forever,' he said, after working his way from big toe to small.

'No,' I answered, before deciding that I owed him more. 'What's in that?'

I was referring to a small clay pot, from which he now removed a cork-stop. The veteran poured some of the liquid on to his hands, and began to massage it into the cracking skin of his feet.

'Toughens the skin up. We've been sitting around too much this summer. Getting soft, every which way.'

'It stinks of piss,' I grunted, wafting the air.

'I think that's an ingredient, yes. Wine, piss, who knows?' He shrugged, unconcerned. 'If a bit of piss on my feet stops them going raw with blisters, then I'm all for it. You want some?' he asked, holding the foul-smelling pot out to me.

I declined, but not out of any sensibility. A year's solitary march across the continent had given the skin of my feet an almost armour-like thickness. Chickenhead had noticed.

'You came a long way,' he offered without accusation. 'Further than the forts on the Rhine.'

'Maybe I was recruited in Italy,' I answered, willing to play the game, if only because the alternative, sleep, was worse.

'Maybe.' The veteran smiled, and I saw his few remaining teeth glinting in the gloom. 'If you were Italian . . .'

We sat in silence as he finished applying the ointment. Soldiers tried all kinds of potions, some created by their own hands, others bought from the sellers that dogged an army. Most were useless, but a salt like Chickenhead was experienced enough to sniff out – literally – the good from the bad.

'You sure?' he asked, holding out the pot a final time. I shook my head, and he replaced the stopper. Perhaps sensing that the foul odour had dispersed, Lupus the kitten now pushed his way from under the canvas and crawled on to Chickenhead's lap.

'Good morning, sir.' The veteran greeted his companion with deep affection, stroking him as he looked up at the skies. 'Shit,' he groaned, snapping back to his more usual sullen self. 'I thought it was a bit dark for this time of the morning.'

I nodded. The clouds had grown thicker under the moon's watch, low and menacing. 'Think it'll break today?' I asked him.

'Tomorrow, latest.' He shrugged. 'Bollocks.'

We sat in silence then. Slowly the camp began to come alive. A short time before dawn, trumpets called reveille, and men stumbled out of canvas to begin the task of stripping down the tents. Work parties were assigned to break apart the rampart, the added labour intended to ensure that we did not hand our enemy a defensive position that we might some day have to assault. Our section was assigned to this task.

'Better to sweat now than bleed later.' Moonface offered the mantra as he swung his pick into the turf.

'Or just don't build the bloody thing in the first place,' Stumps countered, arching his back to ease the stiffness. 'Since when do they attack our marching camps, anyway?'

'That's because we build these, idiot,' Moonface spat, shaking his head. 'Discipline, Stumps. It's what separates us from the barbarians. Maybe you'd be happier with them?'

'Maybe I would,' he mused, breaking again from his labour. 'But no,' the veteran decided, gesturing dramatically at his features. 'It would be a crime to cover this with a beard.'

Moonface showed what he thought of that statement by throwing a sod of turf into his friend's face.

'So who are the barbarians, Moon?' Rufus asked, his brow creased a little in irritation.

'You know who I mean.'

'Oh. Me?' the son of Gaul pushed.

'Of course not. You're a Roman citizen.'

'My father, then? My mother? What about my grandparents?' Rufus pushed. 'Two of my grandfather's brothers died in Caesar's Gallic wars, and it wasn't in this uniform.'

Moonface saw the offence he had caused to his comrade. He made the correct decision, and kept his mouth shut.

'Everyone is a fucking barbarian to someone,' Rufus concluded, turning back to his labour. 'And the ones who don't recognize that, and love the smell of their own shit, are the ones who are buried in it.'

Once the rampart was destroyed and the baggage loaded, the work parties donned armour and fell into formation with the half of the army that had been providing guard.

Slowly and methodically, the force marched from the campsite, leaving only overturned soil in its wake.

The advance north continued, but after an hour of marching, the stop-starts of the column became more frequent. Even Titus, still silent and sullen, noticed with a frown.

'Something's going on up ahead,' Chickenhead mused.

'No shit,' Stumps snorted, raising the cloth about his face to spit on the ground. Despite his jibe, he pressed his friend for more information. 'What d'you think it is?'

'Not fighting. We'd have seen the light infantry called in from the screens. Must be a problem with the track. A bridge, maybe.'

'Shouldn't the scouts and engineers have worked that out?'

'No plan survives contact with an officer,' Chickenhead surmised with a shrug. 'Who knows?'

We would have to wait for our answer. The column continued in fits and starts, the countryside of open fields slowly giving way to more, and thicker, woodland.

'There'll be a forest up ahead,' Chickenhead ventured. 'That's the hold-up. Can't set our battle formations in those bloody trees, so the bosses will be looking for a way around.'

'And if they can't find one?' Moonface asked.

'Then it's hold on to your nuts and straight up the guts,' Stumps answered, his cackle turning to a groan as the column ground to another halt.

'I miss home.' Moonface sighed, his wide face open with reverence as he scanned the surrounding land of sweeping woodland. 'Rolling hills. Blue skies. It's no wonder the barbarians – sorry, Rufus: the Germans – are what they are. Forests are cruel places. Look at it. There's no light. Not like home.'

'This is no forest. Wait until we get further north. Then you'll see forests,' Rufus promised the Italian.

The column lurched ahead, and that afternoon Rufus's words began to seem prophetic, the stands of trees growing thicker until they were unbroken and unending, a shield wall of green. The clouded skies had already cast the day into gloom, but now, despite the fact that sunset was still hours away, the column found itself marching through darkening terrain.

'Going to be hard to keep in touch with the screening troops,' Chickenhead thought aloud. Titus nodded in agreement. Since entering the forest, some warrior instinct had caused the big man to become more alert, yet he remained silent.

Ahead came a familiar shuffle, soldiers cursing as they bumped into the men in front of them, the column shuddering to another impromptu halt, the first for our own century inside the canopy of green. Where one moment there had been the sound of an army on the move, now there was only silence. Awed by the unfamiliar, oppressive forest, the column held its collective breath.

'What now?' Stumps whispered.

I tuned my hearing into the woodland. Leaves rustled in the light breeze. Crows called to each other from the treetops.

'Why are you whispering?' Moonface asked his comrade, equally hushed. Behind him, the youngsters Micon and Cnaeus shot fitful glances at the deep shadows set back in the trees, no doubt wondering what terrors could lurk within. This was alien terrain to the Mediterranean boys, the forest as foreign to them as the bottom of the deepest sea.

The quiet and the muted voices pushed the irritated Titus out of his silence. 'Grow some balls,' he scolded the older pair. 'So it's a fucking forest? So what? A tree can't hurt you, you fucking idiots.' The outburst was harsh, Titus's face harsher still. His comrades reddened and looked away.

'Just think of this place as a city with leaves,' Rufus said softly. His words were directed at the men of the section, but his eyes were on Titus, letting his friend know that he had spoken out of turn, but Titus's scowl showed no signs of slipping.

Not even when a scream echoed through the trees. It was an agonized, rolling shriek. The kind that marked the end of a life.

'What the fuck was that?' Moonface blurted. Up and down the column, hands went to the pommels of short swords. As a reflex, several men tested the fit of their armour, and rolled their shoulders – these were the most salty of veterans. If a fight was coming, they would be ready, muscles loose and limber.

Titus hadn't moved. 'It's a scream, you tart. Did you think the Germans were going to lie back and open their legs for us?'

'Will they attack the column?' Cnaeus asked, doing his best to keep his voice flat. I noticed how he clamped his jaw down to hide any tremor of fear, and perhaps Titus saw the same and admired the boy's effort, for he thawed, just slightly.

'Relax, young 'un, that's why we have the light infantry out there to screen us.'

'Better they get it than us.' Moonface shrugged. 'They're not real citizens, anyway. Just auxiliaries.'

'They're still our soldiers,' Rufus replied coldly. 'Gods, Moon, you are an ignorant bastard sometimes.'

I took from his tone that someone close to him had once served in such a unit.

'My father,' he told me, feeling the question in my gaze.

'Your father what?' Moonface asked, oblivious.

Rufus ignored the question, and the section lapsed into a nervous silence that Stumps was anxious to escape. He spoke up, licking his lips. 'Hey, Chicken. How about you give us a story? Lighten the mood.'

'No,' the older veteran answered flatly. He'd taken Lupus from his pouch, and was concentrating on nuzzling his nose into the creature's fur. 'You'll only take the piss.'

'Nope. Promise. Come on, mate,' Stumps urged, putting his hand on a surprised Cnaeus's shoulder. 'You'd like a story, wouldn't you, you fine specimen of a soldier?'

'Yes please, sir,' Cnaeus eventually managed, his words directed at the gnarled veteran.

'Sir, by fuck!' Stumps grinned. 'You can't let him down now!'

'Fine, a story,' the elder sweat assented, lowering Lupus from his face. 'When we campaigned with General Drusus . . .' He paused at this point, waiting on the anticipated ambush from Stumps, but despite a grin, his younger friend stayed quiet, and so Chickenhead drawled on. 'When we campaigned with him, one of our centuries came across a group of women in the forest. They were all beautiful – stunning, really – with long blond hair, and dressed in bright white robes.'

'Now you're talking.' Stumps smiled, winking at the blank-faced Micon.

'They were priestesses,' Chickenhead explained. 'And they'd been slitting the throats of our men, and collecting the blood in a bronze cauldron. It was almost overflowing.'

'For fuck's sake, Chicken,' Stumps groaned. 'I said something light-hearted!'

'So you wouldn't want to hear about how they cut out the men's tongues, and nailed heads on to trees?'

'Not the kind of nailing I wanted to discuss, mate, but thanks all the same,' Stumps replied, shaking his head. Beside him, Micon and Cnaeus had turned shades of white and green respectively.

'Look at that!' Stumps now laughed, pointing at the pair. 'What's the matter, boys? Little queasy? Well, listen to this.' He embarked on a story that I have no doubt was as crude as it was intimate, but I heard none of it.

My ears were ringing. Blood pounded inside my skull, a tide that I was sure would burst forth through my eyes, such was the pressure. The assault had come without warning, but I expected it was Chickenhead's talk of sacrifice that had breached the walls of my mind's defences. It didn't matter. All that mattered was that I stayed on my feet. I knew that wouldn't happen unless I could clear my vision of the sights in the grove: the withered corpses in cages; the staked, dis-embowelled dead. How had I not heard their screams? How had I escaped the same fate?

The ringing in my ears grew louder, until it was all I could hear. My eyesight blurred, and then it vanished.

But somehow, I stayed upright.

Chickenhead. As my senses returned, I saw that the vet-eran had positioned himself behind me, a casual hand on the belt, and a shoulder against my back, enough to keep me straight. He'd done it so nonchalantly that, standing in tight formation as we were, none had noticed my near collapse.

'Thank you,' I managed, once my muscles would respond.

He leaned in close, so that his words were for my ears only. 'Tonight, you get some bloody sleep. Scream all you want. You can't stand in a battle line like this.'

A battle line. Would it come to that?

Perhaps Pavo read my thoughts and was going to give me the answer, because he now appeared from the head of the century. 'Titus,' he called with his usual frown. 'Screening troops haven't checked in with the legion commander.'

'And?' Titus countered, his patience in short supply.

'And he wants you to find out what's happened to them,' Pavo replied, turning quickly on his heel to avoid follow-up questions.

'Must be nice to have the legate ask for you personally.' Stumps's laugh would have been hollow, had it not been filled with sarcasm.

'Strip off your kit,' Titus ordered us. 'Short swords only. Take off your helmet.' He directed the final instruction to the younger soldiers, who looked confused.

'You'll need your hearing,' Chickenhead explained as he slipped Lupus inside the cloth pouch that hung from his neck.

Moonface snorted. 'Can't you leave that thing here?'

'I'd sooner leave you.'

'Listen up,' Titus rumbled, gathering the section about him. Now that danger seemed close at hand, any sign of his introverted reverie had vanished. Here was a man who knew that, in a fix, it took every scrap of sense, every sinew of muscle, to come through alive. 'No more than ten feet between you. Keep low; try not to make a silhouette. If you see something, make sure you pass it along, but quietly! Keep the line intact.'

'And if something happens?' Stumps pressed, nervously licking his lips.

'Then we're probably fucked,' Titus answered, with no trace of humour. 'Maybe if you're fast, you'll make it back to the column. 'Course, then there's the chance they'll execute you for running.'

And with those words of encouragement ringing in our ears, we slipped off the track and into the long shadows of the forest.

# 19

Beneath the high branches of oaks and sycamores, the leaves still full and green from summer, the forest floor was thick with thriving plant life. Rivulets and gullies criss-crossed the fertile ground – perfect places from which an enemy could spring an ambush – but their random nature made it impossible to methodically search them from one end to the other.

'Keep your spacings,' Titus hissed to the section. We were only twenty yards into the forest, but already the combination of thick vegetation and steep-sided ditches was forcing the men to break formation. Sound seemed deadened by the trees, and yet the slightest crack of a fallen branch rang out like a ship hitting rocks.

I glanced to my left, seeing the wide form of Moonface's head peering anxiously over the lip of a gulley. To my right, Titus was scowling hard. Perhaps he hoped the forest would bend to his whim, as did so many others, and part before him. Dappled light shone through the canopy, the sun painting shifting patterns across the men's armour.

I was not uncomfortable in forests, nor a stranger to them in wartime. I knew that they were not a happy home for the Roman legionary, trained as he was to operate as part of an efficient, brutal killing machine. In situations like this, one had to become an individual, and to rely on the most basic of instincts. Sight would get you only so far in such dense vegetation. Sound, a sense so neglected by the heavy infantry, was your greatest ally here: a rustle when there was no wind;

a clink of metal on metal; muted voices, such as Titus's as he once again ordered the section to hold formation.

I slid down the bank of a dry stream bed, using my left hand to control my descent, my right holding the sword that I had dulled with mud prior to leaving the track. All but Moonface had followed my example, until Titus had ordered him to do the same.

'Save your spit and polish for when we're back in the fort,' he'd growled.

I lay flat on the bank, peering ahead, working my eyesight methodically over what lay ahead of me – first the fore-ground, then the middle ground, and finally the far ground. Once I was satisfied – or as near satisfied as I could be – that there was no German spear waiting in my immediate path, I would resume my crouched advance, cover another short distance, and then repeat the process. No one, no matter how skilled, can concentrate on maintaining their own stealth while uncovering another's, and all while on the move. It had to be broken down.

'You move well,' Titus whispered, joining me in the next gully and lying beside me.

I nodded. Now was not the time for unnecessary words. I put a finger to my lips, and Titus took that as a signal to hold up a hand. From the absence of rustling in the undergrowth, it seemed as though the section had successfully been brought to a halt.

Titus didn't ask me why I held my tongue, or why I stared into the undergrowth like a hunting hound with a scent in its nostrils. He may not have known me, he may not have liked me, but he had seen enough of me to know that in situations like this my instincts were worth heeding.

'Something shining,' I told him finally, so quietly that I saw his thick eyebrows knot as he strained to hear.

'Twenty yards, two knuckles to the right of the oak with the snapped lower branch,' I answered the question in his eyes, and Titus held out his arm in the direction of the tree. Clenching his fist, he used the tree as a marker, and counted two of his scarred knuckles to the right of it. There, certain enough, something was shining, and nature is rarely responsible for such things.

Titus used the flat of his palm to urge me to stay in position, and moved out of the gully. For a big man, he moved well, light on his feet. Little wonder he was a good fighter. He returned swiftly from ordering the others to stay in position, then gestured that he and I should lie down at the bottom of the ditch. It was a good idea. The closer to the ground, the deader the sound of our necessary conversation – or at least, his imparting of orders.

'You move us to it. I'll be a few feet behind you. We get attacked, don't hang around. Just put them down if you need to, then run.'

He must have seen the surprise in my eyes that he had bothered to contemplate my survival, should there be violence. The big man smiled, but offered no explanation. Perhaps he simply reasoned that he could outrun me, and that I'd do enough to distract any pursuit long enough for him to get clear. It was hard to feel optimistic about a man who had nearly killed me on our first meeting.

Titus rose, sitting back on his haunches, and waited for me to climb over the lip of the gully. Instead, I traversed ten feet along its length. I felt his gaze burning into my back, but he didn't push for the explanation, which was a simple one – if someone had seen me slide into that ditch, then they'd be watching the same spot for me to re-emerge. I didn't expect that a few feet would render me invisible, but perhaps it would be enough to force them to shuffle and thus betray their own position, giving me a few seconds to save my skin.

Out of the ditch now, I let my shoulders go loose, but my hand stayed firm about the pommel of my sword. I had my arm half-cocked, the point of the blade angled forward. If an attack came, I would get one chance to drive the iron home.

I stopped to listen, hearing only the shallow breathing of Titus behind me. In the distance, I thought I caught the echo of trumpets and drums, but it was gone before I could be certain. A trick of the mind, perhaps. I stepped forward.

Whatever had been shining was no longer visible to me – the angle of light had changed from my vantage in the ditch – but I had marked the spot well, and was close enough to peer through the branches of the wispy shrub, and to see that it was too thin to hide an ambush. Either that, or its occupants had moved – but to where?

I stalked to the oak, the closest hard cover, Titus moving automatically to the other side. We rounded the ancient tree, blades up and ready, but the only foe we found was one another.

'I was wrong.' I sighed, noticing now the adrenaline thumping through my veins. It is only when the sense of danger recedes that one becomes aware of the body's overactive impulses.

'No.' Titus shook his head, and gestured that I follow him. He moved to the wispy shrub and bent his knee, coming up with something in his hand – a ring. 'Bronze,' he announced, holding it up for my inspection. He was smiling, the owner of the jewellery by default. I was not.

The ring was attached to a finger.

Searching the area nearby, we soon found the traces of more blood, and the signs of struggle – snapped branches and divots in the earth – but Titus was loath for us to wander too far.

'But we haven't found the auxiliaries,' Moonface protested feebly, caught between his desire to fulfil his duty and fear of his section commander.

Titus snatched the severed finger from Stumps, who had been giggling as he held it in place of his own missing digits, and made as if to poke Moonface in the eye. 'This didn't fall off on its own, did it? Now, Pavo said to find out what *happened* to the screening troops. He didn't say we actually had to *find* them, right, Chicken?'

Chickenhead shrugged. He was long enough in the tooth to know that orders could be twisted in more than one direction.

'We found out what happened to them,' Titus asserted, wagging the finger. 'So let's get back to the column before the same thing happens to us. Single file: it'll be quicker. Let's go.'

The men turned back into the forest, Rufus taking the lead, Titus trusting his friend's sense of direction.

'Wait.' It was Chickenhead who called a stop to the withdrawal before it could truly begin. 'Where's the young one?'

Quickly searching the faces of the section, I realized he was referring to Micon. So quiet and unassuming, the young soldier had not been missed, and now no one could be sure when he had last been seen.

'This is fucking great,' Titus snarled. 'I'm going to look like a right cunt if we go back one short. Who was next to him in the line?'

It had been Stumps.

'Just leave him,' he protested, angry at his own mistake. 'I told him to stop. It's his own fault if he kept bloody walking.'

'And have Pavo hold this over me?' Titus snorted. 'No. We find the stupid bastard.'

'I'll find him,' I offered, but my words earned only a look of disdain from the big man.

'Get into formation, and remember whose section this is. The rest of you, spread out. Extended line.'

I took my position to Titus's left. I had wanted to be alone, for more reasons than one. True, I fancied that without the noise and distraction of the other soldiers, I could have found the wandering Micon fast enough – and the sooner he was found, the sooner we could rejoin the relative safety of the column – but the more pressing reason was that I needed to test myself. I needed to know what was in my mind. Left alone in the forest, knowing that my absence would be attributed to death and not desertion, would I run, or would I find my way back to the column, and my section?

I needed to know that answer.

Instead, I moved across the dense forest floor with the other soldiers, trying to take myself out of my own mind and into Micon's. Realizing I had been separated, what would I do? If the boy had any sense, he would go to ground, wait and listen, emerging only when our search party approached.

But Micon was not known for his wisdom.

'Cnaeus!' echoed through the trees in the boy's dull monotone. 'Cnaeus, where are you? I'm on my own!'

'Jupiter's hairy balls,' Stumps groaned. 'The lad must be tired of livin'.'

'Quiet,' Titus ordered, attempting to discern the direction of the voice from the echo in the trees. 'This way.'

'We're not actually going after him, are we?' Moonface spoke up, alarmed.

'Stay here if you like,' Titus snapped. 'Close up,' he ordered the section, and we came together, an arm's width between each man, swords poised and ready.

'Cnaeus!' the idiot kept calling as we advanced. 'Cnaeus, is that you?'

'He's too far away to hear us,' I whispered to Titus, who nodded.

'Trick of the mind,' he grunted, though I could see by the way his hand gripped the pommel that he expected otherwise.

'Cnaeus!' the boy called again.

I could see him now, standing on the raised lip of a ditch, his usually blank face etched in confusion, sword hanging limp by his side.

'Cnaeus!' he shouted, looking over his shoulders in search of his rescuers.

'We go get him,' Titus hissed at me, loud enough so that the others could hear.

We worked as before, myself in the lead, Titus at my back.

'Cnaeus!' Micon hollered.

'Shut up, you idiot,' I shushed him. The young soldier was looking at me as if our situation were the most natural in the world. I took a hold of him by the shoulder, and twisted him back in the direction of the section.

'Everyone went,' he told me matter-of-factly.

And that's when they attacked.

You had to admire their patience, waiting quietly for bigger prey while unwitting bait had bleated in their grasp. From the blur of motion, I knew that there were at least a dozen of them, coming over a gulley's lip like a wave over a breakwater. I had the vaguest impression of spears, bearded faces and a charging war cry, and then I was running, Titus ahead of me, the big man barrelling through the undergrowth like a chariot.

'Run!' I screamed into Micon's ear, half dragging him by the shoulder of his armour. Within moments, we were back where Titus had left the remainder of the section.

Who had vanished.

Titus didn't even break stride, and I followed his example, hoping that he was leading us towards the column and not deeper into a forest that now seemed infested with enemies.

We thudded through the greenery, trying to avoid the ditches, ignoring the thorns that scraped at our skin and the branches that clawed at our eyes. At any moment, I expected to feel a spear's penetrating agony in my back, but I dared not turn and lose my footing.

Micon, however, looked over his shoulder, and then yelled as his sandalled feet hit a root. The youngster stumbled; my grip kept him upright, but the weight on my arm finally dragged us both down, turning me so that I was looking back at the Germans on our heels, their bearded faces flushed with the joy of the hunt and the moment of blood-letting at hand.

They slowed, lowering spears, men jostling for the honour of the kill.

And that's when the section sprang its own ambush.

It was beautifully executed. Later, I would learn that Chickenhead had been its engineer. At the first sign of trouble, he had pulled the section into a ditch, and the Germans, eyes only for their quarry, had thundered past. Chickenhead had led the section in pursuit, and now that the spearmen paused momentarily to see to my own slaughter, their exposed backs fell prey to Roman short swords. Within seconds the economical, brutal stabbing action had worked its way through the spearmen, only one of them having the chance to bring his own more unwieldy weapon to bear.

'They got me!' Stumps squealed, dropping to his knees as the other men stood over their foes, panting from exertion and adrenaline, Rufus coolly dispatching the wounded with a blade to the throat.

I let go of Micon and ran to the wounded man's side. Stumps had his palm pressed to his left shoulder, blood seeping between his fingers. Chickenhead tried in vain to prise back the hand and inspect the wound while Stumps shrieked in fear.

'I'm done! Oh, fuck, I'm done!'

'Shut up and let me look at it,' Chickenhead ordered.

'No! No! I need to keep pressure on. I'll bleed out, Chicken, I'll bleed out! Oh, fuck!'

'There's not even that much blood, you tart,' Chickenhead chided his friend, and I was forced to agree.

'Who asked you, eh?' Stumps shouted back at me. 'You've been nothing but bad bloody luck since you turned up!'

I was spared further insult as Micon appeared on my shoulder.

'This is all your fault!' Stumps cursed the boy, taking his hand away from the wound to point a bloody finger at the young soldier, who simply stared back. 'Do us all a favour and fall on your sword!'

'You're OK. It's gone clean through the flesh,' Chickenhead informed his comrade, taking advantage of the moment to inspect the wound. 'You'll be fine, you baby.'

'I will?' Stumps finally managed, disbelieving.

'Unless you get gangrene,' Moonface couldn't resist adding.

'Oh, shit!' Stumps groaned, fatalistic once more. 'Why is it always me?'

No one had an answer for him. Not even Titus, who had returned soon after.

'Enjoy your exercise?' Rufus ribbed his good friend.

'Piss off,' Titus grunted, but with a smile, relieved to find his comrades intact, at least for the most part.

I rolled a German on to his back, my sandals squelching in dirt soaked by blood. The man had been stabbed several times around the kidneys, and the blood had come from him like a river. Looking at his face, I imagined he was around Micon's age, his beard still patchy in parts.

'Some of these tribes have a tradition of not cutting their beards until they kill an enemy,' Chickenhead grunted, wiping his bloodied blade on the boy's cloak.

Most of the other dead were just as young, and none had any great wealth on them. What little we found was given to Stumps as compensation for his injury.

151

'Just boys.' Rufus spoke quietly, doubtless thinking of his own sons.

'Green troops,' Chickenhead agreed. 'That's not good.'

It wasn't. These were not the grizzled warriors we had faced at the bridge, but young men who had come of age under Roman influence on the region, and an indication that the animosity ran deep. Their motives couldn't have been purely financial, as the army's baggage train would have proved a far more lucrative prospect than clusters of soldiers in the forest.

'Maybe they wanted to get themselves a reputation,' Chickenhead surmised as their eulogy. If he was right, I hoped that the attitude was not widespread.

'Enough of this,' Titus said, eyeing the bodies. Perhaps he was picturing how, if not for Chickenhead's quick thinking, it could have been our own flesh growing cold. 'Let's get back to the column.'

## 20

'Let's get back to the column,' Titus had said.

If only it were that simple.

'Where are we?' Moonface asked no one in particular, his white face creasing.

'Germany, you twat,' Stumps piped up as he used the German bodies as stepping stones. 'Which way back to the column, then, Titus?' he asked as dead air escaped from the lungs of one of the fallen enemy. 'Titus?' he pressed, when no reply was forthcoming.

The section commander stayed silent. The whimsical smile on Stumps's lips began to slide. He stepped on to the dirt. 'Chicken? Rufus? I thought you fuckers had a good sense of direction?'

'Shut up, Stumps,' Chickenhead answered tiredly.

'No. You're always going on about how—' His words ended in a cut-off gargle. Titus's massive paw was around his throat.

'Shut. Up,' the brute whispered with iron in his tone.

Rufus caught Titus's eye with a nod of his head. He stepped up to the big man and whispered something into his ear. After Titus gave a grunt of assent, Rufus began to peel away his armour.

'Where are you off to?' Though rubbing at his bruised throat, Stumps was unable to resist the hushed question.

Rufus gestured with his eyes towards the thick canopy above. 'Find the sun,' he murmured.

It was the only option I'd come up with myself. The column had been pressing north when we left its promise of protection, and our search for the screening troops had taken us east. Since then, however, we had become turned about through ambush and counter-ambush. I was certain that I could track our way back if needed, but that route would be twisting, and perhaps more Germans would come in search of their missing friends. No, better to find the sun and, by its position, launch a new tack through the forest to the legions.

'Spread out. All-round defence. Get down on your belt buckles,' Titus ordered, and so we fanned out about the tree that Rufus now began to climb.

Prone on the stomach, one began to notice the army of insects that busied themselves with their own life-and-death struggle in the forest, their movements as cautious and deadly as our own. Musty dark earth competed with the stink of German blood and open organs to fill my nostrils. Despite the evidence of death around us, the rustle of wind through the trees was tranquil. Calming. I wanted to sleep. I was not the only one.

'Keep your fucking eyes open, Micon,' I heard Titus warn.

I turned to my side, and saw that Rufus was pushing his head through the upper canopy. Within a moment, he was on his way down.

He pointed after he had dropped cat-like from the lowest branches. 'That way.'

Titus squeezed his friend on the shoulder, as much a display of affection as I had ever seen from the man during my time in his company. Then he helped Rufus to slip into his armour, pulling straps tight and double-checking buckles.

'Single file,' Titus whispered. 'Rufus is point man. I'll bring up the back. Don't want to lose any of you cunts again.'

Rufus moved off at a slow pace, his body almost bent double to maintain a low profile. I trusted his soldiering, but I had survived this long by my own skills, and so I made certain that I was behind him in the order of march.

'Be my guest,' Stumps offered, bemused, as I placed myself at the point of greater danger.

We inched our way through the tangle of shrubs and thorns. The sky above the canopy had grown darker, and light no longer played over the men's armour. Instead, long shadows made us think of the threat of ambush and concealed enemies. Hearts skipped beats, breath died in the lungs, only for us to realize a second later that the crouching warrior was a tree stump, the poised spear a branch.

Maintaining the direction westwards was crucial, and so Rufus led us up and over the ditches and rivulets in as direct a line as possible. It was draining work for the man, always wondering if the next defilade held the enemy, and death.

It was as he began to crest a steep-sided bank that the red-headed Gaul stopped suddenly in his tracks, his limbs frozen. He stayed there for a few moments, and the other men of the section bit back the urge to call out, and to know what lay ahead. I fought against my own adrenaline. Was it a trap? How many enemies?

But then I heard it, and it was something that needed no explanation. It was something that I can never forget.

The most hideous scream.

The scream came again. Somehow this one was more awful than the first.

Rufus ghosted his way down the bank, and to my side. His face was drained to the colour of marble.

Titus came up to us. A jut of his jaw asked the obvious. Rufus turned his thumb downwards, indicating that there were enemy warriors ahead. Then he opened and closed his palm twice – ten of them.

'They have wounded?' Titus whispered.

Rufus shook his head. The word dropped heavily from his trembling lips. 'Prisoner.'

As if waiting for the moment, another wail pierced the trees. There was a word within the pain.

'An auxiliary from Gaul,' Rufus said, his eyes closed tightly. 'He's calling for his mother.'

There was nothing to say – but we had to look.

'With me,' Titus mouthed silently.

Leaving Rufus behind, we slithered up the dirt bank like adders. At the crest, I exhaled slowly. I did not want to gasp when I saw the inevitable.

He was naked, tied to a tree, half hidden by the shape of laughing German warriors. His skin was pale from shock, striped red with blood. His chin hung down on a heaving chest.

I wanted to puke. Instead, I watched as a boyish German stepped forward, a dagger in his hand. The screams came as the youngster sliced off the auxiliary's ear.

'Initiation,' I heard Titus breathe, as the trembling young man passed the blade to another barefaced youth.

'We have to do something,' I muttered.

Another slice of the dagger. Another scream.

Titus gestured at the number of the enemy. 'Twelve against eight.'

'Four of them are boys,' I protested, straining to be quiet.

'So are two of ours. And Stumps is injured.'

The scream was weaker this time.

'He's dying,' I whispered to the dirt.

'He's already dead,' Titus said. The words were hard, but not cold. His eyes told me that he burned to save the man as much as I did, but he was responsible for the lives of his section – his friends. I realized then that he would carry this image to his death. As leader, the decision to act or not was his. So was the burden of guilt that came with it.

'There's nothing we can do,' I murmured, hoping to relieve some of it.

Titus said nothing. His eyes bore into German backs.

It took another five minutes, six cuts and four screams for the Gallic auxiliary to die. As the man's life left him, so did the Germans' enjoyment. At an order from their leader, the band of warriors began to pick up their weapons – but not their equipment.

'They're going out to fight,' Titus whispered. 'They're leaving their kit behind.'

He was right. The enemy melted away into the forest, leaving two of the young boys behind.

I looked from them to Titus. A sick smile stretched across his skin.

He held an open palm down towards the dirt – I was to remain where I was. Titus then inched down the bank, and to the section. After a few moments when he must have been briefing the others, I heard the sound of the men moving off through the undergrowth.

Titus reappeared on my shoulder. There was silence. The two German boys sat bored on the equipment. One of them threw stones at the body, which hung limp in its bonds. The missiles made dull thumps as they hit the cooling flesh.

Eventually, Titus spoke. 'Let's go,' was all he said, standing up.

Through practice and second nature, his footfalls on the forest floor were muted, but the big man made no effort at concealment. I joined on his shoulder, guessing at his plan.

We were only twenty paces away when one of the boys chanced to look in our direction. His panicked scream froze in his throat as Titus waved a greeting.

'Hello, boys.'

They ran.

We walked.

'Let's see what we've got,' said Titus as he ripped open the first of the German campaign packs. These were blankets, folded to make a pocket, and tied to staffs with leather string.

I had no eyes for it myself. I was looking at the corpse of the auxiliary. His body was a canvas of cuts and stabs. His ears and his nose were gone. His eyeballs lay at his feet.

'Don't look at him,' Titus told me, biting into a mouthful of stale German bread. 'No good will come of it. This bread's shit,' he added, spitting. 'Fucking goat-shaggers.'

I turned away from the body. The rest of the section were appearing through the trees. One of the German boys was with them, gagged, being shunted forward by Moonface like a sheep.

Titus smiled. 'Hello again.'

Moonface kicked the feet from out beneath the lad. He fell face first into the dirt, head bouncing. There was no need to ask what had happened to the second youth – Moonface's blade dripped blood.

No one made any comment; they were looking at the body. Cnaeus sat down heavily.

'Anything in the packs?' Stumps asked Titus.

'Enough food for a few days. Help yourselves. Bread's shit, though.'

'What about him?' Moonface asked, driving a kick into the German boy's back.

'Take his gag off.'

Moonface obliged, the point of his dagger pressing into the side of the boy's throat. He stayed silent.

'Speak Latin?' Titus asked, tearing off a chunk of bread.

Nothing. Moonface pressed down with the blade.

'Little,' the boy conceded. He was perhaps sixteen, and young enough to have grown up under Roman influence. Latin was the language of trade, so even those who despised Rome were keen to learn it.

His hand full of bread, Titus gestured towards the dead Roman auxiliary. Rufus and Chickenhead were busying themselves with removing him from the tree. They needed to find dignity in death.

'The others,' the boy protested, looking at the kit he had been assigned to protect.

'Was it?' Rufus asked hopefully.

Titus shook his head. 'I saw him, the little cunt.' His voice was as calm as a dead sea. 'I saw him,' he repeated quietly.

Chickenhead pulled a blanket across the body. All was still and silent. I saw Titus look from the covered dead to Cnaeus; the boy's head was between his legs, shoulders shaking with shock. Then Titus looked at the German soldier. He was no older than Cnaeus. The boys were two sides of the same coin.

Titus got to his feet. The bread dropped to the dirt. 'Tie him to the tree,' he said to no one in particular.

Moonface fell hungrily on to the task. 'Help me,' he said to Micon, and the young soldier did.

The German boy resisted, but Moonface drove his fist into his face. As blood poured across the German's chin, he was tied in the auxiliary's place.

'On your feet,' Titus growled, tapping Cnaeus hard on the shoulder with the flat of his blade. 'On your fucking feet,' he said again.

Knees shaking, the soldier obeyed.

Titus shoved the blade into his hand. 'Cut off his ears,' he said plainly. Beside the terrified German, Moonface laughed with glee.

'Titus.' It was Rufus speaking, with friendly warning. 'Titus,' he tried again.

'Cut. Off. His. Fucking. Ears,' Titus snarled.

Cneaus staggered towards the tree. 'I can't,' he mumbled.

'Do it, you pussy,' Moonface goaded him.

'His ears, or yours,' Titus warned the boy, seeing him hesitate; his voice was like the thud of a battering ram against a city's gates. 'This is war, lad, not some fucking parade. You will be a killer, you will toughen up, or you will be a rotting fucking corpse, do you understand that?'

I watched, paralysed. I did not want to see the German boy tortured, and yet . . . Titus was right. This was a war. If Cnaeus were to live, he had to become a warrior. He had to become cold. He had to become a machine that only acted, and never thought.

Thoughts of Arminius pushed their way into my mind. I wished that he were here, certain that he would somehow find a balance. A way to save life, without taking it.

But he was not. There was only the section, and me.

'Just do it, boy,' I heard myself say. 'It will make the rest easier.' I wanted to console him, certain now that this would not be our last taste of death in the forest.

'Who asked you?' Rufus flared.

I said nothing.

'Do it,' Titus ordered again.

Cnaeus raised the blade. He closed his eyes.

Then he was sent sprawling to the floor by Chicken-head's shoulder. In the same movement, the veteran drove his dagger up through the prisoner's chin and into his brain.

He died without a murmur, but not without terror. Piss dripped on to Chickenhead's feet.

'We don't have time for this,' he spat, stepping back as he pulled the blade free. Blood cascaded across the German boy's thin chest.

'Remember whose section this is,' Titus rumbled, step-ping forward to dwarf the veteran.

Chickenhead met his stare. 'I remember whose it *was*.'

The words struck Titus. He hit back with threats. 'The boys need to learn. Maybe I'll teach them on that rat of yours,' he sneered, gesturing to the pouch that contained his kitten and which now hung across Chickenhead's back.

'You'll eat a fucking blade if you touch him,' the veteran pushed through clenched teeth, and I had no doubt that he would kill the man if he did harm Lupus.

'Back off, the pair of you.' Rufus pushed his way between them and faced Titus. 'You want to teach the boys? How about you teach them some fucking leadership? Some fucking discipline?' His face was the same violent red as his hair.

Titus turned away. 'Get your kit together. Take what you want from theirs. I'm having a piss, and then we move off.'

Sullen, angry and shaking with adrenaline, the members of the section split to riffle the enemy packs. Behind them, as Titus's urine splashed against the forest floor, Moonface's blade bit into the neck of the German corpse. Chickenhead and Rufus looked up, but said nothing – the boy was dead, and Moonface, their friend, was scared.

He tried to cover it by placing the severed head on a log. 'For his mates.' He grinned, though his eyes were filled with tears.

We moved on.

# 21

We emerged from the forest far from our own century, and Rufus was forced to dodge a javelin thrown by a nervous legionary – the pathetic attempt earning the young soldier the good-natured contempt of his comrades. Having received directions from a pinch-faced officer, we followed Titus towards the head of the winding snake of troops.

As we went, I saw that Stumps was not the only wounded soldier in the column. We passed perhaps a dozen, and I noticed strike marks on several shields. Clearly, the army had not gone unmolested in our absence, though the damage appeared to be minor, a fleabite to a lion.

'What took you so long?' Pavo greeted Titus. The big man tossed him the severed finger in answer; Pavo caught the digit out of reflex, and inspected the flesh with his standard scowl.

'Found your screening troops,' Titus explained as Pavo let the finger fall into the dirt.

'Old news. Column's been getting harassed the last hour.'

'Harassed?'

'Hit-and-run attacks. Nothing too heavy. None on our own century.' Pavo shrugged, a little disappointed. 'What happened to you?' he asked Stumps, noticing the bloody dressing.

'Heroic stuff,' the wounded man proclaimed, jutting out his chin. 'Should be a Gold Crown in it for me, and double pay.'

'You've got more chance of getting gangrene, and cashing in on your funeral fund.' Pavo smiled slyly before sauntering away to the head of the century.

'Shit me, now even that stuck-up bastard's taking the piss,' Stumps lamented.

We took our place in the century's order of march. The staccato nature of the advance had only increased since entering the forest, and doubled under the Germans' hit-and-run attacks. We passed the evidence of these skirmishes over the course of the next few hours: perhaps two dozen German dead, all stripped of their valuables.

'We haven't lost anyone,' Cnaeus noted of the bodies, his relief causing him to think aloud. Moonface pounced on the chance to chastise him for his naivety.

'We don't leave our own like the goat-shagging scum do. They'll go on to carts, and get a proper Roman burial once we reach the forts.'

'We left that auxiliary in the forest,' Cnaeus mumbled.

'What did you say?'

'I said, do we have enough carts for that?' Cnaeus asked dubiously.

'Of course!' Moonface was full of the confidence and bravado of a people who had conquered half the world. 'It takes ten Germans to kill a Roman soldier. Just look what happened today.'

'We were lucky,' Chickenhead grumbled. 'It could have easily gone the other way.'

Moonface rolled his eyes, and the conversation died.

I was troubled, and I suspected Chickenhead was irritable for the same reason. Looking up between the high branches, the clouds were becoming low, dark and menacing.

'Hope we make camp before that breaks,' the veteran whispered to his feline companion.

We didn't. That afternoon, the skies split without warning. There was no patter of rain, growing to a storm, only a sudden deluge that poured on to the heads of the column with a ferocity that would shame the most berserk of German spearmen.

Titus broke formation to ask Pavo for the wax covers that would stop the hide of the shields from absorbing water, but returned only with a scowl. 'They're all in the baggage train.'

'I'll go for them,' Rufus offered eagerly.

'Forget it. It's at the back of the column. Even if we get them brought up, it'll be too late.'

'It's worth a try,' Rufus pressed.

'I said forget it. It's too late.'

He was right, and in no time the shields were twice their original weight. With a German ambush possible at any moment, slinging the burdens on to our backs was not an option; instead, biceps and shoulders burned with the effort of holding them in position, but it was not an unusual sensation – the army trained with doubly weighted arms and armour to prepare for just such a situation.

The forest track itself was simply a wide path through the trees that avoided the worst of the twisting gullies. Within moments of the deluge, it had become a quagmire. As sandalled feet churned the mud, it became evermore treacherous for the soldiers who followed on behind, and the sound of vicious curses grew in volume and intensity as tired soldiers floundered.

'Why didn't I join the navy?' Stumps groaned as rain beat against his helmet.

'Pavo's coming,' Moonface informed him. 'Why don't you ask for a transfer?'

'Why've we stopped this time?' Stumps asked instead.

'Keep your eyes on the forest,' Pavo snapped, and he was right to. With the darkness of the rain clouds, visibility had fallen. The fringes of the track were ripe for ambush, and a lax moment could be a soldier's last.

Pavo fell in on Titus's shoulder, his voice at a whisper that I strained to hear. 'The bloody scouts have pissed off,' he told the section commander. Why he was imparting this knowledge, I did not know, but from the exaggerated care in his words, I could guess. He was scared.

'They've gone?' Titus asked, eyebrows knotting. 'The Germans?'

The handsome officer nodded, the crest of his helmet spraying water with the motion. 'Felix, I suppose you should know, as you're so friendly with them. The guides have gone. More of the screening troops, too.'

'People don't just vanish,' Titus thought aloud over Pavo's shoulder.

'I said they'd pissed off, not vanished. Probably got no stomach for a fight. Shit, maybe they just don't like the rain? Either way, they were supposed to be showing us the way through this bloody mess.' He waved his arm at the forest. 'So now we have to send our own scouting parties ahead, and make sure we're on the right track.'

Scouting parties. So that was why he was in a sharing mood. I knew what was coming now. So did Titus.

'Not us,' he declared flatly.

'It's from the legion command—'

'Legion commander, my arse,' Titus snorted. 'You just want me out of the picture.'

'Are you saying you won't go?' Pavo straightened his shoulders.

Titus's nostrils flared: a bull in uniform. Eventually he pushed the words out from between gritted teeth. "Course I'll go. Don't have a fucking choice, do I?'

And as Titus had no choice but to follow the orders of the centurion, so the section had no choice but to follow the big man to the head of the column. Only Stumps, owing to his wound, was offered the chance to remain behind, but he refused, cloaking his loyalty to his comrades with a joke.

'If I'm not along for the party, then maybe one of you will have to take a turn getting hurt, and I can't bear the thought of seeing your fat mothers wailing at your graveside.'

At the head of the column, similar groups to our own were receiving orders as they were sent out ahead. One of the army's engineers, squat and tough, made his way over to us.

'I'm Lucius,' he greeted Titus. 'If you boys can keep me alive while I assess the route, then I'd be much obliged to you.' The old veteran smiled.

We pushed out into the forest, but unlike the morning, we were not alone: we caught sight of the other sections to our flanks. The rain continued unabated, dampening sound as well as our persons, and making it safe to talk despite our position.

'This isn't as bad as I expected.' Stumps grinned. 'Kind of nice, actually, not to be stopping and starting every two minutes, and slipping about in the mud.'

'You must have lost more blood than I thought,' Titus grunted, unused to hearing Stumps in anything but a pessimistic mood.

'Missing the desert?' Rufus asked his friend.

'Never. Soaked in this, or soaked in sweat. At least rain stops – eventually.'

Lucius spoke up, his engineer's eye on the widening track ahead of us. 'This is promising. Been used recently, too.' He pointed to the ground and, with the others, I saw the unmistakable mark of hoof prints. 'The German scouts, I imagine,' the short man surmised.

'Your mates ran out on us.' Moonface addressed me, an edge of accusation to his tone. 'You can stick them in our uniform, but a barbarian is still a bloody barbarian.'

I declined to comment, having no wish for an argument. If anything, I partly agreed with his sentiment. I had seen whole cohorts abandon their pledge to Rome; the offer of citizenship was not a potion that could cure all evils. As for Berengar and his men being my friends? No. He was indebted to me, but we were not friends. How could we be? We had never got drunk together. Fought together. Shared stories of lost loves, family, our hopes and dreams. No, I could no sooner call him that than I could these soldiers standing about me. I was at the head of a column of twenty thousand, but I was alone, and that realization caused my mind to wander to a time when I had been surrounded by friends – comrades who knew me better than my own mother did. Comrades who were now nothing but dust and bone.

Those melancholy thoughts, together with the rain hammering the lip of my helmet, made me bow my head, so that I was within killing range of his javelin before I saw him – but neither the man, nor his weapon, could do harm to anyone, now.

'Well, I'll be fucked,' Stumps uttered beside me. Behind him, Cnaeus sank to one knee, his vomit splattering the forest floor with the rain.

Titus, fearless, walked forward. After taking a few steadying breaths, I went with him.

The man was a Roman soldier, his features waxen and grey, blond hair darkened from the rain.

'Batavian auxiliary,' Titus guessed. 'Ever see anything like this?'

I shook my head, the scene causing me to forget to protest that I had not served before. 'Not like this,' I answered, choking back the rising bile in my throat, and it was the truth. I had seen all kinds of unimaginably cruel acts, but this was a first: the soldier had been draped over a fallen log and his javelin forced into his anus.

'Are you OK?' Titus asked, and I nodded, spitting to clear the acidic tang from my throat.

'Shit. There's nothing these goat-fuckers won't do,' he snarled. 'They gutted him, too.'

'Maybe he was dead before they did it,' I offered, seeking any consolation, no matter how trivial.

He shrugged, clearly unconvinced. 'Maybe.'

'There's more over here,' Rufus called from further along the track.

We found four altogether, all butchered and positioned with barbarism that touched on the artistic.

'They need to pay for this!' Moonface growled as he paced back and forth, teetering between collapse and anger.

'Chickenhead, you soft cunt! This is what happens when you show them mercy. This is what happens. They need to pay!'

'They will,' Titus calmed him, his tone firm and unmerciful.

'They need to pay!' the aggrieved soldier shouted again, his white face more ashen than ever. 'Are you listening, Chickenhead, you fucked-up old cunt?'

'They will,' Titus promised once more. Chickenhead let the words wash over him. Lupus was his only concern.

Officers appeared, to inspect the sight. With them came the news that the column had experienced several more, and heavier, attacks. Lucius the engineer said that he would over-see the collection of the bodies, as he was temporarily at a loose end – a good track had been discovered, and it led to open ground.

'Open ground.' Titus grimaced happily as he spoke the words, and as the rain bounced from his wide, armoured shoulders, the section commander's face twisted into a mask that promised murder. I took in the sight of this brutal war-rior, and could not help but feel a moment of sympathy for our enemies.

'Give us a battle,' he prayed.

There was no gradual thinning of forest as we made our way to the open ground. One minute there was the thick, oppressive canopy; the next, nothing between us and the black skies but rain. It hit us with ferocity, but we welcomed its cold touch, anxious to be on ground where we could set our battle lines and dominate our enemies.

If only they would oblige us.

Chickenhead snorted. 'They'd have to be idiots to attack us out here.'

Behind us, still deep in the forest, the clash of arms and armour echoed through the drumming rain.

'Hear that?' Moonface said. 'They're not letting up. Bet it's fun in the baggage train.'

'Want to draw blood while they still can. They'll have to face us eventually,' Titus asserted, clearly still desperate for vengeance. Beside him, his friend Rufus looked pale with nerves. 'What's up with you?' the big man pressed.

'Nothing. Just cold.'

Orders came that the army would establish a marching camp in the open ground within which to lick its wounds and take stock of the situation. Our own century formed part of the guard, a three-deep line of men stamping their feet and rolling their shoulders to ward off the chilling effects of the rain. Behind us, surrounded on all sides by the flesh and armour of soldiers, work parties began the labour of erecting the earthen rampart and waxed-skin shelters.

'Missing a lot of tents by the looks of it,' Moonface observed. 'Told you the baggage train would get smashed.'

'So we'll share fucking tents,' Rufus snapped. The out-of-character outburst was enough to still further conversation.

Standing in the rearmost rank of the century, desperate to escape the elements and my thoughts, I attempted to shut off my mind, focusing on the patter of rain on my helmet and nothing more. The sleepless night and day of spiking adrenaline had taken their toll and, despite the cold, I soon slipped into a trance-like state. It wasn't quite sleep, but the veteran's trick would keep me upright a little longer.

Chickenhead's prodding elbow snapped me from my daze. 'Come on. We're being relieved.'

The rampart was complete, the guard units withdrawn behind its defence. We would be rotated every few hours so that all men could escape the elements, if only for a short while. Hot food was the priority over sleep, and in our own crowded tent, Moonface acted as cook, under the direction of his friend Stumps.

'Crumble in the biscuits, you clumsy bastard! Crumble!' he chided his apprentice.

We sat naked, the veteran Chickenhead having set the example by stripping off his wet clothes. Only Rufus was absent – gone on the hunt for wine, Titus said. I'd helped dig a pit into the soggy wet floor, and the recessed fire was warming our flesh, as well as our dinner.

'Just think, you'd have to pay for this in Rome.' Stumps smiled. 'Finest bathhouse in all of Germany. How's Lupus?'

Chickenhead cradled the creature in his hand, attempting to feed it a morsel of dried meat. 'He's stopped shivering, at least,' he answered, clearly concerned. 'He's not an outdoor cat,' the old sweat added with deep affection.

'I had a cat once.' Micon spoke up, surprising everyone, a warm smile on his idiot face.

'Well, thanks for that great story,' Stumps replied, after no further detail was forthcoming. 'Since you've opened your trap, Homer, why don't you tell us a few more interesting tales? Got any sisters worth shaggin'? Where are you from, anyway?'

'Pompeii.'

'Never been there. What are the women like?'

The young soldier shrugged. 'They're all right.'

'Bollocks.' Stumps laughed, dragging out the word. 'The only inside of a cunt you've seen was your mum's. You're a virgin, aren't you?'

Micon made no reply. His cheeks flushed red.

'Don't worry about it, we've all got to start somewhere. When we get back to the Rhine, me and Moon will show you the best whorehouses.'

'Thanks.' The boy blushed again.

'I went to Pompeii once, with my family,' said Moonface, still stirring the pot. 'My dad was a carpenter. He got work there building a ship. It was a good summer.' He smiled, slipping into the pleasant memories. 'Eight years now since I saw them. They'll hear about this campaign, and know I was a part of it.' There was pride in the soldier's voice.

'Yeah, they'll find out when they get a letter to say you're fertilizing German vegetables,' Stumps teased with an evil smirk.

'They'd taste fucking good if they came from me,' Moonface shot back. 'Here, you stir this sludge.'

Stumps took the spoon from his friend, and the tent lapsed into silence.

Since reaching the relative safety of the marching camp, Titus had once again retreated into himself. We still didn't know why he had withdrawn, but his pensive attitude had taken on a hard edge of anger since the discovery of the auxiliaries' bodies. As Moonface handed the big man a bowl of hot barley, Titus finally drifted back from his silent contemplation.

'Thanks,' he said, and then turned his eyes to the two youngest soldiers. 'You did well today,' he told Cnaeus, who was still shivering. 'And you.' He pointed at Micon. 'Next time you go wandering off alone, we leave you, understand?'

Micon's head nodded dutifully, though his face remained the same blank mask as always. Titus seemed about to add something more, but he was stopped by an act so unexpected that, for a moment, every other man in the tent was struck dumb.

Cnaeus began to cry.

It was a whimper at first, as uncontrollable as his shivering. I wondered if he was even aware of it, but then words formed through the gasps and the tears. 'I want to go home,' he pleaded to no one in particular.

The other men remained silent. Embarrassed. Stumps concentrated hard on stirring the pot. Moonface moved to put more sticks on the fire. Eventually, Chickenhead placed Lupus into Cnaeus's lap; the youth seized the cat as if he were a drowning man clutching timber.

'I want to go home,' he sobbed into the kitten's damp fur.

From out of the corner of my eye, I noticed Titus's considerable bulk stir. The section commander got to his feet, bending beneath the tent's canvas. He took the few short paces towards Cnaeus, and I expected a brutal blow to fall on the boy as Titus attempted to beat the fear from him.

Instead, he sat beside him.

No words were spoken. The only sound came from the constant drumming of rain against the tent's canvas, and the mewing of Lupus as he pawed at Cnaeus's cheek.

The boy soldier sobbed again, but the presence of the gnarled veteran beside him was like a bulwark, and gradually the youngster mastered his emotions. After what seemed like the final snivel, Titus finally deigned to speak.

'We're all scared,' he offered simply.

Cnaeus's wet eyes fell on his commander with a doubtful expression.

'We're all scared,' Titus insisted in a voice like cold iron, 'because we've all got something to lose. Remember what it is, and kill any fucker who tries to take that from you. Fight like that, and you will go home.'

Cnaeus nodded vigorously, rubbing the heel of his hand into his eyes. Titus, with the soft gaze of the veterans upon him, removed himself to his position in the tent's corner and his former reverie.

*We've all got something to lose.* Is that what had pushed the big man into his solitude? What was his to lose?

And what was mine? I was scared – terrified – of dying, but surely all that I had to lose was long gone now, consumed in the fires of rebellion and the bloodshed that had quenched the flames. What kept me fighting? Was I nothing more than an animal, struggling because instinct told me that I must?

No. I knew what it was, though a self-loathing part of myself fought against it as hard as any enemy.

It was hope. It made my throat tighten to even acknowledge its existence, but, deep down, I knew that it was hope as much as fear that had carried me across the continent, pushing me onwards towards Britain: the hope that there I would find a land untouched by Rome. The hope that there I would be beyond the reach of ghosts. The hope that there I would be able to remember who I was, before the blood and the fire.

'Get some sleep,' Titus grunted at the section as he rested his scarred skull in the folds of his massive arms.

Without a murmur, six weary soldiers and one kitten obeyed his command.

# 23

Our rest in the tent seemed to be over before it began. No sooner had I closed my eyes that I was woken by Chicken-head's toes pushing into my ribs as the veteran pulled his tunic on. Immediately, I was alarmed that I was being woken because of my sleep terrors.

'I wasn't—'

'No.' He stopped me, knowing what my question would be. 'It's our turn on the rampart.'

As the rain beat against the hide of our tent, I dressed in my own tunic, the cold damp of the material doing nothing to energize me. The other members of the section were equally subdued, conversation non-existent as they donned armour, collected their arms and shuffled like the dead to take their stations on the low rise that enclosed the encampment.

'This is shit,' Stumps told the storm-filled night.

With our shields and javelins planted in the ground before us, our silhouettes may have looked like statues from a distance, but up close we swayed in the strong winds as fatigue and boredom chipped away at our resolve. I looked for the moon, but it was hidden by thick cloud. It looked as if tomorrow would bring no respite from the tempest.

'Felix.' I heard my name on the wind. 'Felix.'

It took me a moment to locate the source of the sound. It had come from behind me, and there was just enough light in the night for me to make out the transverse crest of a centurion.

'Felix,' Pavo hissed again.

'I'm here, sir,' I answered, no doubt drawing a scornful look from Titus.

Pavo arrived beside me. 'Titus, I'm going to an orders group. I'm taking Felix with me as runner.'

'Him? Runner?' I could picture Titus's thick brow creasing beneath his helmet. 'Take one of the young lads.'

'I need someone I can trust. I'm taking him.'

'Well, OK, then. If you need someone you can *trust*,' Titus seemed to find great amusement in the word.

Pavo turned back towards the camp, and I followed on his shoulder. I did not think that he truly trusted me, but simply recognized me for what I was: the fellow outcast in the century. This march was Pavo's first taste of command in the field, and though there had been no battle, the enemy nipping on our heels might well prove a fearsome opponent. I had no doubt he was wary of his future. In his own mind, he was equally sure that I was an experienced veteran, and he wanted to make use of my knowledge in a way that he couldn't with the other soldiers of the century.

'Today,' he began without preamble. 'What did you make of it?'

It would not be a good idea to dispense with guile completely – Pavo was too ambitious – but it could not hurt to state the obvious.

'The whole world knows that our strength is in our formations, so they hit hard and fast before we could rally. They won't think about taking on this camp, or meeting us in the open.'

'Yes, yes.' He waved impatiently. 'But is that all it is? Is that all we'll bastard get, all the way through this campaign?'

I broke my stride as a dog darted between tents: one of the many camp followers who had stayed with the army on the march, rather than taking the soft route of the Lippe back to the Rhine.

'I'm sure they'll stand when we reach their towns,' I answered tactfully, giving him what he wanted to hear. 'That's when we'll get battle, and the plunder.'

Perhaps my words mollified the man, for he stayed silent until we reached the large command tent at the camp's centre. Dozens of centurions were making their way inside, though most were the seasoned leaders of the cohorts' First Centuries. As to why Pavo, a junior officer, had been summoned to such a gathering I was given no clue, but I thought this anomaly was probably another reason for his apprehension.

'Wait here,' he ordered me at the tent's flap, and so I took my place in the rain amongst a dozen other miserable soldiers. The beating of the downpour against the hide of the tent kept all voices securely within its interior, and I suspect I would have remained ignorant of what passed within had it not been for the sharp eye of an old, frowning soldier – Caeonius, the camp prefect who had been party to my discovery as a blood-soaked ghoul in the sacred grove.

'Gods!' The officer's smile spread genuinely beneath his bulbous nose. 'You must be the only one in the army who's looking better than the last time I saw him.'

'Thank you, sir,' I managed, despite my discomfort at the attention. 'I'm surprised you recognize me.'

'That was a sight I'll not forget until I'm cold in my grave. What are you doing here? Do you remember anything now?'

I regretted that I did not, and then explained that I had been sent to a century as a battle casualty replacement, and how I had accompanied Pavo to the tent as his runner.

'Well, you can't bloody run if you're all rust, can you? Get inside.' He must have sensed my hesitation. 'Just stand at the back and keep quiet. Don't worry about it. Come on.'

What choice did I have? He was one of the highest-ranking individuals in the army, and so I followed the squat man inside, pressing myself against the canvas and hoping that my entrance would go unnoticed in the shadows.

The tent was packed with officers belonging to all of the army's castes: the heavy mob of the Roman legions; auxiliary light infantry; cavalry, both Roman and provincial; engineers; artillery. Their backs to me, steam rising from beneath their armour, they appeared like some army of the dead.

Despite the crowd, Pavo's height let me catch sight of him. He was standing close to the front, and I wondered what could have elevated him to the status he so strongly desired.

'Thank you, gentlemen. Please be seated.' Caeonius's voice sounded from the front and the officers took their places on wooden benches – some aspects of Roman civilization could not be overlooked in the field, no matter the circumstances. Thankfully, there were not enough of these seats to go around, and I was not left to stand conspicuously alone. Then, my view blocked slightly by the chain-mailed shoulders of a cavalryman, I saw Governor Varus take centre stage.

It was no secret that he was a politician rather than a warrior, but even so I marvelled at the effect that only two days in the field had taken on the man. Varus's eyes were dark-rimmed and his skin had the same waxen sheen as the tent.

'Gentlemen,' he began. 'I have some grave news.'

Instantly, the tent seemed emptied of air as men held their breath, military minds churning over possible disasters and responses. I turned them over myself. Yes, the column had come under attack. Yes, the weather was terrible. But these were not incidents that should be insurmountable to an army in the field. What was the grave news? Why did Varus look so ghastly?

And then he told us.

'Arminius is dead.'

# 24

For a moment, discipline slipped, the gathering erupting into hurried conversation, men wondering aloud what could have befallen the German prince, and what effect that would have on the campaign.

I heard none of it.

I felt as if my stomach had dropped past my knees. Knees that were shaking in grief.

Arminius was an enigma: the barbarian-born noble who was an accomplished Roman officer and an embodiment of the Empire. He was that rare kind of man who seemed unshackled by mortal worries, the energy of a dozen legions contained within his skin. He was witty, handsome and kind.

And somehow, I was sure that he was my friend.

And I knew – I *knew* – how ridiculous it was for me to think of a noble-born that way, but hadn't Berengar, the prince's shadow, said as much himself?

But what did it matter? He was dead.

'How?' several voices began to ask.

It was Caeonius who stepped up to answer. Like the legions he had come to embody, his manner of address was direct and brutally efficient.

'Here are the facts as we know them. Arminius was supposed to arrive with his warriors today and join the column. He didn't. Instead, a small group of riders came in. They talked to his scouts, and they immediately rode away together, and at speed—'

'Why?' a legate, commander of the Nineteenth Legion, interrupted.

'All we know is that some auxiliary troops understood part of the exchange between the riders and the guides. They told them that Arminius and his men had been attacked, and that the prince was feared dead.'

Most of the tent held its silence, but the legate was an inquisitive and suspicious man. 'So we don't *know* that he's dead?'

'We don't. At first light, we'll send out cavalry detachments. Their orders are to find Arminius, and to bring his warriors here to join us.'

'And if he is dead? Will they hold by their word to Rome?' The legate, a politician like Varus, sounded doubtful. Caeonius's lack of reply confirmed that he was of the same mind.

Now, Varus seemed to remember his position. The governor struggled to straighten his shoulders and present an authoritative figure, but still he sagged with grief. Perhaps to steady himself, he placed a friendly hand on Caeonius's shoulder. 'I would ask that all commanders now present their losses, and unit strength,' he ordered with the gravity required in such dealings.

One by one, officers stood and reported on their butcher's bill. The legates of the three legions were the first to present; their casualties were light, and mostly walking wounded.

'Slingshot has accounted for most of our injured,' the legate of the Nineteenth observed. 'We tried raising shields at first, but they saw that meant we couldn't return our javelins, and they moved in with spearmen. We lost a few men that way, so now my centurions are ordering the shields kept down. Better the slingshot than the spears. Besides' – he smiled proudly – 'it's not as if my men are ever without black eyes.'

The losses amongst the auxiliary troops had been higher, but a few units accounted for the majority of the number. One had been reduced to half of its four hundred effectives. These had been the lead troops of the army's flank screens, and I thought of the men we had found, butchered and positioned like trophies, and wondered where they came from. Regardless, they had died far from home.

'I've heard stories from the vanguard.' Varus swallowed, addressing the hollow-eyed auxiliary officer. 'What happened to your men?'

'I don't know, sir.' His tone was flat. Almost lifeless. 'They just vanished.'

The direst news came from the commander of the army's baggage train, a colourful veteran whose left arm had been lost on campaign many years ago.

'It's the fucking artillery pieces, sir, 'scuse my fucking language, sir. It was bad enough goin' with it how it was, but now that the fucking rain – 'scuse my language, sir – has started, we might as well be tryin' to pull a bull from out a virgin's cunt – 'scuse my language, sir.'

'Thank you for your report, centurion.' Varus smiled politely, but his eyes betrayed his aversion to barrack-room language.

'It's not just the mud, sir,' the man added. 'Track's narrow, and we're strung out across half of fucking Germany – 'scuse my language, sir. If they break through in even one place, burn a few carts, then we'll be blocked up like my arse after the feast of Saturnalia – 'scuse my language, sir.'

After what had been an inauspicious beginning to the orders group, the eccentric centurion's language – or rather the governor's evident discomfort with it – helped to clear the air in the tent. Invested in Arminius as I was myself, it had become almost natural to assume that all the others were of the same mind, but now, as the assembled officers began to discuss strategy for the army's next move, it became evident that this was not the case.

The legate of the Seventeenth Legion got to his feet. He was a tall, hard-looking man, with a hooded brow and sharp nose that gave his face the look of a hawk. He was also my own legion's commander, though he would know as little of me as did any other officer present, save Caeonius and Pavo, who knew only what I had led them to believe.

'Governor Varus,' the man began, with the diplomacy becoming of a member of Rome's senatorial class. 'Prince Arminius is an excellent warrior, and a loyal friend. I hope that he is well, and that he can join us on the battlefield soon, to share in our glory.

'However, should the Cherusci, for any reason, fail to arrive, then we should not consider this a blow. True, Arminius may well bring eight thousand warriors with him, but we are seventeen thousand, and an elite. It is not for lack of numbers that the enemy has harassed us today, but because we have been hampered by terrain. I would urge, governor, that we make haste to clear these forests, so that we may persecute the enemy in open battle.'

There was a murmur of agreement about the tent. The feeling was that the column had received a bloody nose that day, nothing more. No man was in any doubt that when the army cleared into favourable terrain – and could march in battle formation – the Germans would be forced to flee, or die. Even Varus himself was nodding at the sentiment. If not for his friendship with Arminius, then perhaps he would have agreed to break camp at daybreak and press northwards, but the bonds between governor and prince ran deep.

'The rains will not break tomorrow, and so we shall remain in this camp. Arminius, should he live, shall have one day to join us. Consider, gentlemen, that his scouts offer us the most efficient route from out of this torrid forest.'

Mention of the scouts triggered an alarm in my mind. I dismissed it as a natural concern that Berengar and his men might fall foul of their fellow Germans before they could reach their prince and kinsmen.

'Very well, sir,' the legate assented. 'May I suggest that we use tomorrow as an opportunity to reconnoitre routes, should we have to scout our own way north? The engineers also tell me that the rain and the winds will have brought down obstructions on to the tracks. We can take this time to clear them, in preparation for our advance.'

'Yes, very good. Your legion can see to it? It will be hot work, I imagine.'

'My men are not afraid of hard work, or German spears, governor,' the legate assured him, before gesturing towards the seated men behind him. 'Centurion Pavo has volunteered to lead the work party.'

I could almost see Pavo's shoulders snap back at the mention of his name. Whether this was out of pride, or surprise, I could not tell.

Varus's eyes passed briefly over the handsome centurion. 'Is that so? Good man,' he offered placidly, already moving on to the next in the order of business. 'Now, the camp followers.'

I stopped listening. Instead, I watched Pavo.

Where there had been a solid, implacable statue of a soldier, now there were the smallest signs of anxiety. Slight ticks: the quick pull of his nose; the roll of the shoulders. His face was turned from me, but I could see another's well enough – the legate's.

He was looking in Pavo's direction, a thin smile beneath his hooked nose, and that smile turned my blood to ice because it was not the smile of a proud commander to a brave subordinate, but that of a victor to the vanquished.

With the clarity born of a long relationship with revenge, I knew in my bones what that meant.

Our century had been condemned to death.

# 25

I remained in the tent for the duration of the orders, glad of every moment out of the hammering rain and the rising winds that snatched at the canvas, but I paid little attention to the talk of guard rotations and stores. Instead, my mind turned in circles, wondering why the legate could want Pavo dead. Had the ambitious centurion, in fact, volunteered, and placed his own head in the noose? Or was he as unwitting in this as his suppressed – but visible – display of anxiety would lead me to believe?

I got no answers as we trudged across the greasy ground of the encampment. Pavo's head was down, his pace as driving as the rain.

I trailed a few feet behind and, as I hadn't been dismissed, followed him to his tent. There, I stopped outside the flaps that he pulled violently apart, the waxed hide doing little to suppress the scream of rage and frustration he let out once he was within.

'Cunt!'

I heard what I imagined was his helmet being thrown, then kicked repeatedly.

'Cunt! Cunt! Cunt!'

The outburst was over as quickly as it began, the only sound coming from the rain that bounced from the tent's canvas and the steel of my helmet. I coughed to make my presence known, having to repeat the action several times before Pavo registered it above the downpour.

'Why the fuck are you still here?' he snarled from within the tent, doubtless embarrassed.

'You haven't dismissed me, sir.'

'Fine. You're dismissed. You may as well go and tell the others the good news,' he concluded with vicious sarcasm.

I found them back at the section's tent, their sleeping figures huddled against one another for warmth. I decided the news could wait, but Titus opened an alert eye and was soon demanding information. I kept to the facts, telling him only what I knew for certain: that our century would leave the camp at dawn, alone, and begin the work of clearing the tracks in the forest. Titus's anger soon roused the others, the news eventually making its way to every set of ears.

'Fighting I can handle,' Stumps groaned. 'But fighting and manual labour? That's just not fair.'

'So what else did you hear?' Titus pressed me.

I told them that I hadn't been privy to the orders group, having to wait outside the tent. Only one of the section was savvy enough to see through the lie, and he waited until dawn, when the others were busy donning their armour, to tell me.

'Something's shaken you,' Chickenhead commented quietly. 'What haven't you told us?'

I met the veteran's eyes in the gloom. He had shown kindness to me. After Arminius, he was the only one to have done so.

Arminius.

'He's dead,' I whispered, suddenly desperate to confide in someone.

'Who?'

I told him what I'd heard in the tent, and with each morsel spilled, my shoulders felt lighter. In the moment, I didn't think

189

of the repercussions, I just thought of how Chickenhead was a good soldier – a good man – and deserved to know. I told myself that this was why I opened up. It was all for the veteran's benefit, not mine. This was duty, not friendship.

'I know he was good to you,' he offered, once I'd told him all I'd heard. Like the legate, he seemed unconcerned that the German reinforcements might not arrive, convinced of the superiority of Roman arms and the men who bore them.

'But there's more,' he pressed, his bloodshot eyes boring into me. 'That's not what's shaken you, is it?'

I wanted to tell him how wrong he was, but my sudden openness had already left me feeling anxious, and so I could not share with him how the news of Arminius *had* shaken me deeply. How the feeling of mourning – which had never truly abandoned me during my journey across a continent – was now fresh, an open wound atop the scabs. Chickenhead, immersed in comrades as he was, couldn't have known just how desperate I was to latch on to the first voice that offered a path from the wilderness and the promise of something better. In Arminius I had seen the kind of leader that the world deserved: a proven warrior who would choose the head and the heart to solve disputes, not the sword. My loss paled compared to the loss for Rome, but still I selfishly grieved for him.

But the shrewd veteran was also right, and I almost hated him for forcing me to acknowledge that there *was* more. It had begun as a gnawing uncertainty in my stomach, but the more I considered the possibilities, the more I thought the instinct in my gut was truth. I prayed that it was not, but, right or wrong, I would keep the revelation to myself. Nothing could be gained by sharing it.

In an instant a clarity came to me, and with it, anger. It was wrong of me to have talked to Chickenhead. Hadn't the ugly bastard kicked the shit out of me along with Titus and his friends? They were just using me now that we were in the field, seeing a tool that fit the task. Once we were safe, I'd be the one digging the shit-pits again. The section slave. The shunned.

So be it.

'No, there's nothing more.' I added one more lie delicately on top of all the others.

'You're not worried about today?'

'No,' I answered, this time honestly. I was so sick of being within my own mind that the thought of action almost excited me.

'Then maybe you're not as clever as I thought,' he grunted. 'We've been fixed in place overnight. They've had a chance to concentrate their forces. Even if it's just a few war bands, it doesn't matter. Numbers don't count in the forest.'

I made no comment, and Chickenhead, puzzled at my sudden about-turn, shook his head. 'Just don't tell the others, all right? They don't need to know that our balls are on the chopping-block for this one.'

It was fair to assume that the other men in the section were under no illusions that it would be a parade, but neither did they grasp the significance that only our own century from the cohort would be pushing into the forest and into the killing ground of the waiting enemy. The perceptive veteran had seen the anomaly, and could determine the reason. Despite my sudden change in attitude, or perhaps because of it, he shared with me the reason why.

'Ever wonder how a young lad like Pavo got a century, with no campaign experience behind him?'

191

I half feigned indifference as I pulled tight the straps binding my armour and equipment.

'Depending on who you ask, he was shagging the legate's wife, or daughter, but one of them did the whispering in the man's ear and got him his century. Pavo had his eyes set so hard on the top, he didn't even see that he was walking into a trap, and giving the boss the chance to see him off.'

I shrugged. 'Somebody's got to clear the tracks.' I was abrasive in my embarrassment at dropping my guard.

'Aye, that they do,' the veteran agreed. 'There's always some poor sod that's got to be the first.'

And there had been a time when that would have been me. Willingly. A time when my reckless enthusiasm had bordered on the insane. I had not been alone then, and the reason I was still breathing was because of men like this gnarled veteran before me. Those men had brought me through alive, and what had been their reward?

I shook my head to clear the images that were forming. I needed to concentrate my mind, and so I watched closely as Chickenhead squatted to the floor, worn-out knees clicking, to scoop up Lupus with both hands. 'You're staying here, little one, where it's safe and dry.'

He kissed the creature on its tiny skull, and something in the kitten's contented purring began to soothe me. The bitter anger I had been feeling at myself, misdirected at this man, melted away.

'It was a long night,' I apologized.

'It's going to be a long day.' He smiled, all gums.

A helmet pushed its way through the tent flap, Titus's grimacing face below the steel. 'Get your cocks out of each other's mouths,' he snorted. 'Century's forming up.'

Our short respite was over. We were going back into the forest.

The dawn was dark, the sky thick with clouds that unleashed rain on the tiny marching column, four men wide and twenty deep. Wind buffeted our ranks as we slipped towards the encampment's northern gate.

Sentries from an auxiliary cohort watched us pass, their dark features scowling against the storm, no doubt pitying those who were stepping from within the relative safety of the marching camp.

Pavo strode at the head of the column. With his drawn sword and his considerable height exaggerated by the crest of his helmet, he made for an imposing figure.

'He's keen,' Stumps sneered.

'Just wants to get this over, like the rest of us,' Rufus opined, the usually silent soldier casting restless glances over his shoulder towards the camp's centre.

'Forget something?' Titus asked him.

'My guts.' The Gaul forced a smile.

We cleared the rampart. The forest was three hundred yards ahead of us, silent and sullen. Behind the sheet of rain, it was impossible to make out individual trees in the dawn's gloom, let alone any trace of ambush.

'Cavalry are on their way out,' Stumps commented as the first of the mounted detachments thundered their way from behind us, striking for their own chosen paths. 'Lucky bastards,' he added, enviously eyeing the troopers' steeds.

'You're better off on foot in a forest,' Chickenhead countered. 'Smaller target. Too easy to get picked off from a distance with a horse.'

'I see you're a bundle of joy this morning.'

'Shut it, now,' Titus ordered.

The forest was twenty paces away.

As we entered the trees, I half expected to be greeted by a chorus of screams and war cries. Instead, the barrage of sound decreased, and the foliage gave some small shelter from the wind and rain.

I hadn't been the only one expecting trouble to welcome us, and its absence caused more unease amongst the century than an attack would have done; helmeted heads bobbed and twitched as men scanned their surroundings. Ahead, Pavo forged on, and it wasn't long until we found an obstruction across the track – a tangle of branches brought down by the wind. It was easily negotiable for men on foot, but the already struggling baggage train would need it cleared.

'Work party up,' Pavo ordered. The command was passed along the ranks in a hushed whisper, men daring to hope that they could remain in the forest undetected. Eight soldiers – armed with axes, saws and entrenching tools – made their way up to the obstacle, while the other legionaries of the century turned out to the flanks, crouching behind their shields with javelins ready.

I looked over the iron rim of my protection, trying to methodically scan the woodland ahead of me. The rain made identifying details impossible, and with the dawn a carpet of mist was beginning to rise from the forest floor. There could have been a war band a stone's throw away, and we would have been none the wiser.

The sound of chopping axes and biting saws mixed with the rain, and I turned from my shield to glance at the men dragging the deadfall from the track.

*Deadfall.*

'Don't!' I screamed.

Too late.

Unleashed by the movement of its counterweight, and as if it had been hurled by a god, a thick log came swinging from the canopy.

Some of the work party saw it coming and threw themselves flat into the mud. Some were fortunate to be outside its arc, and watched it glide through the air with wide eyes.

Others were not so lucky.

Two men – either slowed by fatigue, or shock – remained in the deadfall's path, the log swatting them into the air as if they were dolls; the bodies landed with wet thumps only feet away from me.

I don't know what I thought I could do for the stricken soldiers, but instinct compelled me to my feet. I came to the first, who was clearly dead, his chest caved in beneath the armour, blood running freely from his ears, mouth and nose. I looked at the second, and saw Pavo standing over him. The centurion's face was wiped blank by surprise. Before I could move to help, I felt an animal grip on my shoulder.

'Back to your place,' Titus growled, pushing me towards the section.

'Maybe I can help him,' I pleaded, desperate for that to be the truth.

'His head's split like a fucking egg. He's done.'

Titus shoved me down into the crouching ranks. Feet away, and despite the damage, the soldier clung to life for a few minutes more. A few minutes where knuckles went white about javelins, the soldiers certain that the enemy was about to close its trap.

I heard wet footsteps in the mud behind me. Pavo.

'You knew,' he stated simply. 'You shouted, before it fell.'

There was a question there. There were a hundred questions, but Pavo wasn't looking for answers – he was looking to survive.

'I want you at the front,' he told me. 'Titus, get your boys to gather the tools. Julius's section have to carry their dead. You'll replace them as work party.'

The centurion didn't wait for an answer, moving away to stare at the shattered bodies of his soldiers.

'Do you see what you've fucking done?' Titus hissed at me, eyes burning with anger. 'He's always looking for a way to see me off, and you just handed him one!'

'I—'

His arm struck out like a viper, thick fingers gripping my throat. I didn't fight back, and felt the dirty fingernails dig into my windpipe. I felt it closing, being crushed, the sight around my eyes growing black, sound coming to me as if I were underwater. I wondered if this was how it felt to die, and for one blissful moment I almost wished that he *would* kill me, and end the nightmare that had been my journey. My life.

But then, through darkening tunnels, I saw the limp bodies of the dead as they were hefted from the dirt by their grieving comrades, blood and fluids leaking from them like rain, and I knew that if I could have accepted death, then I would have met it an age ago, far from here.

'Get. Your. Fucking. Hands. Off. Me,' I managed, my thoughts growing darker than my vision.

I could see from his face that my bile surprised him, and as Titus released my windpipe, I sucked in a deep lungful of wet air.

'You'd better get us through this,' he threatened, regaining himself.

'I will,' I pledged aloud.

And then, silently, I made a promise to myself.

I promised that I would save Titus's life, and I promised that, once I had saved it, I would take it. I promised this because, as his fingers had crushed my throat, I had remembered who I was.

And that man was a killer.

# 26

The century pushed along the forest track and, with Pavo, I was in the van. The path, barely wider than three men, twisted and turned its way by the most ancient trees and flooded gullies, some of which had overrun, the cold water shin-deep about the metal of our protective greaves.

As I steered the men through this quagmire, I tried to concentrate solely on my survival, but the anger at being placed in this exposed position fought to be heard. The big bastard Titus had threatened that I must keep his section alive. Pavo had ordered the same for his century. I had no intention of disappointing either, but I was one set of eyes, and the forest was a blank canvas for the expert German trappers. How could they ask the impossible of me? I was a soldier, not a fucking god.

Despite my distraction, I *was* able to uncover the enemy's next surprise, though I had the rain to thank for the discovery. The weight of the heavy downpour had cleared away some of the foliage used to disguise the trap: a deep pit lined with sharpened stakes. I used my javelin to remove the rest of the camouflage as Pavo peered down at what would be a hideous and ignoble death.

'Is that shit?' he asked me, referring to the dark matter smeared on to the stakes.

'Carries an infection into the wound, if you somehow got out,' I told him, recalling the results of such injuries. The weeping pus. The tormented screams.

I didn't wait to be told. I pressed on.

The going was slow. I could tell Pavo chafed at the pace, but he had seen the stakes, and I noted how he was careful to remain in my footsteps. The centurion was a quick learner.

Several times we encountered debris across the track. At these potential ambush sites I slid on to my belly, worming my way about the obstruction and searching for the pegs, rope or thick vine that would indicate something sinister. Once I'd given the all-clear, Titus and the section would move up, hacking and dragging the debris clear of the track. Each time, the big man would growl menacingly in my ear, 'You had better be right.'

I was, but I couldn't see everything. It was only a matter of time before the enemy, and the forest that served as their unwitting ally, would get the better of us.

That moment announced itself with a crash, closely followed by a high-pitched scream that sounded like a wailing infant's.

I dropped instantly to a crouch, checked my front for danger, and then chanced to look behind me. A young soldier, not out of his teens, had fallen into a chest-deep pit at the track's edge. His screams cut through the downpour like sheet lightning.

'Titus!' Pavo shouted. 'Take the tools! Get him out and shut him up!'

Titus scowled, but moved away. I moved with them.

The boy's pale face stretched with agony as he screamed. A comrade was holding him from above, his arms under the victim's shoulders, trying desperately to stop the soldier from sliding further on to the stakes.

I knelt by the pit, seeing how one shaft had gone clear through the flesh of the boy's thigh. Another had penetrated his lower back.

'Get an arm!' Titus ordered. 'We'll lift him out!'

Chickenhead stopped him. 'Don't. The stake's packing the wound. We lift him off it, he bleeds out.'

The boy let loose another chilling scream.

'He's gonna bring every tribe in the forests on to us.' Titus cursed, taking the boy's neckerchief and tying it about his mouth. The screams continued, muted, but still loud enough to announce our presence.

'Why haven't you taken him out?' Pavo snarled, arriving at the pit. 'Or shut him up?'

Chickenhead's milky eyes met Pavo's glare. 'We move him, he dies.'

'So move him. You see a surgeon with us? He's already dead, and if he keeps screaming, then so are we,' the young centurion coldly explained.

For a moment, the only sound was the hammering rain and the victim's panted gasps beneath his gag.

'He'll die,' Chickenhead stated finally, and Pavo had the decency to meet his eyes, and then to look at the soldier he was condemning.

'Pull him out.'

We did, the soldier coming free with agonized screams and wet sucking sounds as his body pulled clear of the trap.

We laid him out in the mud, his head in the lap of a crying comrade, no older than his friend. As Chickenhead had predicted, the wounds now leaked blood at an alarming rate; the mud beneath our sandals was soon stained red.

Free of the stakes, the screaming had stopped.

Chickenhead knelt by the boy's side and pulled the gag free. 'Let's give him some fucking decency.'

And perhaps it was a sense of decency that kept us rooted to that spot, unable to take our eyes off the dying teenager, an honour guard all that we could offer his departing spirit. Perhaps that was it, or perhaps it was because the manner of his death terrified even the most experienced of us to our core. This was not how a soldier was supposed to die.

The boy began to mumble, pushing the last of his fleeting strength into his words. 'Mother,' he sobbed. 'I want my mother.'

Chickenhead tried to soothe him. 'Hush now, lad.'

'Mother,' the boy cried again.

'You'll see her soon.'

The torrent of blood became a trickle. The boy died. His friend wept, tears splashing down with the rain on to his young comrade's face.

'Make a litter for the body,' Pavo ordered the section.

We went deeper into the forest.

Every action became automatic, and yet it required a total dedication of the senses. A foot couldn't be placed without scrutiny. A branch couldn't be moved without inspection. Soldiers followed my example, and took to sweeping and probing the ground ahead with their javelins.

Even without the rain and the buffeting wind, the work would have drained a man in hours. With conditions as they were, the century was soon hollow-eyed and gaunt, very different from the troops who had re-entered the forest that morning. We were tired, yes, but the picture of the boy's death was enough to keep us focused – automatic, total dedication to survival.

The track had yielded surprises, and yet the greatest shock of all was that the enemy had not attacked us directly. Why this would be, I didn't have time to speculate, only to offer a quick thanks for small mercies.

'Another log on the track,' I noted to Pavo. 'Looks like a big one.'

'Work party up,' he ordered.

Titus appeared on my shoulder, the axe he carried looking like a child's toy in his huge hands. 'Go on, then, lucky one.' He smiled sarcastically.

I left my shield with the section, using my javelin to test the way ahead of me. The track seemed solid. So, too, from a distance, did the fallen tree.

That was strange. Where the other obstacles had been rotting and wilting, this fallen oak seemed to be in prime condition.

Something was wrong. A familiar tingle began to creep up my spine. The log was the presence of the abnormal. It was a combat indicator. It took me a few more paces before I could see the evidence through the rain.

Saw marks. The oak had been cut.

I expected an instant onslaught of lead slingshot and spears, but nothing changed. The rain beat on my helmet. The wind shook the branches. I quickly moved back to Pavo to make my report.

'Get up there and clear it,' he ordered Titus.

'What? You heard what he said! They put it there. It's a trap!'

'This whole track's a trap,' Pavo replied icily. 'And we've got to clear it, so get up there.'

For a moment, I was certain Titus would plunge the axe into the centurion's neck. Instead, it bit into the fallen oak with a savage rage. Whatever had been building inside the man since we departed the summer camp at Minden came forth in a flurry of blows.

'He's not goin' to stop until I'm dead,' he panted. 'He's not goin' to stop until I'm dead.'

'Pavo?' Rufus asked. As Titus's closest friend, he was the only one in the section who could ask personal questions.

'Of course fucking Pavo!'

'Why?' the ruddy-faced Gaul asked, doubtless on behalf of the section's veterans as a whole.

'Dice.' Titus cackled, pausing to inspect the damage wrought with his axe. 'Day we got paid, he lost every coin he had to me and the QM, and then some. He figures the slate's wiped clean if I'm gone, but fuck that. You promise me, Rufus. You promise me that if I die, you'll get every coin owed to me out of that cocksucker. Get every coin, and then pay some drunk bastard to stick glass in his pretty face. Cut it up like a puzzle, but leave the eyes. No, leave one eye! Just enough so he can see what a mess he is.'

The violence of the words shook most of the men to silence, young Cnaeus open-mouthed at such blatant hostility towards a superior, but Rufus merely shrugged. 'Fine. You feel better now?'

'A little,' he admitted, the axe biting down again.

The oak was thick and strong. I worked a two-ended saw with Cnaeus, Titus's aim being to split the log into sections that could be manhandled on to the track's verge.

'Now, I don't pretend to be Julius Caesar,' Stumps began, panting from the labour, 'but it seems to me that there are a lot of trees in this forest, and not so many tracks. Either Varus is plannin' on opening a lumber business, or we're goin' to have to just make our best effort through the trees.'

Moonface disagreed. 'The baggage train's struggling enough as it is. No way it can make it off the tracks.'

'So maybe we leave it behind?'

'Not going to happen. Too much of an embarrassment,' Moonface concluded, and Stumps kept silent in agreement.

With the sound of their conversation, and the ever-present tempest, it was a moment before I noticed a change in the forest's symphony – the sound of something small, and hard, striking wood.

'Is that . . .' Titus began, pausing as something struck a resting shield with an angry *thwack*!

'Slingshot!' came from several voices.

Almost instantly, adrenaline-fuelled calls echoed from the far end of the century.

'Enemy rear! Enemy rear!'

We weren't the only ones under fire.

'Get the tools. Let's go!' Titus ordered, and we sped with him back to the remainder of the century, the air by my head creasing as a slingshot zipped by. Ahead of me, I saw a man go down, his helmet sent spinning into the air by the impact of a lead weight.

It was Cnaeus. The young soldier staggered to his feet, and began to search for his helm.

'Leave it!' Chickenhead roared, pushing the youngster back towards the century.

The troops on either side of the track were hastily overlapping their shields as lead shot bounced from the protection like angry hail.

We collected our own shields and filed into ranks two deep. I found myself at the front, crouching, my shield covering from the floor. Behind me, Rufus held his shield aloft, raising the height of our barricade. In such a formation, the shot could do little damage to us, but I remembered the legate's words from the orders group, and how the Germans had used the defensive posture of the legionaries in their favour.

'Watch for spearmen!' I shouted, the confidence in my voice causing the call to be picked up and passed along by others. Sure enough, the Germans adopted the tactic.

'Enemy left! Spearmen!' a section commander called.

'Javelins!' Pavo ordered, and behind me the shield wall lowered so that men could hurl the weapons into the on-rushing enemy, a half-dozen screams echoing in reward, some of them ongoing from strikes that had not proved immediately fatal.

'Get the shields back up!' a voice shouted, for the Germans' slingshots had pelted the lines as soon as the defences had been lowered.

A legionary stepped back from the rear ranks, clutching his face and groaning in agony. I was close enough to see Pavo pull away the hands to inspect the wound.

'Shut up! You're fine! Hold the line!' he told the man, whose eye was mashed to jelly.

The two-high wall of shields was intact once more and, not wanting to waste their shot, the slingers in the under-growth held their aim. A weary lull settled over the skirmish.

This was Pavo's moment. He had to seize the initiative from the enemy. He had to clear us from the killing ground. Right or wrong, he had to make a decision.

'What the fuck is he playing at?' Stumps hissed when no orders were forthcoming. 'We can't just sit here.'

But that is exactly what we did. Occasionally, a German light spear would come sailing over the shields, but the enemy were weary of our tight formation, and held back. Crouching and cold, my legs began to cramp. With something of a happy revelation, I realized that I needed to piss. I relished the warmth that spread through what was already a filthy loincloth. Soaking wet as I was, and surrounded by enemies, what difference would pissing myself make?

'I don't like this,' said Chickenhead, working his gums. 'They've probably sent runners to get their friends. No one's coming for us.'

Stumps poked me. 'This is where your mate, the prince, is supposed to ride up the track and save us.'

'Maybe we'll see him soon,' I answered. 'In the afterlife.'

It took the soldier a moment to decide if I was joking, unused as he was to hearing humour pass my lips, no matter how dark. 'You're a strange one, you.'

I took the lull as an opportunity to look at Pavo. He stood in the formation's centre, his eyes on the three dead men that had fallen foul of the enemy's traps.

'He's shitting himself,' Moonface sneered, seeing the same.

'No,' I told him, certain it was not fear that was paralysing the centurion. 'He doesn't want to leave them behind. He knows what will happen to them.'

A German light spear eventually interrupted Pavo's silent debate with the dead, the weapon arcing over the line to graze the thigh of a soldier in the opposite rank, the man's flesh opening in a wound soon washed bright by the rain.

'We leave the dead,' Pavo ordered, his words hard now that his mind was made up. 'Take their weapons. Leave nothing for the goat-fuckers. We're going back to the camp.'

Those were his orders, but their execution would have been difficult enough with only the weather and the glutinous mud of the track to contend with, let alone the enemy that now dogged us as we began the slow march. For the most part, the Germans stuck to the forest's cover, picking at us from a distance with sling and light spear, but occasionally a cloaked warrior – doubtless keen to make a reputation for himself – would charge our shields with his heavy ash spear. Locked in formation as we were, we were unable to reply in kind.

'Bastard!' Titus spat when a German's spear found a soft spot between shields, the iron head slicing across his thick forearm. 'That's fucking it!' he growled, and issued his own, private orders to the section.

The next time a German charged, Rufus and Moonface dropped their shields unexpectedly so the spear passed harmlessly through open air. Titus snatched at the shaft, yanking it forward, the German's momentum carrying his shocked face straight into a thrust of the brute's short sword.

'Shields back up – fuck!' Rufus exclaimed, struck in the shoulder as the lead rain began once again.

'You OK?' Titus asked.

'I think so. Arm's dead, though. Can't raise my shield.'

'Just stay behind me.'

Rufus wasn't the only man hurt; a steady chorus of yelps and shouts came from the century as lead shot found its mark, or a spear slipped between shields.

Suddenly, the retreat came to a shuddering halt.

'Trees on the track!' The call came from the head of the formation.

The enemy had bided its time, dropping obstructions behind us. They'd toyed with us on the path, but now they'd get what they really wanted.

'Break track!' Pavo ordered without hesitation. 'Find a way around!' He pushed his way into the leading rank so that he could look for the course himself. No doubt he did his best, but the undulating ground, waterlogged gullies and thick vegetation soon did to our formation what the German warriors could not.

It began to come apart.

The gaps were small, at first: a dropped shield as a soldier slipped; exposed shins as they crested a mound. Inevitably, however, the gaps widened, men so focused on making headway that the integrity of the whole suffered. Cries of pain echoed from the ranks. I stepped over our first dead of the retreat, the man unmarked but for a small divot in his forehead.

'Maybe he's just stunned?' young Cnaeus pleaded, unable to take his eyes from the body.

'Leave him,' Titus growled. 'Keep that fucking shield up!'

As our retreat began to show the first signs of desperation, nature decided to heap on further misery. The downpour increased, the wind howling in huge gusts that shook the tree trunks. We forged on into the storm – and our enemies closed about us.

We saw them in numbers for the first time, now. They sensed our weakness, but held back in the shadows, trailing us as a hunter would track a wounded boar. They knew that we were still dangerous, and none of them was eager to die. The fact that they were so patient in their stalking worried me.

'There's more of them ahead,' Chickenhead prophesied, but the veteran was wrong; there were more of them every-where, and as the evermore numerous host appeared out of the trees, they pushed closer.

Cnaeus began to shake, almost uncontrollably. 'It's just the cold. It's just the cold,' he repeated, desperate to convince himself.

Spearmen began to rush forward in knots. They did not throw their weapons, but used them to jab and stab at the space around our shields.

'They're not throwing them,' Chickenhead noted, as if it were of importance.

'So fucking what?' Moonface snapped, angry that a spear had slipped by his guard and into his mail. The armour had stopped the blow, but he was still panting from the impact.

'So they've got a limited supply,' Chickenhead explained. 'They're not happy with just seeing us off and going home.'

I grasped his meaning. These tribesmen were preparing to fight a campaign, not an isolated skirmish.

I stepped around another of our dead, his legs coated with bright red blood. Steadily, the number of casualties grew so that I did not note their details.

A blond-haired brute led a charge at our own flank. We braced, as spearheads hammered into our raised shields. Be-hind the protection, Titus and Cnaeus counterthrust with javelins.

'Put some fucking anger into it!' Titus ordered the youngster, who then screamed defiance into the enemy's bearded faces, his voice cracking and breaking with the effort.

Some of the Germans abandoned their spears, leaving them embedded in our shields, which were already heavy from the rain. Now they came with daggers and short swords, and I drew my own, beating aside an eager thrust, and crunching an elbow into the man's face. Stepping back, I whipped the tip of the blade across his throat. The cut wasn't deep, but he sank to his knees, blood bubbling. He'd die a long death.

Good.

Time lost all meaning as the enemy came against us. At first the withdrawal had been a series of short, sharp engagements, a few men involved at most, but now the Germans battered our lines from all sides. Some began to use stones to crash our shields apart, their comrades pouring into the gaps with spear and sword. The screams of the wounded drowned out the wind and the rain.

I glanced at the wild-eyed legionaries about me. I knew that it would take only a single man to run, and the others would follow; and once we ran, we'd die.

I wasn't the only one to see it.

'Hold the line!' Titus bellowed. 'I see your back, I'll gut you and fuck your corpse, you cunts!'

A spear darted towards my face. I twisted, ducking beneath the attack, driving my sword up into the guts of the enemy. Hot blood cascaded over my hand as I struggled to pull the sword free of his sucking flesh.

The action left me momentarily outside of the line, and as I rushed to rejoin them, I saw what remained of our century —

maybe sixty men – a tight knot of red amongst the dark-cloaked enemies.

'My family are in the camp!' Rufus suddenly shouted above the din, his words shocking his comrades even in the desperation of battle. 'If I go down, keep them safe!'

'You stupid bastard!' Titus barked at his friend, pulling his sword free of a German chest.

'Keep them safe!'

'Keep them safe yourself! Stop fucking distracting me!'

Titus bent to the ground, freeing a short sword from a German's dead hand and pushing it behind the leather belts on his waist.

'Not the time for trophy collecting!' Stumps shouted, holding a spearman at bay with feinted thrusts of his javelin.

'You mind your own fight,' Titus growled, ramming his fist into the side of the spearman's head. The blow was enough to drop the German like a stone, and Titus followed through by stamping on the man's skull; an eye popped free of its socket.

'Close up!' he roared, gripping men by their equipment and pulling the formation tighter.

Step by step, foot by foot, the battered century crossed the forest floor, the knot of shields steadily shrinking as German spears found exposed Roman flesh.

'Just let us stand!' Moonface screamed aloud. His wide face was painted in blood, and flushed with battle-madness. 'Let us die standing!'

'I'm not dying here, you mad bastard,' Stumps chided him, hitting his friend across the back of the helmet. 'And neither are you!'

His words held more certainty, his eyes more hope, than they had any right to. I followed his gaze to open ground.

*Open fucking ground.*

We were only fifty paces from the forest's edge, but now, pushed on by our near escape, the Germans pressed home their assault, making us pay for every bloody yard. More men dropped in sight of safety than during the entire retreat, the rearguard wiped out as the formation finally buckled and became a circle of frightened men and overlapping shields. In such a formation, we stepped out of the darkness of the forest and into the open ground, the damp field as welcoming as the forum of Rome.

A few spearmen followed us from the trees to hurl final missiles and insults, but the charge of a patrolling cavalry unit was enough to send them scurrying for cover.

A young decurion, the officer commanding the cavalry squadron, pulled his mount to a halt beside the panting and bleeding men of Pavo's command.

'You're the Second Century, Second Cohort,' he announced.

Pavo emerged from the ranks. The horsehair crest of his helmet had been shorn almost in two by a German sword. His forearms were thick with blood from a dozen spear-nicks. He had not shied from the fighting and, with his proud chin and bright eyes, he made for a heroic figure. 'How do you know that?' he asked, puzzled.

'You're the only ones still out there.'

'The other work parties came back?'

'Some of them did,' the cavalry officer answered ominously, twisting in the saddle to peer at the forest, the trees as much of a barricade as any fort's stone walls. 'Someone doesn't want us to leave this place,' he concluded with a soldier's grim resignation.

Pavo wasted no time, and marched – limped – the century back towards the camp. Through the rain, I took in the men about me. The section had come through the action alive, but not unscathed: Stumps's shoulder wound had reopened, the stitches pulled free as he'd protected others with his shield; a deep gash ran across Titus's forearm, a glimmer of white bone appearing within; Rufus's shoulder was slumped from a slingshot's strike; Moonface pressed delicately on ribs that were deeply bruised, if not cracked; young Micon's helmet was dented and the eternally blank stare of his face was painted red by a cut across his forehead.

I took in these men, and in that moment I knew that I could not abandon them. Not while they were in this forest, besieged by enemies and by the storm. They had kept me alive today, and I owed it to them to return that service. A voice in my head railed against making such a promise, but I told myself that the oath was only to see the section clear of the forest. From there, I would go my own way, north to Britain, and a life free of Rome. Free of the legions. Free of war.

But for now, during the day's struggle and slaughter, something within me had changed. Since my discovery in the grove I had fought against the ties of comradeship, but I could no longer resist those bonds, even if they were conditional, and it would be reasonable to assume that my about-turn had been prompted solely by the trials of combat. Reasonable, but wrong.

Because my decision was born of guilt.

Guilt that my actions had doomed these men, as they had others before them. Guilt that I could not resurrect ghosts. Guilt because, despite the adrenaline that seeped through my veins, despite the horror that we had endured in the forest, and despite the relief of escaping to the marching camp, the decurion's words had left me reeling. *Someone doesn't want us to leave this place.*

With blinding clarity, I knew who.

# 27

'The chieftain Segestes is behind all of this,' I told Pavo. 'Arminius eloped with his daughter, and he wants him dead.'

We were in the centurion's tent, Pavo having begrudgingly agreed to hear my petition. He was scrubbing at his helmet, working away blood that the rain had failed to wash clean.

'He needs the army held up here because he knows Varus will come to Arminius's rescue,' I continued. 'He'll use the other tribes to keep us pinned down until he unites his own, and then we'll be allowed to march on.'

Pavo didn't break from his scrubbing, dismissing my theory with icy sarcasm. 'So the chief breaks an oath to Rome, attacks an army twice the size of his tribe, and all because he doesn't like his son-in-law? It makes no sense,' he snorted, casting an angry eye over the helmet's ruined crest.

'It's a family feud, sir. Sense doesn't come into it.'

I could see that my argument was falling on deaf ears. I needed to try another tack. A dangerous tack.

'The legate,' I said. Pavo's eyes snapped to me at the mention of the man. 'Does it make sense that he'd send a century into the forest with no support? No, because he did it out of passion. He did it for family.'

Slowly, Pavo placed the helmet on the ground, his dangerous eyes never leaving mine as he stood.

'You have no fucking idea,' he warned, but I needed him to take my conclusion to the army's commanders, and so I stepped over the precipice.

'I know you were fucking one of his women.'

I braced myself for the blow. I was expecting it would come to the stomach. Perhaps a knee into my face as I doubled over.

None came.

He laughed.

The laugh was bitter, true to the man, but there was more now, in his eyes, as if he had seen some great irony.

'*You* want to talk about secrets? You? The stranger that a prince ordered me to take into my century? The man who knows more about the Germans' traps than they do? The soldier who claims to be a replacement, but is more of a veteran than any other in my unit?'

He laughed again. I held my silence. Eventually, Pavo spat on the dirt of his tent's floor.

'Forget it. I'm not asking, because something in my head tells me that could be dangerous. But I will tell you this, whoever you are. You're not as clever as you think.'

He looked away from me, and I sensed he was pushing down a tide of bitter reproach.

'You know, all of my life, whenever I've achieved something, people have whispered, *Who's he been fucking*? It never occurs to them – it hasn't occurred to you – that maybe the better question to ask is: *Who* hasn't *he been fucking*?'

'The legate,' I answered quietly.

He spat again, this time with violence. 'He gave me a century and, idiot that I was, I thought I'd got it because I was a good soldier. Because he knew that I was going on to great things. How the fuck did I know that he wanted *that* in return? He couldn't take the command back from me unless I fucked up – and I'm too *good* to fuck up – but he's been looking for a way to get rid of me ever since. I guarantee you that today will not be the last day we get left out to dry because of it.'

The centurion's anger faded, replaced by bitter reproach. A reproach to himself.

'Those men today, they died because of me. I've always known that soldiers have to bleed to get me where I want to go, but these men didn't die for my ambition, but because of my fucking stupidity.'

This was no act. The centurion's scowl, a mask worn so well, had slipped. Here was a young man, heaped with guilt. Little wonder he had been so desperate to wipe the blood from his armour. I dared not tell him that the conscience was not so easily made clean. Instead, I offered the first solution to the problem.

'Give up the rank,' I told him. 'Get a transfer to another cohort.'

He shook his head. Clearly, he'd gone around in circles with the same question. 'It's not about the rank. I turned him down. I know what he is. He wants me dead, no matter where I go, and others will die with me.'

'It's better that one dies than many,' I offered finally.

His eyes became like fire. 'Suicide? I won't go out like that, you cunt. I'm a fucking soldier, and I'll die like a soldier.'

I shook my head. The centurion had mistaken my meaning. I offered him the second solution to the problem.

'Kill the legate.'

Pavo and I talked at length after that, some of it heated, some of it with the cold detachment of butchers. By the time a plan had been decided upon, I felt as if part of the old me had returned.

'You're too good at this,' Pavo noted warily. 'What's in it for you?'

'I keep breathing.'

'There must be something more.'

I considered it.

'Titus. Stop giving his section the most dangerous jobs.'

'You think I give him those details because I want him dead?' He laughed, his white smile brilliant. 'I hate him, I admit. I think he's a bully and a thug, but he's *good*. I know he's my best chance of keeping the men alive. That's why he gets those jobs.'

'It's not the dice?'

'If every soldier in debt tried to kill their way out of it, the army would be down to ten men.'

His reasoning made sense. His eyes told me it was truth. I decided to press my advantage.

'Arminius. You are – were – in debt to him, too?' I asked, pained as I remembered my friend's fall.

'I suppose there's no harm in telling you after what we've talked about. Yes, I owed him, but that was paid by taking you into the century.'

'Why would he do that?'

'Why would I ask? It was a win for me.'

Denied my answer, I moved to the tent flap.

'You're going to want something from me, too.' Pavo's words stopped me at the exit. 'You help me with this, and you have it.'

I made no reply as I ducked into the rains.

Being heavily mauled that day bought the century no sympathy from the army, and later that evening, it was our turn to stand watch on the camp's ramparts.

'I was just startin' to warm up again,' Stumps grumbled. The men had taken the few hours' respite to fill their bellies with hot food. Suffering from the nauseating effects of adrenaline overload, Cnaeus had been unable to keep down a mouthful; both he and Micon were shaking violently from the cold.

'Jump around,' Chickenhead told them. 'Get the blood moving.'

The boys made pathetic attempts to comply, the veterans smiling at the effort.

'Good thing you're soldiers,' Stumps told them with some warmth. 'You'd never make it as acrobats.'

Then the jumping figures produced an unexpected surprise: something was shaken out from beneath Micon's armour.

It was an ear.

Stumps cackled with laughter, bending down to pick up the ragged piece of flesh. He spoke into it. 'Hello. I'm afraid I've got some bad news, mate. The barber took a bit too much off the sides.'

The veterans laughed; only Titus was unmoved by the dark humour. He had a sword in his hands, turning it over as if inspecting every detail. His own short sword was comfortable in its scabbard, and I remembered that Titus had collected one from the enemy dead. I had no idea why. I could only guess that, like many soldiers, he was partial to trophy hunting.

I watched the big man, taking in the bandaged forearm and the scowling face. Only this morning, I had wanted him dead, but my rage had long since faded, quenched by an afternoon of vicious bloodshed. Now, I admired the man who had held

219

his section together, fearless as he herded them to safety. Pavo was right; Titus was a bully and a thug, but he was *good*.

'You hungry?' Stumps asked of Micon, pushing the ear towards the boy's mouth.

He laughed at the youngster's uncomfortable squirming.

'Hey, Moony.' Stumps poked his friend. 'What would you rather lose? Your eyes, ears or nose?'

'My nose, obviously,' Moonface replied without hesitation. 'Then I wouldn't have to smell your arse stinking out the tent.'

'It's a privilege to enjoy my aroma. How about you, Chicken?'

'My ears, so I wouldn't have to listen to you and your stupid fucking questions.'

'And I'll lose my eyes, too,' Moonface added. 'So I don't have to look at your face. It's like a trodden-on bunch of grapes.'

'Gods, you lot are in great spirits tonight, aren't you? Anyone would think you didn't enjoy serving in the glorious Seventeenth Legion. You've got wind, rain and mud. What else could an infantryman want?'

'Shut up, Stumps,' Rufus ordered, his eyes on the treeline. 'Something's coming out of the forest.'

Silence fell. Knuckles went white as men unconsciously tightened their grips on javelins. Eyes strained to see through the sheets of rain that fell in an unending cascade.

'It's a horse,' Rufus announced.

It was a riderless horse, and it was the first of a dozen that appeared over the next hour. Each time, a patrolling cavalry squadron would corral the beast and lead it back to camp. One such sortie brought them close to our position, and we noted the bright red gash on the horse's hindquarters.

Stumps snorted. 'Well, that's the governor's dinner sorted.'

'What happened to the riders?' Micon asked. The dull-witted soldier received only frowns as answers.

But perhaps his question was not as straightforward as it seemed for, shortly after, Rufus again noticed movement in the distance, and this time it was no horse.

It was men.

They were soldiers, the red of their tunics betraying them through the rain. It was harder to make out the dark-cloaked Germans behind them, until they pushed their prisoners onto their knees, and shouted their guttural language into the storm.

'Gods, no . . .' Chickenhead prayed.

From our left, a cavalry detachment had spotted the enemy and were pounding towards them, desperate to rescue the hostages.

I knew that they would not make it.

German blades were raised to the sky, then chopped savagely down into the necks of the captives; the severed heads were held aloft with more native cries of defiance.

The cavalry spurred closer. The Germans ran. They were still short of the forest when the cavalry pulled up, and rode away.

'Slingers,' Chickenhead guessed.

'They took the heads,' Moonface noted, shaken.

I looked at Titus.

Throughout the execution, he hadn't raised his eyes from the captured sword.

I spooned hot barley into my mouth, aware that my respite would be short. Despite knowing what lay ahead, I felt calm. As calm as I had been in a long time. I recognized that the coming

221

mission with Pavo had given me a singular focus that was both terrifying and reassuring. What I was planning was dangerous, and yet, if successful, perhaps I and what was left of the century would come through this campaign alive. Maybe their spared lives would quiet the screams of the others.

Maybe.

Titus and Rufus got to their feet, the pair fully armed and armoured.

'We're going to check on his family,' Titus announced, though why he needed to accompany his friend, I had no idea.

Across the tent, Cnaeus and Micon were still shaking uncontrollably; the watch on the rampart had used up the final reserves of their strength.

'They're coming down with exposure,' Chickenhead assessed. The veteran held Lupus to his chest, the reunion causing a tear to run down the gnarled skin of his ugly face. After the events of that day, no man made any comment or fun of him.

'Come on, lads,' Stumps offered to the youngsters, moving to help them. 'Get those wet clothes off.'

With Moonface's assistance, the veterans stripped the shivering soldiers. Their pale skin was almost blue. Placing the driest cloak at hand over their shoulders, Stumps began to spoon barley into their mouths like a doting mother. With their actions in the forest that day, the boy soldiers had earned their place as members of the section.

The tent flap pulled back, the howling winds causing the fire to dance and shimmy in its pit.

'Felix,' Pavo summoned me, his bitter mask firmly in place. 'Let's go.'

I got to my feet.

'Where's Titus?' the centurion asked the assembled members.

Moonface covered for him. 'Latrines.'

'I've got an orders group. I'm taking Felix as a runner.'

Chickenhead raised an eyebrow, but said nothing. The veteran would know that the army held its orders groups late in the evening, and the sun, hidden as it was, was yet to set. He might have wondered at the anomaly, but he could never have guessed at the true reason for our early departure.

But perhaps someone had, because as we emerged from the hide of the tent, we found a section of the legion's elite First Cohort waiting grim-faced in the rain.

'You.' A scarred centurion pointed at me. 'You're the one they found in the woods?'

'I am,' I answered eventually.

'Come with us,' he ordered. 'Governor Varus wants to speak with you.'

# 28

Pavo had attempted to accompany me upon my summons to the governor, but the senior centurion had ordered him to stand down.

'When will I get him back?' Pavo had pressed. 'I'm already down thirty men, and he's one of my best.'

'Soon enough,' he was told with finality.

So far as I could tell, I was not a prisoner. I still carried my dagger and short sword at my waist, and walked freely with the First Cohort's centurion at the head of his men. To be appointed to a legion's First Cohort was a great honour, and I knew that to press this stringent professional for information would be a waste of time. Instead, as we trudged through the gelatinous mud of the camp, I took the opportunity to think.

What could Varus want with me? Had this something to do with the night on the parade square, where I had intervened to save Arminius's life? How had the governor discovered my identity? I had shared my name with the standard-bearer, but Felix was not an uncommon name in the legions. Would Arminius himself have spoken of me? I couldn't think of a reason why he would.

Shit. Hadn't I spilled my guts when I made my report, blade to the prince's throat? With adrenaline pumping, I hadn't thought to invent a new unit for myself, but surely Varus would have forgotten my words the moment I'd spoken them? The governor didn't strike me as the kind of commander who wished to know the details of his lowliest soldiers.

No, it couldn't have been the night at the square – the centurion had asked me if I was the soldier found in the woods. The grove. Tracing me to my century would have been easy enough. I was the only battle casualty replacement to arrive that day, and the quartermaster's records proved my existence, as did my later drawing of pay. Yes, they could work back and discover my identity, but only as far as the grove, so why the sudden interest?

With a tightening of my stomach, I pictured the centurion and the two dead legionaries that we had pulled from the manure in Minden's streets. I had thought my secret died with them, but had they shared it with others before their throats were slit?

The thought turned me cold. Blood began to pound in my ears. I thought about what they would do to me. It would be crucifixion, and I had seen enough men and women die that way to know how my end would come. I would scream. Piss and shit would run down my legs. I would leave this world disgraced, in agony, and a momentary distraction for others.

Fuck that.

So what to do? I had my blades on my belt, but a section of eight soldiers behind me. They being of the First Cohort, there would be no dull-witted Micons in their ranks. These men were handpicked, and lethal. Cold steel would plunge into my back before my own had even cleared the scabbard. At best, I could hope to take the centurion with me, but what had that man done to deserve death in this muddy avenue between tents? I wasn't afraid of killing my kinsmen, but I

225

had to draw a line between the deserving and the innocent. Wasn't that how I'd come to be here?

And with that thought, it was as if a heavy black cloak had settled over my mind. I knew that I could not resist. Whatever was coming, I would have to face it.

Of course, it was no black cloak but a heavy cloth sack that had been pulled over my head. As its cord was drawn tight about my neck, I heard the rasp of metal as my blades were pulled free of their scabbards, but not by my own hands.

The First Cohort were good. They'd waited to get me clear of my own century, fearing their loyalty, before showing their true hand. Exhaling strongly, I prepared for the blows. As I sank into the cold mud, the kicks rained in.

From the chill beneath my arse, I was sitting on the ground. From the absence of rain on my hood, I was within a tent. I licked my lips and gums, finding my teeth where they had been, and no blood. The First Cohort's section *were* good. My body ached, but nothing felt broken. They had done enough to subdue me, to show that resistance was pointless, and nothing more. If it wasn't for the fact that their professionalism killed any chance of my escaping this situation, I might even have applauded it.

There were voices about me. Numerous voices. Their tones were deep, and rich. Men trained for command and public speaking. Members of the senatorial classes. The army's staff officers, I assumed.

The hood was pulled away.

A half-dozen men stood in front of me. Varus was at their centre, flanked by men in white tunics. Some had broad purple stripes adorning their sleeves, others narrower bands of the same colour. These were Varus's tribunes – the young aristocrats who oversaw the organization of his army.

'Arminius found you in a grove,' Varus stated simply.

I was aware of a looming presence behind me. I was more aware still that the shadow would strike me if I bit back my answers.

I saw no profit in taking further punishment. From the certainty in the governor's words, I would only confirm what he already knew.

'I was, sir,' I answered as respectfully as I could, despite the aching in my ribs.

'And where did you come from, before that?' a broad-striped tribune asked, his aquiline nose twitching with impatience.

'I – I don't know, sir,' I stammered, bracing myself for a blow.

It didn't come.

'You don't know?' the tribune pressed, eyes narrowing in distrust.

'Prince Arminius found me, sir. I don't know what happened before that. He found me, and all my friends were dead.'

This time, the blow did fall. It was a short, sharp punch to my kidney. I hissed in pain.

'Your friends,' the tribune mused, stepping closer. 'And what legion were they?'

'The First, sir,' I answered quickly.

'Ah, so you remember that?'

'I was told, sir. By the prince.'

'Convenient.'

I said nothing. Varus was watching me closely. The governor had not cut an impressive figure the night before. Now he looked as though he'd aged a further ten years.

Something had happened.

I took a chance. 'The prince, sir. He lives?' I delivered the words with an anguish that was not altogether theatrical. The uninvited words earned me more pain, as I knew they would, but I'd also landed my own blow.

I saw the governor's chest swell as he took a calming breath against his grief. 'Arminius is not with us,' he answered cryptically, taking a step forward and grasping my chin in what had been a manicured hand. The fingernails were now dark with dirt. 'I've seen you before.'

One did not become the Governor on the Rhine without a keen intellect, and after a few moments of brief contemplation, Varus had dragged the memories from the depths of his mind.

'It was you. On the square. You saved him, didn't you?'

Now was the time to lie. 'Sir?' I asked, frowning.

There were no punches. No kicks. Instead, Varus's fingernails dug a little deeper into the flesh of my jaw.

'It was you,' he concluded, stepping back.

The strikes were hard, fast and vicious. I toppled forward, my teeth scraping across the mud, and I gagged against the cold slime. Eventually, strong hands gripped my shoulders, and held me up on my knees.

The broad-stripe tribune stepped forward. 'You're a spy, planted by Arminius,' he asserted with far from absolute certainty. 'He killed those men in the grove, and used it to bring you into the army. Why?' he shouted.

His logic was sound, given the coincidence, but I could see that the 'why' bothered him. A spy on Varus's staff would be invaluable. A well-placed centurion would be useful. But a common soldier in the ranks? What use was that?

I didn't think it absurd, however, that they would suspect an ally of planting spies amongst his friends. There was no better way of keeping someone close than knowing their secrets. I would have been deeply shocked if Varus did not have his own moles in the court of every tribal chieftain that claimed fealty to Rome.

'You're an assassin,' the tribune stated, though it was clear that even he doubted this. No assassin worth his blood price would have allowed himself to be meekly led before the governor.

The tribune was grasping at straws, I realized. That was why I was here. There was no evidence to condemn me, only the anomaly that I had been found in the grove and brought into the army, so what had made these men clutch at me?

Arminius. He was the connection. What had happened today to have caused this sudden anxiety? Yesterday, Varus had mourned, but the army's commanders had been confident. Now, I could see the first traces of uncertainty, almost panic, in their eyes.

I looked at Varus. His eyes were haunted. I had seen it in men who suffered from battle-shock, but the governor had not drawn his sword. Had the loss of men from the work parties shaken him so deeply? Impossible.

'You were brought into the army by Arminius,' he now accused me with quiet detachment. 'Why did you not ride away with his scouts?'

The scouts. So I wasn't the only one troubled by their disappearance. The question had circled in my mind on how they – and the few horsemen who had summoned them – had somehow passed unmolested through the forest that teemed with enemies. I had come to the conclusion that they had bribed their way through, maybe even reasoned with their countrymen, but now I saw that there was something more sinister behind their recall. Had Segestes ordered that his Cherusci be allowed to pass, knowing that they would not be able to resist riding to their prince's aid, and leaving Varus and his army blind and fixed in position?

'Sir,' I began, my tone pleading, 'I'm just a soldier.'

'You're a spy,' the tribune spat, answering for the governor. 'And you'll tell us what you know.'

I expected that meant further beatings, and questions at the hands of these men.

I was wrong.

'Take him away,' the tribune ordered the men behind me. 'Find out what he knows, and then send his head to his friends in the forest.'

'Any preference, sir?' a dark voice boomed.

The tribune thought over the question as if it were a mathematical problem; his answer was empty of emotion. 'He's a spy,' he condemned me. 'There can be only one punishment.'

Kneeling in the cold mud, I struggled to choke back a rising tide of vomit, knowing now what my fate would be. The fate I had always feared above all others.

'Crucifixion.'

# 29

The hood was pulled back into place, dampening my senses, and I was dragged from the tent.

The pounding rain was cold against my flesh, but it did nothing to revive me from the numbness that now gripped my mind and senses. Knowing what my fate would be – the most ghastly fate I could imagine – my wits had tried to take leave of my body. Yet they were trapped as if in a cage, and so they rattled the bars of their confinement instead. My muscles shook uncontrollably; my teeth chattered; the sound of blood pounded in my ears. I would have pissed myself, I'm sure, but dehydration saved me from at least that one indignity.

I was dropped to my knees and pushed face down; a few half-hearted kicks fell on to my prone form, just enough to advise me to stay in that position. Prostrate in the soaked hood, I gasped in breaths of wet air made musky by the thick sacking. Incredible what small details you notice, as the end of your life is moments away.

I heard the sound of men's voices; the details were lost in the howling elements, but there was no mistaking the *tap-tap-tap* that announced the construction of the crucifix. I pictured the hammer, and how it would drive the cold steel of the nails through my flesh. I knew I would scream. I screamed in my dreams, for fuck's sake; how could I hold them back under torture?

I don't know how long I lay there, a pathetic worm in the mud. Like the boy soldier who had bled to death on the stakes – had that truly happened this same day? – all I could think of now was my mother. I hadn't seen her in over a decade, and even as I ached for her comfort, I couldn't picture the details of her face. I became consumed with the need to recall her image, and angry that I couldn't. So angry that by the time I was hauled to my feet, my self-pity had been melted away by fury.

I struggled, shrugging off the blows that landed in my stomach. My hands were untied and pulled apart. I felt the skin brush against wood, and threw my head forward, feeling it connect with another man's skull. A curse and a savage blow was my reward.

'Behave yourself, you cunt!' was shouted into my ear, with more punches landing as exclamation.

I wouldn't. Rage had taken over my body now. The human, reasoning side of my mind had departed. All that was left was animal instinct, the need to survive at any cost.

Rough cord was looped over my wrists, finally binding my thrashing limbs to the wood. Inside my hood I snarled, preparing for the bite of the nails.

Instead, the hood was pulled away.

Sometime during my confinement, darkness had come and, shadowed by flickering torches, my captors' faces were black masks beneath steel helmets.

They stood back now, catching their breath, their victim tethered, if not subdued.

One of the men took a step closer. A trickle of blood ran from a nose many times broken. I expected violence, or anger. Instead, the executioner spoke with quiet detachment.

'Look, mate, this is nothing personal, all right? Why don't you stop making a scene, and just tell us what you know? Me and the boys don't really want to be out in the rain, so the longer you keep us out here, the more pissed off and inventive we're goin' to get, yeah? Spill it now, and I promise we'll knock you out before we do anything nasty. You'll go to sleep, and there'll be no pain. Trust me, I've done this a few times, and it's not something you want to put yourself through.'

The placid tone of the words was soothing. For a second, I could almost have forgotten that he was asking me to roll over and die.

I tried to speak, but my mouth had become ash. I ran a dry tongue about my lips, and the soldier got my meaning.

'Give the man some wine.'

I drank greedily from the offered skin, enjoying the rich flavour of the grapes.

'It's good,' I told them, my voice and calm restored.

'So you'll talk?'

'I'll talk,' I began. 'But you may want to do this inside. It's a long story.'

'Nice try.' He laughed before reaching into his pocket, and pulling out a long iron nail. He stepped forward, tracing the point of the metal along the skin of my right arm.

'Last chance to do things the easy way.'

What did I have to lose? I was tied fast to the wooden beams, and even if I wasn't, there were four of them, and they hadn't spent the night getting the shit kicked out of them. My only hope was to talk. Maybe the Germans would be good enough to attack the camp and slit my throat, but until then, I would talk, and these men would hear a lot more than they expected to.

I'd give them a fucking story.

'I'll tell you everything,' I offered, 'but it really is a long story.'

The soldier smiled in the torchlight. 'Go on.'

Instead, I held my tongue.

Maybe it was being so close to death that aroused my senses to heights beyond their usual sensitivity, but I saw movement beyond the flickering torches, and before my captors could land a blow on me for delaying my confession, a commanding voice barked from the darkness.

'Stand down, Hadrian.'

The owner of that voice came to stand before me, and I forgot all about trying to picture my mother. No face could have been as beautiful as this: Caeonius, his hooded eyes and bulbous nose wrinkled with discomfort.

'Get him down.'

The men knew better than to delay, and within moments my bindings had been cut.

'I've cleared it with the governor,' the prefect explained to the soldiers. 'Put him in that tent.'

The soldiers made to pick me up, but stubborn pride compelled me to wave away the help of men who had been about to kill me. The relief of my escape made me weak, and I stalked to the tent like a newborn foal, almost collapsing on the bench within.

'Wine?' Caeonius asked, and I latched on to the skin like a babe to the teat.

'What is it with you and trouble?' he asked in some wonderment. 'Forty years I've done with the eagles, and every now and then, some unlucky bugger like you will come along, and get a legion's worth of shit on his own head.'

'I'm sorry, sir,' I mumbled, wiping away the wine from my chin.

'Sorry for what? Being in the wrong place at the wrong time?'

The prefect must have felt the question in my eyes. My need to know why I had been moments away from a horrific death.

'It's been a bad day, lad, and on bad days, commanders need scapegoats. Unfortunately for you, Tribune Paterculus came up with a theory that Arminius had a spy in the camp, and after a bit of head-scratching, they came up with you.'

'But I haven't done anything, sir,' I protested.

'You were out of the ordinary. That was enough for them. Like I say, they needed a scapegoat.'

His tone told me that they'd found another. I asked him who.

'The Germans aren't the only ones who can hide in the woods,' Caeonius answered proudly. 'I took out some volunteers from the Nineteenth. We ambushed a group of them, brought a few back to get answers.'

As if the prisoners had been waiting for the prefect to mention them, an agonized scream pierced the night.

'The tribune is a real bloodthirsty bugger.' Caeonius got to his feet and placed a fatherly hand on my shoulder. 'Spy my arse.' He smiled. 'I told them that you were more dead than alive in that grove. Now that the tribune's getting his fill, he'll forget you ever existed, but it's best if you don't hang around the headquarters area. I'll have a couple of blokes make sure you get back to your unit.'

'Sir.' I stopped him as he turned to leave. 'There's something I don't understand.' I hoped that I held back the desperation with which I needed to know the answer. A twitch of bushy eyebrows told me to proceed. 'They brought

235

me in because Arminius found me in the grove, but the governor said that the prince is no longer with us? It doesn't make sense, sir. If Arminius is dead, then what does it matter if he did have spies? It's embarrassing, yes, but nothing more.'

Caeonius paused before he answered. His forty years of service had taken him through countless desperate moments, and forged within him a constitution of iron. His words confirmed that the same could not be said of the army's younger, politically appointed commanders.

'There is no sense in fear, lad,' he concluded, and as he turned on his heel, I struggled to stand. I had to know more. I had to.

'What are they afraid of?' I blurted.

'What we're all afraid of,' Caeonius answered without breaking stride, his weathered face grinning as he delivered his verdict. 'Death.'

# 30

I must have looked like a drunk as I struggled to make my way back to the lines of my century, my sandals slipping in mud, head beating like the drum of a slave ship, muscles aching and ablaze. The storm still raged, the gusts threatening to topple me into the muck, but at least the slapping rain was a cold comfort against my skin.

Finally I reached Pavo's tent. I did not stand on ceremony or rank, and threw back the canvas flap.

'Shit,' the centurion said as I stumbled within and sank to one knee. He was quick to his feet. Having pulled the canvas tightly shut against the tempest, he stood over me, his eyes narrow and calculating. 'This wasn't about me, was it?' he asked cautiously, as if I carried the plague.

'No.'

'Then what?' He gestured that I should sit on his bedroll, but offered no assistance. I grunted as I sat back, my head resting on the tent's hide walls.

'The grove,' I told him. 'They thought I was a spy.'

'Are you?' he asked, candid now. After what we had discussed previously in this tent, there was little need for guile.

'No.'

Pavo grunted, as if my near torture and death were of little consequence. He had his own plans, plans which I had helped to engineer, and they had come unravelled owing to my arrest.

'We've missed our chance with the legion commander,' he informed me as he drank from a wineskin. I couldn't help but raise an eyebrow in surprise as he offered it to me. 'He's already issued the orders for the morning. So if he's dead or alive, we're still fucked.'

'The vanguard?' I guessed, and Pavo nodded. There was little anger in the movement, only resignation.

'He's given us the most honourable position.' He managed to smile, and cast out his arms. 'Honourable deaths for everyone.'

'Do they know?' I asked with a gesture of my head towards the other tents of the century, and my section.

Pavo took the wineskin from me, and held it up as his answer. 'In the morning.' He shrugged. 'The boys will have enough to deal with tonight.'

'Why?' I asked, my stomach knotting at the thought of more imminent danger.

Pavo took a deep draught of the wine, replaced the stopper, and got to his feet. 'Can you walk?' he asked.

I nodded, the wine and short rest having done something to restore my balance, or at least I hoped so.

'Then get to your feet, lucky one.' He smiled dryly, surprising me once more by offering his hand. 'Come and see what has become of Varus's glorious army.'

What was left of the century formed up in the darkness, forty-eight men huddled together against the tempest. I was far from the only man battered and bruised, but none of the soldiers bore worse than a flesh wound – those who had suffered more serious injuries had fallen from formation in the forest, and had likely died hideous deaths at the hands of the Germans.

Now Pavo informed us that there would be more suffering before the dawn. 'The governor's ordered that we break camp before first light. The plan is to try and slip away in the dark, before the Germans can work out in which direction we're going,' he said, voice raised against the sweeping rains.

'We're not tearing down the camp?' a veteran asked.

'The camp stays up,' Pavo told him. Beside me, Moon-face's mouth dropped aghast at the deviation from army practice.

'The camp stays up,' Pavo repeated. 'And the baggage train stays here.'

The second part of the announcement brought forth a series of disbelieving cries and curses, for to abandon the baggage train was an acknowledgment that the army was in far more trouble than the soldiers had been led to believe.

I looked over the faces of my section. Chickenhead's pinched face was as cold as marble. Rufus seemed to shake with anger. For my own part, the statement only confirmed what I had been led to believe by the demeanour of the army's commanders — that they were running scared.

'This is bollocks!' a voice cried out to a chorus of loud agreement.

Pavo called for silence. After a fraction of a second, he got it. His actions in the forest had earned him the respect of all but Titus, and he had become the century's leader in more than name.

'There's something else,' he announced, taking the helmet from his head so that he could address his men soldier to soldier, man to man.

The action was so unlike the cocky bastard that I braced myself, for it could only be the most grave of news that was making the centurion behave in this way.

And it was.

'The badly wounded. They aren't coming with us.'

The howl of the wind and rain was drowned out by indignant curses at the idea of such an order. Where before there had been surprise and hurt pride, now there were only shouts of anger, reproach and fear.

'For fuck's sake!' Stumps called out. 'Just how fucked are we?'

Pavo had no answer, standing like a statue as the rain pelted his uncovered face.

'This is a bloody disgrace!' a veteran roared. 'We can't leave them! The goat-fuckers will skin them alive!'

Optio Cato stepped forward to the front of the assembly. Pavo's second in command, Cato was largely redundant in the century, every man knowing that it would be Titus who would step into Pavo's shoes should the centurion fall, the natural laws of leadership and survival trumping the chain of command now that the army was in such dire straits.

'Lads,' Cato began, holding up his hands, 'calm down! We don't have any seriously wounded in the century. We're not leaving anybody behind!'

The words did something to restore order, loud curses reduced to grumbles.

Pavo gestured that Cato should rejoin the ranks, then put his helmet back on, its shorn crest billowing in the wind. 'We don't,' he agreed, his words directed at all present. 'But other centuries do.'

'What are you saying, Pavo?' Titus growled from the rear ranks, sick of dancing around the matter. 'Just tell us what the fuck is going on.'

The centurion sought out the big man. There was no doubt that he had to force the bitter words from between his teeth, and when he spoke, even the hardest of the men swallowed.

'We're to report to the camp hospital and separate the wounded from their comrades,' Pavo ordered, and I knew that with his next words, his eyes would become as dead as the night's darkness. 'We're to make sure that they're left behind.'

## 31

Formed into two ranks, Pavo led the century through the camp's tented avenues, the mud a viscous oil beneath our feet.

Everywhere in the darkness soldiers hurried about in preparation for the army's early departure, taking what they needed from the baggage train and stowing it with their own personal equipment. Unlike the departure from the summer camp at Minden, these measures were accompanied by an air of desperation, and Chickenhead clucked at the army's anxiety.

'Wasting their time. They should just worry about sleep,' he opined beside me. 'We're gonna have to fight our way out of this forest, Felix. All the stuff on the carrying yokes will be dumped by the time the day's out, I promise you. Shields, sword and wineskin, that's what we'll be carrying.'

We tramped on through the dirt, the veteran's eye catching my own.

'This bit's going to be hard,' Chickenhead added quietly, with a glance towards the younger members of the section.

I said nothing. There was nothing to say. I knew what the old soldier meant: it would be down to the old sweats to take on the horror of separating the casualties from their friends, and to heap it on to our already polluted souls.

'Century,' Pavo called from the head of our pathetic formation. 'Halt.'

Our sandals slapped down into the mud. We were at the hospital. Braziers and lamps lit the area, and from the light that they cast, flames struggling and flickering in the wind, I saw other bodies of men. We were not the only century dispatched to this task.

We waited a few minutes in the rain. Then, given away by the silhouette of their transverse crests in the darkness, I saw that Pavo had been joined by another centurion. Likely he was the commander of our cohort's First Century, disseminating orders. Sure enough, Pavo then came down the line, issuing his own orders to each section. Eventually, he reached Titus.

'Titus, I don't have another section as salted as yours,' the centurion began.

'You can't dress up a turd.' Titus cut off Pavo's speech, his deep voice resigned. 'Just tell us what we're doing.'

Pavo did, and as we heard the words, our hearts sank.

'I was hoping we'd get perimeter duty or something,' Stumps said, echoing my own thoughts.

But we did not. We were to pull the wounded and dying from the arms of their comrades.

'Let's go,' Titus grunted. 'Anyone hesitates, I'll beat the shit out of him.' The big man's words were harsh, but well meant. He knew as well as anyone that this task would make our life-and-death struggle in the forest seem like a pleasant walk on a summer's day. There was no adrenaline here to carry us through the suffering, only the acid in our stomachs and the lumps in our throats.

Titus led us towards the large tent that acted as one of the marching camp's hospital wards. By torchlight, I saw other sections enter the canvas to our left and right. Titus's broad shoulders obscured my view as he pushed through the flap, but as I ducked within, I knew from horrid experience what I'd find.

A brazier had been placed in the tent's centre, its orange flames dancing on the waxed hide canvas. The grey smoke was thick, but it did little to mask the stink of wounds and shit. A narrow walkway crossed the tent's mud floor, and to either side lay the wretched forms of men with appalling injuries clad in blood-soaked bandages. These poor souls ignored our presence, but their vigilant comrades, eyes burning as they glared at us, did not.

They knew why we had come.

'You're not from the Nineteenth,' a veteran accused us, rising from beside a soldier whose leg had been amputated below the knee.

'We're not,' Titus stated simply.

'Then what the fuck are you doing here?' the soldier asked as half a dozen other men of the Nineteenth Legion also got to their feet.

Titus said nothing, which was answer enough.

'No.' The soldier's hand reached involuntarily for the pommel of his sword.

'You don't have a choice,' Titus cautioned him, his tone grim.

'I have a choice.' This time, there was nothing automatic in the way that the veteran gripped his weapon.

'Your friends are already dead.' Titus grimaced. 'Don't join them.'

'He's my *brother*.' The soldier forced the words out from between clenched teeth, and then his voice began to falter. 'He's my brother,' he pleaded, and I could see that his eyes were becoming as wet as the night. 'The Germans will show no mercy,' he finished.

It was Chickenhead who stepped forward, the old soldier moving past Titus to stand alone at the tent's centre. 'You're right,' he said, meeting the legionary's tear-filled eyes. 'They'll show no mercy here, and they'll show no mercy in the forest. Do you want to put your brother through that pain? Your comrades?' he asked of the other soldiers. 'This campaign is becoming a rout, friends. Give your brothers the chance to go with honour, and dignity. Not as some amusement to barbarians.'

The silence in the tent was as heavy as the rain that beat the canvas. Despite the downpour, screams and shouts could be heard as other men were dragged from their comrades' sides throughout the camp's hospital tents.

'There's no hope?' the veteran asked Chickenhead.

I swallowed the lump in my throat and spoke. 'None for the wounded.' Instantly I felt their stares burn into me. 'I heard it from Varus's lips myself,' I finished, my skin flushing. 'Arminius and his allies aren't coming. We're on our own.'

'It's over.' Titus's tone was final.

The veteran recognized a battle lost. Slowly, he lowered himself to one knee and took the hand of his oblivious brother. 'Forgive me,' he managed. Tears ran down the leather-like skin of his cheeks.

Then, throughout the temporary ward, other soldiers bade farewell to men they had sworn to protect. Men they had promised never to leave behind, no matter the odds or dangers. Mercifully, the most badly wounded had been placed within this tent, and none were conscious of their abandonment. The same could not be said of all within the camp, and cries for mercy pierced the night, raising the hairs on our already frozen bodies.

'Report back to your units,' Titus ordered and, slowly, the men began to file past our section, their heads down in shame.

Only two refused to leave, clinging on to their comrades' stretchers, eyes mad with grief.

Titus handled one alone, lifting him as a father would his struggling child. It took myself, Moonface and Rufus to pull the second soldier away.

'Leave me! Leave me!' he screamed, thrashing in sorrow. 'You cowards! Stand and fight! Stand and fight!'

We threw him down hard into the dirt beyond the tent's flap. It did little to dampen his rage, and instantly he sprang to his feet and rushed at the tent's opening. Titus stepped forward and drove a huge fist into the side of his head, felling him like a tree. Then, as the man hit the ground, our section commander rained kicks on his prone form. Finally, the soldier was dragged to lie face down in the slippery filth, a warning to others.

Re-entering the tent, Titus saw the faces of young Micon and Cnaeus filled with terror. The section commander's blood boiled over at the sight of their naivety.

'This is a fucking war,' he snarled, stabbing his finger at the dying men. 'This is it. This is what you signed up for. Are you enjoying it?'

The boy soldiers had no answer for him. What man did?

'Out!' he bellowed. 'All of you, out!'

We complied with haste, the rain pelting our faces as we stood in the darkness, thankful to be away from the condemned. No one spoke, no one dared make a sound, and so I do not imagine I was the only one to hear Titus's sword slide clear of its sheath, or hear it puncture flesh, or hear the wet sucking sound as it was pulled free from its victims.

It was a few minutes before Titus rejoined us. When he finally did leave the tent, his eyes were as sunken and dark as a mine shaft. If it were possible for a man to age years in mere moments, then he had done so.

No one could meet his eye. Still no one spoke. Knowing that the horrors were far from over, we merely followed.

## 32

Dawn was a few hours away. The century's rotation at guard duty had come again. During the interceding hours between the hospital ward and the camp's ramparts, no man had spoken, eaten or slept. Instead, the soldiers of the section sat and considered their own fates. Now even Micon and Cnaeus carried the thousand-yard stare of a veteran, their sight fixed on nothing, yet taking in everything.

So deep in misery were we that not even the chilled rains or thundering winds could disturb our dark thoughts. I was picturing my own death, choking away my life on a cross, when I caught sight of movement in my peripheral vision.

Pavo.

'Titus.' The wind carried his words to us. 'Your section with me. We're pushing out a hundred yards beyond the rampart. If there're any Germans probing the lines, then it's kill or capture. I'll make the decision on the ground. Nobody acts unless I do.'

I expected our section commander to make some protest, but Titus's grim face didn't change as he drew his short sword, and I realized that he was eager to spill blood.

We followed Pavo in silence, the storm dampening any sound that our footfalls or equipment could make. Perhaps I should have been frightened to leave the camp's rampart, but I wasn't. The exertions of the night had drained me to a point where I was beyond caring about my own life and death. I could almost welcome the chance to die on an enemy spear, rather than under torture from my own comrades. If death was anything close to sleep, then it would be bliss.

'Down,' Pavo hissed and, following his example, the section prostrated itself in the soaking grass.

Even in such a miserable position, sleep fought to overwhelm me. To resist, I dragged my fingernails across my cheeks until the skin broke. I pushed at my eyes until I felt the socket wall. None of it helped. I just wanted to sleep.

Just one hour's fucking sleep.

Instead, I lay there. I do not know how long we were in that drenched position, with the chill of the earth rising through my sinewy flesh to shake the marrow in my bones, but when we stood, my joints groaned and clicked as if I were a man of a hundred. I heard a puppy-like whimper from Micon; the wretched boy soldier was on the edge of breakdown, his mind and body stretched to their limits.

At least so he thought. I knew from experience that there was always more punishment that a human being could endure. His mind might break, but the body would go on, and I was equally certain that we would find such trials with the dawn.

'Back,' Pavo ordered with another hiss, satisfied that there were no enemy lurking in our sector.

I was not so convinced. Given the weight of the downpour and the howl of the winds, I felt it would have been possible for an army to pass within ten yards of us and remain undetected, but it was not my decision to make, and I followed our leader back through the darkness.

Another weary century had taken up position on the rampart, and challenged us half-heartedly with the night's watchword. Pavo answered, and as we were allowed through, he stood atop the earthworks to count each man in as he passed, and ensure that we were all accounted for.

'There's no need for that,' Titus grunted, offended, but Pavo continued.

And he was right to, because we were one man short.

Someone had been left with the enemy.

'It's Rufus,' Titus said immediately, without needing to look over the faces of his section.

Pavo's own was hidden in the darkness, but from the suppressed anger in his words, I could imagine the handsome face twisted into a snarl.

'Where is he, Titus?'

'The baggage train,' he answered curtly.

'Why?'

'His family's there.'

'Gods,' Pavo groaned. 'He brought his bloody family into this fucking mess?'

'Yes, Pavo, he brought his bloody family,' Titus answered, growing hot.

'And you let him?'

'I had no fucking idea, but it's done now, and if we're about to abandon the baggage train, then I'm not going to stop him seeing his family.'

'It's your job to stop him,' Pavo hissed. 'You're his section commander, and he's a bastard-deserter.'

The final word was too much for Titus. His arm shot out like an arrow, gripping Pavo by his mail and making as if to lift him by the throat.

To give him his credit, the centurion kept a remarkable kind of calm. 'Moon,' he said, his words measured, 'What's the punishment for attacking a superior officer?'

'Death,' Moonface answered after a moment.

From the venom in his next words, Titus could not have cared less. His face loomed within an inch of Pavo's. 'I put my sword through eight Roman soldiers tonight, you pompous piece of shit, because the governor was going to leave them to be gutted and tortured by the bastard goat-fuckers, so don't you go telling me that one man looking after his family will make any difference to this cunting army!'

Titus's heated admission left the section and centurion open-mouthed. Deep down I had known Titus had carried out mercy killings within the tent, but hearing the confirmation made my knees shake and my bowels loose, for there was no more harrowing act than taking the life of a comrade, no matter how justified.

'You did that?' Pavo asked finally.

'Of course I fucking did.' Titus's voice was as flat and as hard as his iron sword. 'What choice did I have?'

Gently, Pavo pushed Titus's hand away from his throat. After a moment, the big man allowed it to be moved.

'You had none,' Pavo agreed heavily. 'But I can't let Rufus desert, Titus. Do you think he's the only one with a family in the baggage train? If it gets out that he's gone with no repercussions, then the century will be down to twenty men by dawn.'

'So say you dispatched him on a task,' Titus offered, as neutral as it was possible for the hard man to be. 'Do that, Pavo, and I wipe your debt clean. You hear that?' he asked the section. 'The centurion's debt to me is wiped clean. Write him off as one of the badly wounded, and I'll write off what you owe me. If we're going to die out here, then let Rufus die with his family.'

It seemed like an age before Pavo replied, after turning the possibilities over in his mind. Finally, he addressed his words to the section as a whole.

'Rufus was killed tonight on sentry duty. His body could not be recovered. If anyone ever speaks differently, then I'll gut them myself.'

'You're finally sounding like a leader.' Titus's words were heavy with bile. Then he smirked. 'Now fuck off.'

Pavo's temper flared at the words, but he had accepted a bribe to overlook desertion and was in no position to assert his authority.

I watched the silhouette of his tall figure and shorn-crested helmet stalk away into the darkness, thinking of the complexities of the man. Within the space of the day I had seen him be a heroic and natural leader in battle, an ambitious and remorseful man in private, and a greedy and unscrupulous commander in the face of debts. He was not a man I could ever trust, but when the century formed up before dawn and marched into the forest, that is exactly what I'd have to do.

Until then, I was left to shiver in the darkness.

# 33

I was alone in the trees. It was dark, and yet I could see every detail: the branches, withered and decayed; the ground, red and violent.

'What are you doing here?' I called out, knowing that I was being watched, and knowing by whom.

They gave me no answer.

I staggered on into the trees, desperate to find the forest's end. The stink of decaying flesh made me retch. The ground groaned in agony with each of my steps.

'Shut up!' I hissed, knowing there were souls trapped beneath the muck. 'Shut up!'

They would not.

Feathers began to fall from the sky. They were black, caked in burned blood.

'Get out of my head!' I screamed.

The dark feathers clung to me like insects. I wiped at them with frantic hands.

'Get out of my head!' I screamed again as the rain began to pour. A rain of blood. It ran into my eyes and beneath my armour. It covered me.

It was too much. I wept.

Then, through my tears, I heard the laugh. A laugh that I knew so well. 'Marcus?' I croaked.

A harsh voice greeted me from the depths of the blood forest. 'Coward.'

'Why are you doing this?' I pleaded.

'You know why.'

'I'm sorry!'

'You're not.'

I dropped to the floor, my knees sinking into the red ooze.

I heard footsteps behind me. I tried to turn, but my body was frozen. Paralysed.

'You left me,' the voice accused.

With slow paces, he moved into my eyeline. I saw him through blood and tears. Marcus. My oldest friend. My centurion.

'You left me,' Marcus rasped through his severed jaw.

I cried.

He spoke again, toying with a coil of intestine that protruded from a ripped belly. 'You left me.'

'I'm sorry.'

'You're sorry?' he asked, with another laugh made ugly by the wounds to his face. 'You're sorry?'

I had nothing to say. Blood poured from the sky. I wanted only to die.

'Then finish it,' Marcus finally offered, and a blade landed at my feet. 'Kill me.'

'I can't,' I stammered. 'I can't.'

Marcus sneered. I looked at the blade, wondering if I had the strength to turn it on myself.

Then a second voice spoke from the trees. 'Kill him,' it told me. 'Kill him.'

The voice was powerful. Certain. Somehow, it filled my limbs with purpose. I stood. The blade was in my hand.

'Kill him,' the voice said again.

'I can't,' I lied.

'Kill him.'

Marcus smiled. His jaw flapped beneath what had been a handsome face. The face of my closest friend.

'Kill him.'

He was still smiling as I drove the blade into his heart.

# 34

My eyes snapped open.

'Welcome back,' Stumps grunted.

'I was screaming?'

'Who isn't?' He shrugged, ending the matter.

As I took in deep breaths to overcome my sleep terrors, I looked about me. The section sat huddled inside the tent beside a pathetic fire, its flames as weak as our desire to leave the camp and re-enter the forest. We sat crowded for warmth, pruning hands pushed into armpits or groins. Only Titus sat alone, his hard stare fixed upon a sword that lay across his lap. The sword that he had recovered from the Germans in the forest.

With no warning, he got to his feet and left the tent.

'Titus?' Stumps called to the man's wide back.

There was no response.

'Probably gone to see Rufus,' Moonface managed through chattering teeth.

It was the logical explanation, and yet I could not accept it. Nor could I explain why I got to my weary feet and left the sanctuary of the tent for the violence of the storm, the others watching me push my way out of the canvas as if I were a madman. Perhaps I just wanted to be awake, and away from my terrors.

Outside, I saw my section commander easily enough. Even the darkness could not hide him, his massive figure like the silhouette of a mountain against the ink-black sky. I followed at a short distance, making no great attempt at stealth – the storm was enough to hide my presence.

Following the man through the tent-lined avenues of churned mud, I soon became aware of our destination despite the darkness – the ingrained map in my brain of an army's marching camp told me that we were headed towards the quartermaster's.

I was not wrong.

The area about the quartermaster's tents was a hive of activity, soldiers and slaves unloading equipment from carts so that it could be carried on the backs of men and mules. Muleteers, those slaves that tended to the animals of the baggage train, looked to their charges. I noticed how they packed the mules' bells with straw and wrapped them in cloth, a precaution against noise that could give away the army's pre-dawn departure. I almost smiled at their optimism. I fully expected that the Germans would know we had set foot outside the camp before our own generals did. The tribesmen had been one step ahead of Varus at every turn, and I did not foresee that tomorrow would bring a change in our fortunes.

What I did see, by torchlight, was Titus moving amongst the slaves and soldiers, his stern face questioning. I had no doubt whom he was looking for. Eventually, as a slave pointed in the direction of the latrines, it would seem that Titus had found him.

Hidden by shadow, I followed on.

The latrines were nothing more than a waist-deep slit trench dug into the dirt, the spoil deposited on the camp's ramparts. Given the ferocity of the storm and the predicament of the army, I did not expect that many soldiers were using them, preferring the promise of at least a little shelter between tents. My hunch seemed justified as I saw only a lone figure squatting over the hole. A lone figure that Titus now approached. Downwind as I was, I caught the full stench of the trench, but the wind also trapped the big man's accusing words, and they were full of hate.

'You lying bastard,' Titus snarled.

The squatting man raised himself to his full height. I could not see his birthmarks, but I recognized the voice well enough – the quartermaster.

'Who do you think you are, interrupting a superior officer when he's taking a shit?' the man spat with no trace of humour.

'You told me they were going to Britain,' Titus snapped.

'They were,' the man answered after a pause.

'Then why am I finding them killing our men!' Titus shouted, stepping forward and shoving his superior hard in the chest.

'Calm yourself!' the quartermaster ordered, an edge of alarm in his tone. 'We can talk.'

But Titus wouldn't calm himself.

'We can talk,' the quartermaster almost begged.

Then, for the briefest moment, the dark storm clouds slid apart and a slither of moon showed itself against the black.

It was enough light for me to see the fear on the man's face.

It was enough for me to see the hate on Titus's, and the sword in his hand.

He drove it upwards into the quartermaster's throat.

Somehow, I mastered my own desire to call out, and in that silence I heard the man's gurgled struggle as he tried to scream. Leaving the blade embedded, Titus pushed the man backwards; the quartermaster toppled into the trench with little grace. Had I not known what he was like, I could almost pity the bastard: his final breaths would be drawn lying in the filth of an army.

Instead, I crouched in shadow, anxious that the moon might show itself again and reveal me. There, I watched as Titus took a moment to stand over the man he had killed, as if savouring the murder.

*Murder.*

For what?

I had to know.


Titus followed the same path back towards the century's lines, doubtless confident that the storm could provide better cover than any meandering route. He seemed oblivious to my stalking of him, and as the questions about his murderous act raced through my mind, I grew careless in my pursuit.

And that momentary lapse was enough for Titus to kill me.

Somehow, the man had melted into the shadow of a tent, and now, as I passed, his thick arm swung out, the oak-like forearm hitting my throat and dropping me to the mud, where I lay wheezing like a landed fish.

'You,' the giant accused me. I looked up into his eyes, seeing nothing but cold calculation – and murder. I had underestimated him, and now I would die for it.

'You.' He spoke again. 'Did you see it?' he asked finally.

I still struggled to breathe, but I saw little point in denial. If Titus wanted to kill me, he would kill me, and so I nodded.

'And you want to know why?'

I nodded again, expecting a blade. Instead, I got a hand.

Titus pulled me to my feet, the big man grimacing as he saw the confusion in my eyes. 'The sword,' was all he told me.

It was enough.

'The weapons under the straw.' I managed to choke, referring to the weapons I had seen smuggled out of Minden under Titus and the quartermaster's supervision.

'They were supposed to go to Britain,' he confirmed. By his tone, it was clear that they hadn't.

'You found them in the forest.'

'I found them in the forest.' His voice was bitter. 'Roman blades in German hands.'

'Doesn't mean that they were yours,' I offered, rubbing at my burning throat.

'They were mine.' Titus held up a scarred fist. 'There was only one supplier working out of Minden, you understand? I made sure of that.'

'And now he's dead.' As I spoke I thought of the quartermaster's body in the shit-filled trench.

'Quicker end than the cunt deserved,' Titus grunted as the man's eulogy.

I said nothing. The rain beat against our faces as we held each other's stares.

'So what now?' I asked. As witness to Titus's murder of a superior officer, I still held little hope that I would be leaving the filthy avenue alive.

The killer snorted. 'Rufus has gone to his family. He won't be coming back. Chickenhead's a good soldier, but this storm is turning him to rust. The others? They're sheep.' Titus spoke harshly, his eyes hard.

'So you won't kill me?' I asked, almost jumping in surprise as the big man bellowed out a bark of laughter.

260

'You're as guilty as me, *Felix*.' He smirked. 'I don't know of what, exactly, but you have blood on your hands. I'd bet my life on it.'

I said nothing, and Titus smiled again, enjoying his sport and, perhaps, seeing life with the clarity that can only come when one is so near to death.

'I don't promise you'll live through today,' he told me, 'but it won't be my blade that guts you.'

I imagined that was as heartfelt a truce as I could ever get from this man, and so I put out my hand. I had nothing to gain from denying our transgressions. 'To secrets, then.'

Titus paused, his thick lips twisted in amusement. 'To secrets.' He took my hand and stared deep into my dead eyes. 'And to killers,' he finished, walking away into the darkness.

I watched him go. He knew who I was. Despite our differences, we were the two most alike in the section.

Then such thoughts were cut away as I was suddenly forced to bend at the waist. Perhaps it was being a moment from my imagined death that made me vomit, or perhaps it was the irony. Either way, as I wiped the acidic bile with the back of my hand, I echoed Titus's salutation in my head.

*To killers*, he had said.

*To killers.*

# 35

I followed Titus into the section's tent.

'We thought you'd gone to get Rufus,' Stumps mumbled, relieved to see his leader return.

Titus made no reply. Instead, he cast his eyes over the section's soldiers, seeing the five men clustered about the weak flames, their stares as empty as the pathetic brazier. In them, I saw the look of men who were on the edge of surrender. Titus saw it too, and acted.

'Look at me,' he ordered.

They did, heads turning slowly on aching shoulders. At Titus's back, I took in the sight of them, and one fact was painfully clear: these were not the men who had marched from Minden.

Chickenhead's pinched face was gaunt and grey. He had wrapped Lupus the kitten in a scarf, and held him to his chest as if the feline were a precious jewel. Moonface and Stumps, young veterans in the prime of their years, had the hollow-eyed and desperate look of criminals condemned to the arena. Micon and Cnaeus, mere boys, seemed to have aged a decade in a day, Cnaeus's temples having developed a shock of white like a rabbit's tail.

Yes, this was a section on the edge of breaking. In times of crisis, men show themselves to be leaders or followers, wolves or sheep.

Our own wolf stepped forward. He pulled away his helmet, dropping it to the ground. 'What happened tonight, at the hospital,' Titus began, looking at each of the shivering men in the eye, 'that's not going to be us. That will never be us.'

Titus paused with his next words still in his mouth, and I wondered if the gnarled veteran was about to fill his comrades with false promises of invincibility, everlasting life and glory.

He was not.

'Our section will never leave a wounded man behind. If any of us are too fucked to go on, then . . .' Now he did falter, his thick jaw grinding like a millstone. '. . . then what needs to be done will be done.'

His words finished, I watched as Titus seemed to swallow what looked like a rock in his throat. The sorry figures before him stared back, their already assaulted minds struggling to accept the thought of dying at the hands of their friends. It was not a concept they were eager to face, but Titus gave them no choice.

'Do you all agree?' Titus pushed them, volume rising. 'Well? Fucking talk!' he finally snapped, when no answer was forthcoming.

It was Chickenhead who was the first to break his silence, his head bobbing as he shrugged and grimaced. 'What choice is there? We've all seen what the goat-fuckers do for sport.' At his chest, Lupus made a mewling sound, and the veteran turned his attention back sharply to his beloved creature.

It was enough of an agreement for Titus, and he cast his eyes about for further confirmation.

'I agree,' Moonface managed on his second attempt.

'Stumps?' Titus pressed.

'I'm going to live forever,' the soldier forced out, using every ounce of his spirit to muster a smile. No one laughed, but Titus's lip twitched in affection at the effort. 'But if I don't,' Stumps continued, 'then please, do what you must. Please.'

'Boys?' Titus asked, turning his attention to the section's youngest soldiers. 'It's time to man up. Wipe the fucking snot from your faces, and give me an answer.'

'I agree?' Micon said, as if unsure he was being given a choice, his tone as flat as ever.

'I agree,' Cnaeus stuttered a second later.

Titus rubbed a huge hand across his stone face. 'And I expect the same treatment from any one of you, if I get fucked up. No one left behind. Now get off your fucking arses and prepare to move,' he ordered, and the five ex-hausted forms roused themselves from the floor, so bone-weary that even the usual litany of curses was absent.

As Titus turned from them, he saw me on his shoulder and met my look. 'What?' he asked, eyes narrowing.

'You didn't ask me,' I told him, wondering why. Maybe, even after all we had been through, I was still not a part of this section.

The man's face twisted into a savage smile as he gave me my answer. 'I've got a feeling you'll outlive us all, lucky one,' he said, brushing by me to the tent's flap and calling over his shoulder in a voice of iron: 'Come on, boys. Dawn's coming.'

I turned my eyes from him to the other members of the section, seeing the gaunt-faced men hauling armour over their heads and down on to tired shoulders. I was sure that my own appearance was no better – worse, even – than theirs, and yet in this pitiful state we had to face the violence of nature and of our enemies, for it was time to break camp.

It was time to go back into the forest.

## 36

We formed up in the darkness, our depleted century standing shivering in three files. Despite the burden of shield and equipment, we pressed ourselves together tightly for warmth and reassurance in the face of the unknown.

I found myself on the right flank of the century, which gave me the uncomfortable choice of wielding my sword in my left hand – a pointless task against anyone but the most poorly trained enemy – or leaving my right side open to the forest and its dangers. To the left of me was young Cnaeus, Titus having ensured that the youngest and greenest soldiers were packed into the formation's centre, encased by a solid shell of veterans.

We had left the section's tent standing, Pavo having issued the orders that the century's baggage would be left behind. As Chickenhead had predicted, we would be carrying only our arms, armour and the most basic of foodstuffs with us into the forest. A certain amount of extra equipment would be carried on the legion's mules now that they were relieved of their carts, and amongst that would be tents, but the soldiery expected that these shelters would be reserved for the higher echelons of the command, and perhaps the legion's elite First Cohort of veterans. For the foot-sloggers in the meat of the army's fighting arm, the promise of an escape from the elements lay beyond the forest, and in a Roman fort on the Rhine.

'May the gods help us,' I heard Moonface pray. The devout soldier had doubtless come to the same conclusion, and knew that our days of misery were far from over, even if the Germans were to quit the battlefield. Despite his begging, the divine ones seemed disinclined to interfere with war or weather, and as the first band of dirty yellow light appeared on the horizon, we were given the hushed order to march with wind and rain lashing our pale faces.

Gone were the trumpets. Gone were the drums. This morning, an army slunk away towards the west like a whipped dog.

Such was the section's misery that no one commented when the order of march became evident in the gloom: our own Second Cohort was leading the legion, and therefore the army. As the Second Century in that division, I found myself some thirty ranks back from the tip of the army, a hundred men ahead of me, more than fifteen thousand to my rear, and the gods only knew what host of enemies all around, though I expected we would meet some of their number soon enough.

With such grim thoughts in mind, I narrowed my eyes against the sheet-rain that drove hard towards us. The gale was so strong that it was almost as if the winds wanted to save us the horror of the forest, trying to drive us back within the earthen ramparts of the marching camp.

But we pushed onwards towards the black line of the forest. Towards the terror of the enemies' traps and ambushes, just as infantrymen are supposed to.

No voices could be heard, only chattering jaws and the rattle of equipment. By the thick black belt that stretched across the horizon, I saw that we were almost within the forest. Then, as the first men entered, what had been a smooth march across the open ground became a stop-and-start stutter, those soldiers who had not yet withdrawn into themselves cursing as their sandalled feet hit half-buried tree roots or slipped on the cloying mud. Was this how Varus planned for his army to slip away from the German tribes who had shown themselves to be a step ahead of us at every turn? If I hadn't been so terrified, perhaps I could have laughed. We were fucked, I knew deep down, but to survive I had to pretend otherwise.

Knowing that my balance could make the split-second difference between life and death during the ambush I was certain was coming, I tried to empty my mind of anything but my foot's placement on the forest's treacherous floor. I was tired, wet, hungry and bruised, but the sad truth was that I had been existing in such a state for months. My new life in the legions had brought me my first real shelter and proper food in as long as I cared to remember, but now I found myself drifting back to the most basic of animal instincts, shutting my mind to my wretchedness, and concentrating on the sounds and sights – as few as they were – about me. That meant I was one of the few soldiers who did not stalk into the back of the man in front as the column came to a shuddering halt and the whispers began.

'Obstruction on the track.'

'Fuck. What do we do?' I heard from muted voices.

What we did was to wait in the darkness, senses tight. Men turned out to face our exposed flanks, shields pulled tightly against their chests like babes to their mothers. As we crouched in the gloom, I knew that scouts would be inspecting the barriers in our path, officers conferring over the course of action. I thought I knew what it would be.

'Second Century to the front.' My pessimism was justified.

We moved off at a half-step, the First Century having pushed out on to the flanks of the track, allowing us to stumble our way through their middle, the wall of shields a gutter to funnel us in the direction of the trail's obstruction.

'There're logs across the path,' Pavo whispered, joining us.

Even in the darkness, I could see that his skin shone bright and pale. He was shaken.

'I've sent two sections to clear the closest ones,' the centurion went on, the slightest of tremors in his voice. 'Titus, you take your section and clear the smaller logs on the other side to them.'

'Protection?' the big man rumbled, his tone sounding like distant thunder.

'First Century have men pushed out.'

'Ahead of us?' Titus pressed.

There was no answer, which gave us all the answer we needed – we were putting our head into the bear's jaws.

Titus had heard enough. He pulled his sword free of his scabbard and, without a word, made to lead off.

Before he could take a step, Pavo gripped him by the mail of his sleeve.

'There's more,' the centurion whispered, attempting to be a voice of calm and order. He failed, his tone cracking. 'Above the logs. There's . . .' His voice trailed away as he sought out the words.

After a moment, he gave up trying to find them. 'Be careful, Titus,' he said instead.

Behind me, I heard Stumps utter a curse. Every other man was silent, doubtless picturing, as I was, the nightmarish surprises the Germans had left for us. We would have to find them in the darkness, for the rising sun was struggling in its battle with the gloom, and despite the beginnings of a ruddy red glow on the leaves, it was in the long shadows that we moved forward.

Titus led the way, and this time Pavo did not stop him. A natural motion now, I slipped in behind the big man, the other members of the section following on in single file. Chickenhead, as solid as any man, brought up the rear, ordered to do so by Titus in case any of the section tried to run in the face of the enemy.

In this order, we drew level with the first work party, soldiers of our own century, their yellow teeth grimacing in the gloom as they worked to haul the thick oaks from the army's path.

'Quieter!' a voice of authority hissed from the shadows.

'Come and do it yourself, you cunt,' came a reply, the in-subordination cloaked by the night.

Led by a soldier of the First Century, Titus skirted the work party, the section winding its way through the labouring soldiers towards our own task. A scream carried from far into the trees somewhere in the night. The sound of it made my balls climb up into my stomach.

'We're at the head of the army,' I heard Stumps whisper behind me. He had come alive now that he was beneath the canopy of leaves, his adrenaline pumping. 'Our section, at the head of the fucking army.'

But he was wrong. There were soldiers ahead of us. Roman soldiers.

They were waiting for us.

Vomit pattered the forest floor. I stood open-mouthed.

'Gods,' Stumps whispered. 'Fucking fucking gods.'

The waiting soldiers were merely silhouettes at first, but as my eyes focused in the grey dawn, I could make out the straps of their sandals, the cut of their tunics and the rope that was twisted thickly about their necks.

The men hung from the branches like rotting fruit.

My stomach wanted to leave my body as I looked over them, seeing dead faces twisted in agony or mutilated beyond recognition.

Then, beside me, I heard a gasp of pain so terrible that I thought we had come under attack. I turned on instinct, bringing up my shield, expecting to find bloodshed and enemies.

Instead, I found Titus, a titan frozen in grief, choked words fighting to make their way out of his tight throat.

I had never thought to see him so shaken, so *human*. I followed his eyes to the cause of this pain, and saw a soldier who waited to greet his comrades in the trees.

It was Rufus.

Our comrade's body swung from the branch with the storm's violent gusts, each motion causing the tree to creak, the groan as lifelike as if it were coming from Rufus's own mouth. I looked from the body to Titus, seeing a mountain that was close to toppling.

'No,' he breathed heavily as the picture sank into his mind. 'No, Rufus, no.'

He stepped forward. I looked over my shoulder. In the dirty light of a storm's dawn, I saw the faces of the section wide-eyed in horror and grief.

'Keep them with the century,' I told Chickenhead, slapping his shoulder hard to drive home the point. The man acknowledged me with a nod. Then I closed up on to Titus's shoulder.

He did not acknowledge me as he paced slowly forward, his limbs seeming to struggle with the effort, his eyes never leaving his friend's face.

My own eyes were sweeping the forest floor, desperately searching out some trap that the enemy might have laid in our path, using our fallen comrades as bait. Then, as the rope and its branch creaked again in the wind, I looked up at the man who, for a short time, had been my comrade. A man who I knew was a loving father and a trusted brother to his friends.

Even in the gloom, I saw enough to know that Rufus had not died a good death. I wanted to look away, but some sick sense made me stare at the carnage. The image seared into my mind, where I knew it would dwell forever, with all of the others.

I fought down the wave of nausea as I took in the sight of him. Rufus's guts hung from him like uncoiled rope, his belly sliced apart like a sow's. His jaw was hinged open grotesquely, likely broken before death, the mouth now held wide by his own cock and balls.

'Fuck,' was all I could utter, for it was as ignominious an end as any man could suffer.

The defilement was too much for Titus – it would have been too much for any comrade of the dead men in the trees – and that, I knew, was what the Germans had been counting upon.

'Bastards!' he roared, regaining some of his strength and making as if to climb the tree and cut down his friend's body, desperate to restore some dignity to his comrade.

I could see no traps in the shadows, but experience told me that what he was doing would only bring more death to our section.

'Bastards!'

'Titus, don't,' I hissed against the wind.

I was ignored. He began to climb.

'I'll kill all you bastards!'

'Titus,' I hissed again as he began to make progress into the branches.

There was no getting through to him. I knew that my next action would as likely kill me as an enemy snare, but fuck, what choice did I have?

I grabbed one of Titus's exposed ankles and jumped, putting all of my weight on to the man who was already straining the tree's thin branches. They snapped instantly, and we fell the short distance to earth, the air driven from my lungs as the giant collapsed on top of me.

'You cunt,' he growled, raising his thick fist.

I had been expecting the attack and rolled away quickly; Titus's knuckles pounded into the dirt beside my head. I prepared for the second attempt, but the big man soon forgot me as he caught sight of his friend's swinging feet; once again, he was lost to grief and not in control of his actions. Titus scrambled from the slippery mud of the forest floor and made to pull Rufus down from the branches as I had done to him.

'Don't!' I called, rushing to his side.

But I was too late.

Titus pulled on his friend's bloodied legs with all of his might, snapping the branch, and Rufus and his entrails dropped to earth.

Bringing the enemy's trap with him.

It was a solid mass of deadfall that crashed through branches as it plummeted towards us, splinters showering the forest floor like confetti at the games. I was already moving, my momentum giving me enough power to hit Titus side on with my shoulder, the big man spinning backwards and clear, but the crash sent me tumbling. I hit the ground alongside Rufus's body, my hands sliding into the cold slime of his guts. I had no time for disgust; using every ounce of strength in my battered body, I pushed with my arms and rolled away to my side.

The deadfall smashed to earth a split second later, obliterating the corpse of the man who had been Titus's closest friend and showering me with his blood and churned dirt.

'Rufus!' Titus wailed. Beyond grief, the big man pulled his helmet from his head and cast it like a pebble into the forest's shadows – where I heard it hit metal.

Before I could breathe, the enemy attacked.

# 37

The Germans charged from the gloom with a violence that matched the storm, their war cry promising murder.

Titus seemed to smile as he turned to face them. He'd lost his sword in the chaos of the deadfall. He would meet the enemy with bare fists and bared teeth.

'Titus!' I called, tossing him my own blade and pulling my shorter dagger from its sheath. There was no time to run back to the shields of the century – German spears would impale our exposed backs long before we made it – and so there was nothing to do but face the rush and fight like dogs for every extra second of life. I did not assume there would be many.

The Germans' silhouettes looked huge in the gloom. I intended to use my smaller size to my advantage, placing my back against a tree so that my own shadow was faint, my rear defended from German blades.

The first tribesman was on me in moments, axe raised high, shield low. With such poor handling of his weapons, I knew that he was a green soldier – this would be his first and final taste of combat. I stepped inside the arc of his unwieldy swing and killed him with the first thrust of my dagger, the blade punching through his unarmoured chest to burst his heart; his death cry came as a strangled gurgle.

I took up the dead boy's shield with no more than a second to spare; there was a harsh clang of metal on metal as a weapon struck against its surface. I whipped my blade low, slicing across shin, then drove it upwards into an exposed groin, the man howling in agony as he stumbled away into the trees. I let him go. From such a wound, he would be dead within minutes.

I pressed my back against the tree and held the shield across my chest. I saw the shadows of the enemy coming from the mist-shrouded trees like ghouls: an army of the undead, it seemed. Many of them ignored my presence, charging instead towards the battle that I could now hear raging behind me. The vanguard of the army had been engaged, and myself and Titus were inconsequential distractions for those few soldiers who yearned for single combat.

In the gloom I caught sight of the roaring section commander. Titus stood like a volcano on the forest floor, death to all those who came within arm's reach, his blade chopping and hacking like a berserker's. Consumed by rage, not content to stand on the defensive, he ploughed into the enemies who had so cruelly killed his friend.

Titus reaped a terrible revenge. With my own eyes, I saw him dispatch more than a dozen men. The sword I had thrown him abandoned in sucking flesh, Titus wielded an axe in each hand, the metal heads chopping into meat as if he were the butcher and the enemy the frightened sheep.

In all my days of combat, I had never seen a man so single-minded in his slaughter.

I pushed a dead German from my blade. Wiping blood from my eyes, I saw the beginning of daylight penetrating the forest. There were no rays of sunshine, only a gradual raising of the gloom, but it was enough for me to see the faces of our enemies now, some defiant, others terrified. It was enough for me to see Titus, more gore than man.

His animal instinct honed through adrenaline, he felt my gaze and looked my way. I saw no recognition in his eyes, only death. My stomach lurched at the sight of it.

Suddenly I realized that the skirmish was over. One minute we had been besieged by enemies, the next we were alone, the only Germans we could see the dead and dying. Titus hunted these men one by one, taking great pains to prolong their suffering.

I could hear battle still raging in the trees beyond us, but the distance had grown. We were in danger of being separated from the army.

'Titus,' I called. 'We have to get back to the century.'

I was ignored.

Slowly, as if approaching a hungry lion, I stalked towards him. I held a German sword in my hand, ready to bring it up and defend myself should the big man strike, but Titus was too engrossed in his task to notice my presence. On his knees, the veteran was pressing his thumbs into the eyes of a wounded spearman.

The man's screams cut through my core.

'Titus!' I called, louder this time. 'Fucking look at me!'

He did, and my bones froze as if winter had come. He was a beast. Nothing in his eyes was human.

'Titus,' I managed to murmur.

The killer then got to his feet, leaving his victim groaning in agony and clutching at a destroyed face. I looked at Titus's hands, seeing the viscous fluids dripping from his thumbs.

'Gods,' I managed again, tasting bile in my mouth. 'Leave him. We have to get back to the others.'

As Titus looked me up and down, I was gripped by fear. I knew that, if he chose to do so, this hate-filled animal could kill me within moments.

Instead, he spoke. 'Rufus is dead,' he told me in a voice of stone.

'I know,' I answered. 'We need to get back to the section, and look to the others.'

He seemed to consider my words, even turning his head in the direction of the sound of battle, but when he spoke again, I knew that he would not be rushed from the site of his friend's body – not when there were still German wounded lying scattered in the mud.

'Rufus is dead,' he said again, and then set to torturing his enemies.

# 38

Titus took his time in killing the German wounded. A few were lucky, too far gone to offer the man any sense of sport in his retribution, and these he dispatched quickly by blade. The conscious were not so fortunate, and died in agony, Titus beating them to death with stones, or choking the life from them with his gnarled hands.

I didn't see most of it: I turned my back – for our own safety, rather than from unease. The sounds of fighting could still be heard, but the trees and the storm made it impossible to guess at what distance – I didn't want to be surprised by a rush of German reinforcements heading to the battle. Then, as the last German took his final gasp, I became aware of a new sound.

Crying.

I turned, seeing Titus sitting back on his heels, his killer's bloodied hands tight over his face as his body was racked with sobs. I turned my eyes back to the trees, not wanting to linger on his grief, but unwilling to leave him alone in the forest. Consumed by misery as he was, I was certain that he would not survive without me.

I was wrong. As quickly as the flood had come, the well of Titus's tears dried. The sobs lasted for mere seconds, and then, with the silence of a predator, he pushed his huge form to its feet and stared in my direction.

Tracts of tears had cut through the blood on his face. His eyes empty of all emotion, Titus looked like some creature of nightmare.

He looked as I had appeared to Arminius.

'We need to find the column.' He spoke as if the dawn's bloodshed had never happened and his closest friend were still drawing breath.

Surprised by his about-turn, I cast an involuntary look at the deadfall that had crushed Rufus's mutilated corpse.

'Rufus is dead.' Titus spoke coldly, and I recognized in the tone a man who had spent all sentiment, and was now reduced to an empty vessel.

'We need to find the column,' he repeated, cocking his head at the sound of battle. 'Rufus is dead.'

And so we left our comrade to the forest.

The forest floor was littered with the dead and dying, Roman and German spread beneath the trees like decaying apples. When the storm's winds finally abated, flocks of crows would feast, but for now, the bodies lay unmolested in the tangles of undergrowth.

The clash of sword on shield was a constant echo as we made our way back towards the column, the dead our signposts towards our comrades, who I hoped yet lived. Titus seemed solely focused on finding yet more enemies to slay.

'Soldier,' I heard through the wind, the word a desperate plea. 'Soldier!'

I found the source, a veteran of our own legion, not long for this world. I took in the man's sorry state, recognizing that he had been left for dead at the bottom of a water-filled ditch. Somehow, he had found the strength to crawl to the trench's top before his reserves had finally run out. His guts were spread beneath him.

'Please,' he grunted through clenched teeth, gesturing at a blade in his hand. 'I can't.'

Meeting the man's blood-red eyes, I stepped forward. The hand that I placed on his shoulder was more to steady myself than he. Then, before I had a chance to rethink my action, I drove my dagger into the veteran's heart. I felt him shudder, crimson running from his lips as his red-raw eyes rolled back into their sockets.

I turned my head away from the man I had killed. Titus was looking at me. He made no comment. He simply walked into the trees.

And so I staggered on behind him.

I do not know how many of the fallen we passed in the forest, nor how long we wandered. I know only that I hastened two more of our own on to their ancestors, their dying stares seared into my own eyes, a mix of pathetic gratitude that the pain would end and dreadful fear of the unknown beyond.

'The column,' Titus grunted with no visible relief. Only when he slapped me hard across the face did I realize that I had not seen our soldiers through the trees because my own eyes were filled with pitiable tears.

Titus called out to the nearest troops. They were not engaged by the enemy, and shuffled slowly along the dirt of a narrow track, wild eyes searching the forest for the next ambush.

'Your cohort's up ahead,' a veteran told us. He had taken command after both his century's centurion and optio had been killed during a few minutes' combat. 'What's left of it,' he added, spitting on a German corpse.

Titus used his bulk to forge us a path ahead through the column, though the body of men had long since ceased to bear a resemblance to the proud formation that had marched out of the summer encampment at Minden. More and more, the army was becoming a group of frightened men who huddled beside their comrades as they headed into a storm of wind, rain and spears. I had seen an army coming apart at the seams before, and I knew that once the thread of discipline was pulled, there was little to stop the unravelling. Unless we cleared the forest, I was certain that the Germans would kill us with a thousand cuts.

With such dark thoughts in my mind, I almost lost myself to tears when I heard a familiar voice call along the trail.

'Titus! Titus!'

I turned with the big man, and there I saw Stumps.

He was alone.

'Where are the others?' Titus demanded.

Stumps didn't answer at first. Instead, he embraced his friend and, without hesitation, myself. 'Further up the column,' he then explained. 'I came back to try and find more javelins.' He swallowed. 'I thought you were dead.'

'Rufus is.' Titus spoke tonelessly.

Stumps had no reply. He only nodded, and swallowed again.

'Take us to them,' Titus ordered.

We pushed onwards, the mud beneath our feet like churned butter stained crimson. In a short time we had reached the remainder of the section. Miraculously, they were all still alive; not all of the legion had been so fortunate.

'Casualties are bad, Titus,' Moonface explained once he had finished kissing Titus's stone-like face. 'Fucking bad. Optio Cato's dead – took a spear in the neck. Quintus and Gnaeus are both gone. Horsehead lost an arm and bled out.

281

Even the legion commander's dead.' He cursed. 'A tribune took over, and rotated the cohorts. Fourth Cohort's in the lead now, so we're just following on and trying not to get killed in the harassing attacks.'

I looked towards the side of the tracks, seeing a half-dozen German bodies, and a few of our own. Stumps noticed.

'They put a big effort in when we broke camp, but they've slackened off since. If only the fucking weather would do the same.'

It was only now that I was reunited with my comrades that I became aware once again of the howling wind and driving rain, a sensation that had been lost to me as I concentrated on finding the column and avoiding German steel.

Looking ahead at what remained of the century, I saw the distinctive shorn crest of Pavo's helmet. The centurion yet lived.

'He hasn't stopped smiling since the legate was gutted,' Stumps commented.

I looked over the faces of the section, finding no smiles there, only the worn-out stares of soldiers who had already been forced to witness and endure more than any man should. In such circumstances, I expected the boy soldiers to suffer the most, but as my eyes settled on Chickenhead's pinched face, I saw a soul twisted with torment. In the hours since I had last seen the soldier, he had aged by a hundred years.

I felt a hand on my shoulder.

'The kitten.' Stumps shrugged beneath his armour. 'It's really gone downhill this morning, and Chicken's not taking it well. I don't think Lupus is goin' to make it out of this forest.'

I couldn't meet the man's eye, and made no reply – because I was certain that none of us would.

We trudged on in silence broken only by mumbled prayers and the absent-minded muttering of curses. Occasionally slingshot or spear would be spat forth from the forest. Sometimes a Roman voice would cry out in agony and fear, often pleading for a mother or loved one. As we marched on, I saw these victims beside the tracks, their pathetic moans hardening some men's souls and breaking others.

'For the gods' sake, don't leave me!' an auxiliary trooper begged in his thick Latin. 'Don't leave me!'

What choice did we have? We left him.

We left him, and so many others.

'Keep your fucking eyes front,' Titus ordered, desperate to hold his section together. 'If their mates can't do it for them, then it's not down to us.'

Slowly but surely, the idea of a unified army was being watered down so that the soldiers' sole concern was the survival of their closest friends, and themselves.

'Kill me! Kill me!' a maimed soldier begged.

'Kill yourself!' Stumps screamed, at breaking point.

The march through the abandoned wounded proved too much for many. Veteran and boy soldier alike broke in the face of the dying and the constant threat from the forest, charging into the trees with mad cries of vengeance. None were seen again, but some were heard as their screams echoed through the branches.

'This is a fucking nightmare,' Moonface choked.

'You wake up from a nightmare.' Stumps hit his friend hard across the shoulders, and then across the steel of his helmet. 'This is a test! Fucking get a grip, you cunt!' he hissed into the face of his comrade, slapping him hard to drive home the point.

The blows worked, and Moonface rallied. Then he steadied himself by cursing beneath his breath, promising to bring revenge and murder to every home in Germany. He vowed that he would torture the men, rape the women and enslave the children. Such heated bile brought him some consolation from the misery around him. It even galvanized the others. I began to dare hope that, in this mass of misery, perhaps our own section had the fortitude to survive with our minds intact.

But it wasn't to be. Hope for Chickenhead's sanity fled with Lupus the kitten's final breath, the tiny creature losing its battle against the elements as we floundered in the mud.

'No!' the veteran wailed, as if he held his own child. 'No! Don't! Don't!' He dropped to his knees on the filthy track, his ugly face pressed into the soaked fur of the tiny body, now rigid, beyond any hope of salvation.

'Chicken . . .' Stumps tried, reaching out.

'Get away from me!' his comrade screamed as he drew his sword and threatened his friends. 'I want to die!' he pleaded, and then made to break for the forest and death on the German spears.

It was the quick action of Stumps and Moonface that stopped him, their shields raised to block his path. They risked death in doing so, for their friend was so consumed by grief that he resembled the animalistic Titus I had seen spreading murder.

'I want to die!' Chickenhead called into the trees. 'I want to die.' He dropped his sword into the mud, tears cascading across his pockmarked cheeks.

This was not the time to beat and threaten. Not knowing what else to do, I stepped forward and embraced the man.

'Just leave me,' the veteran sobbed into the armour of my shoulder. He had spent twenty years killing and losing comrades on Rome's behalf, but the death of his tiny companion was one blow too many for the man's fragile mind.

I looked at Titus, and saw nothing on his face. His eyes were empty and dark. When he moved, I expected a blow that would try to restore the veteran to his senses. Instead, Titus hoisted the old soldier on to his shoulder as if he were a sack of grain. Chickenhead made no motion to fight it, as limp as a young child carried by an impatient father.

I looked at them with a sense of disbelief. While other soldiers lay dying in the mud, guts in their hands and pleading for mercy, a man I knew to be a murderer carried a heartbroken veteran and his dead pet towards sanctuary.

*Sanctuary*, for word now spread that there was a clearing up ahead.

At least for a moment, we were leaving the forest.

# 39

Wind and rain pelted my face. My throat was dry, my stomach empty. There was no muscle in my body that didn't ache with every shuffled step. No bone that was not bruised to the marrow.

And yet, leaving the trees, I felt as if the weight of the world were lifted from my shoulders.

Open ground. Roman battle lines. Here lay sanctuary in our formations, and victory – if only the Germans would oblige us with combat.

Of course, I did not expect that they would, but at least for a moment we did not need to fear the next step, or shadow.

And a moment was all it would be for, scanning the horizon, the smudge of unbreaking trees was visible through the grey gloom.

'We're not out of the forest,' Stumps groaned. 'When does the fucking thing end? Do we even know if it ends?'

No one had an answer for him. Instead, Pavo's clipped tones called through the winds. 'Century! Move from column to line!'

Despite our fatigue, hours of drill practice ensured that we quickly changed formation, our depleted century forming a unit that was eleven men across and four deep. I found myself in the front rank, which allowed me to lean forward and see the wings of the army begin to stretch out in both directions as the troops cleared the nightmare of the forest.

It also allowed me to see that no enemy formations stood ahead of us.

Moonface spat. 'They won't come. Fucking goat-fucking cowards.'

Now that we were in position, Titus placed Chickenhead down on to the earth, the veteran still trembling from grief.

Moonface spoke again. 'They won't come.'

Something in those tired words triggered the volcano of Chickenhead's sorrow to erupt in anger. The old soldier's hand flashed out to snatch a javelin from young Micon's grip, and before anyone could lay a hand on him, he charged forward from the formation.

'Come on, you bastards!' he cried, sprinting across the wet grass and brandishing the weapon in the air. 'Come and die! Come and fucking die!'

'Titus!' I heard Pavo call in frustration, but we didn't need to be told: the veterans of the section were already running with me after our errant brother. Moonface was the first to reach him, and brought him down by leaping on to his back.

'They won't fight!' Chickenhead snarled, pinned to the earth, his teeth gnashing like a hunting dog.

'You'll be killed by our own commanders if you run like that, you mad old bastard!' Moonface shouted into his friend's face.

'So let them kill me!' Chickenhead shot back, and from the wild abandon in his eyes, I knew that he meant it. 'Let them kill me!' he challenged again.

Instead, we dragged him back to the century.

Pavo, his face freshly scarred since I had last seen him, stormed across to us. 'It's been a hard day. But the next man who leaves the formation will be broken for it. Fucking broken,' he promised.

'His cat died, sir.' Young Micon spoke up as if the words explained everything, and an army of thousands was not being torn apart in the German forest.

Pavo's mouth dropped open at the insubordinate answer, but such was the absurdity of the comment that the centurion was silenced.

'The Germans won't fight us here,' he finally managed, turning on his heel. 'So get ready to make camp.'

Only minutes later, the centurion's prediction came true. Governor Varus had survived the forest, and now ordered that his legions build a marching camp in the open ground.

'His cat died?' Stumps asked, pulling his battered helmet from his head and shaking his head in wonder at Micon's insubordination. 'His fucking cat died.'

After the long morning of bloodshed, it was time for the army to lick its wounds.


I swung the pick into the dirt. The power behind the blow was pathetic, my muscles spent. All around me, other soldiers battled fatigue to dig the ditches and build the ramparts of the army's marching camp.

Against the wind, I heard the sound of soft sobbing. Looking over my shoulder, I saw that Stumps was digging, the soldier seemingly oblivious to the tears that cut through the thick grime on his cheeks.

'His fucking cat died,' I heard him repeat to himself for the thousandth time.

Chickenhead sat apart, his head between his bony knees as rain bounced from the steel of his helmet.

'Keep digging,' Titus grunted, seeing my stare. 'He'll come through.'

I wasn't so certain. Chickenhead's kitten had been the anchor that kept his mind from drifting into the waters of depression, and worse. Now there was nothing to hold the man back. Experience told me that he was as broken as any man with a spear in his guts.

Unfortunately, I had a long time to think over such dark matters. There were hours of backbreaking labour before the camp's defences were completed. The men of the legions were exhausted and, despite the threats and cajoling of the centurions and optios, construction took twice the time that day as it had done when the army first took to the field.

Despite my own discomfort, I was grudgingly pleased to see that our commanders insisted on maintaining the regulation defences of the camp, an important step towards sustaining the discipline that was our best chance of survival. Still, that solace did little to soothe my blistered hands.

Pavo finally nodded, atop the earthen bank. 'Good enough. Get some rest, and some food.'

'We got any tents?' Stumps asked in hope.

Pavo said nothing.

'Felix,' Titus said. 'Come with me.'

I looked at Pavo, but the centurion made no protest as the section commander led me away, leaving our comrades to huddle together on the wet ground, a solitary blanket pulled over their heads for protection against the storm.

'Where are we going?' I asked Titus once we were out of earshot.

'To find the camp followers.'

'Rufus's family?'

He nodded. So he hadn't forgotten about his friend. I felt as if I needed to offer something.

'He was a good man, Rufus,' I tried feebly.

'He was a great man,' Titus grunted. 'And a great soldier.'

'He won the Gold Crown?' I asked, referring to his decoration for valour.

'Four years ago. We went on raids across the Rhine, nothing large scale. We went into a stinking village to raze the place. It looked deserted.'

'It wasn't,' I guessed from his tone.

'It wasn't.' He grimaced. 'Half the century went down, including our centurion and optio. Rufus held it all together.'

I was surprised. Titus had always seemed the natural leader of the pair. Perhaps he read my thoughts.

'I was one of the ones that went down.' He smiled sadly. 'Rufus pulled me out of a burning hut. He saved my life.'

I said nothing. No wonder the men's bond had been so close.

'They offered him the century after that, but he didn't want rank. That wasn't him. Just his family and his mates, that was enough.'

And so we looked for his family.

The camp followers – or, at least, those who had made it this far – were huddled in the camp's centre, hundreds of wretched individuals who shuddered in the rain. Many had armed themselves with a mixture of Roman and German weaponry, for they would receive no mercy from Rome's enemies. At best, these civilians could expect to be taken and sold into slavery. At worst, there was rape, torture and death.

Tradesmen of every colour and country had followed the army in the hope of riches. Now their stores were abandoned to the Germans, and these merchants would be lucky to escape the forest with their lives. Amongst them were the prostitutes, and I saw one of these hard-eyed women stare at me as we trod through the grass of a field that was quickly being churned to mud.

'Go and fight them, you fucking tarts,' the whore cursed, desperate to vent her spleen.

'Fuck off, you rat,' Titus growled. I had no doubt that he would beat her down should she retort, and the prostitute must have sensed it too, for she held her tongue, though her eyes screamed oaths.

'Whores,' Titus grumbled beneath his breath, and I saw dozens more, but where some followed the army for profit, others had done it out of love. These were the families of the troops, though all were unofficial.

These civilians made for pathetic figures now. I swallowed as I took in the miserable sight of them. Children wailed, their skin waxen and grey from exposure. Mothers, eyes wide and red, held dying babes to their chests and cried into their wet hair. I wondered which would survive this day, or the next. Very few, I was certain. Their bones would litter this field and the forest, sport for the German warriors and food for the woodland creatures.

'Felix,' Titus grunted, poking me in the chest with a thick finger and snapping me from my dark musings. 'Stop standing there with your head up your arse and start asking for Rufus's family.'

I did. Most of the families could tell me nothing, their eyes empty wells. Others told me to leave them alone, fuck off, or worse. None were forthcoming with any useful information.

It was Titus who found someone who had answers. She was married to a veteran of our own cohort, and her family had encamped near Rufus's own within Minden town.

'They were with us,' the hard-faced woman confirmed, wiping snot from beneath a constantly running nose. 'But they made a break for it in the forest. Reckoned they had a better chance on their own.'

'But they were alive?' Titus pressed.

'They were then.' The woman shrugged. Like the soldiers, she had seen too much, and death no longer had the impact it had done only a day before. 'And Rufus?' she asked.

Titus's only answer was to walk away.

I followed, but I could not help a final look over my shoulder, where I saw the hundreds of innocents that shuddered in the cold, lambs awaiting the Germans' slaughter. They had followed the army expecting riches and glory, but instead, they had found only death.

I do not know what Titus had planned to do had he discovered his comrade's family, but the option had been taken from him. It seemed certain that Rufus's loved ones would join their husband and father in his grim resting place.

'I'll never know what happened to my mate,' Titus suddenly said out of nowhere, breaking me from my thoughts.

'What?' I asked, flustered.

'I'll never know. I told him to go, when we were outside the ramparts. I told him: "Go and be with them." And then what? Did he get lost? Did the fuckers get into our camp, and snatch him? I'll never know, Felix. All I can hope is that he was dead before they did . . .' He faltered. '. . . that fucking shit to him.'

'It's war, Titus,' I managed, certain that, as a veteran, he would know what I meant. In war, some things go unanswered, and good men die.

I wanted to try to say something more to the man, hardened though he was, but my words died as I saw him peering through the grey gloom. A body of men and animals moved within the marching camp's walls.

'What is it?' I asked.

'Cavalry,' he grunted, eyes narrowing. 'They're getting ready to ride out.'

'Why?' I asked, puzzled, unable to guess why a large body of horsemen would be forming now that the army had fixed itself in position behind the relative safety of ditch and rampart.

'I don't know,' he answered, but I could tell by the curiosity in his voice that we were going to find out.

## 40

Titus and I walked towards the body of horsemen. The troopers were busily checking the hooves of their mounts and tightening straps of both saddle and armour. Many of the beasts and their riders bore scars and bandages, the cavalry having come through the day no less punished than the foot-sloggers.

'Brother.' Titus hailed the nearest veteran. I saw that the green trousers beneath his tunic were stained almost black by blood.

'My second mount of the day,' he told us, seeing my look. 'This one belonged to a friend of mine.'

The trooper was anxious to share his experiences, even with a stranger. I recognized this as the sign of a man who was filled with nervous anticipation.

'You look like you've had a shit day,' Titus offered, putting a hand on the horse's soaked flank. There was comfort to be drawn from the company of beasts that held no malice. Little wonder that Chickenhead was suffering so much from the loss of his feline companion.

The cavalryman shrugged, taking in our battered and bloodied appearance. 'No worse than yours.'

'And now?' Titus asked, looking about at the men who were taking long, fortifying pulls from wineskins. 'Looks like you're planning a party.'

The trooper snorted at the jest. 'The governor is,' he explained, offering us a drink from his own wineskin. We declined, knowing that every man in the army was short on rations, and not wishing to deprive a good man of his own.

'Varus is sending us out. North, then west,' he told us after a hearty swig. 'We're to link up with the legions on the Rhine, and bring reinforcements.'

The trooper's words were hollow, holding little hope of success, and no wonder: the army had already abandoned its baggage train, and with it the majority of the campaign stores. Every hour in the marching camp would only weaken the fighting capacity of the legions through exhaustion and exposure. We could not hold out forever, and the Rhine forts were a long way away.

'How long's the ride?' Titus forced himself to ask.

In answer, the man simply offered the wineskin. This time, we were both eager to take it.

'Keep hold of it,' the cavalryman insisted. 'I'll either pick up some more on the Rhine, or in the afterlife.' He cackled at his own dark thoughts.

'Thank you for this.' Titus offered his hand and gave the man his name and unit. 'Look for me when we're back in the forts and I can repay the favour.'

'Atticus,' the trooper introduced himself. 'And if you'll excuse me, friends, it looks as if we're leaving.'

'Mount up!' a voice called, and Atticus hauled himself up into the saddle.

'Until we meet again.' He smiled, and trotted his mare to join the formation of grim-faced horsemen.

Without speaking, I walked with Titus to the nearest stretch of rampart. We did so not only because we had both been taken by the genial trooper and wished to see him on his way, but also because we knew that the army's hopes rode with these men. As we stood on top of the earthen bank and watched the depleted squadrons forming up, we recognized that Varus was rolling the dice in desperation, for without cavalry, even a Roman army in open battle would be hard pressed to win, as German horsemen would be able to harass our formations with impunity, picking apart the ranks until they finally broke, and the foot-sloggers could be run down in the open.

We were not the only soldiers to sense this, and soon the ramparts were thick with troops from every legion and auxiliary cohort in the army.

'It's the beginning, or it's the fucking end,' I heard a salt say behind me.

'Good luck, lads!' another shouted, and several others echoed the call.

I turned and looked at Titus. He held my gaze. Neither of us had the stomach to cheer.

At a command, the horses began to trot northwards, slowly gaining speed, riders anxious not to overwork the animals that had already endured so much.

I watched through the driving storm, seeing them approach the curtain of forest where they would hope to find a passage to the Rhine. All about me was silent now, the cheering long finished, the only sound the slap of the wind and rain against armour. The forms of the cavalry mounts began to blur into one mass with the distance.

The first sign of disaster came a moment later.

'Fuck, no!' came the curse. It was from the mouth of a young soldier, his sharp eyes having picked out something in the gloom a moment before the veterans.

But we saw it now.

Horsemen. A host of them. And not our own.

They came from behind a wall of trees, their formation thick and promising death, war cries carried by the wind. Even from so far, it was clear to see that our own battered troops were severely outnumbered. They had no chance.

No chance.

I heard the clash of arms and armour a moment later as the German cavalry enveloped the smaller number of our own exhausted horsemen, some of whom tried to forge ahead through the storm of steel, while others reined in their mounts and bolted back towards the encampment.

Within the space of a few breaths, the army's hope of salvation had been routed.

'The gods help them,' a veteran prayed, but his words fell on deaf ears, and I watched blank-eyed as our cavalry were hunted down like deer by the cheering Germans.

I saw none make it to the safety of the ramparts, but as the final screams died on the wind, a body of horsemen did ride towards us, the proud men in the saddle flushed with victory.

At the head of these German warriors, one nobleman rode alone, the wealth about his neck shining splendid even through the grey of the storm. He held a severed head aloft by its hair, and paraded it in front of the watching eyes of the Roman army, a harbinger of their doom. With a detachment brought on by exhaustion, I realized that this was a leader who not only wanted to destroy his enemy, but wanted them to know that their end was near, and terrible. He wanted them to suffer, and so without doubt he hated them. He hated Rome. He hated the legions. He hated me.

I looked at that magnificent warrior in the saddle, and I was surprised by all of this. Surprised and sickened to see the face of our enemy, and the architect of an army's destruction.

Because it was a face that I knew well.

It was the face of Arminius.

## 41

Arminius, a traitor.

For a moment, I almost laughed at the irony of it all. Then, as the gorge of bile rose up from my stomach, and my legs threatened to buckle beneath me, I reached out to Titus. He sensed my weakness, a rough fist taking hold of the back of my armour and holding me upright as a father would his unruly child.

He spoke tonelessly. 'We're fucked now.'

All around us, panicked whispers took flight as the identity of the lone horseman was spread, men desperate to know the answers to their most feared questions: had all the German tribes risen in revolt? Were our bases on the Rhine overrun? Would the German prince treat with our leaders, and negotiate terms, or was he bent on the wholesale destruction of our forces?

'He wants us dead,' Titus grunted, considering the last one. 'Look at him.'

I did.

Seated astride a powerful grey mare, Arminius appeared as the God of War himself, shoulders thick with armour and bearskin, long blond hair tangled by rain across the handsome face that betrayed not the slightest trace of a smile. Arminius was unmoved by the howling storm, a Roman head in his blood-covered hand. He appeared as confident as a man who was seeing the game unfold five steps ahead of his adversary.

'He planned all this,' Titus breathed, and looked at me.

I met his eyes, expecting suspicion in them, but I found none. I should not have been surprised. We had been through too much together – suffered too much together – for my own loyalty to be questioned now.

'I'm sorry.' Titus shrugged, in one of the rare gestures that betrayed his stone-like exterior. 'I know you liked him.'

'He's your enemy,' I managed, and then corrected myself. 'He's our enemy.'

I do not know if Titus would have replied, for a murmur ran through the ranks of watching troops on the rampart, and I turned to see the approach of the army's staff officers. These panicked members of the senatorial class needed to confirm their fears with their own, wide eyes, and as they climbed the slippery battlement, some even wailed as they saw the lone figure on horseback.

'Traitor!' others called in anger.

Arminius was unmoved by it all.

He waited.

He waited and, eventually, he was given the audience that he desired – Varus.

The governor came to the ramparts like a cripple, the trials of the field, and now of treason, too much for a man who had considered Arminius a son. Varus slipped as he tried to scale the mud of the earthen bank, dropping to his knees in the dirt, and, seeing such feebleness as a portent, soldiers began to whisper that the gods had forsaken the legions, and that the army was doomed to be destroyed at the hands of Varus's wayward child.

Knowing how much the older man had loved the prince, I expected that there would be some kind of exchange

300

between governor and German. Some demand for an answer, or a prayer for peace.

There was none.

No accusations, or explanations. Arminius simply turned his hard eyes on to Varus and then threw the severed head towards the rampart. It hit the dirt with a wet thump and rolled away grotesquely into the grass. Then, his message delivered, Arminius simply pulled on the reins of his mount and trotted back towards his greatest ally, the forest.

With that simple act, he sealed the destruction of an army.

Varus was the first to fall on his sword.

There was no speech. No great oration. For the first time during the campaign the man drew his blade, turned it towards himself, and fell forward so that the weight of his flabby body carried the steel through his chest. Perhaps because his hands were shaking from cold, or nerves, Varus missed his heart, and lay floundering for a moment as his torn lungs gasped for air.

With those on the rampart, I watched this without comment. Like the men about me, I had already seen too much. This act of cowardice left me open-mouthed in shock, but such were the horrors of the forest that I could not be any more revolted by it than I could the rising and setting of the sun. The actions of the governor – and, moments later, those of his staff officers – unfolded so quickly that I seemed to be watching them in slow motion. Within an instant of Varus pulling his own sword, many of his staff lay dead by their own blades, their blood pooling in the mud of the camp they had hoped would prove their bastion.

'Fuckers,' Titus growled besides me. 'Come on,' he urged, pulling at the sleeve of my tunic. 'No good's gonna come of standing around here and watching these cunts do themselves in.'

Equally disgusted, many of the other soldiers began to move away, returning to their centuries, but not all. Some sat back in the mud, or dropped to their knees. Some wailed, while others gave in to despair in silence.

It was the beginning of the end, I knew.

As I stumbled along beside Titus, I recognized an old soldier standing amongst the dead of the army's staff, his worn face twisted into ferocious anger. It was Caeonius, the camp prefect who had found me in the grove with Arminius, and who had saved me from crucifixion. Betrayed by both the German prince and the governor, and now left as the senior soldier in the army, it seemed that the weight of the legions would have to be borne by this man's wide shoulders.

I pitied him. This was an unwinnable battle, but what choice did he have but to fight it? What choice did any of us have? We were not blinded by the same shame and honour that had forced the aristocratic leaders to fall on their swords. We wanted to live.

'Felix,' I heard, and turned.

The standard-bearer from the parade square, the bearskin over his head and shoulders thick with matted blood. Dirty bandages covered a wound on his arm. Here was a man who had stood in the thickest of the fighting.

'Standard-bearer,' I greeted him.

'Your friend has come to kill us,' the man said, though there was no malice in his words. He was resigned to his fate.

*My friend.*

'He's my enemy,' I said, though I heard the uncertainty in my voice. 'He lied to me.' I told him, unable to see my hypocrisy.

The man turned his head away, looking at the crowd who had gathered about the bodies of the staff officers. 'Look to your comrades, brother,' he told me, offering his hand. 'It's going to be a long road home.'

I took it, and then watched as he stalked towards the frightened soldiers. I knew that we would never speak again.

We left the scene, walking in silence as Titus led us through the lines to our own century, but my mind screaming: Why – *how* – could Arminius have committed such treason? He had been raised a son of Rome. He had fought for Rome. Bled for Rome. Why this treason? A treason that had clearly been plotted carefully for months: the honeyed words into Varus's ear; the disturbances that had required the legions' response, all the time directed into the jaws of Arminius's carefully baited trap.

I was no sentimental idiot, and knew Rome's flaws better than most, but I could not understand how such a passionate, popular prince had been able to plot and deceive while maintaining his charisma and inspiring loyalty in those he sought to destroy. That, to me, was the greatest mystery of all.

Rumour of this treason had spread through the legions like wildfire, and when we reached the huddled forms of our comrades, Titus and I were assaulted by a barrage of desperate questions, Moonface dropping to his knees in the mud as Titus gruffly confirmed that Varus and his staff were dead.

'Pick yourself up,' Titus ordered. 'Varus was a fucking coward and a cunt. Don't sit crying in the mud for him.'

It took Stumps and Cnaeus to haul the distraught soldier to his feet. The myth of Roman glory was the air that Moonface breathed, and in a matter of days he had seen the illusion of invincibility and grandeur shattered.

'We're dead,' he groaned, and no one disagreed with him.

I looked over the faces of the section, seeing all hope abandoned. Chickenhead had ceased to function as a soldier and a man, a hollow-eyed ghost clad in armour. Young Micon and Cnaeus were gaunt-faced and vacant. Stumps veered between moments of outlandish optimism and soul-crushing depression.

'I don't want to die,' Micon stated simply, his blank face showing no sign of emotion.

But die it was certain we would, for the trap had been sprung and an army was leaderless in the killing ground. With such doom in mind, I remembered something Pavo had said in Minden. Something he had told me before the forest and the bloodshed.

*No one should die amongst strangers.*

He was right.

I did not want to die an outsider, and so I opened my mouth to speak.

'My name isn't Felix,' I told the six soldiers who had become my brothers.

Their dark eyes widened as I laid bare my poisonous soul. 'It's Corvus.'

I swallowed, sealing my fate.

'And I am a traitor.'

# PART THREE

# 42

'I am a traitor.' I breathed the words again, as if hearing them myself for the first time.

The section did not respond; they simply stared. So exhausted and battered were they that my confession bounced like a pebble off the armour of their minds.

'I'm a fucking traitor!' I shouted into their faces, desperate now to unburden myself before the bloody end that awaited us beyond the ramparts.

Titus rallied first. He shrugged. 'This isn't your first time under the eagles.' It was a statement rather than question. I knew that Titus had had his suspicions all along, as had the other veterans, and even the boy soldiers. A soldier's ways were too hard to disguise. From drill, to my movement amongst the trees, I had been betrayed by my experience.

'Just speak,' he ordered.

And so I did. 'Not my first time under the eagles,' I confirmed, forcing the words out. 'But my first time on this frontier. My old unit, they were in Pannonia.'

*Pannonia.* Just speaking the name of the province was torture. When I had first set eyes on the place there had been no land more beautiful, but I had seen that utopia torn apart by bloody rebellion. Since my desertion, the details of that campaign had been mercifully vague in my mind, leaving me only with the impression of chaos and suffering.

'You were in the war there?' Stumps asked.

I nodded, but that was as far as my answer would go. I wanted to tell them more – I was desperate to – but that time was a blur of blood and misery, and if I tried to describe those few vivid memories that I could recall, the words would stick in my throat like hooks.

'I ran,' I finally choked.

'Why?' Stumps asked.

'I – I don't remember. I just ran. It was a slaughter. I don't remember much, but it was slaughter. Every day, it was . . . slaughter. I couldn't watch them die any more.'

I don't know what I expected, then. Perhaps it would have been different had we not been on the edge of our own destruction, our leaders having died within the hour by their own blades. Hard to question a foot-soldier's honour when his senatorial leaders, his supposed betters, had taken their own lives rather than face the enemy. And so, instead of fists and accusations, I faced only questions.

'I was going to Britain,' I answered several voices.

'Britain?' Titus asked.

I shrugged. 'No Roman law. Across a sea. It seemed as good a place as any, and I had friends. Maybe they're still alive,' I added, certain that if they were, then I would never see them. Not now that our head was in the bear's jaws.

'A long way to walk from Pannonia,' Titus commented. Pannonia sat against the Adriatic, an entire continent away. I had crossed countless miles of field, forest and mountain range before I had found myself in the sacred grove where I had been discovered by Arminius. I told them as much, my shame-filled eyes focused on the dirt.

A bark of laughter caused me to look up.

It was Stumps. He looked at me in pity. 'You ran from one war, and ended up . . .' He let his words trail away, but spread his arms to encompass the misery and squalor of a dying army.

No one caught the infection of his smile. Instead, Moonface took a step towards me. I saw a flash of something in his eyes. Despite the collapse of Varus's army, Moonface still believed in the Roman ideals.

'Cunt,' he spat.

And then he hit me.

It wasn't a good strike, his muscles tired and his aim awry, but I made no move to defend myself, and it caught my cheek, the bone beneath my eye singing with heat.

'Back!' Titus growled, hauling the soldier away as if he weighed no more than an empty tunic. 'What the fuck does it matter now if he ran? Have you seen where we are? Have you seen what's coming?'

'You're giving up?' Stumps asked, suddenly sour.

'Fuck you, I'm not giving up,' Titus declared. 'I'm going to live through this, and so are you, little pricks. Moon!' he growled, and Moonface met his glare. 'Forget your fucking eagles, the emperor and every other thing that they ever told us was important. Look around! Seven of us. Seven of us here to fight our way out of this. If you don't believe we can do it, then fall on your sword now like that fucking governor and his wet-cunt officers.'

Titus's words hit home like a war-hammer. I looked at the brute and saw a figure that was so large in life that perhaps death would not have the stomach to take him. Maybe – maybe – here was a man who could pull us through the impossible to safety.

Stumps snorted, his eyes lively. 'Nice speech, Titus. At least if I die, you'll keep me entertained until the end.'

'Are you in this or not?' Titus demanded, in no mood for jests.

'Of course I am, you soft bastard,' Stumps told him, spitting for emphasis.

'And the rest of you?' Titus challenged them.

None answered with the same enthusiasm as Stumps, but a grudging nod was enough for the big man. Only Chicken-head stayed alone, mute and unmoving.

'I'll get him to the Rhine if I have to carry him,' Titus promised, glancing at the veteran, and I had no doubt that he meant it.

That left only me.

'I'm a traitor,' I told him again, as if that explained everything.

'You're a soldier,' Titus snorted. His open palm hit the side of my helmet, and with that blow I knew that I would die for him. I would die for a man I had planned to kill, and I would kill a man that I had adored.

Arminius.


We sat huddled like sheep, a sodden blanket held over our heads. Without warning, it was tugged back.

'Fuck off,' Stumps moaned, his eyes closed.

'Get up,' a voice commanded.

Pavo. I looked up at him, silhouetted against the grey skies. The striking centurion had been smiling in the hours following the death of our legion's commander, knowing that the man's end had increased the chances of his own survival. There was no smile now. Only the two words that every tired soldier dreads to hear.

He spoke, his words clipped. 'Work party.'

And so, with every sinew of our bodies aching, using hands and weapons to push ourselves up from the mud, we struggled to our feet and followed behind Pavo with the rest of our depleted century. Looking around, I sensed that our numbers had thinned further still since we had made the marching camp. My suspicions were confirmed as I overheard two veterans talking – three men in the century had taken their own lives. Another had died from exposure.

They would not be the last. Arminius could sit back in the trees and watch us wait and bleed our way to oblivion. We would have to break out, I knew; it was our only chance. A small, terrifying chance, but one that would have to be taken, and soon.

But before that, there was a task to be performed. A task that our section had been assigned to. We needed to bury the dead.

'Mass grave,' Pavo informed us. 'Just dig.'

We did. It was slow work. Miserable work. The ramparts that day had been agony enough, and that was before our leaders had abandoned us to our fate.

'I bet they're not going into a mass grave,' Stumps said, and he was right. A veteran of the Nineteenth Legion, a friend of Titus, explained that Varus and his staff officers had been cremated before their individual burials so their bodies could not be desecrated by the Germans.

'But the lads got sick of waiting for the fucker to burn,' the veteran spat. 'So they just filled the hole in once his hair had been singed off.'

'Better resting place than he deserves,' Titus opined, and his friend agreed before going on his way. Watching the men exchange goodbyes, I knew that neither of the veterans expected to see the other again in this life.

The mass grave was only knee-deep before a call came from the centurions that put a stop to the digging. We were then ordered to begin filling it with the dead of the common soldiery.

'I fucking hate this!' I heard Stumps call out. Looking at him, I saw that he held an arm in his hand, the shoulder joint ragged with flesh.

'It came off when I lifted him,' he explained, half smiling as tears flowed over his cheeks.

Many more of the bodies showed wounds from the morning's fighting, but dozens were intact and unscathed. Often these were the youngest soldiers, the boys having succumbed to a combination of terror and exposure. Not all of the wax-faced corpses were soldiers, and amongst the red-tunicked bodies were dozens of camp followers – women and children of all colours and ages.

'I knew him,' Titus grunted, referring to a veteran who had died from a chest wound. 'Good bloke.'

'What was his name?' Cnaeus asked.

'What's it matter?' Titus shrugged, suddenly prickly. 'What the fuck does it matter,' he repeated to himself.

There were other familiar faces. Moonface was grieved to see his favourite whore amongst the dead. Stumps buried a comrade from his days as a recruit. As he had done when digging the rampart that day, the man wept silently to himself. Chickenhead sat alone and undisturbed. Like the dead in the grave, he had no further interest in this world. He was a shell now, already resigned to death. I suspected that, when it came, he would welcome it, and that pained me, for the man had shown me kindness and comradeship. I struggled to think of a way to bring him back, but failed. How do you tell a man that life is worth living, and all is good, when you are standing up to your knees in the corpses of those who had been your friends and comrades?

'We need another grave digging,' Pavo ordered, seeing that the first was full and bodies were still stacked above ground in the mud.

And so we dug.

The skies were dark before the final body was dropped into the dirt. Then began the task of covering the fallen with soil, condemning them to a grave that would surely be dug up by the Germans as soon as we departed the marching camp. Our enemies would be keen to make sport of our dead by desecrating their bodies.

I cannot tell you how long the task took. Only that, at times, I was at peace with my place in the world, feeling not a care for my past, or my future. At other moments, I felt as if a boulder were on my chest, crushing me with the weight of my depression. Then at other times I simply wept, and I could not have told you whether it was from joy or grief.

If not already broken, I would say that my mind was breaking.

I was not the only man on the edge of insanity or, more truthfully, with a footstep inside its boundaries. Some men fled the camp in the darkness. Others took their own lives. Some, however, held their nerves in an iron grip. It was down to these men that we were still an army, and not a rabble.

One of these men was Caeonius. The man had served long enough to have stared disaster and death in the face many times, and though nothing could have compared in scale to the tragedy in which we now found ourselves, Caeonius was undeterred as he took control of the army.

'We're going to form two battle groups,' Pavo informed his huddled century. We were at full strength now, our depleted ranks merged with another unit that had lost their own centurion. 'Prefect Caeonius will lead the first, and we'll be in there with him. When dawn comes, we break out.'

Despite his best efforts, Pavo's words sounded hollow, but no one could blame him. We were an army of exhausted, starved men, battered by nature, and surrounded by a ferocious enemy that hated us. What chance could there be of our successful escape?

None.

But what other choice was there?

And so we would fight.

# 43

The hours of darkness passed in misery and squalor. As a section, we sat huddled and shivering beneath sodden blankets, our breath thick and stinking beneath the wool. From somewhere, Titus produced a handful of hardtack biscuits, which he rationed out amongst our seven. No one asked where, or how, the big man had come by the food, but I had little doubt that we had his scarred fists to thank for it.

We took our turn on the rampart, too tired to care if the Germans should attack. In darkness or in the dawn, we would have to face their spears eventually. Some men decided to take their chances and deserted during the night.

'Best of luck to them,' Stumps said with a shrug when we heard that a pair from our own century had run. The news earned nothing more than a nod or an empty stare from the other veterans – let them take their chances, was the muttered opinion. If our leaders would not stand for us, then why should the rank and file stand for them?

I wondered if my former comrades had been as understanding of my own abandonment of them. Perhaps Varo and Priscus would have forgiven me, but despite my best efforts to convince myself, I knew that I was forever damned in the eyes of my oldest friend, Marcus. Perhaps he watched me now from the afterlife, eager to see my end.

I spoke to the wind. 'Not long, Marcus.'

I saw echoes of past battle-brothers in the men who sheltered with me now. Priscus and Stumps would have become great friends, I was certain. Varo and Titus would have clashed at first, but I could envision the pair of brutes ruling the army's black-market trade with an iron fist. Marcus and Moonface could have fawned together over the grandeur of empire and the nobility of conquest.

I shook my head in grief for the comrades I had lost, and the ones I was certain would follow.

'Let's go,' Pavo called.

The rain-filled sky was still dark as we shuffled from the ramparts, our guard duty finally at an end.

'Get close,' he ordered, and our century huddled as one mass around the silhouette of our centurion. 'We're forming up to march at the end of this watch, so if you need to shit or pray, then do it now.'

Their orders received, most of the century stayed in position, too tired to seek out sanctuary that they knew by now did not exist, but I saw Titus's large shadow break from the ranks. Despite the fatigue of my body and mind, I wanted to think, and to move, and so I followed, falling into step alongside the brute.

'Where are you going?' I asked, feeling as though the experiences of the past few days had earned me the privilege of such questions.

'We need food.'

We found it amongst the camp followers. Unburdened by arms and armour, some entrepreneurial souls had saddled themselves with the supplies Varus had ordered left behind when the baggage train was abandoned. Now these morsels were selling at a hundred times their worth.

To protect their investments, the tradesmen had taken on the service of a section of auxiliary soldiers, whose cohort commander had doubtless been paid off handsomely for the guard force. It was to one of these Batavian soldiers that Titus spoke. A pouch of coins was produced from within the big man's tunic, and in return he was given a small parcel wrapped in cloth. It was barely the size of Titus's gnarled fist, but he made no objection.

We walked away in silence. I knew that to procure the food for the section Titus had given up a considerable slice of his personal wealth – perhaps all of it. It was a selfless act of comradeship, and I muttered as much to the man.

'If you're all too weak to fight, then I die,' he grunted in response.

'If you say so.' I shrugged, certain that his reply was nothing more than the keeping up of appearances.

'Can I ask you something?' I pushed on, desperate to distract myself.

'If you have to,' Titus replied, no doubt for the same reason.

'Why did you come back to the eagles?' I paused to gauge the man's reaction. His thick brow knotted, but there was no sign of his anger flaring, and so I continued. 'You did your twenty years in the desert. How did you end up here with a new legion, half a world away?'

Several wet footsteps passed, and I expected that his answer had passed with them.

It had not.

'As part of my discharge, they gave me a farm,' Titus told me, his hard voice bitter. 'A *farm*. Barren scraps on a slope so fucking steep you could hardly stand on it.'

'So you couldn't work it?' I asked naively.

'Of course I fucking worked it,' the man shot back with anger and pride. 'I dug out that slope until it was flat. I carried in rich soil from miles away. I made it work.'

'Then why come back to the legions? To this?' I gestured at the chaos around us, wanting to take advantage of Titus's brief openness.

'You know why.' As he spoke, his tone was the softest I had ever heard it, oiled wood instead of steel. 'A man needs family.'

I wanted to ask him more, but something in those last words told me it would be a mistake to do so. I had got as much as I could from the big man.

We reached our own family shortly afterwards, and it *was* a family, I knew. It wasn't as simple as thinking of the section as seven brothers, for Titus was both mother and father, and Chickenhead the distressed uncle, but it was a family nonetheless. Dysfunctional but fiercely loyal.

'Here.' Titus handed out the food to his charges. 'Get this scoff down your necks. Water, too.'

'You're not eating?' Stumps asked, and Titus shook his head.

'I had mine on the way back,' our leader lied. 'Now shut up and eat.'

We did, while the slate sky above us began to grow a lighter grey with the dawn.

'Form up! Prepare to march!' came the order that we both dreaded and welcomed, knowing that the enemy were now only heartbeats away. One way or another, we would soon see an end to our suffering, and so, as we took our places in the ranks, we not only prepared to march. We prepared ourselves to die.

In the darkness, it was impossible to tell how deep the ranks of our formation were, but it was evident that Prefect Caeonius had elected to form the two battle groups into short, dense units, rather than the long column that had been strung out through the forest in the previous days.

I found myself on the outside of the formation, with Titus in front of me and Stumps to my right. Behind me was a soldier from another section, his jaw chattering uncontrollably – from cold or fear, I did not know, nor would I blame him for either.

The wind whistled through the ranks, carrying with it the sound of shield bumping against shield, steel pulled free of its sheath and final words of encouragement between friends. From other parts of the camp, it carried the terrible cries of the wounded. Once again, those too maimed to march would be left behind, sentenced to die hideously at the hands of the Germans. I only hoped that their comrades would do the right thing and end their misery quickly before the army took flight.

Looking at the shadowed faces of the section, I saw men grown hard against such sounds and thoughts. Even young Micon and Cnaeus were unflinching as tortured screams tore through the gloom.

It was Chickenhead who broke, the once solid veteran cut free of the bonds of discipline now that he no longer cared for his life.

'Out of my fucking way,' he ordered, and began to push his way out of the centre ranks, where he had been placed by Titus.

'Out of my way!' he shouted again, his red eyes furious as Titus's hand shot out to grip him by the sagging flesh of his throat. 'Let go of me,' he choked.

'Get back in your place,' Titus growled.

'Fuck you,' Chickenhead managed, and tried to spit, the pathetic fluid dribbling across his chin.

'And where will you go, you daft cunt?' Stumps asked his friend.

'I'll stay with the wounded.'

'The wounded are already dead,' Stumps replied coldly.

A strangled bark of laughter forced its way from the veteran's throat, Chickenhead's red eyes bulging with amusement. 'We're all dead, you soft bastard! Better to get it over with here and now, than drag it out in that fucking forest.'

Titus's patience ran out. His free hand slammed into the breastplate of Chickenhead's armour, driving the air from his lungs with such force that the man's already bulging eyes looked like they would burst, and his knees buckled.

'Enough of your shit,' Titus swore, taking his hand from the veteran's throat and allowing Moonface and Stumps to hold him upright. 'Find your balls.'

'Battle group!' a voice called from the darkness. 'By the centre, quick march!'

There were no trumpets. No horns. No unified slap of sandals against the dirt. Instead, a dense mass of men stirred muscles that had passed the point of endurance, shuffled across the earthen ramparts and marched towards the dark horizon of the enemy's greatest ally: the forest.

As we moved, a figure appeared to my left, outside of the ranks. It was Pavo, come to talk to Titus ahead of me.

'Two battle groups,' he told his most trusted section commander. 'We're in the lead one, Caeonius commanding. We hit the Germans and push through.'

Titus made no comment. This was neither the time nor the place for elaborate plans. Only brute strength and the will to survive could carry us to safety.

'I don't see there being any chance for open manoeuvres and drill,' Pavo concurred. 'This is going to be a brawl, Titus.

Just keep your boys tight, and push forward. Keep them tight, and don't leave anyone behind. That's all we can do.'

With those words, the centurion took his leave.

'Obstacles up ahead!' came the calls from several voices, and the body of men shuddered as the march across the open ground ended and the battle group's vanguard entered the forest. Obstructions would no longer be cleared from the army's path, and each man clambered up and over the fallen trees as best as he could. This opened up holes in the formation and destroyed any chance of cohesive movement, but the forest had already proven that to attempt such unity was fruitless.

'Help each other,' Titus ordered as we came across our first fallen tree trunk. Fresh and fit, we could have leaped across it while burdened with a full load of equipment, but drained and bruised, we crossed the obstacle like a gaggle of aged spinsters.

And yet progress was good. The blanket of fog lay thick on the ground, but my mind was attuned to movement in such conditions, and I reckoned that we were making good distance, while still under some cover of darkness.

I was not the only man to sense it, and a murmur of encouragement rippled through the ranks as men dared to believe that we had passed through the thickest parts of the forests, and that maybe today would offer us the chance to hold our formations, and dare the Germans to attack us in open battle.

The Germans . . . they were not idle as we fled, and in the distance came the first sounds of steel on steel. The challenge of war cries. The screams of the dying.

'They're attacking the rearguard,' Stumps thought aloud.

If that were true, then Arminius was not content to bleed the army slowly to death in the forest. No matter if it was a harassing attack, he was facing us openly.

'He has all the cavalry, doesn't he?' a voice asked.

It was young Cnaeus. In a matter of days, the boy soldier had gone from a student of war to an academic. He knew that without our own cavalry to beat off the attacks, the German horsemen would be free to swoop on to our formations of infantry, picking them off with javelin and spear. It seemed that now, whether in the forest or in the open, Arminius would hold the advantage.

Still, the attacks in the open seemed brazen from a man who had been so calculating in his every move. Why would he give up the advantage of the forest now? Why were his troops attacking our rear in numbers, when they could far more easily bleed us from our flanks in the trees? This was their homeland, their turf. Our nearest sanctuary was days away, even without the need to fight our way there.

Then, as the fog began to lift, we were given our answer.

'What is that?' Stumps asked, squinting at a thick smudge that ran below a crest on the horizon. 'Battle formations? Are they goin' to stand against us?'

'No,' young Cnaeus replied, his youthful eyes sharp. 'It's a wall.'

And as the fog burned away, and we marched ever closer, I saw that the boy soldier was right.

It was the final piece of the trap. Arminius had built a wall, and if we were to have any hope of escape, then we would have to cross it.

The skirmishes of the forest were over.

Battle was upon us.

# 44

The rampart ran along the lowest slope of a crest, below which was the track that the battle group would have to follow to avoid marshlands to the east and thick forest to the west. Once again, Arminius had shown his guile, and instead of placing his defensive works directly across the line of the Roman advance, he had placed it at an oblique angle that would allow the tribesmen to pelt our units with stone, javelin and spear should we try to manoeuvre by it. The wall was constructed from intertwined withies – strong and flexible willow stems – and into this barricade Arminius had included sally ports from which his men would be able to rush down and exploit any breach in the flanks of our bedraggled battle groups.

'The bastard built this weeks ago,' Stumps observed, and no one argued with him. Considering the scale and the quality of the works, there was no doubt that Arminius's treachery had been planned long ago. Through guile and deceit, he had led Varus's army to its place of execution, and this rampart was the chopping block on which the legions must lay down their necks.

'We can't march past it,' I thought aloud. 'With the high ground they can pick us apart. They'll hit us with missiles and harassing attacks until we break; and when we do, Arminius will have his shock troops ready to smash into that gap and tear us apart. Once we break, it's all over.'

Titus considered my words, and showed his agreement by spitting. 'Hit-and-run with these bastards is over. It's a frontal assault on that thing, and clear them out from behind it.'

At the head of the battle group, Prefect Caeonius came to the same conclusion. What other choice was there? His orders reached us through Pavo moments later.

'We're going in *testudo*!' Pavo called, adrenaline raising his voice an octave. 'Keep your shields tight! Hold together! When we break through, hold formation and we'll slaughter these goat-fucking cunts!'

His words were met with little enthusiasm. Only Stumps seemed to smile. 'All fucking campaign, all I've heard is "wait till we get to fight them in formation".' The man cackled manically. 'Well, here's your chance, boys! It's hold on to your nuts, and straight up the guts! What a fucking riot!' he concluded, spitting for luck.

Looking around me, I saw that the morning's fog was nothing more than a whisper now. The German wall and rampart were stark against the slope, the shape of men visible as they climbed its heights to taunt us. All around me, tired red eyes peered out from beneath the steel peaks of helmets. Other sets of eyes were squeezed shut, while below them cracked lips moved frantically in desperate prayer. I caught the smell of shit, and knew that more men would paint their thighs before we ever reached the walls.

We waited like this for the order to advance. Who knows how long we stood for? I have heard some soldiers say that in battle, time becomes a blur. For others, the wait was stretched out as if into infinity. Some suffered it in silence, while others beat at their armour and chanted mantras or promises. No one man was like another in his preparation for or experience of combat, yet each action was born of the same reason – the terror of the unknown.

The terror of death.

'Battle group!' the order came. 'Form *testudo!*'

The sound was like a thunderclap as men on the outside of the formation overlapped their shields by their sides, while those in the centre raised them overhead with tired arms. At once we were cast into darkness, thin slits of grey light doing little to illuminate our gaunt faces. The stink of sweat, breath and infected wounds filled my nostrils.

'Come on, you fuckers,' I heard Stumps curse. 'Let's go. Let's fucking go. Straight up the guts! Woo!'

He was answered by a trumpet note, and the formation of shields lurched forward at a slow march, footing insecure thanks to the darkness and slippery ground.

Knowing that every step carried us closer to the enemy, men became more vocal now, promising death to the enemy or begging to be delivered from it themselves. For others such as I, now was the time for deep, ragged breaths as we sought to control shaking limbs.

Fuck, I was scared.

I didn't want to die, but I knew that every step carried me towards that likely fate. All I could hope was that it would be quick. Please, if it should come, let it be quick.

*Fuck. Fuck. Fuck. Is it too late to run?*

Of course it was. Run, and the Germans would have me as a grotesque plaything, as they did Rufus. Did I want to die with my cock and balls stuffed into my mouth? No. If I was going to go, then better it be over in a burst of adrenaline and chaos.

My breathing sounded as though it came from a terrified bull, and over the sound of these breaths I now heard the guttural challenges of the German tribesmen. They were confident in victory, and almost mocking in their war cries. To hear them so clearly, the rampart must be close.

Close enough that I could die here.

Our arrival was announced by the sound of stone striking hide as the Germans began to pelt the leading shields with slingshot and rocks. Men began to cry out, some from wounds but most to gain the confidence they needed to press forward into the storm.

I was one of them.

'Fuck you!' I screamed at no one and everyone. 'Fuck you!'

Then, without warning, the formation came to a shuddering halt, and my nose pressed against the cold metal of Titus's mail – the leading troops had reached the rampart.

'Tools forward!' came the order. 'Tear it down! Get the fucking wall down!'

Under cover of the leading shields, men on their knees began to frantically hack at the withies that made up the wall, desperate to open us a hole through which we could push in, and engage the enemy.

But the Germans above them were not idle, and stones began to rain on to shields and skulls. Even strong arms would have struggled to hold off this hellish downpour, but weakened by fatigue, the leading troops had no chance, and as the rocks broke down the protection, German spears and javelins found Roman flesh. Screams echoed beneath the shields. The smell of piss and shit grew stronger.

'Get us up there!' I heard called again and again, finally realizing that the demand came from Chickenhead, spittle flying from his mouth.

'More men on the tools!' came Pavo's shout, though I could see little of the man, or anything else, my entire vision taken up by Titus's wide back. 'Second Century, push up! Push up!' he ordered, and we struggled to obey, moving in half-steps.

To my right, I saw the first of our wounded crawling back between the legs of their comrades, blood trailing in their wake. Others lay where they fell, skulls caved in from the rain of rocks, limbs twitching as their bodies gave up the fight.

The sound ahead was chaos now, screams and war cries, taunts and defiance. Somehow, orders cut through the madness, and our century was amongst those pressing through the ranks ahead, shields held aloft above our heads as we collected tools from the hands of the dead and dying.

'Bring down the wall!' Pavo called, and I saw it now through a tangle of legs and armour, the wood chipped from Roman tools and spattered with Roman blood. Shafts of light broke through the ceiling of shields as spear and stone poured down from above.

Into that carnage, we forged ahead.

Clarity of thought and action was lost. Adrenaline and fear took hold of my body. I shouted, but I could not say what. I do not know where the axe in my hand came from, only that I found myself on my knees, frantically swinging it into the wooden barricade ahead of me, splinters of wood thrown back into my face as my muscles burned with the effort.

While some of us struggled to break through, others attempted to fight back against those who assailed us from above. It was an impossible task; our javelins were shorter than the Germans' spears, and any Roman brave enough to expose his body to take aim and throw was pierced by German steel before he could loose his own weapon.

And that was how I saw Chickenhead die.

Desperate to draw blood, the veteran had pushed away his neighbour's shield, which was covering him from above, and was arcing his javelin back to throw when the first spear plunged down to hit him on the armour of his shoulders. The mail held, but a second speartip found flesh between shoulder and neck, driving deep into the veteran's body. Blood spurted into the air as he cried out in anger and pain. Before Titus could pull his shield over our fallen comrade to protect him, a rock the size of a child's torso came tumbling across the rampart and crushed Chickenhead's helmet as if it were made of glass. In a heartbeat, the veteran had been reduced from our beloved comrade to a broken, mangled corpse.

'Leave him!' Titus ordered, seeing Stumps about to drop to Chickenhead's side, his own safety forgotten. 'Leave him! Pick up the tools! Get this fucking wall down!'

What choice did we have?

And so we struck the wood of the German defences with axe and pick. Like wild animals, we pulled at it with our bare hands until our fingernails tore away. Spear and javelin stabbed down from above, and the screams of the dying outsung the victorious war cries of those behind the wall.

How long the attack lasted for, I could not say. Once Chickenhead fell, I was barely conscious of my own part in it. There was the noise, the labour, the feeling of hot blood against my skin. In that scrum against the wall, time lost all meaning. There was no room for fear, only the most basic instinct to draw the next breath, and to live through the next second.

I did not hear the trumpets or orders that sounded the retreat. Likely I would have remained at the wall, hitting it pathetically with a blunt axe head until I was finished by a German spear, had Titus not dragged me from the carnage.

Somehow, I escaped the wall intact but for the most minor of injuries. Looking back, I could see that hundreds of our comrades had not been as fortunate – beneath the withies was a red carpet of fallen legionaries. This carpet seemed to rise and fall as the wounded tried to crawl to safety, but they would never be able to escape the Germans who now poured howling through the wall's sally ports, determined to dispatch the injured and harass the retreat of those that still stood.

'Jog-trot!' came the order, relayed by voices hoarse from fear. 'Jog-trot!'

I flashed my wild eyes about me. Chickenhead was gone, but the other members of the section somehow lived, their faces painted in gore and terror. As a unit now, we shuffled at a trot away from the wall, our muscles beyond fatigue, but carried on by adrenaline. As the German horde poured downhill towards us, the trot became a run, men pushing and shoving their way to escape.

The army was in danger of becoming a rabble. Retreat was becoming rout.

Prefect Caeonius recognized it, and knew that there was only one decision to make.

'Halt!' the centurions called, relaying our leader's order. 'Halt, you bastards! Form up! Form up! Battle formation!'

Somehow, discipline took hold, section commanders and veterans pulling their comrades to a stop, and pushing them into a formation that could face the onrushing tribesmen.

They knew that it was our only chance now. A chance so pitiful that to do anything but prepare for the end was foolishly optimistic.

And so, with shaking muscles and panting lungs, we prepared to make our final stand beneath the legion's eagles.

# 45

Our army was dying. The Empire was being brought to its knees. The rampart beneath the hill was thick with our dead, across which now streamed a mass of German warriors, flush with the sense of victory. All about us, the jaws of Arminius's trap were slamming shut.

Suddenly, the irony of it all hit me like an arrow. I had walked a continent to escape war, and now here I stood, part of a colossal defeat that I knew would echo across the entire world. Despite the death around me, or more likely because of it, I suddenly choked out a laugh.

'We're fucked.' I smiled at young Cnaeus beside me.

I knew it was a hollow smile. The smile of a man who had one foot in the earthly realm and one beyond. But, surrounded by death, I had the choice of laughing in its face, or shitting myself at its touch.

And so why not die with a smile on my face?

The Empire meant nothing to me. Enlightenment? Romanization? They were fancy words for corpulent politicians. My world was the section, the mates on my shoulders. My world was now nothing more than the few yards to my front, seen over the axe-ravaged horizon of my shield's lip. It was a small world, and one full of terror.

My smile dropped as I heard Pavo shout, 'Here they come!' The warning was redundant. A wave of screaming Germans sprinted towards us, a solid mass of shield and spear.

These were fresh troops, unbloodied, their eyes still sparkling with life. They hadn't fought in the forest. They hadn't bled on the wall. I hoped that their inexperience would allow me to see a few more seconds of this grey morning.

'Brace!' Pavo called, and I overlapped my shield with Cnaeus's, putting the pathetic weight of my body behind my front leg. My limbs were weak, dying, and yet they obeyed. Adrenaline had fed them to this point. I felt the slip of the mud beneath my sandals, and ground them in deeper, knowing that every inch of push and shove would be a matter of life and death.

With a sidelong glance, I caught Cnaeus's eye. Three days ago, this comrade had been a young warrior. Now, he was an old man. Even the stubble on his unguarded throat had grown white. He had done his duty, and showed the promise of a fine soldier. In another life, he could have risen far. In this one, he seemed certain to die on this track.

I pushed such thoughts from my mind as I turned my eyes back to the front. The Germans were now a few paces away, their faces screaming, cursing, twisted by both hatred and the scent of victory.

We clashed. It was shield on shield, grinding, creaking and splintering. It was metal into flesh, the resistance of bone, the break in through ribs, and the suction as the blade was drawn free. It was gnashing teeth, spitting faces and eyes dead with resignation or ablaze with defiance.

It was battle.

Once again in the face of death, time became meaningless. I measured life in breaths and sword strokes.

Beside me, young Cnaeus screamed like an animal as he thrust his blade into a German's body. Pulling his sword free sent a cascade of hot blood spurting into the air and across my own skin. I tried to call out, more beast than man, as my own steel tore open a stomach, conscious of the hot entrails that fell across my sandalled feet.

'Die!' I screamed into the bearded faces of my enemy. 'Die!'

And die they did. How many on my own sword? What does it matter? Only survival was important, and for that we needed victory.

But victory belonged to our enemy.

I stood, but hundreds had fallen. The line finally broke, Germans pouring into the breach like an infection, the fight of ordered battle lines descending into a melee of individual skirmishes.

Warrior after warrior came at me. Most were a blur – cut, parry, thrust and move on – but some details fought their way through the carnage to etch into my mind, destined to dwell there until my own final gasp: a legionary staring quizzically at the stump of his arm, hacked off by a German axe; a woman, a whore from the baggage train, holding spearmen at bay with wild swings of her own staff; a mule, thrashing in agony, eyes bulging from its skull in terror.

'Rally, rally, rally! Form on me! Form on me!' I heard the harsh call for order pierce the riotous cacophony of battle, and saw the broken line of soldiers fighting their way to my side. I did not know it at first, but the barking voice had been my own. Like the well-drilled strokes of a sword arm, my tongue had acted on its own initiative.

'Kill them!' Stumps screamed, blood pouring down his skull from a half-severed ear. 'Kill them!' he demanded of us.

We tried. Cut, parry, thrust: the endless repetition of death's machinery, broken only when I felt a hand grip my sword arm.

I turned, and saw young Cnaeus falter.

The boy buckled to his knees, one hand desperately fighting for my attention, the other pressed to a wound on his neck that spewed crimson like a grotesque waterfall.

I knew that he was a dead man. His wide, terror-filled eyes told me that he knew the same.

The Germans gave me no time to delay the inevitable. No time to assure him that all would be well. No time for good-byes. All I could do was cover the boy with my shield, fighting off attackers as he whimpered and choked to death on his own blood. Finishing off a swordsman with a thrust into his stomach, I finally had a chance to look down between my feet. Cnaeus lay there, his eyes open and unblinking.

The boy was dead.

I had no time to mourn him. Our small knot of men had to stand firm as the tide of German warriors swirled around us. Other groups of soldiers closed ranks, shields overlapped, swords and javelins held in shaking hands.

Here was the lull in the battle. Such hostility could not be continued indefinitely, and now was the point where men collapsed from exhaustion, or backed away to fill lungs with air and stomachs with wine. Men still died, but the initial clash of forces had dissipated into a handful of stand-off skirmishes and the dispatching of wounded. Tortured cries for mothers rang out in every language of the Empire and the German tribes. I knew battle, and recognized this lull as an inhalation before further exertion. The fight was not over. The forest seemed to hold its own breath, waiting for the next move.

'Felix, are you all right?' I turned, seeing Titus. He held a German longsword in one hand, an oval auxiliary shield in the other.

'Cnaeus is gone,' I managed, after spitting to clear my throat.

Stumps and Moonface were still with us. Micon too.

'Stop crying!' Titus shouted into the boy soldier's face.

'Cnaeus,' the boy sobbed.

'Do you want to join him, you tart?' Titus challenged the youth. 'Or do you want to live?'

'I want to live,' Micon finally stammered.

'Then pick up your fucking shield,' the man growled, and the boy did so, coming to stand beside me.

'This isn't over.' Titus spoke confidentially into my ear, though any man could see that truth.

We cast our eyes over the German ranks opposing us, a mass of men that swayed with anticipation.

'They're waiting on something,' I agreed.

It came a moment later from the head of the track: thunder – the thunder of hooves.

Titus spat. 'Cavalry. Fuckers.'

Stumps grimaced. 'See you on the other side, boys.'

The horsemen burst forth like blood from an artery, pouring into the narrow space between the trees.

'Shields!' Titus called. 'Hold! Hold!'

The irrepressible flow of the cavalry swept up those Romans who did not hold their formations, men dying as they were trampled beneath hooves or spitted on the end of cavalry spears.

Other knots of soldiers broke in the face of this brute force, discipline replaced by animal instinct to flee for the illusion of safety in the trees.

Some men resisted this urge. Forced it down with clenched teeth and empty stares. They were the backbone of a legion, but the spine had long since snapped.

'Get back, you cunts! Get back!' Pavo called at the soldiers who ran for their lives. 'Get fucking back here!' This was the moment he had longed for: glory-drenched battle. The chance to carve a name, reputation and career.

It all came to an end in a clatter of hooves. I saw the centurion disappear beneath the trampling steed of a German nobleman, the shorn-crested helmet tossed into the air as if it were an afterthought.

'Pavo's gone!' a veteran of our own century called.

And so it was that our own band split apart, soldiers I knew by sight bolting for their supposed salvation. Only the survivors of our section held together. We were blood-brothers who had slept, ate and shat together so often that we were almost of the same organism. By some mercy, our solidarity bought us a moment of respite, the cavalry mounts swerving around our unyielding shields, leaving the diehards to go in search of easier or more glorious prey.

And there was nothing more glorious than a legion's eagle. The silver totem was the heart and soul of a legion, and as the soldiers of Rome died in the dirt, or fled for the trees, the eagle wavered. The standard-bearer whom I had met on the parade square was forced by wounds to his knees, the bear-skin cloak about his shoulders thick with matted blood.

I saw the man sag, a witness to the last stand of the infantry who fell in defence of the eagle. Only when the standard-bearer made no further move to fight did I realize that the man had died with his hand on the sacred staff. That decorated warrior had told me it was better to be lucky than brave, and now his words were proven as the boot of a German cavalry soldier pushed his limp body to the dirt, a rush of blood pouring from his open mouth. The wild-maned German warrior then hefted the totem into the air, cheering himself hoarse, and his countrymen broke from their slaughter to revel in the capture of one of Rome's most sacrosanct possessions.

It was the final blow. The last cut. Seeing the symbolic eagle fall into the hands of the enemy, the minds of Rome's soldiers turned to their own survival.

They broke.

'Go. Run!' Stumps screamed into my face. 'Get to the trees! Fucking run. Run. Go. Run!'

I looked down and saw Cnaeus's lifeless face. The wound to his neck was as raw and open as his dead eyes – they told me to run.

And so I did.

I crossed the open ground littered with the dead and dying, my eyes focused on the forlorn sanctuary of the woods. I ran like an Olympian, and as I hurdled a fallen cavalry mount, I saw a ward of the legion that had slunk, unnoticed by almost all, into the deep green shadow of the forest.

It was a mule, and I knew what was contained within the boxes on its sweat-shined flanks – they were the legion's pay chests, and in this forest of ghosts, they offered me the promise of being reborn.

I intended to take it.

# 46

Branches whipped across my face as I rushed into the tree-line, desperate to leave the sound of the tortured screams behind me.

Clear of enemies – at least for a moment – the ruined muscles of my legs finally buckled as my sandals hit a tree root, and I collapsed to the floor like scythed wheat.

I lay there panting, spittle dripping between my teeth. Like a baby, I tried to regain my feet, frantic to find the mule that I had seen disappear into the forest with the legion's pay chests on its back.

Instead, as I pushed myself up with shaking arms, I found a blade pointing at my throat.

'You ran,' the man accused me, and I swallowed at the sight of him.

His huge frame dripped with gore. His eyes burned with hate. He was a vision of nightmare.

'We all ran,' I forced myself to say.

Titus lowered his blade. 'We need to keep going,' he told me, offering his hand and pulling me to my unsteady feet.

He was right. We had to keep running. The unending chorus of screams told us as much. And yet . . .

'There's a mule,' I told him. 'I saw it come in close to here.'

'We don't have time to fuck around—' he began.

'The legion's pay chests are on its back,' I finished, and Titus's eyes grew wide.

'You're sure?'

I nodded, and I knew that there was no way Titus would run with the promise of riches so close at hand. The man was a survivor, but deep down his soul was touched with greed. He had risked much in his sale of arms with the quartermaster. He would risk much to come into possession of a pay chest.

'Show me where the mule came into the forest,' he ordered, and I did, taking him the short distance to the edge of the track and a break between the trees. From there, finding the beast was a simple enough task, the mule having followed the path of least resistance through the trees. Avoiding our enemies was not as easy, but Titus was a god of war, and he cut them down as if they were children. Some almost were.

'There!' He pointed. The mule made no effort to avoid us, and as I took hold of the loose reins about its neck, Titus hungrily tore open one of the chests on its dirty flank.

'Fuck me,' he whispered, his eyes wide as they took in the mass of coin. 'Something brought us to this point for a reason, Felix. We can take this. You can go to Britain – I've got the connections. With this coin, we can do it.'

Britain – the land I had striven for with every torrid step across a continent. The land I had dreamed would offer me redemption. The land I had dared hope would offer me sanctuary from ghosts.

This was it, the moment I had been waiting for since Arminius had first found me in the sacred grove. I was free of the army, its discipline and its punishments. I had coin – more coin than I could have ever imagined. I even had a warrior and a comrade with whom to share the road.

And yet.

'We can't leave without the others,' I heard myself say.

It was a moment before Titus spoke.

'You saw what happened back there. They're dead, Felix. The others are dead. It's just you and me now.'

'Did you see them fall?' I pressed. 'Cnaeus is dead, but Micon? Stumps? Moonface? Did you see them fall?'

Eventually Titus shook his head.

'Come back to the track with me. We can stay in cover. Maybe we'll see them. If not,' I promised, 'then I'll come with you. We'll make a break for it.'

Titus held my eyes. He was no coward, far from it, and yet we both knew that with every moment delayed, the chance of us escaping the forest grew ever smaller.

'One look,' he told me as he spat, and so, pulling the mule's reins, I led us back towards the track where an army had been destroyed.

At least so we thought.

'Fuck. How?' Titus whispered, peering out from the trees.

We were looking at an army of ghosts. A cohort of Roman soldiers. Somehow, this band of bloodied men had survived the collapse, and had rallied in an area of open ground. There were perhaps a thousand of them, from all three legions and all manner of auxiliary cohorts, bound together now as a single unit, fighting for survival.

'It must be the second battle group,' I guessed. 'I didn't see what happened to them. Did you?'

The big man shook his head slowly.

To see such a cohesive force still alive was a surprise not only to myself and Titus, but to Arminius's army. The Germans had thought the battle won, but this thick tangle of

Roman soldiers had hung on doggedly to life. Flush with victory, no German warrior was anxious to die now that the battle's outcome had been assured, and so a tense lull had descended over the field.

'It's stopped raining,' I heard Titus say in wonderment.

I looked up. For the first time in days, the skies had closed. I noticed then that the branches had ceased to tremble, the winds dying away to nothing. The final act of Arminius's deception would be played out beneath a beautiful blue September sky.

I ran my eyes over the assembled ranks of the Roman soldiery. What I saw was no surprise, and I recognized men who were resigned to death in this place. Their eyes were hollow. Their cheeks were gaunt. There would be no escape. Only the manner of death was to be decided.

The death of my comrades. The death of my friends.

Stumps. Micon. Moonface. I saw them in the front rank, with overlapping shield, and bloodied blades in hand. For now, they lived, but the German horde was stirring. This lull would end. The tempest had cleared, but death was coming again with more violence than any storm.

'Titus.' I pulled at his tunic, but I could see that the warrior had already sighted the men of his section, for his eyes were huge and wet.

And then, without a word, he walked back into the forest.

# 47

'Where the fuck are you going?' I hissed at Titus as the big man led the mule away from the army's survivors in the open ground and deeper into the forest.

'Home,' he said simply.

'Titus,' I tried. 'Those are our mates out there. They're still alive. Didn't you see them?'

'I saw them.' He pushed a branch out of the way of his face.

'Then where the fuck are you going?' I demanded again.

'Home.'

It was too much.

I raised my blade. Its edge was thick with congealed blood that smeared across the coarse hair of the big man's throat.

'Kill me, or get out of my way,' he ordered, and I had never seen the brute so calm. So at peace. What reason could possibly compel him to walk away from his comrades' side with such serenity?

'I've got a son,' Titus answered the question in my eyes. 'He served with the fleet, and three years ago, his ship was lost at sea.'

I didn't know what to say.

'That's why you rejoined the eagles,' I managed eventually.

Titus nodded. Having lost his boy, he had gone back to the closest thing he had to a family. A family he was now abandoning.

In pleading tones, I told him as much.

'My boy's alive,' Titus answered me, and almost smiled. 'Just before we left Minden, I got word. My boy is alive, Felix. He's in trouble, but he's alive.'

I thought back to those days when we had marched out of camp, Titus withdrawn into himself, sullen and despondent. I had assumed it was due to the prospect of the upcoming campaign, but it was the scars of the past that had troubled him.

'Titus,' I began, 'you have a son, but those are our brothers out there. We can't leave them to die.'

'You and me? What can we do?' he whispered, his eyes flickering across the forest. 'We're two bastard-soldiers, Felix. Arminius has almost wiped out three fucking legions. If it was Stumps and Moon standing here now, and you and me out there in the open with our balls in our hands, I'd tell them to run as fast as they fucking could.'

I couldn't argue with his logic. I would do the same.

And yet.

'We can't just leave them to die.'

Titus ran a gnarled hand over the cracked skin of his face. His chest rising like a mountain in earthquake, the man sighed. 'We all died when we came into this forest, Felix, but for you and me, this is our chance for a new life. Out of all the people in this army, you should be the one to understand that.'

I made no reply, and so those were the last words that Titus spoke to me. I wanted to talk, but no words would come, so I simply watched as he led the mule and the legion's pay chests into the forest, until his thick shoulders were swallowed by the green.

I wanted to scream. I wanted to cry. From an army of thousands, and a handful of comrades, I was once again alone.

343

But I did not have to end my life that way, I realized. I had a choice.

I turned my back on Titus, and sought out death.

Moving through the trees, I collected a spear from a German corpse. The man's lips had twisted in death, giving him a bemused expression. Even the dead seemed to chide me for the decision I was making.

Finding the Roman survivors was a simple enough task. The battle was still in a lull, but the screams of wounded men, and the taunts of those who were still thirsty for blood and glory, guided me through the trees like a ship following a lighthouse.

Wanting to be nimble on my feet, and knowing how drained my body was, I discarded my battered helmet and slipped the chain-mail shirt over my head, gasping at the pain – my shoulders had been rubbed raw beneath the summer tunic.

Finally unburdened, but with my muscles screaming at even such a simple effort, I began to stalk my way at a crouch to the forest's edge. Aside from the dead, I seemed to be alone within the trees. The foe had his eyes on a bigger prize than the lone stragglers of the army.

*The army.* I looked at it now, all that was left of it. A thousand bloodied men who had already gone through everything that nature and the enemy could throw at them. Somehow, they still stood, though I did not deceive myself that any of these brave warriors thought that they could come through this ordeal alive. Like myself, they had committed themselves to death here, beneath the blue German skies.

Not so the warriors of the tribes. Under Arminius, the Germans had won a great victory. It was a victory that would spread ripples of fear throughout the Empire, and yet their glory had been secured at a terrible cost, and the open ground was littered with German dead. With my own eyes I had seen hundreds fall in the forest. To break apart the final Roman stand would likely take hundreds more German lives, and a man is far less likely to throw himself against sword and shield when he knows that the spoils of victory are so close at hand. That was why the Roman soldiers were left swaying on their feet, their enemy watching them, poised, yet nervous.

And so it was for Arminius to ride forward towards the men he had once called allies, comrades and brothers.

It made my skin itch and crawl to see him, but I realized instantly that it was not because of his treason. It was because, in every movement, and every ounce of his poise, Arminius showed nothing but grace and dignity. Despite the horrors, despite the bloodshed, this man was totally assured that his cause was just.

Could I argue that it wasn't?

'Soldiers of Rome!' he called in a voice that commanded attention from every man, no matter how battle-shocked. 'It is time for you to end your suffering.'

'Fuck off, cunt!' came shooting back from the Roman ranks; the call was picked up by a dozen voices, though most men remained like stone, too drained to offer challenge.

'Your leaders abandoned you, soldiers!' Arminius countered, undeterred. 'They fell on their own swords, instead of standing by your side. Why should you fight for weak men like that? Why should you die? You have done all that honour could demand, and a thousandfold more. Like Hector's, your defeat will be remembered in history for its glory. There is no shame in it! None! It is time to end this bloodshed.'

I did not expect any further taunts from the ranks, nor were there. The Roman survivors were being offered the slightest chance of life, and every man was weighing that in his mind, playing out the most hopeful of scenarios.

The Roman leader stepped forward from the ranks.

Prefect Caeonius. He lived. This man had ultimate authority, and would determine the course of the Roman army, and so I found my fate once again in the hands of the two warriors who had discovered me as a bloody apparition in the sacred grove.

With his thick shoulders drawn back, Caeonius walked out from between the shields. Even from a distance, I could see that his armour was bent and bloodied. Here was a true leader, one who had been in the thick of the action. The most salted veteran in the legions, who loved and valued the soldiers beneath his command. He would not fritter away their lives needlessly.

'What are your terms?' he called.

I had expected that Caeonius would have made some comment about Arminius's treachery, but he was so long in the tooth that he had seen Roman allies – even Roman senators – cast aside their allegiance for vainglory.

Arminius had proved himself to be a great commander. Now he recognized Caeonius as an equal, and climbed from his saddle so that both men stood on the bloodied turf.

Arminius's words were simple, the tone neutral yet un-yielding as they carried across the field. 'Your soldiers will surrender, Caeonius, and be taken into slavery.'

*Slavery*. The word struck like an arrow. Depending on the conditions, it was as much of a death sentence as defying

Arminius and his tribesmen on this battlefield. Backbreaking labour in mines and fields – what terms were those?

But the damning conditions of surrender offered one thing that a last stand could not.

Hope.

There was the hope that a Roman army would swoop in to avenge the defeat of Varus. There was the hope of escape from farm, or slave barracks. There was the smallest hope of a benevolent master. Every Roman survivor was now convincing himself that *he* would be the one to defy the odds and resume his former life. That *he* would be the one to see his homeland and town once again, and be reunited with loved ones.

Caeonius, I'm sure, would have known that slavery was a harsh sentence to inflict on his soldiers. I am equally sure that, had he known a handful would escape and survive the ordeal, he would have seen the enslavement as infinitely preferable to a final stand in which all his soldiers perished, however gloriously.

Hope. It had driven me across a continent. Now it opened Caeonius's mouth.

'We surrender.'

# 48

No man seemed to dare breathe in the moments following Caeonius's surrender. The Roman soldiers held their ranks, battered shields overlapping, eyes hollow beneath steel helmets. The German tribesmen stared at their foe, desperate to finish their enemy, but wary of the wounded animal that could still kill and maim in scores.

It was Caeonius who acted first, drawing his bloodied blade from its sheath and casting it down into the wet dirt. Then, with that signal, shields, javelins and swords began to fall from Roman hands. A few men began to weep. Most stared vacantly at nothing.

It was over.

Arminius climbed back into his saddle and called something aloud in German. With fierce eyes, he repeated it with force, and I can only assume it was a savage order that his men must respect the surrender, and not butcher the Roman prisoners, as so many clearly wanted to do. I had seen surrender before, and the moments following the laying down of arms were critical. If blood spilled now, it would not stop until the last drop had run into the dirt. If calm could prevail for a time, then the Roman soldiers would live to see their enslavement.

'Caeonius,' Arminius then called in Latin. 'Leave your arms here, and march your men to that camp.' He pointed towards the army's final marching camp, where Varus and his staff had taken their own lives the previous day.

Caeonius hesitated for a moment. He knew that once his soldiers were separated from their arms, there would be nothing to prevent a massacre.

'Form up in ten ranks!' the prefect finally called, realizing that he had no choice, and I watched as the desperate-looking mass of men shuffled their way into formation. Many had to be held aloft by their comrades, and I knew that the end for these wounded soldiers would be near. A crippled slave was of little use.

Eventually, the remnants of the army formed up. Knowing that they were ten ranks deep, I could now make an estimate of the cohort's size. The mathematics left my stomach sour.

Fewer than a thousand survivors.

Fewer than a thousand from an army of seventeen and a baggage train of three.

The forest had swallowed us whole.

'Formation!' Caeonius called, his voice showing no recognition of the tragedy. 'By the centre, quick march.'

Of course there was nothing quick about the shuffle of exhausted and wounded men. A few of the most stubborn held their shoulders back, with some reserve of pride, but most stumbled and staggered towards their enslavement, herded by the German warriors who followed in their wake like hungry dogs.

The army's path to the fort brought them closer to my position, and as they came, I sought out the faces of the men I had known. Only a short time had passed between my laying eyes on Stumps, Moonface and Micon, and then Caeonius's capitulation, and I was hopeful that my comrades had survived those final moments. And yet, try as I might, I could not see them amongst the mass of hobbled soldiery.

But I could see Arminius.

I could see him well enough, the cunt, sitting astride his war-steed like a god, his blond hair cascading over his thick shoulders, his face serene. It made me hate his treason all the more that he showed not the slightest smugness at its success. It was as if he had known all along exactly how the campaign would unfold, and so he felt no relief. Surely he knew that his actions here would shake the world, and yet . . . nothing. No smile. No oration. No beating of his thick chest. He simply walked his mare behind the army that he had butchered, and, in doing so, he walked it into killing range of the spear in my hand.

I knew I would not miss him from my vantage point; he was too close to have time to evade the missile. My initial movement would give away my position, but Arminius's instinct would be to turn towards me, not shy away, and that action would present me with twice the target width to hit. My muscles were beyond fatigue, and yet they now raged with hate for this man, and so I knew they would not fail me. My aim would be true, and though it was too late for my comrades, perhaps I could do something to stop the landslide that was about to pour from Germany into Roman-occupied lands.

My grip went loose about the spear's shaft as I considered those words: *Roman-occupied lands.*

Since when had I cared about Rome, Germany or any other country or tribe? With shaking hands, I knew the truth was that I did not. I was not Moonface, a patriotic chest-thumper. I was not Rufus, proud of my heritage.

Lines on the map meant nothing to me. I was wearing one uniform, but I could just as easily be wearing another.

Perhaps it was for this reason that instead of hurling the spear into Arminius's chest, I held it limp by my side as I stepped from the trees and on to the corpse-strewn track.

'Arminius,' I called, though the prince was already turning to face me, his troops sprinting towards the threat with murder in their eyes.

He stopped them with a raised hand. Like a pack of hunting hounds, the German warriors waited to tear me apart at a signal from their master.

Arminius's eyes burned into me, and then he gave the slightest shake of his head. I saw his lips move as he spoke in silent German.

I expected honeyed words from the man who had talked Governor Varus and his army to their deaths. My ego even flattered itself that he would wish to justify his treasonous actions to me.

Instead, Arminius simply looked at me with the same bemused detachment as he had done in the sacred grove. Yet again I had appeared to him as a bloodied, savage-looking thing, though now that I had given up the element of surprise, I was as little threat to the prince as a gnat to his mare.

'You could have killed me?' he said finally, with a gesture of his chin towards the spear in my hand.

The words were a question, the answer to which I had not fully understood myself until I replied.

'You said that I owed you two,' I forced from between my broken teeth. 'On the parade square at Minden, you said that I owed you two. I won't die in debt to you.'

And with those pathetic words of defiance, I threw my spear to the floor, and prepared for death by closing my eyes, clamping my jaw tight and squeezing my muscles so that I would not shake or shit myself as the German warriors came for me.

I expected it would be the strike of a sword into my flesh that would force me from this state of dreadful anticipation. Instead, it was a bark of the happiest laughter.

I opened my eyes.

The bastard. The bastard was smiling. He was looking at me with wonder, as gleeful as I had ever seen him.

'I don't want you to die, my friend.' He beamed and chuckled, throwing himself gracefully from the saddle, and walking towards me with his hands free of weapons.

I tried to muster the courage to attack him with my own bare hands and teeth, but something in his grace held me rooted to the spot.

And then, with a few words, Arminius spilled my insides as well as any blade could have done.

'I want you to join me. I want you to join me, Corvus.'

*Corvus.* He knew me – *he knew me* – and as the black closed in around my eyes, and the ringing built in my ears, I knew now that I had known *him* long before the sacred grove.

My vision swam, blurs of bodies and entrails stretched out across the ground, but these were not the men of the German legions. This was Pannonia. This was another life.

'Corvus.' Arminius spoke again, but I could no longer see the man, nor reply – my every sense was focused on the wall of blood that rushed towards me, thousands of corpses churning endlessly in the red froth, screams assailing me from their dead mouths.

I wanted to scream myself. I needed to.

But I couldn't.

And so the wave of blood hit me, and I remembered it all.

# 49

I hadn't lied when I told the section that my true name was Corvus. I hadn't lied when I told them that I was a deserter. At that moment, with our leaders dead by their own hands, and staring at our own end in the morning, I had wanted to unburden myself fully to the comrades I had come to trust and love as brothers.

I had thought that I had done so.

Now, confronted by Arminius and my own name, the memories that I had pushed down into the blackest part of my soul came forth like an eruption, the force of it sending me to my knees. Acidic bile burned my throat as my body and mind ached to purge itself. I had once believed that the terrible things could never be forgotten, but I now saw that my mind, so damaged, had tried to save me like blood clotting a wound.

'Corvus,' I heard from somewhere, the scab tearing free.

I tried to lift my head. My vision swam as if I'd been kicked by a horse. I saw the form of bodies littering the ground by the hundreds. The details of their faces and uniforms were lost, but I saw the minutest things – the insects hopping on the gore. A woman's golden hair dancing with the wind.

'Corvus.'

The name stung me like a whip, because I knew now that Corvus was not an ordinary soldier who had, like so many others, tried to desert his legion during a time of war.

No. *I*, Corvus, *was* my legion. The rising star. The hero. The killer who had climbed from boy soldier to standard-bearer in only five years. I was the guardian of the legion's eagle, its heart and soul. In Rome's Eighth Legion, there was no man more admired, no warrior more feared, than Corvus.

Than *me*.

That was three years before I found myself at Arminius's feet in a German forest. Since then, throughout the Danube legions, the name of Corvus had become a curse.

Because the hero became a traitor.

The reason was war, though it all began peacefully enough. I had never forgotten the early days of it. Like Germany, the province of Pannonia was on the fringe of the Empire, and as such its subjects wished to enjoy their own customs and traditions. They asked the Emperor of Rome for a degree of autonomy, but the rule of that demi-god and city was iron, and so peaceful request became bloody revolt. The citizens of the province were tired of being ground beneath the Roman heel, and Roman garrisons were attacked. Politicians were murdered.

The Eighth Legion, where I carried the proud eagle standard, formed a part of Rome's response.

I remember how eagerly I awaited it. Like young Cnaeus, who had died at my feet, I ached to prove myself. Like Pavo, who had been trampled by a German horse, I yearned for glory. I had seen combat against bandits and brigands, but this was to be my first taste of war.

It was nothing but butchery.

Our mission to restore order saw us raze towns, enslaving the women and children and executing the men. After only a few days on campaign, I could no longer count in my mind the women I had seen raped, or the atrocities I had been a part of. My conscience was bloodied, and my blade more so. As standard-bearer, I was always in the eyes of my comrades. Respect and esteem meant all to me, and so I had slit the throats of elderly men as they knelt trembling in their own piss.

It was a mercy when our 'enemy' offered resistance and some kind of blood-letting that could be described as combat. I was at the front of every charge against the fortified positions, desperate to lose myself in the chaos. Soon I began to realize that I was hoping for an enemy spear to find its way through my armour and into my black heart.

None did, my work as a butcher continued, and so it was that I found myself within my campaign tent, resting on my knees, with the point of my short sword pushing between the junction of my ribcage.

I let my weight move forward, slowly, and felt the blade pierce skin. I held it there, savouring the balance of life and death. I knew that with one sudden movement I could end it all. I could remove myself from a world that had shown itself to care only for death and darkness. I could stop myself being a piece of that macabre machinery.

But I did not.

I did not, because I had already seen too much. I had already *done* too much. Before my death could come, there had to be some repentance. Some way to give peace to the men that I had killed.

I would find it.

The campaign continued. My search to bring balance was fruitless. Like a coward, I took to finding excuses to avoid the bloodshed. I explained to my commanders that, rather than be in the thick of the fighting, I wished to study it from a distance. My courage was famous by this point, my leaders eager to groom me for future appointments, and so it was that I found myself on the crest of a low-slung ridge, watching the town below as our troops pulled screaming families from their homes in the dawn's light.

It was there that Arminius found me.

He wore the uniform of a cavalry officer, though there was no sign of his mount. His face was open and whimsical, as if the tortured screams of rape and murder below us were a prelude to a joke. The handsome man's cavalry squadron was attached to my own legion, and I had seen him often. Often, and never comfortable with what was unfolding.

'Corvus, sir,' I greeted him.

'Arminius.' He offered his hand, man to man, forgetting rank and the privilege of noble birth. I took it, and in that moment I saw the confirmation in his eyes that he loathed this campaign as much as I did. Loathed an empire's organization that relied on butchery to survive.

'Those are our own citizens we're killing,' Arminius observed, his tone low. In the closest street, a man was being hacked apart by inexperienced boy soldiers. It was a bad death. A long one.

I turned my eyes from the sight, not in disgust but because I wanted to take the measure of this man before I uttered words that could condemn me to an end on the cross should he betray my trust.

I do not know how he gained my confidence, but it was given to him as easily as a babe loves its mother. Perhaps it was because I had developed such contempt for my own life that I no longer cared for its preservation. I simply needed to unburden my soul.

And so I spoke.

'I can't serve an empire that does this,' I heard myself confess.

Arminius considered my words. Beneath us, the man in the street had ceased his screaming. Other citizens, found cowering in their hiding places, were beginning theirs.

'I look to my own people,' the German said, and gestured to the death in the town. 'When they feel as though they deserve a voice in the running of the Empire that they are told they are a part of, will this be their reward? Will I be asked to carry my sword against those of my own blood?'

I said nothing. We both knew the answer.

'Rome is a light in the world.' As Arminius spoke, I could feel his love for that place, and its principles. 'But the torch is carried by the wrong people.'

'How do we change that?' I asked suddenly, needing to know the answer, certain that this man possessed it, and anxious to play my part.

'What are you willing to do?' he asked me, his blue eyes burning into mine.

I placed my hand on the pommel of my sword.

And so, as the screams of Roman justice echoed beneath us, Arminius told me how we would defeat an empire.

War is expensive. Neighbouring kingdoms must be bribed to either interfere, or not. Armies must be provisioned. Soldiers must be paid.

It was this last reason that gave me the chance to hurt Rome. As standard-bearer, the legion's coffers came under my watch. I was supposed to be scrupulous, and incorruptible.

But I was set on my path to become a traitor.

And so, one night, I deserted my dear comrades, and fled my legion with those pay chests, taking them into the hills where the rebels were mustering to form a resistance against Rome's iron fist. It is enough to say that I was distrusted at first, but chests full of gold did much to persuade. The final act of my confirmation into the rebel ranks left me with shaking knees and a belly of acid, and yet I did what needed to be done. The details of that act can wait in my soul's black pit with all the others.

I was an accomplished warrior, known throughout Pannonia, and so I was placed on the staff of the rebel generals. It would not be unjust to say that my expertise was a large part of the reason that the war then dragged on for two blood-soaked years. It was only when Rome dispatched an army of unprecedented size that we finally became trapped in the harsh mountains.

It was then that I ran. I had already abandoned one set of comrades, though I knew that my reason for that desertion had been just. Leaving the hilltop fortress as the legions swarmed over the mountainside like lava, I had no such justification. The rebellion seemed lost. Rome had won. I simply wanted to live. When Marcus took his last gasp, I ran.

I ran. I ran northwards, because Britain was the only place where I – maybe – still had a friend.

I could not tell you when my mind ceased to function as Corvus the traitor. One moment I was running from the flames, the next I was alone in the mountains – it was only when I slept that the memories came back to me, but they began to grow distant, individual horrors replaced by the wall of blood that would wash over me and wake me screaming.

Like a fort besieged by catapult and ram, my mind had crumbled in war. Now, on a battlefield a world away, it had been rebuilt by the man who had cut down an army.

Arminius.

I felt his hands on my shoulders, and opened my eyes.

It was then that I screamed.

## 50

I screamed.

I screamed again, and again, and again. Screams of frustration. Of hate. Of self-loathing.

Arminius pulled me to my feet and held my face tight in the iron vice of his hands. 'Corvus.' He smiled. 'Stop this shit. Look around you.' He gestured. 'We've won.'

I did look around me. I saw bodies on top of bodies. I saw the ruin of an army. I saw an end to the ambitions of an empire. Three legions destroyed. Could Rome ever recover?

'I did this?' I managed to mutter.

For once, Arminius let a prideful smile play across his handsome features. 'This was my work, Corvus, but the gods had their hand in it too. Why else would I have found you in that grove? They sent you to me.'

'Why didn't—'

'I tell you?' He smiled again. 'Tell you what? That you were a traitor? A turncoat? Why? So that you could have been put up on a cross, and taken me with you?'

'You should have killed me,' I murmured.

'I thought about it,' Arminius admitted, still holding my face. 'But the gods spoke to me in that place, Corvus. They told me that you would play your part in this, and you did. *You* saved me on the square. When my uncle wanted me imprisoned, or dead, you saved me. And so, yes, you made this possible.'

I looked about me at the bodies that would soon be flyblown and bloated. I wanted to throw up.

Arminius recognized my weakness. 'I know an ally when I see one, Corvus. You showed your true heart in Pannonia. It is a good heart. The heart of a man who cares for ordinary people, and not the pampered life of a senator half a world away. I have seen broken warriors before, and I just had to let you come to me in your own time. Until then, I watched you. My men watched you.'

I looked up from the carpet of corpses.

'The two legionaries and their centurion, buried in the manure,' I realized. 'They knew me. They knew what I had done. That was you.' I meant that Arminius had killed them to keep my secret.

'Berengar,' Arminius confirmed, with a nod towards the giant bodyguard who now walked into my eyeline, his thick muscles painted with Roman blood. 'Berengar took care of you, Corvus, because you're one of us. You've seen the rot in the Roman Empire. Together, we can stop it spreading.'

'We can,' I heard a voice say, stunning myself as I realized that it was my own. 'We can,' I said again, and believed it.

For what was Rome?

Seeing the purity in Arminius's eyes, I knew exactly what it was. It was a bully that masqueraded as a teacher. It was a tax collector that disguised itself as a philanthropist. It was a bloodthirsty executioner that paraded as a guardian.

Rome was poison.

'Rome's poison,' I said aloud, as more wretched memories came rushing back, and I knew that I spoke the truth.

Had I not deserted the Eighth Legion in sound mind, desperate to prevent – or at least delay – the atrocities committed against the people of Pannonia? It was only bizarre fate that had seen me once again clad in the red tunic of the legions and marched off to war on Rome's behalf. It was only the bonds of brotherhood to a few men that had kept me in the armoured ranks when the chance to escape had presented itself. The shared ordeal was the fabric of our binding, not the notion of Rome, or empire.

And now those battle-brothers were gone. Dead, deserted or missing. My ties to Rome were cut.

'Follow me,' Arminius offered, taking his hands from my face.

And so I did, and when I followed, it was not as a prisoner, but as an ally of the German prince.

It was as such that Prefect Caeonius now saw me. He had cast his hollow eyes back to take in the sight of the man who was his victor, and now the sole determiner of his fate, and by his side he saw the wretch that he had rescued from a tortured death on a cross. A man who, it must now be clear to him, had been a traitor all along.

I expected some fire in his eyes. A curse.

There was nothing. He had seen too much. Endured too much. I was simply one more blow in the barrage of deceit and misery.

'What will you do with him?' I asked Arminius, and the prince tracked my eyes to the leader of the Roman army's remnants.

He did not answer. It was the first and only time I ever saw indecision cross his face.

I did not press him, my mind still swimming from my own revelation.

We followed the sorry survivors of Varus's army through a gap in the ramparts of the final marching camp. Within the raised dirt walls, hordes of German tribesmen and camp followers picked through an army's litter, searching for anything of value.

'Stop your men there,' Arminius called, and Caeonius ordered a halt at the camp's centre. Men came to a stop as if in a dream, bumping and shuffling into each other's backs.

Arminius walked forward and, given an encouraging push in the back by Berengar, I assumed that I was to follow on behind. So it was that I found myself within a javelin's length of the Roman commander.

Prefect Caeonius had no words for me. I, though I tried, had none for him.

'What now?' He spoke instead to Arminius.

'Show me where Varus is buried.'

Caeonius shrugged, as if he had been expecting the order, and led off.

Berengar called something in German, and a dozen of Arminius's household warriors ran off, quickly returning to their leader's presence with picks and shovels.

'Here.' Caeonius pointed to the earth, the position seared into his memory through shame and anger.

It took only moments for the strong German warriors to dig up the corpse. As we had been told by Titus's veteran comrade, Varus should have been cremated, but only his hair was singed, his lips twisted from the heat. There was no mistaking the man.

Arminius now pulled down his breeches and, to the cheers of his followers, pissed all over the charred face of a governor who had been amongst the most powerful men in Rome.

Caeonius said nothing. Nor did he protest when Berengar stepped forward and used the edge of a shovel to brutally hack the governor's head from his shoulders in a series of wet slaps. He held it up for Arminius's inspection, the prince's eyes flashing with venom as he spat into the dead face.

'Send it to King Marabodus,' Arminius ordered, translating for the benefit of myself and Caeonius.

'Why?' I found myself compelled to ask.

'His tribe are the Marcomanni. You won't find any of them on this battlefield, Corvus. It's time for everyone to choose a side,' he finished ominously, and from those words, I knew that the bloodshed would not end here, in this forest. This was only the beginning of Arminius's rebellion against Rome.

'What now?' I asked him, picturing those future battlefields.

Arminius did not direct his answer towards me. Instead, his eyes stayed fixed on the headless corpse of Varus. Perhaps it was his hatred for the man, and all he embodied about Rome, that caused the answer that Arminius snarled.

'Kill all of the officers,' he ordered.

# 51

Caeonius made no attempt to dissuade Arminius from the sentence of death that the prince had proclaimed. He did not beg for his life, or beseech him for mercy. He simply held back his shoulders, his weathered face a blank mask as he awaited the inevitable. Perhaps it was this stoicism that compelled Arminius to speak.

'You are a good man, Caeonius,' he offered to the soldier he had condemned to die. 'Too good to be left alive. This will be a long war.'

The Roman veteran nodded. 'It will.'

But his part in it was over. Berengar's blade hacked into the prefect's neck with such force that Caeonius's spine was severed instantly, his head flopping forward uselessly as an arc of blood gushed into the air.

Cries of alarm rang out from the Roman prisoners who had witnessed the act. The body of men pushed and crowded together like sheep stalked by hungry wolves, no man wanting to be on the unprotected outside.

Arminius called something in German, and his men moved forward to begin separating the rank from the file, pulling centurions and tribunes away from the common soldiery.

Following the prefect's example, many marched out with their shoulders back and heads held high. Others were dragged from the body of men like screaming toddlers.

'You said they would be slaves,' I protested.

Arminius placed his hand on my shoulder as if I were a naive child. Perhaps, after all that I had endured, I still was.

'These people are a disease, my friend. An infection that must be cut out, as if we were surgeons. The soldiers I can spare, but the officers will never overcome this defeat. Shame will push them to act, and to encourage dissent amongst the ranks. For some to survive, the leadership must die.'

I wanted to find fault in his words, but I had seen enough of war, and man's ways, to know that he was right. Perhaps if the executions of the Roman officers had been clean and merciful, like the surgery Arminius claimed it to be, then I would have stood firmly by his side through all of the coming storm.

But they were not.

In all the horrors that I have seen, little can compare to those moments following Arminius's order to kill the officers. The German warriors fell on the assembly of prisoners with glee, dragging away those whose rank and station were given away by the ostentation of their uniforms.

The screams began moments later.

Tribesmen pinned centurions to the dirt as their comrades sawed tongues from crying mouths. Bodies were hacked into pieces as if they were logs for a fire. Heads were cut from shoulders, gathered into grotesque piles and taken to the forest to be nailed on to trees. Seeing this horror, some Roman officers took their own lives rather than suffer the drawn-out torture – I saw one split open his skull with the very chains that bound his wrists, grey jelly spilling from his smashed eye socket as he collapsed into the bloody dirt.

'Stop this, Arminius,' I finally hissed as my vision swam. 'Stop this!' I shouted, taking hold of the prince's arm.

He met my look. There was no pleasure in his eyes at the suffering, only a grim acceptance that his men had endured their own hell in the forest, and that now they would make their enemy suffer for every freezing night and bloody skirmish.

'Please stop it,' I begged.

Arminius looked away, and I knew then that I had been a fool. Not because I had thought the Roman Empire was corpulent and cruel, but because I had thought that it could be replaced with something better. Something just. As I watched the blades chop into the screaming Roman faces, I saw laughter, terror and confusion. I saw the face of power through bloodshed, no matter the uniform, language or banners. I saw that all I had endured, all I had fought for, had been pointless, a horrifying ordeal that offered no end, only the promise of more suffering.

And so I had only one last thing to ask of Arminius.

One last thing to beg for.

'Just kill me. Please. Just fucking kill me.'

'Why would I kill you?' he asked, bemused.

I threw out my arms at the horrors that were unfolding about us. 'Roman emperor or German prince, it's all the fucking same!' I cursed him. 'Look at this! This isn't war!'

'It *is* war.' Arminius shrugged, and the shrieks of the tortured Roman officers added weight to his words.

'It's fucking murder!' I shouted into his face, and saw his bodyguards bristle at the open hostility towards their leader. 'It's fucking murder, Arminius! It's what you said we would stop!'

'It's war,' he said again, his tone low. 'And you can either accept that, Corvus, or you can't.'

I spat at his feet. 'I can't accept it. I won't accept it. So just fucking kill me.'

'No.'

'Berengar!' I shouted at the brute, who was eyeing me as if I had gone mad. 'Kill me!'

The giant shook his head.

I wanted to call them both cowards, but how could I? I was the coward. I was the man who could not stomach war.

And so I sank to my knees in the mud.

'I won't kill you, Corvus,' Arminius told me as he saw the fight flee from my wretched body.

'I can't be a part of this,' I murmured.

'You can. You just need a rest. Then you'll see things clearly.'

'I do see things clearly,' I breathed, watching as another Roman head was hacked from its shoulders, blood pumping from the stump of the neck in violent spurts. 'I've seen too much, clearly. I don't want to see clearly! I just want to die!'

My words were pathetic. Pathetic words, from a pathetic creature. Arminius looked me up and down then, doubtless wondering how he could ever have considered me a worthy ally.

'I can't kill you.' The prince shook his head out of sympathy. 'But our journey together ends now.' He turned to Berengar. 'Put him with the other common soldiers,' he ordered in Latin, and then turned back to face me, the blue of his eyes alight with bitter disappointment. 'You had your chance to stand with me, my friend. It hurts me that you turn your back now, when our work has begun, but I cannot kill you for it. As you refuse to throw off the chains of Rome, you will become a slave, Corvus. It pains me, but you will become a slave.'

I could see that his words were heartfelt. So too were my own. 'Fuck you,' I spat.

Berengar's huge backhand swatted me a split second later, and I rolled on to my face in the filth. When I looked up, Arminius was gone.

Two German warriors pulled me to my feet and shoved me in the direction of the herded Roman soldiers. I swear I could almost smell the panic.

'Here, brother,' a veteran of the Nineteenth Legion offered, helping me to my feet once the tribesmen had dumped me. 'You talked to their leader.' There was astonishment in his voice.

I wiped blood from my mouth. Berengar's blow had knocked free a tooth. 'Yes,' I managed, and felt accusing stares from the soldiers about me. Those who could still care. I had to cover myself. 'I knew him from Pannonia, when I served with the Eighth.'

The explanation did something to dispel the suspicion, and the troops withdrew into their own misery. Exhausted and fearful, the mass of men were silent but for the ever-present chorus of muttered prayers, curses and crying.

I had no wish to be idle. I had left Titus and chests of coin to find my friends, and so I called out: 'Second Cohort, Seventeenth Legion? Second Cohort, Seventeenth?' I repeated, and looked at the German warriors who acted as our wardens. They showed little interest in me. Unarmed and emaciated as I was, that was no wonder. I was not a threat.

'Second Cohort, Seventeenth Legion?' I shouted again.

'Over here!' came back from behind the wall of men.

I pushed my way through the soldiers towards the voice, calling again, and was answered.

'Second Century,' I greeted the man whose eyes sought me out.

'Fourth,' he acknowledged with a grunt. 'Have you seen any of my boys?' he asked, daring to hope that some of his comrades yet lived.

I shook my head, and asked him the same.

'Over there.' He jabbed a thumb across his shoulder.

I gave the man my thanks and pushed hastily on, stepping over men who had collapsed from exhaustion. Despite their proximity to death and their imminent enslavement, some even snored in the mud.

'Second Century, Second Co—' I began.

'Felix!' A plaintive voice cut me off. 'Felix!'

I half turned and saw Stumps struggle to pick himself up from the dirt. My heart beat faster to see him, and I pulled the soldier into a tight embrace.

I wanted to say something – I'm sure that he wanted to say the same things – but neither of us spoke. How could we? A look was enough. A look to confirm that, despite the misery and the horror, we still had a brother amongst the chaos.

'Titus?' he asked finally, swallowing in anticipation.

I could not speak. Stumps was already battered emotionally and physically to the edge of his limits and beyond, as every man was. If he knew that Titus, his leader, his friend, had abandoned him . . .

'Dead,' I muttered. 'Titus is dead.'

370

The soldier dropped his head on to my shoulder, trying to weep tears from eyes that had long since run dry.

'Titus, Chicken, Rufus, the boy,' he choked. 'I don't know where Moon is, Felix. I don't know where he is, or Micon. I think they're dead. I think they're all dead.'

'There's hope,' I promised him, and meant it.

How could I feel that way? Strewn across the forest was the carcass of three legions. The soldiers' bodies were condemned to be pulled apart by animals, their bones bleached by sun and rain. It was the worst defeat a Roman army had suffered in longer than living memory, and I knew that Arminius would not stop here. This battle was a statement of intent, a declaration that Rome was not invincible. It was the beginning of an age of war.

And what would be my part in it? Which mask would I wear? Which standard would I carry? For Rome I had been a soldier, and called a hero. Against her, I had been a turncoat, and a rebel. Wherever I had marched, death had followed.

But now I was a slave.

'On your feet!' a German voice called in thick Latin. 'On your feet!'

Somehow, the walking dead obeyed.

'That way! Move! Go!'

And so we marched, leaving the blood forest behind us, the thousands of corpses lining the route as if it were a parade of nightmare. Besides me, Stumps began to whimper.

'They're all dead,' I heard him mumble between sobs.

Were they dead? Most likely. Even Titus, force of nature that he was, would struggle to survive alone in this hostile place. Chickenhead, a man who had grown to be my friend, would rot beneath the German wall. Rufus was lost to the forest, as was young Cnaeus, but try as I might, my battered mind could not mourn them now. Instead, I envied them.

I envied them, because as we shuffled our way north towards the German hinterland, the terrifying weight of my position came crashing down, and I knew that no battle, no forest, could be as terrible as the torment I was soon to suffer.

For I was a slave.

# Author's Note

I'm not sure when I first became interested in the Battle of the Teutoburg Forest – as the decimation of Varus's army is known – but I do remember Adrian Murdoch's *Rome's Greatest Defeat* accompanying me to Basra when the insurgency there was in full bloom. Through books like Murdoch's I began to see how Varus's campaign was an ancient echo of the one I found myself involved in. Where a supposedly superior force – of a supposedly advanced culture – was bloodied at the hands of an enemy they had underestimated, in a land that was unconquered, and amidst a people they did not understand. For me, Iraq seemed to be a case of history repeating itself, and I felt an affinity to those ancient foot soldiers who would have trodden the dense German forests with as little familiarity as I paced a desert city.

As far as military disasters go, Varus's defeat ranks alongside Stalingrad as a pivotal moment in history that echoed far beyond the local borders. Stalingrad signalled the end of Hitler's dreams of expansion eastwards, and so too did the loss of three legions mark the end of Rome's attempts to conquer German lands east of the Rhine. Who knows how the Empire would have grown with that powerful fighting force intact and in capable hands.

The scale of the loss of Varus's army cannot be overstated. Forgetting for a moment the thousands of unfortunate auxiliary soldiers that were lost, the might of *three* legions was wiped out in a matter of days. There were twenty-eight legions active at the time of the massacre, and so Arminius's victory deprived Emperor Augustus of more than *ten per cent* of his heavy infantry. Ten per cent of the soldiers that were the lynchpin of the Roman Empire both in attack and defence. Furthermore, Varus's defeat came on the heels of a war in Pannonia that had bled the legions viciously, and so it was little wonder that the news of the German victory caused such panic in Rome; able-bodied men were pressed into service, whilst slaves were freed and formed into cohorts sent urgently to bolster the Rhine garrisons.

*Blood Forest* features several characters that were known to history at this time. The first, Governor Varus, I have presented as I found him. Then, as now, army leaders were not necessarily the greatest soldiers or even expert tacticians. Birth and political connections played a huge part in appointments, and Varus seems to have been totally outmatched in leadership by his enemy, Arminius, whose conduct of battles as well as his ability to band together an alliance of tribes, showed great strategic capability as well as prowess on the battlefield.

Arminius is one of my favourite characters in history. He was born into German nobility, raised in Rome, and served with distinction in the Roman army. Varus was enamoured with the man, which seems to have directly contributed to his demise. There is no record as to why Arminius turned on Rome, but I have explained my own theory in this book. There was no unified nation or notion of Germany at the time, but certainly the Germanic tribes held common ground and tongues, and some men would have viewed Rome's growing power in the region as an act of attempted domination rather than assimilation. Arminius was one of these men, and his victory would see him remembered in his homeland as a hero who defied the invader.

Prefect Caeonius is remembered in the classical texts for marshalling the army after the suicide of Varus and many of his staff officers. I admire the man's courage, and could just as well imagine him giving encouragement to a young soldier at Rourke's Drift: 'Hitch, do your tunic up.'

Felix and his section mates were born in my imagination, but their personalities and traits are drawn from the soldiers that I was privileged to serve alongside. Reading the accounts of infantrymen at war has always fascinated me, and I am stuck in my belief that soldiers are soldiers, regardless of the uniform or era. There's something in our blood that makes us do the things we do, and say the things we say, and I think that Felix would have been just as at home in Helmand province as he would have been in Germany. Very at home actually, as by strange coincidence, the name of my patrol base in Afghanistan was Minden – I'm not lying!

It is precisely because no account of the Roman rank and file exist that I wanted to write from their perspective. The leaders of the time are well documented in fact and fiction, but a commander is only as good as the men who execute his orders. For the soldier, there is no big picture to a battle. They do not see the masterstrokes, or the turning points. They see only their own struggle for survival, and glory for their leaders comes when enough soldiers are triumphant in their own microcosms of battle.

Further to this point, I wanted to explore in *Blood Forest* the mental aspect that conflict has upon the soldier. We are only just beginning to understand the mental scars of war, and I do not believe that Rome's soldiers would have been easily shrugging off the loss of their comrades, or the acts that they were forced to witness and endure.

Though I believe I have an understanding of how soldiers think and behave, I consider it important to point out that I am a storyteller and not a historian. Rome's legions and their battles have gifted me the setting in which to place Felix and his comrades, but this book and the ones that will follow are not intended to be definitive in their detail. I humbly piggy-back on academic experts, and whilst I endeavour to be as accurate as possible, there are times where I feel that story trumps fact, and that the beautiful power of artistic licence can be deployed. I am mindful too that no one alive today has lived through the days of the early Roman Empire, and that means – in my mind at least – that there are no definitive answers. If there are lessons to be drawn from *Blood Forest*, then I hope that it is through metaphor, and my deep belief that the character of the soldier transcends time.

As I've already alluded to, I could not have completed this novel without the work of historians and academics. For anyone interested in learning more about this era or battle I strongly recommend Michael McNally's *Teutoburg Forest AD 9*, the aforementioned *Rome's Greatest Defeat* and the definitive *Legions of Rome*, by Stephen Dando-Collins. All were ever-present during the writing of *Blood Forest*, but that being said, any mistakes are my own. Feel free to tweet them to me, and I'll get down on my face and give you press-ups.

The loss of three legions is a brutal blow for Rome, but the Empire is not known for its forgiveness. With Arminius a threat, and Felix a slave, there's a lot more blood to shed.

# Acknowledgments

I could not have written about soldiers without having served with them, and so first thanks goes to the men and women that shivered beside me in training areas, sweated with me in the desert, and listened patiently to my ideas during sentry duty in the early hours. Above all that, thank you for having my back and bringing me home.

I would not be where I am in life without my parents and family. They gave me confidence to take on any challenge, inspired me to travel the world, and supported me no matter what my decisions. I can't imagine that my choice of careers as soldier and writer ever gave my mother a sound night's sleep, but she is responsible for giving me my passion for history and books, and without her *Blood Forest* would never have happened.

Huge thanks to the entire team at Furniss Lawton, particularly to my friend and agent, Rowan Lawton, for her guidance and belief in me. I sent Rowan my first manuscript whilst floating on an overcrowded tug boat off the coast of Sudan, and her confidence in my work helped me realize the dream of becoming a professional storyteller, and took me away from the circling sharks that were hungrily eyeing up my Welsh beef.

The seeds of *Blood Forest* were planted at Penguin with the help of Rowland White, my editor and fellow lover of all things military. Rowland 'got it' from the start, and I could not have asked for a better team to bring my vision to the page. Alongside Rowland, Jillian Taylor of Michael Joseph provided invaluable insights, and has helped me take strides as a writer. There are many others at Penguin who made this book possible, and I have the greatest appreciation for their efforts, with special thanks to Richard Bravery for the most amazing cover art I have ever seen!

Thank you to my good friends Tim King, Gareth Emery, and Tom Wilkinson, my unpaid proofreaders who have always given me such great feedback. You will all be rewarded for your help by receiving further unedited manuscripts in your inboxes, and my best wishes.

Final thanks goes to the incredible archaeologists and historians whose tenacity in uncovering the past makes my work not only possible, but also so thoroughly enjoyable.